CW00345019

The Wolf Mat

The Royals Of Presley Acres:
Book 3

Roxie Ray
© 2024
Disclaimer

This is a work of fiction. Names, places, characters, and events are all fictitious for the reader's pleasure. Any similarities to real people, places, events, living or dead are all coincidental.

Contents

Chapter 1 - Liza

A sharp pain pierced my skull, forcing me to wake up. The room swirled around me like a carousel, blurring the unfamiliar surroundings into a disorienting mess. I blinked in an attempt to clear my vision, but the pounding in my head only intensified.

"Where am I?" I muttered as I carefully got up from the cold, hard floor. My limbs, heavy and uncooperative, seemed to belong to someone else.

Hints of light filtered through the dark curtains drawn across the windows just enough for me to make out the antique furniture—a large wooden wardrobe, an ornate vanity mirror, and a plush velvet chair—but nothing looked familiar.

"Think, Liza, think." I rubbed my temples to try and ease the aching in my head, willing myself to remember what had happened and how I had ended up here, but my memories were shrouded in a thick fog, leaving me grasping at fleeting images.

"Ty." The name slipped past my lips like a lifeline. My mate, my rock, my anchor. If anyone could find me, it would be him. The mere thought of Ty made me a little braver, a little stronger. He wouldn't stop until he found me.

I had to believe that.

"Focus." I inhaled deeply. If I couldn't remember how I got here, maybe I could at least figure out where *here* was. I stumbled over to the window, the heavy drapes rustling reluctantly as I pulled them back.

Outside, the world was a sea of darkness, broken only by the silhouettes of towering mountains and dense groves of trees. Wild and untamed. Something about the landscape was strangely familiar, like it was calling to some distant part inside me.

"Well, I'm in Texas." I stared out at the vast expanse before me. The terrain definitely looked like that of my home state, but beyond that I had no idea where I might be, or who had brought me here.

I jumped when a soft, familiar voice suddenly echoed in my head.

Holy shit.

"Easy, Liza," he said soothingly, sending an involuntary shudder through my body.

"Who are you?" I said out loud instead of inside my head. "What's going on? Why am I here?"

"Please, calm down." His voice was gentle. *"You're safe here, I promise. No one is going to harm you."*

"I'm having conversations with a voice in my head that's telling me I'm safe. You'll have to forgive me if I find that a little hard to believe."

"I understand how strange this must seem, but trust me when I say you're not losing your mind," he assured me. *"I can't explain everything right now, but soon, I will."*

"Who are you?" I asked again with mounting frustration.

Again, there was no response, and my anxiety only grew.

"Listen," I said, about to lose control. "My mate is going to find me. Ty won't stop until he does, and when he does, you'll all be sorry."

The voice in my head remained silent, leaving me with nothing but my own thoughts. No comfort there. They were nothing but a jumble of worry, anger, and fear. I couldn't stay trapped in this room any longer. I needed to get out, find answers, and get back to Ty and my family.

Hoping for a quick and easy exit, I inspected the windows first, but tugging on the handles only proved they were locked tight.

"Of course," I said under my breath, rolling my eyes. Why would my captors make it easy for me?

Next, I turned my attention to the door, which was just as locked as the windows, naturally. I ran a hand through my tangled hair, but I refused to give up. There *had* to be some way out of this place. I searched the room more thoroughly, checking every nook and cranny, even the floorboards, for hidden exits or weaknesses. So far, nothing.

"Why am I here?" I asked myself out loud, resting my forehead against the cool glass of the window, willing the answer to come. The world outside remained stubbornly silent, offering no clues.

A short distance away from the window, I spotted an odd-looking tree branch that seemed out of place, almost like it was beckoning me. Maybe I could use the branch to escape? It was a long shot, but I was desperate.

"'Kay, then. Windows it is." I cracked my knuckles and gave the locks another determined look. "Let's see if you can stand up to a pissed-off wolf shifter."

I backed away from the pane, giving myself enough room to charge forward with all my strength. If I could break the glass, I could climb out onto that branch, and make my way down the tree. It wasn't much of a plan, but it was all I had, and I clung to it.

"Here goes nothing." I launched myself at the window.

Every bone in my body jarred as I slammed into the glass, yet the window held firm. Pain flared through me, but I gritted my teeth and prepared for another attempt.

"You won't keep me here." I growled, glaring at the stubborn barrier between me and freedom. "I will get out of this place. I will find the truth. Then..." The full weight of the situation settled over me. What would I do then? What if the truth was worse than the nightmare I was currently trapped in?

There was no time for doubt or fear. I needed to act. I steadied myself and charged at the window once more, fueled by desperation. This time, I vowed, I would break free.

Damn it all to hell. I stumbled away from the unyielding window, breathing hard. Desperation clawed at my insides like a living thing, but I refused to let it consume me. I needed to stay focused and find a way out of this place back to those I loved.

"Get a grip, Liza." I paced the room like a caged animal. The scent of polished wood and fresh linens filled my nostrils, but it did little to soothe my frayed nerves. I racked my brain for any detail that might help me determine my captor's identity or their intentions. All I had were questions; questions that multiplied with each passing moment.

An unwelcome, familiar voice echoed through my mind, causing me to freeze in place. *"Calm down."*

That was impossible, given my every nerve was on edge. "Who are you? What do you want?"

"Everything is going to be fine," he assured me, though his words provided little comfort. *"You're not in any danger here. I promise no harm will come to you. You're safe."*

"Safe?" I scoffed, incredulity warring with fear. "I've been kidnapped, locked in a room, and I'm speaking to a voice in my head. You'll have to forgive me if I'm not particularly in a *safe* state of mind right now."

"Trust me, you're not losing your mind," he said with surprising gentleness. *"You have many*

questions, and I promise I'll do my best to answer them soon. For now, you need to remain calm."

"Who are you?" I asked again, more insistent this time.

"My identity will become clear soon enough," he said evasively. "For now, all I can tell you is that you'll be allowed to leave this room if you can prove you're not a danger to anyone here."

"Prove I'm not a danger?" Of all the... "You're the ones who kidnapped me. What kind of twisted game is this?"

He stayed silent, leaving me fuming and confused. I paced the small room, my anger and frustration building with each step. The walls closed in, taunting me with their confinement.

My thoughts shifted to my family. Were they safe? Did they know what had happened? I desperately wanted to know, but the voice remained maddeningly silent. The events in my mom's kitchen flashed through my memory.

"Hey, voice in my head!" I shouted, trying to get his attention. "What about my mom? Is she okay?" There was no response. My frustration and fear grew, mingling into a toxic cocktail that threatened to overwhelm me. "Answer me, damn you!" I was so close to losing it.

Still, the voice didn't say a word.

The silence was deafening, drowning out everything except my ragged breathing.

"Fine," I growled as I wiped away tears that had managed to escape. Resolve settled over me like a cloak. I'd do whatever it took to escape and reunite with my family.

The voice in my head remained silent, leaving me to face my fears alone.

"Ty will find me," I said. "You'll be sorry when he does."

I knew with every fiber of my being that Ty would never stop searching for me. My mate was a force to be reckoned with, and he wouldn't rest until he'd rescued me. I just had to hold on, keep fighting, and find a way to make it easier for him to track me down.

The door to my prison creaked open, and I tensed, readying myself for whatever might come next. A young woman entered; her arms laden with food. She appeared nervous, like she expected danger to leap out at any moment. She looked so young and innocent—nothing like my captors in my imagination.

Too bad, so sad. I ignored the pang of sympathy I felt for her. This was my opportunity to escape.

"Thank you," I said softly, trying to put her at ease.

She nodded, but her hands shook as she set the tray down on a small table near the bed.

"Please, can you tell me where I am?" I asked, keeping my voice gentle.

She shook her head, clearly too afraid to speak.

"Who's keeping me here?" Desperation put an edge in my tone.

She remained silent; her attention fixed on the floor.

"Fine," I snapped. "Don't help me."

The woman flinched but still didn't respond. With a huff of frustration, I turned my back on her, focusing instead on the food. It smelled delicious, but no way could I trust it. There was no telling what might have been done to it, and I refused to let my guard down, even for a moment.

As the woman left the room, I made my move. With a surge of adrenaline, I lunged for the door, slipping through the narrow opening just as it began to close. The hallway beyond was well lit and unfamiliar. Any other day, I'd have said it was beautiful, but I didn't hesitate as my bare feet pounded against the cold stone floor, and I sprinted toward what I hoped was freedom.

"Hey!" the woman yelled, her voice high-pitched with alarm.

I ignored her, pushing myself harder, faster.

"I wouldn't do that if I were you."

Footsteps echoed behind me, but fear lent me speed, and I refused to give up. I would escape this place no matter what it took. "Fuck you."

As I turned the corner, I skidded to a stop. A massive, burly guard, with his arms crossed beneath his broad chest, and a menacing scowl etched on his face, stood in the corridor. His imposing figure blocked my path. I wasn't going anywhere without a fight.

"Going somewhere?" he asked in a deep, gravelly voice. He did not sound amused.

"Get out of my way," I snarled, trying to sound brave. If Ty were here, he'd fight for me. But I was alone—I had to be my own hero.

"Nice try, but you're not going anywhere." The guard took a step toward me, cracking his knuckles menacingly.

"Watch me." I tensed my muscles, preparing for the fight of my life.

He lunged with surprising speed for someone of his size, but I was quicker. Ducking under his outstretched arm, I tried to slip past him. However, he recovered rapidly, and he grabbed me by the waist before slamming me against the wall. Pain exploded in my back, and I barely bit back a cry of agony.

I thrashed wildly in his grip. "Let go of me!"

The goon was too strong. His iron-like fingers dug into my neck, making it nearly impossible to breathe.

"Give it up, girl," he growled in my ear, his breath hot against my skin. "You're not getting out of here."

My vision blurred. If I didn't act fast, I'd pass out. With one last surge of strength, I slammed my elbow against the side of his head. He grunted in surprise and released me just long enough for me to slip from his grasp.

My victory was short-lived. Before I made it more than a few steps away, the guard tackled me, pinning me to the floor under his massive weight. My arms were trapped, and no matter how hard I struggled, I couldn't break free.

"Enough," he said. "You put up a good fight, but it's over now."

As he hauled me to my feet and dragged me down the hallway toward my prison, despair crept in. My escape attempt had failed. I was once again at the mercy of my captors.

The guard's grip was unyielding, his face an emotionless mask as he shoved me into the room. I stumbled a couple of steps before regaining my balance and spinning around to glare at him just as the door slammed shut with a loud bang. The lock clicked into place, sealing me in my prison once more.

"Damn it." I kicked the door in frustration. Pain shot up my leg, but it did nothing to quell the anger boiling inside me.

"I tried to warn you."

"Fuck you." I was right back where I'd started, locked in a room with no way out.

"I'm not surprised you tried to escape, but even if you managed to get out of this house, there's only miles of forest waiting for you. You'd be lost in no time."

"Thanks for the pep talk," I said sarcastically. "Really helpful." Despite my snarky response, I had a sinking feeling the voice was right. I'd never been good with directions, and the thought of wandering around aimlessly in the wilderness was almost as terrifying as being held captive.

Okay, a bit less terrifying.

"Your safest bet is to remain in the house," he continued. Yeah, right. *"At least here you have some chance of staying alive."*

"Alive, but still a prisoner." I flung myself onto the bed and stared up at the ceiling."

"Sometimes survival is all we can hope for," he said softly. He sounded almost sad, as though he understood the gravity of my situation better than I did.

"Who are you?" I hissed. "Why won't you help me?"

There was a long pause, and for a moment I thought he'd abandoned me. Then he spoke again, more hesitantly than before. *"I can't help you. Not yet, anyway. There are complications."*

"Complications?" I scoffed. "You're just a fucking voice in my head. How complicated can it get?"

"More than you can imagine," he said cryptically. *"Believe me when I say that I'm doing everything I can to keep you safe."*

"You owe me an explanation. Why was I taken? Who are you people?"

"Everything will be explained in due time," he said, his tone annoyingly serene. *"For now, I need you to trust me."*

"Trust you?" Disbelief dripped from my every word. "That's rich coming from the person holding me hostage."

"Much is at stake," he said with a hint of urgency. *"I cannot reveal more until I'm certain it's safe to do so. Please, try to understand."*

He went silent after that.

Good. I didn't want to talk to him, anyway.

Hours passed as I prowled around the room. My stomach growled like an angry beast, reminding me of the hunger gnawing at my insides.

My body ached from the scuffle with the guard, and my thoughts ran wild as I tried to piece together how I'd ended up in this bizarre situation.

Without warning, the door swung open, revealing the terrifying guard from earlier. His massive frame filled the doorway, and he stared at me with a stern expression. I froze mid-step and glared back at him. What was he going to do?

"Your dinner." He stepped into the room to place a tray of food on the table, then picked up the other one.

The mouthwatering aroma wafted through the air, causing my stomach to protest even louder. I eyed him warily, not daring to make a move toward the tray.

"Go ahead, eat." He nodded toward the food. "Clean clothes are in the closet. You can use anything you find in the room."

"Thanks, I guess," I said, taken aback by his slightly more hospitable demeanor. Still, I didn't trust him or anyone else in this place, and I certainly wasn't about to try and escape again—not with him standing right there, anyway.

"Can you tell me why I'm here?" I asked cautiously.

His gaze locked onto mine, a hint of sympathy flickering in his otherwise cold eyes. "Can't do that," he said gruffly. "Not my place."

"Whose place is it, then?" My anger flared. "I deserve to know why I've been taken from my home—from my family."

"All your questions will be answered in due time. For now, take care of yourself. You'll need your strength."

I rubbed my arms and looked around.

"Tomorrow." The guard's deep voice resonated within the room, making me jump. "If you behave and do well tomorrow, you can leave this room."

"Behave?" I gritted my teeth, trying to stay calm even though anger heated my blood. "What does that even mean?"

"Follow instructions," he said matter-of-factly. "Eat. You'll need your strength. It's not poisoned."

He turned and left, shutting the door with a heavy thud. I stared at the closed door, with fury and confusion raging inside me. What kind of game was this? Why had they brought me here?

"Answers in due time," I muttered under my breath. "Not good enough."

Despite my reservations, my stomach growled loudly, reminding me how hungry I was. Cautiously, I approached the tray. My nose caught the scent of perfectly seasoned chicken, roasted vegetables, and buttery mashed potatoes. The aroma was heavenly.

"Is it poisoned?" I asked, staring at the plate. The food looked amazing, but I couldn't trust anything or anyone in this place.

I hesitated for a moment, weighing the risks, but I couldn't bring myself to touch the food, no matter how good it looked and smelled.

Instead, I pushed the tray aside and scanned the room for something, anything, that could make me even the tiniest bit safer. My gaze landed on a pile of blankets in the corner.

"Better than nothing," I said, grabbing a few and clutching them tightly.

The bathroom was my best option, being the most secure place in this unfamiliar prison because it locked from the inside. Grabbing the blankets and pillows from the bed, I shuffled into the bathroom and locked the door behind me with a resolute click.

"Ty, where are you?" I whispered as I sank down to the cold tile floor, my back pressed against the door. The thought of him out there, searching for me, gave me a small measure of comfort.

I wrapped myself in the blankets, shivering despite their warmth. The hard floor beneath me and the chill of the tiles were nothing compared to the fear that tightened its grip on my heart. As I lay there, I thought about my brothers. Ever since we were kids, Mason and Michael had always been so protective of me. If they knew what was happening, they'd tear the world apart to find me.

I forced my mind away from the terror before it could consume me. I'd faced worse than this. I'd get through this.

Sleep was fleeting and restless, filled with nightmares of shadowy figures, and cold, unforgiving eyes. It felt like mere minutes later when footsteps outside my door jolted me awake.

"Is someone there?" I called.

"Stay calm," that familiar voice in my head said, spiking my fear even more. *"You're not alone."*

"Who are you?" Damn it. I wanted to see the person behind the voice. All I got in response was silence—a silence that stretched on for an eternity.

"Please." Tears stung my eyes. "Tell me what's going on."

"Tomorrow," the voice was, gentle but firm. *"All will be revealed tomorrow."*

With a heavy heart and a resolve made of steel, I tried to sleep again. Tomorrow would be a new day. One thing was for sure—I would not back down. I would fight with everything I had to get back to Ty and my family, no matter the cost.

Chapter 2 - Ty

The scent of blood permeated my nostrils when I stepped into Liza's parents' house. Isaiah was right behind me, his concern and anger etched on his face.

"Where is she?" My voice shook with barely contained fury. The once warm and inviting kitchen looked like a war zone. Glass crunched under our feet with every step we took. The table, where I'd shared so many meals with Liza's family, lay on its side, the chairs tossed across the room, and there were splatters of blood everywhere. The bitter taste of fear and helplessness coated my mouth, making it difficult to swallow.

"Stay calm," Isaiah said, placing a hand on my shoulder. His touch was meant to be reassuring, but all I wanted to do was to find and tear apart whoever had taken Liza and hurt her loved ones. "We'll find her," he added quietly as he began inspecting the wreckage, his sharp gaze scanning for any clues that might lead us to Liza.

I took a shaky breath to regain some semblance of control, but my wolf was agitated, pacing restlessly within me. The need to protect Liza, to have her safe in my arms, gnawed at my very being.

Isaiah gestured to something on the floor. I moved closer, clenching my jaw at the torn piece of Liza's shirt, the delicate material stained with blood. The metallic tang of blood rose in the back of my throat when I picked up the fabric.

"Who did this?" I growled, my vision blurring.

Liza's laughter, her smile, the way her face lit up when she was happy... those images haunted me now, taunting me with the possibility I might never see her again.

I looked up at a security camera mounted in the corner of the room. "Maybe we can find something on the footage."

We huddled around the screen in the tiny security room. We needed to find Liza, and we needed to find her now.

"Got it." Isaiah's fingers flew over the keyboard as he pulled up the video feed from earlier that day. I scanned the screen for any clue that might lead us to Liza's captors.

"Wait, pause it right there." I pointed to one of the figures on the screen. Isaiah complied, and I leaned in closer, squinting at the image. "Can you enhance that? I think I recognize him."

"Yeah, just give me a minute," Isaiah clicked a few more buttons, then the enlarged image filled the screen. As the face came into focus, my blood turned to ice. It was Liam, Liza's brother. The bastard had taken her right from under our noses.

"Son of a bitch." I growled, clenching my fists so tightly, my knuckles turned white. "Liam."

"Who?" Isaiah asked, confused.

"Liza's brother. He must have planned all of this. If that son of a bitch is involved, God knows what else he has planned for her. Fuck!" I slammed my fist onto the table. "We need to find her."

Liam stared at the camera with an alarming intensity. He'd taken her. It ignited a rage within me I couldn't tamp down. If he hurt Liza, I'd tear him apart limb by limb.

"Let's get this to the estate," Isaiah said, his voice tight. "We'll put together a team to track them down."

As we left Liza's parents' house, my heart clenched with the need to find my mate. I was supposed to protect her and keep her safe from harm. Now she was gone, and her family was suffering. I couldn't—

wouldn't—let the guilt consume me. I had to do whatever I could to find Liza and bring her home.

"Isaiah, gather all the security footage," I said before I climbed into my car. "I have to go to check on Dad."

"Understood." Isaiah nodded, his face set as I shut my door and drove off.

I hurried through the estate to my parents' home. Five minutes later, I watched my father struggle to sit up in his bed. As much as I wanted to be there for him, my only concern now was Liza and her safety. My gut churned with anxiety, but I needed answers.

"Ty," he croaked, his voice hoarse. "I'm so sorry."

"Tell me what happened, Dad." I tried to keep the growl out of my voice. I needed him to focus on the facts, not self-pity.

He winced in pain from the movement. "Liza rushed inside to check on Rory after we heard her scream. I was right behind her, but someone ambushed me before I even sensed them." He averted his eyes, and I could see his self-blame eating away at him.

"Did you see who it was?" I knew who it was, but I wanted him to remember it all. "Did they say anything?"

"No, I didn't get a good look at them, but they must have been skilled to get the drop on me like that," he said shamefully.

"Hey." I met his gaze, our eyes so similar in their stormy-gray hue. "This isn't your fault. We're going to find out who took Liza, and we'll bring her back home. Safe."

He nodded, swallowing hard. "I just... I let you both down."

"Stop that. Right now, we need to focus on finding Liza." I kept my voice firm but not unkind.

"Okay." He managed a weak smile. "You're right. We'll find her."

My phone buzzed in my pocket, cutting through the tension in the room. I glanced at the screen. Scott, Liza's father.

Swallowing past the tight anger in my throat, I answered the call. "Scott, what's going on?"

"Rory's been rushed into surgery." He sounded like he was on the last threads of sanity. "The injury to her head was worse than we thought. There's bleeding on her brain."

"Shit." The situation just kept getting worse and worse. Not only was Liza missing, but now Rory was fighting for her life.

"Ty, focus on finding Liza," Scott pleaded. "I don't know what I'll do if I lose them both."

"I promise we're doing everything we can to find her," I assured him. "We won't stop until she's back home, safe and sound."

"Thank you," he said before ending the call. As I slipped my phone back into my pocket, I turned back to look at my dad.

He was out of bed and already halfway dressed.

"You sure you should be doing that?" I asked.

He grunted. "Scott shouldn't have to wait alone, and I'm already healing."

He wasn't a man to argue with. "Let's go." There wasn't a second to waste. He told my mom he'd be back soon, and we walked outside.

The cold air bit my skin as we climbed into the car, but it was nothing compared to the icy atmosphere inside the vehicle.

I gripped the wheel tight enough for my knuckles to ache while Dad stared out the window, my thoughts a whirlwind of anger and fear.

"Are you going to be able to keep your emotions in check when we get there?" Dad asked.

"I'll try." My anger would only make things worse for everyone involved. "But I can't promise anything."

Dad exhaled slowly. "You're not the only one who's hurting here. We all love Liza and her mother. We need to focus on finding Liza and making sure Rory is okay."

"I know." I rubbed a hand over my jaw, keeping the other clenched on the steering wheel. "I just... I can't shake this guilt. I should've done more to protect them."

"None of us saw this coming, but what matters now is how we handle it. Let's be there for Scott and the boys, and you do whatever it takes to bring Liza home."

"Right." As we pulled up to the hospital, I steeled myself, determined to do whatever was necessary to make things right.

We entered the waiting room, the harsh fluorescent lights casting stark shadows on the faces of Liza's brothers. Mason's and Michael's expressions were thunderous, and I braced myself for their wrath.

"Where the hell is Liza, Ty?" Mason's rage was barely contained. "You were supposed to protect her."

"Believe me, I'm doing everything I can to find her. My team is combing the security footage now." Frustration had me balling my fists. "Right now, we need to focus on your mom and dad. They need our support."

"Support?" Michael sneered, his eyes cold and accusing. "Is that what you call it when you let our sister get kidnapped and our mother attacked?"

"Enough." My father's voice commanded the attention of everyone in the room. "We're all upset, but pointing fingers won't help anyone. We need to work together if we want to find Liza and bring her home safely."

"You blame me, and maybe you have every reason to. But I swear to you, I will do whatever it takes to make this right," I told them.

Mason's jaw clenched, his eyes burning with anger. After a moment, he nodded curtly. "Fine." He turned his attention back to their father, who sat hunched over in his chair with his face buried in his hands.

"Thank you." My heart ached for them. It was my responsibility to fix it—to save Liza and mend the rift that had formed between our families.

The door to the waiting room opened, and a doctor in pale blue scrubs approached us. His expression was calm and professional, and I sensed the slightest hint of relief coming from him. It was enough to make my heart skip a beat.

"Mr. Mims?" the doctor said, his gaze settling on Scott. "Your wife is out of surgery. She's in recovery now if you'd like to see her."

"Thank God." Scott's shoulders sagged with visible relief. A weight lifted off my chest, too. At least Rory was safe for now.

We followed the doctor through a maze of hallways, my ears picking up every conversation and beeping monitor along the way. It was disorienting, the constant barrage of human sounds and scents, but I kept my focus on the task at hand: being there for Scott and Rory.

When we finally reached Rory's room, she was awake but groggy, her eyes glazed over from the painkillers. The bandage wrapped around her head was stark white against her dark hair. She looked so fragile. So vulnerable.

"Hey, sweetheart," Scott said as he approached Rory's bedside and reached a trembling hand out to touch her face.

"Scott," she croaked. "Where's Liza?"

Scott's jaw worked, and his eyes darted to me. He couldn't hide the truth from Rory, but how could he say it?

Before he could answer, I stepped forward, needing to take some of the burden off his shoulders.

"Rory, Liza is... well, she's not here right now." I chose my words carefully. "We're doing everything we can to find her and bring her home."

The sterile scent of the hospital room burned my nose, and the quiet beeping of machines monitoring Rory's vital signs assaulted my ears. She looked pale and fragile in the dimly lit room, her eyes barely open, but she was alive and awake.

We didn't bombard her with questions, as she had just had brain surgery . Shifter healing or not, it was important to give her time to recover. Scott remained at her side, holding her hand gently, his gaze never leaving her face.

It was Rory who broke the silence, her voice weak but determined. "I need to tell you what happened." She looked at each of us in turn, drawing strength from our presence.

"You don't have to do this now," Scott said softly. "You've been through so much already."

She shook her head slightly, winced, then continued. "No, I need to tell you. There were three men. They came into the house and threatened me. They made me text Liza."

My fists clenched involuntarily, and my wolf rose to the surface, its protective instincts on high alert. The thought of these men threatening Rory and using her to get to Liza made my blood boil, but I forced myself to remain calm for her sake. We needed to focus on the information she was giving us, not our emotions.

"Did you recognize any of them?" I asked, hoping for any clue that might lead us to Liza, considering we knew very little about Liam's whereabouts.

Rory shook her head again, more carefully this time. "No, but one of them seemed familiar. He looked a lot like Liza."

"Take your time, Rory." I tried to keep my own impatience in check. "Every detail helps."

"His eyes," she said, her gaze distant as if she was reliving the moment. "They were cold and calculating. He knew exactly what he was doing. He was the one who made me send the text—told me that if I didn't cooperate, they'd hurt Liza."

"Rory, that man was Liam. He's Liza's half-brother," I said.

"Her half-brother?" Rory's eyes widened in disbelief. "But... why? Why would he do this to his own sister?"

"Because he doesn't see her as family." I growled, digging my nails into the palms of my hands. "He sees her as a pawn in his twisted vendetta against our pack. Against us."

"Against me, too, it seems." A shudder passed through Rory's body. "That explains why he was so adamant about protecting Liza from 'those people', as he put it."

Those people. She was talking about us. Our pack. Our family.

"Rory, what do you mean Liam seemed determined to protect Liza from 'those people'?" I asked, trying to remain calm.

She looked at me, her eyes still glassy from the anesthesia. "When the other two men were in the house, Liam was trying to convince me that he could keep Liza safe. He claimed that the people she was with..." She hesitated for a moment, glancing at me with uncertainty. "That they were a danger to her."

The very idea of someone claiming we were a danger to Liza was preposterous. We had done nothing but care for and protect her since she joined our pack. Yet, there would be no reasoning with Liam. He saw us as his enemies, which was evident in the way he had orchestrated this entire mess.

I clenched my jaw, my teeth grinding together. Dad placed a hand on my shoulder, a silent reminder to stay focused.

"Rory," he said. "Did Liam say anything else? Anything that might give us a clue as to where he's taken her?"

Rory shook her head, looking apologetic. "I'm sorry. One of the other men came into the kitchen and grabbed me—he was the one who hurt me, not Liam. I wish I could remember more, but I was so scared. And after Liza appeared, everything happened so fast."

"We understand," I said gently. "You've been through a lot. Just try to focus on your recovery now."

Tears welled in Rory's eyes. "Thank you."

We left Rory's hospital room, but I couldn't shake the feeling that there was more to Liam's actions than just misguided protectiveness. He had some hidden agenda—something that went beyond his apparent vendetta against our family. But what?

Dad drew me from my thoughts. "Liam clearly believes we're a threat to Liza, and her brothers seem to agree with him."

"Then, we'll prove them wrong," I snapped, unwilling to let their mistrust hinder our mission. "They have no idea how much we love her or how far we'd go to protect her."

"Damn right," Dad added.

As soon as we got back to the estate, I jumped out of the car. My heart pounded, each beat only intensifying my need to find Liza. With Dad following closely behind, I burst through the front doors with fury and desperation coursing through my veins.

"Where's the footage?" I scanned the room for anyone who could help, barely containing my wolf's growl.

Isaiah looked up from a table, where multiple monitors were set up, displaying security camera feeds from around the house and property. He gestured for me to join him. "We've already got it pulled up."

I rushed to his side, my gaze locking onto the screen that showed Liza being carried away by a stranger, her treacherous brother leading them to a truck. The sight of her limp form in his arms sent a fresh wave of rage surging through me. How could he do this to his own sister?

"Can you zoom in on that truck?"

"Already tried." The room was silent but for the sound of Isaiah's fingers tapping rapidly on the keyboard as he clicked through different angles of the footage. "We can't get a clear view of the plates. The streetlights were out.."

"Damn it." I cursed under my breath as I stared at the blurry image of the vehicle. Every second that passed was an eternity, and it was driving me mad knowing that she was out there, trapped and terrified, while we remained helpless to rescue her.

"Keep looking," I said, my tone brooking no argument. "There has to be something we can use to track them down."

Isaiah nodded. "Of course."

The tension in the room was palpable. Nico approached me, his expression grim. "We've been looking into Liam's properties." Nico had dark circles under his eyes. "These are a few potential locations." He spread out a large map marked with red circles across the table.

"Call in a scout team." I pointed at the locations on the map. "I want eyes on every one of these places, and I want it done discreetly. We can't risk tipping Liam off."

"Already started." Isaiah tapped his cell phone on the table. "The teams are on their way now."

"I appreciate that." I gave him a curt nod. My wolf paced within me, eager to hunt down the man who'd taken our mate.

Before I could delve deeper into my thoughts, my phone rang, the sound jarring in the tense atmosphere. I cursed as I glanced at the caller ID. Castro, the bastard.

"Castro," I said tersely, my mind already racing with questions. "What do you want? I haven't got time for you right now."

"A little birdie tells me you're missing someone, and I can't say I'm happy about it. How could you let her be taken, Ty? You were supposed to protect her. Let me go against my nature and give you a little... help. Liam Petrov has taken Liza. He has a vendetta against the Kellers."

Hearing Liza's name from his mouth only served to make my anger and fear flare more intensely. How the fuck had Castro discovered so much already? But I couldn't let my emotions cloud my judgment. I had to focus on getting her back.

"His hatred for you Kellers runs deep," Castro continued. "He has a lot of reasons to hate you and your family, Ty. Like me, he blames them for the fall of the Wylde pack. It's worse for him because they killed his father, and essentially kidnapped Liza. Unlike me, he thought she was dead until you pulled your little stunt and put her on national television."

His words settled on my chest, making it difficult to breathe. As much as I wanted to lash out at Castro for reminding me of my own guilt, this information was invaluable.

"Thank you." I forced the words out through gritted teeth. "I appreciate your help." Ugh, thanking him was fucking gross.

He hesitated before continuing. "Just be careful. Liam is dangerous, and he won't hesitate to use Liza against you."

"Why are you telling me this? I would have thought you and Liam were on the same side."

"Because I hate him, Ty." Castro's voice was dark with loathing. "Liam may have a right to be angry with your family, but he's taken it too far. He's obsessed with revenge, and he knows how to utilize Liza's full potential. He doesn't care who he hurts along the way, including Liza."

"What do you mean, Liam knows how to utilize Liza's full potential? What does he want from her?"

"Power," Castro answered bluntly. "Liza is a weapon whether she realizes it or not. Her latent abilities could be used to wreak havoc on anyone who stands in Liam's way, and he knows it."

"We need to find her before Liam can use her against us." I growled. "We can't let him win."

"Agreed. Good luck, Ty." With that, Castro hung up.

I wasn't sure what he meant when he said Liza was a weapon, but I needed to find out, because as long as Castro knew more than we did, he was a danger to us all—especially Liza. As much as I'd have liked to pick apart Castro's words for their hidden meanings, my mind was already racing with plans and strategies to save Liza.

"Isaiah, Nico." I turned to face them. "We need to step up our search. We're dealing with forces beyond our understanding, and time is running out."

Castro's words hung like a black cloud in the air as I paced back and forth with questions and fears racing through my mind. The dim lighting in the room cast eerie shadows on the floor, giving an unsettling atmosphere to our already tense situation.

"Ty," Isaiah began cautiously. "What if Liam knows about you and Liza being fated?"

The thought chilled me to the bone, and I stopped pacing to turn toward him. "I don't know. It's possible, but we can't be sure."

"Maybe that's why he took her," Nico's brow furrowed in concern. "He could be using her as leverage against you."

"Or he could be planning something far worse," I added, my gut twisting. "If he knows how to use her powers, who's to say he won't try to control her? To turn her against us?"

Chapter 3: Liza

I opened my eyes to the cold, unforgiving floor of the bathroom. My body ached from sleeping on such a hard, unyielding surface, but it was better than lying on a bed that felt more like a trap than a place of rest.

I barely registered the female voice outside the door. "Breakfast is ready."

My stomach growled at the mere mention of food, but I couldn't bring myself to trust whoever had left it for me.

"There are fresh towels on the bed for you as well."

I waited until her footsteps faded and the door shut before I got up. My muscles protested, reminding me I was a prisoner here, no matter how soft the bed, or how clean the bathroom. I needed to find a way out, but first, I wanted to see what food they'd left for me.

The smell of bacon wafted through the room as I approached the breakfast tray. It was almost too tempting to resist, but I couldn't afford to let my guard down. If my captors wanted to poison me, this would be the perfect opportunity.

I pushed the tray away and turned to the bed, where a pile of fresh towels awaited me. They were warm from the dryer and plush beneath my fingers. I buried my face in their softness. It was a small comfort, but one I desperately needed.

"Are you really going to starve yourself?" the male voice echoed in my head, and I gritted my teeth, forcing myself not to react.

"Maybe if you tell me who you are and why I'm here, I'd be more inclined to eat your food," I shot back out loud.

"Fine, don't eat, then." There was a hint of annoyance in his tone. *"You're only hurting yourself by not eating. It's not poisoned if that's what you're worried about. Why would I go through all the trouble of capturing you just to poison you? If I wanted you dead, you'd already be dead."*

As much as I hated to admit it, his logic made sense. I stared at the food for a moment longer before giving in to my hunger and devouring every single bite. The bacon was crisp and salty, the eggs fluffy and perfectly seasoned, and the golden-brown toast had just the right amount of butter. Even the orange juice tasted freshly squeezed. It was a meal fit for royalty, and yet most likely it was all a ploy to keep me complacent and under their control.

"Happy now?" I bit out once I'd cleared the plate.

"*Thrilled,*" he replied dryly. "*Go ahead and take a shower. You'll feel better once you're clean.*"

I rolled my eyes but did as he suggested, stepping into the luxurious shower, and letting the hot water rain down on me. The showerhead was adjustable, allowing me to choose the perfect spray pattern and pressure. I sat on the built-in bench where I let the water wash away my fatigue. The toiletries were high-end, with fragrant soaps and shampoos that left my skin tingling, and my hair silky smooth. I took my time, savoring every moment of this small reprieve from my captivity.

A good hour later, I stepped out of the bathroom wearing a warm, plush robe, feeling somewhat refreshed, despite my circumstances. I checked around the empty room, searching for any signs of change since I'd left. As far as I could tell, everything was just as I'd left it.

Then I remembered the cameras hidden throughout the room. My captor must have seen me enter the bathroom. They were probably still watching me. Ugh, freaking gross.

My mind drifted to the dream I'd had the night before—a dream filled with Ty's strong arms and heated kisses. Even though he was nowhere near me, my need for him found its way into my subconscious. It was ridiculous, really. Here I was, being held captive, yet all I could think about was how desperately I longed for Ty to ravish me.

It took every ounce of my willpower, but I finally managed to put some distance between myself and those tantalizing thoughts of Ty. I began rifling through the clothes that had been left for me. I didn't want to stay in this robe for too long.

The clothes were simple yet stylish, consisting of a pair of dark jeans and a soft, white blouse. I dressed quickly in the bathroom. The clothes were comfortable enough, but it unnerved me how well these items fit. Whoever had chosen them knew me intimately.

"Are they dressing me up like a doll now?" I said under my breath, my fingers absently playing with the hem of the shirt.

As I looked up, with my damp hair clinging to my neck, I froze at the sight of the guard standing at the open doorway. My heart hammered, and I instinctively took a step back, calculating the distance between me and the bathroom door.

"Easy." The guard held up a hand to placate me. "I'm not here to cause you any harm. You've been granted a few hours of freedom outside this room."

Erm, no. This was too good to be true, like a trap just waiting to snap shut around me.

"Where are we going?" I asked cautiously.

"Somewhere you can stretch your legs and pass the time. Don't worry; you'll be perfectly safe."

Safe was a relative term, but I kept my mouth shut as I followed him out of the room. I hesitated in the doorway, my heart pounding as I weighed the risks and potential benefits of taking this supposed freedom being offered to me.

"Look, you can stay cooped up in this room if you want." The guard's impatience was palpable, and he crossed his arms. "I couldn't care less what you do."

His words served as a reminder that this could be my only chance to gather information about my surroundings. If I wanted to escape this place, I needed every advantage I could get.

I took a step forward. "Fine. Let's go." I straightened my posture and tried to exude confidence, despite the uncertainty swirling within me.

The guard nodded curtly, and we began our journey through the expansive house.

As we walked, I marveled at the grandeur. Tall windows draped with luxurious silk curtains allowed natural light to pour into the hallway, casting an ethereal glow on the polished marble floors. Intricate woodwork adorned the walls, and crystal chandeliers hung from high ceilings like sparkling constellations.

I tried to focus on memorizing the twists and turns of the labyrinthine corridors, but then I remembered what my captor had told me: nothing but miles of trees. If there was even a sliver of a chance I could escape this opulent prison, though, I had to take it.

"Here we are," the guard said, stopping before a heavy wooden door carved with ornate designs. He pushed it open to reveal a large study. A plush armchair sat in front of a stone fireplace. The fire burning in the heart cast flickering shadows across the room.

"Is this where I'm supposed to stay?" I asked, my gaze darting around the space, already searching for potential exits or hiding places.

"Yep." The guard leaned against the doorframe. "You're free to read any book you'd like while you're here. Just don't try anything funny."

"Wouldn't dream of it." My tone dripped with sarcasm, and I rolled my eyes. Real mature.

The study was a sanctuary of knowledge, its walls lined with floor-to-ceiling bookshelves that seemed to stretch into infinity. I ran my fingers over the spines of the books, feeling the smooth leather and rough fabric beneath my fingertips. The scent of old paper and ink filled the air, mingling with the faint aroma of polished wood and leather-bound volumes.

"Make yourself at home," the guard said gruffly, leaning against the doorframe. "Lunch will be served to you in here later." His tone was dismissive, but I could have sworn I detected a hint of pity in his demeanor.

"Can I ask you something?" I put some space between us and turned to face the huge man.

He sighed, clearly exasperated. "What is it?"

"Who is my captor? What does he want from me?"

He simply glared at me.

"Can you at least tell me if my mother is okay?" I swallowed hard, anxiety gnawing at my insides. The image of her pale, terrified face flashed through my mind.

"Your mother is going to be fine," he answered, and there was a ring of honesty to his words.

"Thank you." Relief washed over me like a cool ocean wave. At least she was safe...for the time being. How long would that last if I didn't find a way out of here? How long could any of us hold on to hope?

"Now, quit asking questions." His patience was obviously wearing thin. "Just enjoy your time here while you can."

With that, he closed the door, leaving me alone in the vast room. I swallowed hard, trying to tamp down my growing frustration and fear. If I wanted to escape this place, I needed to gather information, and fast. If the guard wouldn't tell me anything, maybe I'd find some clues among these books.

I wandered through the rows of shelves, scanning the titles as I searched for anything that might provide insight into my captor's motives. There were volumes on history, politics, science, art, and even a shelf dedicated to rare, ancient texts written in languages I couldn't begin to decipher. My captor had eclectic tastes, but what did any of it have to do with me?

As I continued my search, I became increasingly aware of the silence enveloping me. It was almost suffocating, pressing in on me from all sides. Without the guard's presence, I felt vulnerable, exposed, and more determined than ever to find a way out.

Ignoring the books, I paced the length of the room. What did I know about this man? What could he possibly want with me?

My thoughts raced in circles as I racked my brain for any shred of information that might help me understand my situation. All I had to go on was the voice in my head that seemed to know everything about me, yet remained infuriatingly elusive.

I sighed, my predicament bearing down on me like a heavy stone. It was no use. I was trapped here, with nothing but miles of trees and an enigmatic captor standing between me and freedom.

I had a nagging feeling I was being watched. I scanned the room for any sign of cameras. It didn't take long for me to spot the small, unassuming devices tucked away in the corners of the room.

"Great, just great," I said under my breath. I was a bird in a cage, trapped and monitored every second of the day.

The large bookshelves lining the walls caught my attention. I went back to looking at the books. One stood out among the rest: *The Dark History of Sex Toys*. Curiosity piqued, I pulled it from the shelf and started flipping through the pages.

Holy fucking shit. I couldn't believe a book like this even existed. My gaze stayed glued to the detailed illustrations and descriptions as I imagined Ty and me using some of these toys. After the dream I had, I was still horny, and this book wasn't helping at all.

"Focus," I admonished myself, forcing my thoughts back to the task at hand. I couldn't afford to get distracted by my stupid sex drive right now. There was too much at stake.

Footsteps approached the door, and I quickly shoved the book back onto the shelf, trying to act casual as the lock clicked and the door opened.

"Here's your lunch," a female voice said, cutting through my anxious thoughts.

I turned to see the same woman from before—the one I'd bowled over in the hallway. She looked even smaller and more fragile up close. Darn it. I didn't want to feel guilty on top of everything else.

"Thank you. I'm sorry about yesterday, by the way. I didn't mean to hurt you."

She gave me a small smile and nodded, setting the tray down on a nearby table. "It's okay. I understand. I just hope that one day you'll see the master is a good man."

Her words caught me off guard. *The master?* Did she really believe that? Was she a captive too, or was there something more going on here?

My curiosity got the better of me. "Are you a captive as well?"

She looked genuinely shocked at my question. "No. The master saved my life. I owe him a great debt."

My eyebrows knitted together as I tried to make sense of her words. Was she truly happy to be here, serving this man who was holding me against my will?

"Can I ask your name?" I asked, hoping to learn more about her.

She gave me a hesitant smile. "It's Anna,"

"Nice to meet you, Anna. I'm Liza."

"Likewise." Her eyes softened. "I hope you enjoy your lunch."

The word *master* echoed in my mind as Anna motioned to leave the room. It didn't sit well with me, and I couldn't shake my unease. Why would someone insist on being called that? What kind of power did he hold over people like Anna?

"How did he save your life?" I asked before she could disappear through the door.

Anna hesitated and bit her lip. "I was in a bad situation before I came here. The master found me, took me in, and gave me a purpose. I can never repay him for that."

I studied her face, searching for any hint of deception or fear. I found none. Her words seemed genuine. Heartfelt, even. How could that be? How could the man who kidnapped me also be a savior to this girl?

"I understand why you're afraid," Anna said softly. "Please, trust me when I say the master is a good man. He has his reasons for doing what he does, even if they don't always make sense."

If he was such a good man, why did he kidnap people and lock them up? There had to be more to the story.

"Enjoy your lunch." Anna gave me one last reassuring smile before she left and closed the door behind her.

Alone again, I stared down at the food, my appetite momentarily forgotten as I pondered Anna's words. Who was this mysterious master? What had he done to earn such loyalty from her?

I picked up my fork, hesitating for a moment before taking a bite of the tender chicken.

The rich flavors exploded on my taste buds as I ate, though I was reluctant to admit it was delicious. In front of me lay a salad mixed with fresh vegetables topped with a tangy dressing, a heavenly piece of grilled chicken cooked to perfection, and a side of creamy mashed potatoes that melted in my mouth. The aromas wafting from the plate were irresistible, but still, I kept reminding myself that I shouldn't be enjoying this, no matter how delicious it was.

"Ugh." I took another bite. "It's not fair that the food is so good when I'm stuck in this situation."

Sometime later, long after my meal had settled, the door to the study opened, revealing the same guard who had brought me here. He stood tall and imposing, his arms crossed over his broad chest like usual. I studied him carefully, trying to gauge his intentions.

"Time to go back to your room," he said gruffly and motioned for me to follow him. I hesitated only for a moment before deciding to comply, figuring I'd use this opportunity to learn more about this master and his motivations.

"Can I ask you something?" I blurted as we walked down the elegant hallway, our footsteps echoing softly on the polished marble floors. The guard glanced at me, his expression unreadable.

"Sure. Shoot." He sounded almost bored.

"Are you indebted to the master, too? Or do you really just not care that you're helping keeping someone captive who's done nothing wrong?"

He didn't break his stride or give any indication that he was bothered by my blunt inquiry. After a moment, he sighed and said, "I do owe him, but that doesn't mean I don't care about your situation."

"Then, why help him?" I asked, trying not to sound whiny.

"Because he saved my life once," he replied without hesitation. "In this world, loyalty is everything."

His words echoed Anna's earlier statement. What kind of man could inspire such devotion from two completely different people?

"Is what you're doing worth it, though?" I was genuinely curious. "Keeping someone captive like this?"

"Look." He stopped in front of the door to my room. "I won't pretend to understand everything that's going on or why you've been brought here, but I do know that the master isn't a cruel man. He's got his reasons for doing what he does. If you give him a chance, maybe you'll see that, too." The guard's words hung in the air, heavy and suffocating. "You're lucky. If any of the people wanting that bounty on your head had gotten to you, you'd likely be somebody's fuck toy right now."

My stomach twisted at the thought, and bile rose in my throat. The idea of being captured and used like some disposable object made my skin crawl. It didn't make sense. If that was all this master guy wanted from me, why was I here? Why hadn't he just done whatever he wanted with me already?

He stepped aside so I could walk into the bedroom, which I did. No point in trying to fight him again.

"Then, why am I here?" I asked defiantly. "Why go through all this trouble if not to use me as an omega?"

He leaned against the doorframe, his arms taking up their usual residence over his broad chest as he regarded me with an unreadable expression. "That's not for me to say. All I can tell you is that the master has his reasons."

I recoiled instinctively, clenching my jaw, and doing my best not to let the full impact of his statement show on my face. Even though he was trying to make me feel better, in his own blunt and brutal way, it had the opposite effect.

If anything, the thought of what might have happened if things had gone differently only served to heighten my fear and confusion.

Before I said anything else, a sudden crackle filled the room, followed by the familiar voice that had been haunting me ever since my abduction, this time over the speaker.

"Enough." The stern tone left no room for argument. "Leave her alone."

I glanced at the guard, who looked unconcerned. He simply shrugged before turning to leave the room.

On the one hand, I was glad the conversation was over. On the other, I had been cheated out of the answers I so desperately sought.

Once the door clicked shut behind him, I slumped against the wall, momentarily overwhelmed by my situation. The guard's words echoed in my head, reminding me just how precarious my position really was. I didn't know who the master was or why he had taken me, but I couldn't afford to waste any more time trying to figure it out.

I pushed away from the wall. "Who are you?" I shouted. I didn't know if he was still listening, but it was worth a shot.

"Patience," he said in my head after a moment. *"All will be revealed in due time."*

"Due time?" I was getting sick of all this evasiveness. "I've been kidnapped, held captive, and now your staff is telling me I'm lucky because I could've ended up as someone's sex toy? Sorry if I don't find that particularly comforting."

"*Your anger is understandable,*" he said, his voice calm. "*Your situation is not as hopeless as it seems. You are here for a reason, and that reason has nothing to do with the twisted fantasies of those who seek to harm you.*"

"Then, what is it?" My pulse pounded in my ears. "Why am I here?"

"*Like I said before, patience.*" His infuriatingly calm reply only exasperated me even more. "*In time, everything will become clear.*"

"Fine." I wasn't going to get more answers right now. "Don't expect me to just sit here quietly and wait for you to decide I'm ready."

"*Wouldn't dream of it,*" he said with a hint of amusement. "*After all, what would be the fun in that?*"

"Who are you?" I asked again, slapping my palm against the wall. "Why don't you come out and show yourself instead of hiding behind speakers?"

"*I promise that tomorrow, over dinner, we will have a proper face-to-face introduction, and I will answer all your questions.*"

"Tomorrow?" I couldn't keep the incredulity from my voice. "You expect me to wait another day just to find out who you are? Why should I trust anything you say?"

"*It's not like you have much of a choice in the matter, but I can assure you that I am a man of my word. Tomorrow, you'll get your answers. Get some rest.*"

How could I rest when I was locked up in a strange place with no idea why I was here or who was keeping me here?

Despite my racing thoughts, the exhaustion from the past few days finally caught up with me. Reluctantly, I crawled into the bed. While I waited for sleep, I tried to focus on anything other than my current predicament, especially since tomorrow promised a confrontation with my mysterious captor.

Chapter 4 - Ty

The dim glow of the fireplace cast dancing shadows on the walls of my office. Dad sat across from me, his face marred with concern and memories long buried. We were discussing the threat Liam posed to our family and whether we should take Castro's warning seriously.

"What I did to that pack all those years ago... it was brutal but necessary at the time. I can't imagine the hate Liam must harbor for us." Dad rubbed his temples, clearly wrestling with his past actions.

"He wants revenge, Dad." I leaned back in my chair, gripping the armrests hard. "Then there's Liza. We practically kidnapped her after killing her biological parents. It's no wonder he's furious. But would he go as far as murder?" My wolf bristled. "Would he be willing to kill his own sister just to get back at us? If so, why kidnap her in the first place?" I asked, trying to understand Liam's twisted plans. Dad shook his head slowly, his posture filled with uncertainty.

Before either of us could speak further, the door burst open. Nico and Isaiah strode into the room, holding rolled-up blueprints, their urgency radiating off them like heat from the sun.

"These are properties we found associated with Liam. We've marked the ones reported to have the most traffic." Isaiah tapped the roll of blueprints he carried.

The men spread the paperwork all out on the table, tracing the outlines of various buildings and properties.

Nico pulled out the closest location's layout, scanning it for any sign of weakness or vulnerability. "Let's focus on this one first." He tapped the paper. "It's only a few hours away from here, and it looks like it has some potential weak spots we could exploit."

Dad, Isaiah, and I gathered beside Nico to examine the blueprint and aerial map. Thick woods surrounded the property, and a winding road led up to a secluded house. It looked like the perfect place for Liam to hide Liza.

"Here's what we're going to do," I said, my wolf howling in anticipation of finding our mate. "Isaiah, you and I will approach the property from the east. We'll move through the trees, staying hidden as much as possible. We don't want to alert anyone inside that we're coming."

Isaiah nodded.

"Meanwhile, Nico and a couple of guards will circle around to the west side. You'll be our backup, ready to step in if things go south."

Nico nodded silently, his face betraying no emotion.

"Once Isaiah and I reach the house, we'll scout the area and look for any signs of movement or activity. If we spot Liza, we move in quickly and quietly, and we get her out of there."

"Are we sure this is the right place?" my dad asked. "What if she's not there?"

"Then we'll move on to the next property." I tried to sound confident, even though uncertainty gnawed at my insides.

A heavy weight settled on my heart as I stared down at the blueprint, working out the worst-case scenarios in my mind. My wolf paced restlessly within me, equally anxious to find Liza and bring her back to safety. Ordinarily, I would send a team of wolves to scout out a location like this, but this was different. This was my mate we were talking about.

"Are you sure you want to go by yourself?" Dad asked. "We can have a team ready to go in minutes."

I shook my head, my resolve unwavering. "This is Liza, Dad. If she's in danger, I need to be the one who saves her."

He pressed his lips into a thin line. "At least let me come with you."

"No." My firm tone had him meeting my gaze. "I need you here. If anything goes wrong, I trust you to make the right decisions for the pack."

His expression softened slightly. "Just be careful, son."

I nodded, swallowing the lump that had formed in my throat. "I will. I promise."

Isaiah, Nico, I, and a small contingent of wolves set off toward the property under the cover of darkness. As we approached, a sense of foreboding crept over me, the shadows closing in tighter around us with each passing moment.

"Stay sharp," I told the others. "We don't know what we're walking into."

The moonlight cast a ghostly glow over the secluded house and eerie shadows on the ground that danced in time with the wind rustling through the trees. I crouched behind a thick bush, scanning the area for any movement. The silence was nearly suffocating, broken only by our own breathing.

I turned to Isaiah and Nico. "Anything?"

"Nothing yet." Isaiah held up binoculars, his attention never leaving the house. "But we've got to be careful. This place is giving me the creeps."

Nico nodded in agreement, his usual bravado replaced with a tense seriousness.

We moved cautiously, each of us taking up our agreed positions around the perimeter of the house. My wolf urged me to charge in and tear apart anyone who dared to harm Liza, but I knew better than to give in to those primal instincts. We needed to be strategic if we were going to rescue her.

As I peered through the foliage, trying to catch a glimpse of anything that might indicate Liza's presence, frustration washed over me. Why did Liam have to drag her into this? She didn't deserve to be caught in the crossfire of our twisted pasts.

"Ty," Nico called softly over the radio from his position on the other side of the house. "I think there might be someone inside. There's a shadow moving near the window."

My gaze snapped to the indicated spot. A flicker of movement caught my attention, but it was gone as quickly as it had appeared.

"Is it her?" he asked after a moment.

I nodded. "Has to be." Even as I spoke, a nagging doubt began to gnaw at the back of my mind. If it *was* Liza, why didn't I feel the magnetic pull of our mating bond?

"Wait." I trusted my gut, and it was telling me something was off. "Something's wrong. Look closer."

As the seconds ticked by, I studied the woman in the window. She moved slightly, raising her hand to brush a lock of hair from her face—an action so distinctly Liza-like that I nearly rushed in. Still, the absence of our connection plagued me, refusing to be ignored.

"Ty," Nico murmured. "It's not her."

My heart sank. He was right. The woman standing in the window was too short—not by much, but it wasn't her. "It's a decoy. Liza isn't in this house."

Our failure pressed down on me, but this was not the time for self-pity. We needed to regroup and figure out our next move.

"Let's fall back." My words cut through the quiet night air. "We need to rethink our plan."

The damp earth beneath my feet did little to ground me as the night air buzzed with the tension radiating off me. Nico and Isaiah flanked me, their unwavering loyalty a solid comfort despite our current predicament.

"Alpha Keller?" A strange voice cut through the darkness, and I stiffened at the unexpected intrusion. A man stepped out of the shadows, his bearing confident, yet not entirely hostile. Something about him seemed familiar, but I couldn't quite place it. "I'm here on behalf of Liam."

Nico growled low in his throat. I held up a hand, silencing him. Something told me this man had information we desperately needed, and I wasn't about to let my pride get in the way.

"Speak." I steeled myself for what was to come.

The man eyed us warily, then cleared his throat. "Your little operation here has been... well, noted, shall we say? Liam wanted me to inform you that your efforts are futile. You won't find Liza."

I balled my hands into fists, barely holding back a snarl. How dare he speak so casually of my mate, as if her life were nothing more than a game to be toyed with?

"Where is she?"

"Ah, well, that's not for me to say," the man said with a smirk that made my blood boil. "But know this, Alpha. Liza will have to make a choice soon. When she does, she'll choose her brother. Liam has no intention of harming your precious Liza. Liam also wanted me to tell you that he's impressed. He thought you might be reckless enough to storm in here without thinking, but it seems you're more cunning than that."

"Is that supposed to be a compliment?" I asked, my voice dripping with sarcasm.

"Take it however you'd like." His smirk widened. The asshole knew he'd struck a nerve. "Liam will be pleased to know you're not a complete idiot."

"Very well," I said through gritted teeth, forcing myself to remain calm. Easier said than done. "Tell Liam that I will find her, and when I do, he'll have to answer for everything he's done."

The man merely smiled before melting back into the shadows.

Nico stepped in front of me, his hand gripping my arm firmly. "Ty, don't. If we go after him now, we'll be playing right into their hands."

"Let go of me, Nico," I snarled, my wolf itching beneath my skin to give chase. "He knows where Liza is. He's our best chance at finding her."

"Listen to Nico," Isaiah said, his eyes locked on the man's retreating form. "We can't afford to lose our cool right now. Liam's got the upper hand. We need to be smarter than he is if we want to get Liza back."

Molten lava coursed through my veins, but they were right. Charging after the messenger wouldn't help anyone, least of all Liza.

Reluctantly, I nodded, letting the fire in my blood subside to a steady simmer. "Let's regroup and figure out our next move."

The taste of defeat lingered in my mouth, bitter and acrid, as I trudged back to where we'd left the cars. The shadows followed me like spectral wraiths, mocking my failure. I swallowed down my self-pity. Liza was depending on me. We climbed back into the vehicles and returned to the estate.

***

"Ty," Dad called from the armchair in my study. He scrutinized me with concern and curiosity. "There's something you need to see."

He handed me a heavy, worn envelope, its edges frayed with age. My fingers traced the inked letters that spelled out *'From Castro'* on the front.

"What is this?" I asked warily.

"It's a delivery from Castro. Open it and see for yourself." My father watched my every movement.

I tore the envelope open, revealing a battered, leather-bound journal. It looked ancient, its pages yellowed and fragile. As I cautiously leafed through the entries, realization dawned on me. This journal had belonged to Liza's biological father. Questions swirled in my mind like a tempest. How had Castro obtained such a prized possession? What secrets did these pages hold?

"Have you read it?" I glanced at my father before turning my attention back to the journal.

"I skimmed through," he said. "There's a lot to learn from it."

I frowned as I continued to leaf through the entries, each word ingraining itself onto my soul. My wolf was restless and agitated. There was something hidden between the lines that we needed to understand, and I vowed to uncover it.

"This could be the key to finding Liza."

"Let's hope so." I didn't miss the sadness in my father's voice. "We need to bring her home, Ty. We owe her that much."

Nodding, I clutched the journal as if it were a lifeline. I skimmed through the worn pages, my eyes darting over the writing as I searched for any clues that could lead us to Liza. The scent of old leather and ink filled my nostrils—a reminder of the secrets held within its bindings. As I flipped through the pages, my heart raced, each word holding more significance than the last.

I paused on a page that sent a chill down my back. My blood ran cold as I read the words written about Liza, the implications twisting my stomach into knots. It was worse than anything I could have imagined. What I held in my hands was a ticking time bomb— one that threatened not only Liza's safety, but also the very foundation of our pack.

"This just got even worse."

Dad's brow furrowed with concern as he leaned closer, trying to catch a glimpse of the page that had so thoroughly shaken me. But I didn't want to reveal it to him—not yet. I needed time to process the information before I shared it with anyone else.

"What is it?" he asked. "What did you find?"

"Something dark." I swallowed hard. "I can't tell you yet, Dad, but this has raised the stakes much higher."

He sighed, a look of resignation crossing his features. "Very well. Just remember that you don't have to carry this burden alone."

"Thank you," I said, my gaze returning to the damning words on the page. As much as I wanted to confide in my father, I couldn't bring myself to speak the truth out loud just yet. It was too terrible. Too dangerous.

As I continued to read, my mind raced with thoughts of Liza entangled in a web of darkness and deceit. She was out there somewhere, likely unaware of the secrets hidden within her past. Unaware of the danger that loomed over her head like a dark cloud.

Chapter 5 - Liza

A sharp knock jolted me from my uneasy sleep, and I blinked groggily at the bathroom door. Streaks of sunlight filtered through the tiny window near the ceiling onto the cold tile floor where I'd made a makeshift bed for myself. Unwilling to trust my captor enough to sleep in the bedroom they'd provided, I'd sought refuge on the bathroom floor again before I got too comfortable on the soft bed.

"Breakfast," the familiar female voice called from behind the door, making me pause before getting up from my makeshift bed. I ignored the discomfort in my muscles and gritted my teeth. I wasn't about to let them see any weakness.

"Coming." I opened the door and nodded at the same girl who had delivered my meals before.

Her dark hair was pulled back into a low ponytail, and she held a tray laden with steaming food. The scent of bacon and eggs wafted toward me, making my stomach grumble involuntarily.

"Thanks." I accepted the tray with a tight smile. "So, Anna," I said, making a concerted effort to start a conversation. "How long have you been working here?

Apart from delivering food, what else is included in your job description?"

"Uh, well." She glanced nervously at the door as though expecting someone to barge in at any moment. "I've been here for about two years now. I mostly clean and help with other tasks around the house."

"Two years?" I tried to hide my shock. "That's a long time. How old are you?"

She didn't meet my eyes. "I'm twenty-two."

"Really?" Her admission surprised me. "You don't look a day over eighteen."

"Thank you," she said, her cheeks flushing pink.

"Did you grow up around here? Do you have a family nearby?" I continued, hoping to establish some sort of rapport with her.

"Uh, no, I'm not from around here." She fidgeted with the hem of her uniform. "I don't really have any family left."

"I'm sorry to hear that," I whispered gently, feeling a pang of sadness in my chest. I knew what it was like to lose loved ones, and I wouldn't wish that pain on anyone. "So, uh, earlier you mentioned that the master saved your life. Could you tell me more about that? How did he do it?"

"It's nothing," she said quickly, a nervous smile playing at the corner of her lips. "It's not important."

"Come on, Anna," I pleaded gently. "You can trust me."

She shook her head. "Sorry, I can't talk about it." Her face paled slightly as she glanced at the door again. "Please, let's not discuss this. I shouldn't be talking to you about these things."

"Anna, I need your help." My desperation became more pronounced. "I don't know what's happening or why I'm here. You're the only person who's shown me any kindness since I arrived. Please, just tell me something, anything that might give me a clue about who the master is or what he wants with me."

She looked torn, her gaze darting between me and the door as though weighing the risks of revealing more information. Finally, she said, "All I can say is that the master has his reasons for everything he does. He's not a cruel man, but he's also not someone you want to cross. I suggest you do as you're told, and maybe, just maybe, things will work out for you in the end."

"Anna, please—"

She cut me off with a frantic shake of her head, her eyes wide with fear. "I've already said too much. I have to go. Just... be careful." With that, she hurried out of the room, leaving me alone with my swirling thoughts.

"Bothering the staff again?" asked the mocking presence inside my head, and I clenched my fists in frustration. My captor seemed to be a constant presence in my head, invading my thoughts and making it impossible to forget that I was being watched at all times. I had to pray he couldn't actually *hear* my thoughts, only project his voice into my mind.

"Leave me alone," I snapped. "You kidnapped me and locked me in this place. What the fuck do you expect?"

"Fine," he said curtly. *"But I don't understand why you insist on sleeping in the bathroom when you have a perfectly comfortable bed available."*

"Maybe because I don't trust you," I shot back as I stared down at the food on the tray. "Just so you know, I'm not going to stop trying to escape."

As I paced back and forth across the room, the plush carpet soft beneath my bare feet, I racked my brain for any other possible strategies to learn more about my captor and his motives. If I couldn't get through to Anna, maybe there was someone else among the staff who would be more willing to help.

"Listen, you son of a bitch! You've cut me off from the world, so excuse me if I crave some human interaction."

He remained silent for so long, I thought he'd retreated, but he spoke again, and when he did, his demeanor was surprisingly gentle.

"*Very well. I understand your need for connection.*" He almost sounded apologetic. "*As for sleeping in the bathroom, you really should trust me more. You're safe here.*"

"Safe?" I snorted, slamming my fists onto my hips. "You keep saying that, yet I've been taken from my home, my family, my life. Trust isn't exactly high on my list right now."

"*Perhaps I can change that. I've already told you we'd be having dinner together tonight. We can discuss this further then.*"

My stomach churned at the prospect of meeting the mysterious man in person. What would he demand of me? I tried to push that thought aside and instead focus on the opportunity it presented. If I managed to get close enough to the person behind all this, maybe I'd find a way to escape.

"Fine," I said, my fingers instinctively pulling at the hem of my shirt. "I look forward to meeting you properly at dinner."

Once again, I was left alone with my thoughts. As I stood there, I tried to steel myself for what was to come, drawing on every ounce of strength and courage I possessed. I would not allow fear to hold me back, not when my freedom was at stake.

I picked at my breakfast, worry nagging at me like a relentless itch. The food was delicious, but the anticipation of the dinner I'd been promised with my captor made it difficult to enjoy. The eggs were fluffy, the bacon crisp and savory, yet each bite tasted bland and unexceptional on my tongue.

"Get a grip, Liza," I muttered, forcing myself to take another bite. My stomach churned, but I needed the energy now more than ever.

As soon as I finished eating, I darted into the bathroom for some much-needed privacy. I had barely begun to wash my hands when there was an insistent knock on the door, followed by the sound of it creaking open. I hastily dried my hands on a towel and squared my shoulders, bracing for whatever was coming next.

"Miss Liza," the guard said gruffly, visually inspecting me as if assessing my readiness for... something. "The master says you are to be given more freedom."

"More freedom?" I asked, surprise momentarily drowning out my fear. Was this some kind of trick? A test to see how I would react? Or was it a genuine offer? A small taste of the life I so desperately longed for?

"Within the house, yes," he clarified, his face blank. "You may explore certain areas, but you must not venture outside. Understood?"

"Of course," I said cautiously, trying to gauge his intentions. His body language remained guarded, revealing absolutely nothing. "Thank you."

"Follow me," he said, turning on his heel and striding out of the room. I hesitated for a moment, then trailed after him, curiosity getting the better of me.

I followed the guard through the house, my bare feet padding silently over the plush carpets and polished marble floors. We passed through a corridor lined with ornate, gilt-edged mirrors, and intricately carved wooden panels that appeared to stretch on for miles. Yet, for all its splendor, the place was cold and empty—a beautiful prison that offered no true comfort or solace.

"Here," the guard said abruptly, stopping in front of a set of double doors. He pushed them open to reveal a breathtaking indoor pool, its crystal-clear water shimmering under the soft glow of the overhead lights. It was like something out of a dream. A sanctuary hidden within the confines of my gilded cage.

"The master believes physical activity is important for maintaining health and wellbeing," the guard said a little less gruffly. "He's made this room available for your use, should you wish to take advantage of it."

"Thank you." I gazed at the inviting water. As much as I hated to admit it, the idea of swimming, of the cool embrace of the water against my skin, was incredibly tempting. Perhaps it would provide a brief respite from my constant anxiety and help me clear my mind.

"Remember, you are not to leave the house under any circumstances. If you do, there will be consequences."

"Understood." When he turned away and left me alone in the pool room, I wondered what this newfound freedom really meant. Was my captor growing more lenient, or was it simply another means of control?

As I walked around the pool, taking in my surroundings, it became apparent that this room was just as private as the bedroom. Security cameras were discreetly mounted on the walls, their lenses positioned in such a way to ensure the entire room was covered. Clearly, my captor wanted to keep a close eye on me, even during what should have been a relaxing swim.

The space was drenched in natural sunlight thanks to the tall windows that towered almost three stories high, and I drifted over to them. The picturesque sight of landscaped gardens and the thick forest beyond greeted me. Unfortunately, it didn't give me any clue as to where I might be. I could be anywhere. The view was stunning, but it only amplified the cruel reality of my captivity.

The windows were designed to only open at the top, and there was no way for me to grip the smooth glass and climb.

Well, I striked that off my list of potential escape routes.

"Focus," I whispered. "There must be a way out of here. You just need to find it."

I continued my exploration, taking note of every detail that could potentially aid in my escape. Even though the pool area didn't provide me with a quick way out, any information I could gather was worthwhile.

"Nothing's impossible," I said firmly, trying to banish the doubts clouding my mind. "You've faced worse than this, Liza. You'll find a way out."

With a renewed sense of purpose, I turned my attention back to the pool. I'd enjoy the freedom it offered while I could. For now, I needed to stay strong, stay focused, and most importantly, stay alive.

I opened the door to the pool house bathroom and found a brand-new swimsuit waiting for me on the smooth marble countertop. With its elegant gold accents, the sleek, black one-piece exuded a sense of style and sophistication. I raised an eyebrow at the unexpected gift but figured there was no harm in going for a swim.

"Better than sitting around here feeling sorry for myself," I said under my breath as I changed into the swimsuit. Once on, I admired how well it fit me, and it struck me, once again, that whoever chose it appeared to know my size perfectly. I tried not to let it creep me out.

The instant I stepped out of the bathroom, the invigorating touch of the pool area's cool air against my skin made me shiver with goosebumps. I took a deep breath, allowing the scent of chlorine and the earthy aroma of the potted plants around the pool to fill my lungs. It was a welcome change after being cooped up inside the lavish prison of the bedroom.

The water lapped invitingly at the edge of the pool, and I waded in until I reached the perfect depth for swimming. With each stroke, I tried to let go of the tension that had been building since my abduction. The water was nice against my skin, and my taut muscles started to relax. For a moment, I allowed myself to forget about my predicament.

It didn't last long.

While I swam, I studied the cameras. They followed my every move, providing a constant reminder that I was being watched. I realized that the bathroom I'd been sleeping in was the only area I was confident did not have cameras. The fact that my captor might have been watching as I'd changed into the swimsuit made me feel queasy.

"Yes, Liza," I ridiculed myself, the sound echoing through the room. "Because watching me change is the most unforgivable act he's done."

No matter where I went or what I did, there was always someone watching and monitoring my every move. The thought both infuriated and terrified me, but I refused to let it break me. Instead, I used it as fuel for my resolve to escape.

Floating on my back, I stared up at the ceiling. "You need a plan. A real plan."

I took another moment to assess my surroundings, committing every detail to memory. The tall windows, the potted plants, the cameras—they all held potential clues for my escape. I just needed to find the right combination of elements, and the perfect opportunity to make my move.

As I sliced through the water, I was sure of one thing: I wouldn't rest until I had reclaimed my life and escaped from this nightmare. No matter how impossible it seemed, I would find a way out, and when I did, there would be hell to pay.

After completing my laps, I treated myself to the whirlpool, where the gentle pulsing of the jet against my back was soothing, yet it also sent a whisper of desire through me. I pressed my hand to my stomach. This was not the time or place for such thoughts. I was still a captive. For now, I had to keep my focus on escaping.

"Get a grip," I said under my breath as I moved away from the jet and swam toward the edge.

"Miss Liza?" Anna's voice echoed through the pool house when she entered with a tray filled with delicious-looking food. "I brought you some lunch."

"Thanks, Anna," I said, quickly hoisting myself out of the pool and wrapping a towel around my body. I'd use this as another opportunity, but I'd learned to stay away from anything personal with Anna. This time, I'd try to learn more about the house itself and its occupants. Maybe even figure out where the staff slept.

"Can I ask you something, Anna?" I tried to sound casual as I took a seat at the table.

She poured me a cup of coffee, the aroma strong enough to mask the scent of the chlorine in the air. "Yes, Miss Liza. I'll... I'll tell you what I can." She was so hesitant. Was this master genuinely that daunting?

"Where do the staff sleep? Is there a certain area of the house for that?" I asked, watching her closely for any hint of unease or suspicion.

"Um, well, we have our own quarters in the east wing," she said hesitantly, giving me a curious look. "Why do you ask?"

"Curiosity, I guess." I kept my tone light. "I'm just trying to get a better idea of this place, since it looks like I'll be here for a while."

Just as she was about to leave, I said, "Anna, one more thing. Do all the staff live in the east wing?"

She paused and turned back toward me, her brow furrowed. "Not exactly," she said hesitantly. "Some of us do, but there's also a separate house on the property where some of the others live."

I cheered internally at gaining this new information. "A separate house? Where is it?" I tried my best to sound casual, as if it were just another question to satisfy my curiosity.

Anna glanced around nervously, as though she wasn't sure if she should be sharing this information with me. "It's... a little farther away, toward the northwest part of the estate. Just beyond the gardens and past the stables." She pointed in the general direction with a trembling hand.

"Thank you." I spoke softly, trying to convey my gratitude without raising any suspicion. Once she nodded and left the pool house, I allowed myself to smile. At least now I had a general idea of direction, and I knew where to avoid if I managed to escape this opulent prison. It was a small victory, but it rejuvenated my hope.

I concentrated on my lunch, despite my nerves and excitement. I needed to keep up appearances and not arouse any suspicion from those watching me. While I ate, my mind raced with escape plans and strategies.

Were the people living in the other house staff members, or were they, like me, being held captive for reasons unknown? What secrets might be hiding within its walls? Perhaps some clue about the identity of my captor, or even a means of contacting the outside world?

I had a feeling this new piece of information was crucial. It was a small but significant step forward in my quest for freedom. Yet, I couldn't act rashly or let my excitement get the better of me.

For now, I'd watch, wait, and gather as much information as I could. When it was time to make my move, I would be armed with the knowledge and conviction I needed to break free from this gilded cage and return to the life I'd so cruelly been torn away from.

As I contemplated my situation and tried to quell the mixture of fear and anticipation coursing through my veins, a glimmer of hope shone through the darkness. The road ahead might be long and fraught with danger, but at least now, I had a direction to move in. A starting point on the path toward reclaiming my freedom.

"Stay strong," I whispered, my fingers intertwined tightly, and the pressure in my hands echoing my determination. "You can do this. You will survive. You will escape."

The pages of the glossy magazine that had been left out on the table slid under my fingers as I flipped through them absentmindedly. All I could think about was my potential escape and my mysterious captor. The scent of chlorine lingered on my skin as a reminder of the deceptive freedom offered by the vast indoor pool.

"Miss Liza, it's time to go back to your room now."

The guard's voice startled me, and I jerked my head up to look at him. God, he was huge. He seemed to fill the entire expanse of the double doorway. He was stern but not unkind—a contradiction that only heightened my anxiety. The contrast between his uniform and my damp bathing suit made me flush with embarrassment before fear flashed through me.

"I'll just go and put on something else." I dashed into the changing room and grabbed the robe hanging behind the door, securing it around myself. I'd shower and change in my bedroom, where there were no prying eyes of any hidden cameras.

I bundled my clothes in my arms and followed the guard back to the room. The guard's quick strides made it difficult to make a mental map of the route. He opened the door and stood to the side as I stepped into the room with my head held high, the door closing with a definitive click behind me. But this time, I didn't hear the click of the lock. For a fleeting moment, I thought to make a break for it, but the more rational side of my mind warned me there might be a trap waiting for me on the other side of the door.

After showering, I wrapped myself in a fluffy towel, luxuriating in its comforting warmth, only for that small comfort to be obliterated when I came out of the bathroom and found a fresh set of clothes neatly arranged on the bed. I couldn't stand this complete lack of privacy. Glaring up at the camera in the corner of the room, I grabbed up the items left for me and scurried back into the bathroom to dress for dinner.

With no clock, and no way to tell how many hours had passed except for the lengthening shadows outside the window, time crept by slowly. Each passing moment was a cruel reminder of my situation. Despite my best efforts to lose myself in a book, I kept glancing out the window, entertaining myself with absurd escape scenarios. I was lost in this contemplation when another guard opened the door and discovered me with my forehead pressed against the cool glass, pondering the logistics of my potential escape.

"Miss Liza, the master is waiting."

I stood up, the soft fabric of my fresh clothes brushing against my skin. My heart thumped against my ribcage, its beats echoing like the wings of a caged bird, desperate for flight. Refusing to be viewed as weak, I steadied myself and regained my composure.

"Let's get this over with." I groaned internally. I'd been aiming for nonchalant, but to my ears, my words lacked confidence.

"Who is he?" I questioned the guard, curiosity winning out of over my fear. "Why go to all this trouble just to keep me here?"

The guard didn't say a word, and his stoic expression betrayed nothing.

Taking a slow breath, I tamped down my growing frustration. I needed to stay alert and observant if I wanted to stand a chance to escape this place.

When we approached another set of ornate double doors, my palms started to sweat, and my heartbeat grew erratic. The unknown captor, the reason for my imprisonment... It all lay beyond those doors.

The doors swung open at the guard's push, revealing a lavish dining room with a soaring ceiling and gleaming marble floors. Against the backdrop of opulence, the beautifully arranged table for two stood out with its simplicity and charm. The chairs were positioned directly across from each other in a clear sign of what was to come: an intimate dinner with my captor.

This was it, the moment I'd been dreading and anticipating in equal measure.

I hesitated at the threshold, scanning the room for any clues of my captor's identity. More priceless art adorned the walls, and flames danced in the enormous fireplace.

I thought of my family and friends—the people who had been ripped away from me without warning or explanation. Rage and fear warred within me, tempered only by the knowledge that if I wanted to be with them again, I needed to stay focused and in control.

"Show yourself," I said, my voice stronger than I expected. "Tell me why I'm here,"

"Have a seat, Miss Liza." The guard gestured toward the table, then turned and left, closing the heavy door behind him, leaving me alone in the silence.

The table called to me, and my attention was immediately captured by the photo album placed in the center. Its age and simplicity were a stark contrast to the surrounding luxury. A small white envelope with my name written in graceful, flowing script sat on top of the album.

My birthname: *Liza Wylde.*

With a single breath, the bravado I'd been holding onto evaporated.

I was Liza Mimms. Liza Keller. Very few people beyond my mate and our families knew the truth about my birthright. Most people believed Liza Wylde had died with her family in the massacre at Heather Falls. Dread consumed my entire being. Fuck. Castro could be behind all this. Was it possible I was being held captive by the one man we'd fought so tirelessly against?

"Take a look," said the all-too-familiar voice in my mind, softer than ever before. *"It may help explain a few things."*

I bit my lip as I stared down at the note, then cautiously lowered myself onto the seat, my unsteady fingers grazing the cover of the album. Blood rushed in my ears, and my fingers trembled with anticipation. What secrets would I discover within these pages?

Gingerly, I opened the album to the first page, and I gasped and slapped my free hand to my mouth. The photo was charred around the edges and crumpled, but someone had taken the care to have it properly mounted inside the album. I stared down at the image of a baby girl, her wide eyes filled with curiosity, a tuft of white-blonde hair on top of her head, with her arms reaching out to the unknown photographer. I didn't need anyone to tell me that I was looking at myself.

Tears welled in my eyes as I turned the page, the rustling sound breaking the heavy silence around me. Seeing the countless photos of me as a baby was a surreal experience. I'd never seen them before. With my adoptive parents, Scott and Rory Mimms, the photographs began after Dominic Keller left me with them, and they adopted me at age four. In these images, I was a newborn cradled in the arms of my birth parents, Josef and Portia Wylde, or playing with them. It was a surreal experience to witness these precious moments. Moments I had no memory of.

"Mom... Dad..." My finger trembled as I traced the contours of my mother's image, my throat tight with emotion. I wiped away a tear, trying my best not to cry. I needed to stay strong to understand what this all meant. The kidnapping, and now this album... it was like trying to solve a jigsaw puzzle without a picture. A challenge that seemed impossible to overcome.

Flipping through the pages, I witnessed my growth from a newborn with innocent eyes to a toddler with an insatiable curiosity. In many of the pictures, there was another constant presence—a little boy, a few years older—that shared a noticeable resemblance with me. My brother Liam. In the captured moments, our laughter and playfulness served as a testament to the undeniable strength of our connection. As all the puzzle pieces fell into their rightful spots, the door swung open once more.

Caught between fear and a sense of possibility, I slowly shifted my focus from the album to the doorway. I was in a state of shock and disbelief as I took in the sight before me. Even though I hadn't seen him since I was a toddler, I recognized him instantly. The boy in the pictures. The boy from my dreams.

"Liam," I gasped, my vision locked on the unbelievable figure standing in front of me. "You're here. You're really... How?"

"Hey, Liza." He offered a small, sad smile, and his voice sounded familiar. "You must have so many questions."

"Questions?" I scoffed, shaking with a combination of relief and anger. "You have no idea."

"Let me explain." Liam took the chair across from me. "There's a lot I need to tell you. First, I need you to understand I never meant for any of this to happen. You were never supposed to be involved."

"Involved in what, exactly?" I asked, my attention flitting between him and the photo album.

"Everything that's happened, you being brought here—"

"Me being kidnapped, you mean," I snapped.

"You being brought here," he reiterated calmly. "It's all tied to our family, to secrets that go back generations."

"Secrets? What are you talking about?"

"Please, just listen." Liam reached out to take my hand. As much as I wanted to pull away and reject the comfort he was offering, I couldn't. I needed answers, and he was the only one who could provide them.

Chapter 6 - Liza

The tension in the air was suffocating as Liam and I stared at each other. Confusion spiked inside me. He looked exactly like the one picture I'd found of him on social media, only older. His brow had a few more wrinkles, and a few gray hairs were sprinkled among the darker locks.

What had happened to him during the years we'd been separated? How had this man transformed into the kind of person who would scheme to harm an innocent woman who wasn't involved in whatever was going on? He'd arranged for me to be kidnapped. He'd taken me from my mate and family.

As I pondered on the events that had unfolded in my mother's kitchen, I could feel my anger intensifying, like a bonfire gradually engulfing my body.

Vivid flashbacks surged through me, as if I were reliving them. I could hear my mother's voice calling me, urging me to come quickly. I sensed something amiss, yet I hastened to her side.

In my mind, the night unfurled before me in a series of distressing images. I arrived to find the front door ajar, inviting uncertainty. Entering the house, I discovered my mother lying motionless on the frigid kitchen floor in a pool of coagulated blood. Her pleas for me to flee and abandon her echoed in my ears, her words a desperate warning. The memory of my frantic attempts to lift her, to get her to safety, engulfed me with a heart-wrenching ache.

I could still feel the stickiness of her blood staining my hands. Then as we burst out of the house, believing we had found refuge, a figure emerged from the shadows. He brandished a weapon, directing his demands toward me while my mother stood defenseless.

The shock of the memory was amplified by the realization that this man was acting under the orders of my own brother. My own flesh and blood had betrayed me and orchestrated a situation that led to physical harm being inflicted upon my mother. It was an unforgivable act.

As I pushed myself up out of my chair and paced the grand dining room, I couldn't help but notice the strong smell of freshly polished wood, which only heightened my restless state. The anger that welled up within me became so overpowering, it took over my entire being. The flooring beneath me started to shake, and the fine china on the table made a chiming sound as plates collided with each other.

I was beyond angry at this point. The images replayed back over and over like flash photography.

The man who'd kidnapped me had been hired by own brother, and he'd hurt my mother. The man in question remained silent and still, not moving from his seat at the table, his fingers steepled before him as he observed me with the same curiosity one might expect from a child examining an insect.

"How dare you hurt my mom? All she is guilty of is loving me. She had nothing to do with you, Liam. What the hell is your motive for hurting an innocent woman?" I couldn't even tell if the things I was saying were making any sense at all. The power that coursed through me was so strong, I struggled to keep it under control.

"*Rory wasn't supposed to be hurt,*" Liam said suddenly, though his lips didn't move.

I stopped, stunned. That's when it hit me. He'd been the person speaking in my head this entire time. My anger momentarily gave way to astonishment as I stared at him.

It was all too much to take in. I was a volcano on the verge of erupting. The vibrations in the room escalated as a testament to my barely contained fury.

"Is that supposed to make it better?" I said, shaking with rage. "It's still your fault she was hurt. Without your involvement, she'd never have been in harm's way." The room trembled even more violently, the vibrations reflecting the tempest within me.

The quake I was causing didn't seem to bother him in the slightest. "Rory was only meant to be detained," he said, speaking aloud this time. "The man responsible for hurting her is no longer an issue."

I stared at Liam, the tremors quieting while a million questions whirled through my head, but one rose above the rest. "What do you mean, 'no longer an issue'?" I whispered.

Liam avoided the question, and the unsettling darkness in his gaze made me shudder. As the room suddenly grew colder, an involuntary chill ran through my body. My imagination painted a vivid picture of what might have happened to the man who hurt my mother, and it filled me with a strange mix of horror and satisfaction.

"Tell me what happened to him," I hissed. Part of me needed to know the truth, even though I was sure I might regret it.

Liam hesitated, then sighed. "Let's just say he won't be hurting anyone else ever again."

The finality in the way he told me was all I needed, and cold realization settled over me. Despite the fact the man had hurt my mother, the idea of Liam taking such drastic actions left a bitter taste in my mouth. I was torn between relief and fear.

Sensing my thoughts, the house began to rumble again, matching the agitation that coursed through me. I clenched my fists, trying to regain control, but it was like grasping at sand.

"You need to slow your breathing down, Liza. Find the anger inside and lower it." It was a command, but his tone was soothing.

I attempted to center myself. Slowly but surely, the room stopped quaking, and my ears popped at the sudden silence.

Now that my anger had subsided somewhat, I didn't bother to mask my disbelief. "Liam, is that really you?"

"Unfortunately, yes," he said with a bitter smile. "It's been a long time, Liza."

"Too long." It felt like I was staring at a ghost. Not just a ghost, but a distorted reflection of myself. The resemblance between us was astonishingly uncanny, from our strikingly similar eye color to the identical shape of our jaw lines, and even down to our noses. Nevertheless, there was an indescribable and unsettling aura surrounding him that had unease twisting in the pit of my stomach.

"Are you okay?" Liam asked, genuine concern lacing his words. "You look like you've seen a ghost."

"What do you think, Liam? Just as soon as I think I have all the pieces of the puzzle, someone snatches them away at the very last moment. The pieces keep shifting, never allowing me to see the full picture."

"Sit," he said. "I'll explain everything."

"Where do you even begin?" The question slipped unbidden out of my mouth. It was more of a rhetorical statement than an actual question, but Liam offered me a wry smile as he reclined in his chair.

"Let's start with our father," he said, running a hand through his blond hair that was a shade darker than my own. "To be honest, he wasn't a good man.

There's no point in pretending otherwise. I won't do it. Not only was he a bastard, but he was a cold-blooded murderer, and to top it all off, he was the undisputed leader of a notorious crime organization. Ironically, I now find myself at the helm of that very organization." He paused, his eyes darkening. "Whatever he was, I have to believe he loved his family. Despite the twisted nature of his beliefs, he genuinely thought his actions were for our benefit."

I sank down into my chair and wiped my damp palms on my trousers.

"Your mother carried the omega gene," he went on. "Our father was a strong alpha, but he was also a covetous man. He hired a geneticist who told him that if he and Portia were to have a female child, there was a very good chance she would be an omega as well."

Liam pinned me with a scrutinizing stare. "An omega stronger than any alpha. Feared by those who didn't understand our kind. There's a reason omegas were hunted down and killed, even by members of their own species. Because of the threat they posed to others, they would outlive their usefulness and become a liability. Our father believed there was another way. He believed omegas could be better controlled... *molded* into something useful if, rather than waiting for an omega to emerge during adolescence, they began training young."

His jaw worked for a moment, and he was full of sympathy when he continued. "That's why you were born, Liza. You were created for the sole purpose of becoming a weapon. Josef was sure there was a way to train you so he could control you."

"By brainwashing them—me—from birth," I spat, rage coiling in my belly like a snake.

"Essentially, yes," Liam said, never breaking eye contact with me. "He began your training as soon as you were born. He died before it could be completed."

"Training?" I asked, struggling to wrap my head around the idea. "You make it sound like I was some sort of pet project."

"Not a pet project... a weapon," he corrected, though it was without malice. "Liza, our father considered you nothing more than a means of achieving his desired outcome. A way of guaranteeing power and wealth for himself and his bloodline."

As Liam's words penetrated my mind, I found myself pondering the man who had given me life not out of genuine affection, but driven solely by his own self-serving motives. Knowing Liam spoke the truth only heightened the impact and made it that much more real.

Tears stung the back of my eyes. "Are you saying our parents only had me to use me?"

"Unfortunately, yes," Liam said, regret and sympathy blazing in his eyes. "Omegas are powerful, but they're also dangerous. If the wrong people control them, they can cause great harm. Our grandmother was an omega, and her handler murdered her when they could no longer control her."

A violent shiver racked my body at the thought of such a fate, and I dug my fingers into the wood of the table as if it could somehow anchor me to reality amid the storm of emotions raging within me. Was this why Liam had kidnapped me? To pick up where our father left off and become my handler? What in the ever-loving fuck was a handler?

"Is that why you brought me here?" I asked, my resolve wavering with fear and uncertainty. "Are you planning on taking Josef's place and becoming my handler?"

Liam's face contorted with disgust as he quickly shook his head. "No, Liza. That's not why I took you. I had to protect you. That's why I took you from the Kellers. I couldn't let them have control over you."

"Ty would never do that," I bit out. "The Kellers weren't even aware I was an omega."

Liam's jaw dropped at that, and if I looked hard enough, I'd be able to watch the cogs turning in his head as he tried to process this new information.

He frowned and shook his head. "Of course they knew," he said, more to himself than me. "They were just pretending not to. That's why they married you to Ty Keller. They wanted to use your power for their own purposes."

"No," I snapped. "You're wrong. They didn't know. The Mims knew. My parents—my *adoptive* parents," I clarified. "When I began showing symptoms at thirteen, they took me to a doctor who put me on hormone suppressants to keep the symptoms at bay. Not even the doctor knew what to expect from me. As for the Kellers..." I closed my eyes and breathed deeply to cool my blood. "They treated me like one of their own, and when they did find out, they went above and beyond to protect me and never once tried to exploit my abilities."

Liam shifted in his chair and avoided my gaze. After a moment of tense silence, he looked back at me. "I, uh... I had a plan." He rubbed the back of his neck awkwardly.

Dread surged through me. "Which was?"

He gave a resigned sigh. "I was planning to kill the Keller pack."

My senses were jarred, as if I had just been punched in the face. I gasped for air, my chest tightening. "You were going to kill them?" I choked out in horror.

"Only because I believed they'd kidnapped you and were trying to turn you into their own weapon of destruction," he said defensively.

I shook my head. "That doesn't make it right, Liam. They're my family. Ty is my mate." Then I remembered something else—something he likely didn't know. "We're fated, Liam. Ty and I are fated mates."

He groaned and twisted his hands through his hair. "Well, that definitely does change things. There's no way I'd be able to kill Ty now. Not without killing you, too."

"Damn right you can't," I hissed. The room vibrated again, but I couldn't bring myself to care. For a moment, I considered giving in to my power and bringing the whole fucking house down, but maybe not yet.

My head swam as I tried to process everything Liam had just revealed.

"Is this what you do, Liam?" I asked barely above a whisper. "Take matters into your own hands like our father?"

"Sometimes it's necessary," he said, unapologetic. "But I'm not our father, Liza. I'm just trying to protect you."

"By kidnapping me? By hurting my family?"

"Your mother was never supposed to be hurt," Liam said, smacking his palm on the table. "As for taking you, I did it to protect you, to save you from a fate that would have been much worse. I won't apologize for doing what was right."

I wanted to argue, to keep lashing out at him, but... he believed he was doing what was best for me, even though it went against everything I had ever been taught. It didn't make it right, but it was getting harder and harder to stay angry at him.

"Can you really protect me, Liam? Or are you just dragging me into the same darkness that consumed our father?"

For a moment, Liam didn't answer. Then, with determination lacing his words, and his eyes full of sadness, he said, "I'll do everything in my power to keep you safe."

I studied him, looking for any sign of deception, though I saw nothing but the truth. I was certain that no matter what the future held, Liam would do whatever it took to protect me, even if it meant following in our father's footsteps.

Slowly, the house stopped rumbling, leaving a tense silence hanging in the air. Liam watched me intently, as though waiting for another outburst, but I was spent, the anger that had fueled my power now replaced by a hollow ache deep within.

"Wait a minute," I said, suddenly remembering something that had been bothering me. "You. You've been talking inside my head... even back at the Keller Estate, right? How did you do that?"

Liam's expression softened as he relaxed in his chair. "Ah, yes. Telepathy. I discovered it when I was a kid. As far as I'm aware, I'm the only one who has it.

From the research I've done, all alphas in our bloodline have a special gift. This is mine. It comes in handy when I'm... working."

I frowned. A pang of jealousy struck me somewhere in my belly. "So, I can't do it?"

"No." He chuckled. "You're an omega, Liza. You have your own gifts, like those incredible healing powers of yours."

"Great," I said under my breath. "I can heal people, but I can't talk to them in their heads. That's convenient."

Liam laughed softly, and for a brief moment, he didn't look like a dangerous mob boss, but just a brother trying to connect with his long-lost sister.

"Come on," he said, standing up from his chair. "I want to show you something."

He led me down the hall to his office, which was a room filled with floor-to-ceiling bookshelves, antique furniture, and an enormous desk covered with paperwork and files. He gestured toward a stack of documents on one corner of the desk. "This is everything I've gathered on the Kellers over the years," he said. "When you mated with Ty Keller, I assumed they'd taken you in because of your powers and wanted to use them for their own gain."

I stared at the files, and an icy chill ran down my spine. Liam had come very close to making a devastating mistake.

"They were completely unaware that I'm an omega. No one apart from my adoptive parents and the doctor knew." I looked up at him, searching for some understanding. "It was only recently that they discovered what I really was. Dominic took the Kellers down a different path after everything that happened at Heather Falls. All their businesses are legitimate now."

Liam had the good grace to blush.

I hesitated to think what that meant. "Whatever you've done, Liam, make it right. The Kellers are good people."

He nodded. "We'll figure this out together. Whatever it takes."

Relief mingled with trepidation as I eyed the files. Liam might not be the brother I remembered, but he was family. I had to believe that now he knew Ty and I were fated mates, he really wouldn't proceed with his plans.

Liam's demeanor suddenly became serious as he leaned against the edge of his desk. "Can you tell me everything you remember about the night our father, our pack, was destroyed?"

I chewed the inside of my cheek, wondering where to start.

"Castro." I paused, finding it difficult to even say his name without being nauseated. "He played a big part in what happened that night. He orchestrated the massacre of the Wylde pack, then used the Kellers as a scapegoat for our father's death."

Liam's face twisted with fury. "I remember him." He growled as he spat out the words. "He was fixated on you, Liza. Obsessed. His every action proved that. It was unnatural. Unhealthy. It's partly why Josef had to send me away from the pack. He still met with me to train me to be a good alpha, but it had to be away from the pack, and especially away from you."

"You don't need to remind me." The memory of Castro's relentless pursuit made me uncomfortable. "He's still obsessed with me now, possibly more so."

"He's still alive?" Liam exclaimed. His aura radiated such power, my skin tingled.

"Yes." I swallowed hard. "I wish he wasn't, believe me. My life would be so much different if he'd died when the rest of the pack did."

"Damn it," Liam cursed, his hands clenched into fists. "I'd hoped that bastard had been wiped out with the others."

"Me, too." I wrapped my arms around myself, trying to find some comfort. "He didn't, though, and now... he's more dangerous than ever."

I told Liam what had happened since the day 'Stone' had tried to come between Ty and me, then all the crap Castro had pulled since, up to and including me believing he was the one who'd kidnapped me. Again, Liam had the grace to turn an endearing shade of tomato red.

"I'm sorry for adding to your worries, Liza," he said remorsefully. "But you mustn't underestimate the seriousness of Castro's threats. Obsession like that... it can drive someone to do terrible things." Liam gave a slow shake of his head. "We need to protect you from him."

"Protect me?" I scoffed. "I don't need your protection, Liam. Ty has been more than capable of handling Castro. We've been managing fine without you." Even as I said it, I knew it was a lie. We weren't handling Castro, but damn if I was going to let Liam put my mate down.

"Are you sure about that?" he asked, searching my face for any hint of doubt. "If he's still as obsessed with you as he was as a kid, he's dangerous. From what you've told me, he's spent the years planning, gathering resources and allies. Do you have any idea of what he's capable of now?"

I shook my head. "I won't hide from him, Liam. I won't let him control my life any longer."

"Good." Raw emotion emanated from him, and his expression darkened. "Now, let me help you deal with this threat once and for all. Castro knows you're an omega, but if he learned anything about the destructive power you're capable of, and the role a handler plays in controlling them... the last thing you need is that evil fucker having that kind of power over you. You'd have no free will. You're hardwired to obey any order your handler gives. *Any* order," he emphasized.

"Castro? A handler?" The thought of that twisted man controlling me, using me for his own warped purposes, made my veins ice over. My skin crawled.

Just what did fate have in store for me? Was I destined to be nothing more than a pawn in someone else's game?

"Exactly." The fierce protectiveness in Liam's voice both warmed and frightened me. "We can't let that happen, Liza. I won't stand by and watch you become a victim of his sick desires."

"Then, what do we do?" Desperation crept into my words. "How do we stop him?"

"We'll figure that out. We're family. No one messes with my family."

"Thank you." My heart swelled with gratitude and something akin to love for this brother I'd only just met. It was strange to find comfort in his presence, especially after the way he'd taken me, but it was undeniably reassuring.

"Promise me one thing." Liam's eyes bored into mine. "You'll let me make this right. If Castro ever comes near you again, if he ever threatens your safety or the safety of those you care about, will you come to me and let me help you?"

"I promise." Unshed tears lay on my lashes. "I promise, Liam."

"Good." A small smile flickered on his lips before disappearing just as quickly. "Now, let's figure out how to get rid of that fucker."

My confusion still lingered at the edges of my mind as I tried to understand everything Liam had told me. One question in particular nagged more than the others, though.

"Liam." I cleared my throat. "How does one become an omega's handler?"

Liam sank down in the armchair next to me. As he leaned back and drummed his fingers on the armrest, he looked every bit the mob boss. "Think of it this way. You're like a sleeper agent," he said slowly. "Our father put your wolf's main omega powers to sleep with a word—a word only certain people would have been told. I believed Dominic had forcefully extracted that word from Josef before ending his life, but now I know he wasn't aware of you being an omega..." Ice flashed in Liam's eyes. "That word will fully awaken your wolf. The person who knows that word and says it will become your handler, and you will be under their complete control."

Chapter 7 - Ty

Nico and Isaiah were catching up on sleep, and I couldn't begrudge them for it. I wanted to be out looking for Liza, but it wasn't safe to go alone—not after Liam's goons sighted us so quickly at the last property. He had far more security than we'd expected. I couldn't sleep while Liza was out there. Not when I didn't know what that fucker was doing with my mate.

The phone rang, shattering the silence in my office like a gunshot. I blinked, momentarily stunned by the sudden intrusion. A bolt of adrenaline coursed through my body as I reached for it, the leather from my chair creaking under me, and the lingering aroma of coffee from the cup of my desk bringing me back to the present. My lawyer's name flashed on the display.

"Ty speaking." I tried to control the tremor in my voice. The last few days had been a whirlwind of emotions that had drained me completely. Liza's disappearance felt like an anchor around my neck, dragging me down into a sea of worry.

"Ty, it's Mark Jameson," he said. "I've got some good news for you."

"Good news?" Unless he was calling to tell me Liza was with him, I couldn't think what good news he could possibly have for me.

"A worker from the warehouse came forward this morning," Mark continued, pausing for emphasis. "He confessed the drugs found in the factory were his. The DA has just told me all charges against you have been dropped."

The news hit me like a lightning strike, sending shockwaves throughout my entire body. I leaned back in my chair, both relieved and incredibly confused. If this worker was telling the truth, why was everything inside me still screaming that Liam had planted those drugs to set me up and ruin my name? Why was someone suddenly confessing?

With my brow furrowed in confusion, I asked, "Are you sure?"

"Positive. One of the press operators, George Dale, came forward and admitted the drugs were his."

"Thanks, Mark." This was really fucking strange. "Keep me updated if anything else comes up."

"Of course." With a click, the call ended.

It didn't sit right with me. There had to be more at play here.

I leaned back into my chair and propped my feet up on my desk. I had been so sure Liam was behind the planted drugs to set me up and tarnish my reputation. Was it part of some larger plan? Or had someone else intervened?

I breathed in the scent of wood and furniture polish to calm my nerves. The quiet ticking of the clock in the corner of my office reminded me that time was moving forward, even if my world was currently standing still. My wolf's unease mirrored my own, evidenced by the low growl reverberating through me.

I shook my head to clear it and slapped my cheeks. "Stay focused." There were too many unknowns, and I couldn't afford to lose myself in speculation. The pack needed me and Liza...

God, I needed her back safely more than anything.

No sooner had the thought crossed my mind than the phone rang again. I stared at the screen certain I was hallucinating. Liza's name was flashing across it. A waterfall of relief quenched the burning fire of anxiety that had been consuming me for days. My mood instantly lifted, and I answered the call, unable to contain my excitement.

"Liza? Is that you?" My voice cracked, and I clenched my fists, desperately seeking something tangible to cling on to.

"Ty, it's me. I'm okay." Her voice was shaky, but she really did sound okay. My wolf stirred within me, aching to be near her.

"Where are you?" I worked hard at remaining calm despite the tornado of emotions inside me.

"I'm not sure exactly, but please trust me. I'm safe, and I'm coming home.."

"What happened?" The tidal wave of relief was tempered by a thousand questions.

She gave a weighted sigh. "It's... it's a lot, Ty. I'll explain everything when I get there, but you have to promise me something first." Her plea pulled at my heartstrings, and I would've promised her the moon if she asked.

"Anything, Liza."

"It will be a lot to process. I need you to listen without judgment, and I need you to stay calm." She sounded so vulnerable.

I frowned. What could possibly warrant such a request? But I swallowed down my fears. All that mattered now was Liza coming home. Together we were capable of tackling any challenges that lay ahead.

"Please, just promise me," she pleaded. "Promise not to attack Liam when we come back."

The name sparked a fierce reaction in me, and my body tensed. "What the hell is going on, Liza?" I snarled.

Her loud, frustrated exhale rumbled through the phone. "It's complicated, Ty. Please, just trust me on this. We'll explain everything when we get there. I need you to stay calm and promise me you won't harm him."

For her, I fought back the rage. "Fine, I promise, but the moment he poses a threat, I reserve the right to ensure our safety, and that of my pack. He took you from me, Liza. That's not something I can easily overlook."

"He had his reasons for that. I understand why you're angry, Ty. I can't imagine what it's been like for you, but it hasn't exactly been a walk in the park for me, either. I need you to hear him out." In the background, a man called her name.

"Are you ready?" he asked her.

I growled. "Okay. I promise. Just… just hurry, I need you."

"Thank you," she whispered so tenderly that her words carried a profound sense of gratitude and love. "I'll be home soon."

"I love you," I murmured.

"I love you, too," she said, and then the line went dead.

I stared at the screen, the muscles in my jaw ticking. For now, Liza was out of danger, but my gut told me something was very, very wrong.

Each possibility I came up with was more troubling than the last. What could be so important that Liza would beg me to listen without judgment? We knew Liam had kidnapped her, but how was he connected with everything?

***

Time crawled by with agonizing slowness, each tick of the clock like a roll of thunder in my silent office. It had been six hours since she'd called. Six long, torturous hours that only made the three days she'd been missing seem even longer. My wolf snarled and paced restlessly on the edges of my mind, desperate to do something—*anything*—other than wait. We were powerless, and it didn't sit well with either of us.

"Ty," my mother said from the doorway. I tore my attention away from the window, where I'd been staring at the driveway. "You need to eat something. You've barely touched your food. And you need to rest."

I glanced down at the untouched plate in front of me and pushed it away. "I'll eat when Liza's back, and I can't rest when she's out there with Liam."

"Your father and I are here to help," she said softly. "We'll work through this as a family."

She was right, of course. Not that it eased the ache or anxiety that had taken root in my gut. I wanted Liza home, safe in my arms. Until then, the world was off balance—or as Liza would say, like a cake without its frosting.

"Son, you need to keep up your strength," my father said. "For Liza's sake, not just your own."

"Fine." I shoveled a few bites into my mouth before dropping my fork with a resounding clatter.

The food tasted like ash, each bite a bitter reminder of how I'd failed to protect the woman I loved.

"Where are they?" I slammed my fist against the wall. The searing pain that shot through my hand only fueled the tempest brewing within, yet it served as a poignant reminder to stay composed—for Liza, for my family, and for my own sake.

My phone buzzed with a text, and I jumped up from my chair. "Liza's back. Security just informed me she's on her way down the drive."

I rushed out of my office, and my parents followed behind me, concern and hope written all over their faces.

The three of us stood on the porch, our collective anticipation palpable as we waited for Liza to arrive. My ears picked up the distant rumble of an engine, growing louder as it approached our home. A sleek, black SUV came into view, kicking up dust as it stopped a short distance away. I struggled to contain the anxious energy that coursed through me, my wolf snarling and huffing, eager to be reunited with his mate.

After the passenger door swung open, Liza emerged, her hair disheveled and eyes puffy from crying. Despite that, she was the most stunning vision I had ever encountered. My heart swelled with relief and love, the mating bond pulling me toward her like a magnet.

"Ty." Liza's voice cracked with emotion. I barely had time to react before she was in my hold, her arms and legs wrapping around me. I buried my face in her neck and held her as tightly as I dared. Her sweet vanilla and calming lavender scent grounded me, and some of the tension seeped out of my muscles. My wolf let out a contented sigh.

"God," I murmured in her ear. "I was certain I'd lost you."

"Never," she said, stroking my hair. "You'll never lose me, Ty. I promise."

I raised my head, and Liza cupped my face, her own paling as her stare intensified. "My mom?"

The intensity of her fear heightened, overshadowed by her fear of the answer, and the overwhelming guilt for not having asked sooner.

"She's okay. Rory's fine. She had to have surgery, but the doctor discharged her earlier this morning."

Liza dropped her head onto my shoulder and sobbed.

"Let me look at you," I said softly, reluctantly pulling away to assess her. Leaning back slightly, I searched for any sign of injury or harm. Though she appeared unharmed, the worry etched on her face spoke volumes.

"I'm fine," she said, her bottom lip quivering slightly. "I promise, Liam didn't hurt me. He made mistakes, Ty, but he believed he was doing the right thing and was saving me."

"Saving you?" I frowned. "But, why? From me? What does he want with you?"

"Like I said on the phone, it's complicated. There's so much I need to tell you."

"Then, tell me." My heart ached at the uncertainty in her tone. "I can't help until I have all the details, and the longer you delay, the more disturbing scenarios my mind makes up."

Before she could respond, the closing of a car door, and the crunch of gravel underfoot reminded me that Liza hadn't come home alone.

Liam approached us, his attention locked on Liza, and she slid off my body and stood next to me. My wolf snarled, ready to defend his mate from any threat.

"Stay back," I said, glaring at Liam as he stepped closer. He didn't look like the ruthless mob boss I'd heard so much about. He was surprisingly unassuming, with a lean build and a clean-shaven face. But I wasn't going to let appearances fool me. I was acutely aware of how dangerous and sinister this man was.

Liam's expression remained impassive, but I could've sworn I detected a hint of sadness in his hooded eyes. "I want to help you," he said simply. "We can put an end to the danger your pack faces, and to the danger Liza faces, if we're united."

"Help us?" I raised an eyebrow, my wolf growling within me at the thought of trusting him. "After everything you've done?"

"Your mistrust is understandable." Liam's tone was measured and calm. It was unnerving how he was so in control despite the precarious situation he found himself in. "But you need to understand that I would never harm my own sister."

"Then, why did you kidnap her... hurt her mother?" I said with barely restrained anger. "Why put her through all of this?"

He pulled back his shoulders and straightened his spine. "Rory was never meant to be hurt. And I took Liza because I needed to learn the truth."

"Your methods are twisted," I spat, and my wolf snarled in agreement. "You could have come to us with your suspicions. Instead, you kidnapped her, terrified her, and put our entire pack in danger."

"Ty," Liza said softly, putting her hand on my lower back. The warmth of her touch was a calming anchor amid the storm of emotions swirling inside me. "He had his reasons."

"That doesn't justify his actions," I said, but my anger had lost some of its edge. I hated to admit it, but Liam seemed genuine. It made me question if he truly was the monster my intel made him out to be.

"Perhaps not," Liam said, his eyes darting to Liza before returning to me. "But now that I'm aware of the truth, we have a common enemy—someone far more dangerous than either of us ever thought. The only way to stop him is to cooperate and work as a team."

"Work together?" I snorted. "Why would I trust you after everything you've done?"

"Because you're going to need me if you want to put an end to Castro." His words were as smooth and unruffled as his demeanor.

I couldn't stop the bitter laugh that escaped me. "You expect me to believe that? After everything you've done to us?"

A storm raged within me. The last thing I wanted to do was to trust Liam, but Liza's faith in him, after everything he'd put her through, gave me pause. If there was even a sliver of truth to his words, then we couldn't afford to turn away any potential allies. Not with the stakes this high.

I fixed Liam with a glare. "Let's say I believe you. What do you propose we do about Castro?"

Liam leaned against the car. "First, we gather information. Castro is cunning, and he's been hiding in plain sight for too long. We need to uncover his plans and find out where he's hiding."

I bristled at the idea of working side by side with Liam, but my wolf was well aware of the importance of protecting our pack and, most importantly, our mate. The enemy of my enemy is my friend, as the saying went.

Didn't mean I had to like it.

"Ty." Liza traced comforting circles on my back. "Please listen to him. He's telling the truth."

"Fine." I curled my fingers into fists to keep my claws from extending. "If you double-cross us, if you hurt Liza or anyone else in our pack, I won't hesitate to end you. Liza's brother or not."

"Understood." Liam met my eyes, and the intensity in his stare affirmed the unspoken pact between us. As much as I hated to admit it, the fire burning within told me that perhaps, just perhaps, we could find a way to work with one another for the sake of those we loved.

I led Liam, Liza, and my parents into my office, trying to ignore the suffocating atmosphere. My wolf paced restlessly, ready to strike if the need arose. The thought of working with Liam and trusting him set me on edge, but for now, I had no choice. If he could help us put an end to Castro's threat, I'd grit my teeth and bear it.

I positioned myself next to Liam as we gathered around my desk. "Tell us everything."

***

We all gaped at Liam and Liza after what he'd just revealed of her past. I was struggling to wrap my head around the fact that her own father had planned to use her as a weapon. A tool for his twisted ambitions.

"Your father…" I struggled to find the right words. "He really planned to do that to you?"

Liza nodded, her eyes glassy and unfocused. "So it would seem." Her words were barely audible. "He wanted me to be the key to his power."

The pain etched on her face infuriated me. The one man who should have loved and protected her had instead chosen to exploit her, to turn her into something she never asked to be. My wolf snapped his jaws together, demanding retribution, but there was little we could do now. Her father was long gone, and we needed to concentrate on stopping Castro.

"Are you okay?" I asked, taking her hand. She gripped it tightly, as though I was an anchor she needed to keep her boat afloat in a wild storm.

"I… I'm not sure." She shrugged. "It's just… it's a lot to take in. My whole life, I always believed my father loved me. Now I've got to come to terms with the realization that he saw me as nothing more than a weapon. A tool to be used at his discretion."

"Hey," I said softly, gently tilting her chin up. "You are not a weapon, Liza. You are a strong, amazing woman, and no one has the right to judge you otherwise."

"Thanks," she said, a ghost of a smile flickering across her face.

"Darling," my mother said, her voice filled with compassion. "You are not alone in this fight. We are all here for you, and we will do everything in our power to protect you."

"Thank you," Liza said, blinking back her tears.

Liza's gaze shifted uncertainly back and forth between her brother and me. She worried her lower lip between her teeth before she finally spoke. "Castro is planning something big, Ty. He wants to use me, my abilities as an omega, to control other packs. And Liam thinks…" She cleared her throat. "Liam thinks he might have learned the trigger word my father used on me."

My stomach lurched, and I swallowed down the bitterness in my throat. The idea of anyone using Liza like that enraged the fuck out of me, but I forced myself to stay calm for her sake.

"Son of a bitch," my father grumbled, and I could feel his anger radiating off him. My mother stood beside him, her face pale, and her hands shaking ever so slightly.

"Are you certain?" I growled, turning my glare back at Liam. "How did you learn about this trigger word?"

"When I came of age, a safe deposit box was passed down to me. It held the details of our father's business empire, and a book—essentially an omega training manual. But I was aware of the word's existence long before that when I overheard our father talking about it, even though I may not have had the details of what the word was then." Liam spoke with a chilling undertone.

He paused to let the meaning of his words sink in before he carried on. "Castro was always hanging around the house when Liza was little, so it's only logical to assume he would have also heard Josef, and he would have definitely taken steps to ensure he learned the word. That's makes him a bigger danger to Liza."

"Speaking of danger." I growled. "You have no proof Castro has the word. The only person we know can trigger Liza's power is you. That makes you the most dangerous person in this room."

Liam's gaze never wavered as a knowing smile played on his lips. "True." He shrugged. "But I have no intention of using this against her. We're family, after all."

"Family doesn't always have each other's best interests at heart," I shot back, thinking of Liza's father and the horrors he'd planned for his own child. The thought of anyone hurting her made my blood boil, and I barely managed to keep the snarl from creeping into my tone.

Liam leaned forward. "Look, we haven't started off on the best foot, but we have a common goal: keeping Liza safe and stopping Castro. We'll need to trust each other if we want to succeed."

The problem was that trust wasn't something easily given or earned, especially not between two alphas with so much at stake. Despite my doubts, I knew deep down that working with Liam was our only chance to protect Liza and foil Castro's evil plans.

Fury coiled around my intestines—I would not let anyone use her, especially someone from her past—

but I shoved my emotions down and focused on the task at hand. We needed a plan, and we needed it fast.

"So, how do we stop him?"

"First, let me assure you"—Liam's sincerity shone through in his expression—"I have no intention of ever using Liza's trigger word or doing anything to harm her. If anything, I want to help deprogram her, to free her from the chains our father placed on her. And I believe you can help me with that, Ty."

That caught me off guard, but I heard no lies in his words. Despite our rocky start and the inherent mistrust between us, there was also an undeniable bond, and a connection born from our shared love for Liza.

"Deprogram her?" I asked, my eyes narrowing. Was it even possible to undo the damage that had been done?

"I've researched it," Liam declared confidently. "With the right combination of therapy, support, and time, we can help Liza break free from her trigger word."

I swallowed the lump in my throat, my taut muscles slowly relaxing. "I'll help you, but on one condition. You keep us updated on all the information you have about Castro and his plans."

"Deal," Liam said without hesitation.

"If we're going to stop Castro, then let's get started. The sooner we put an end to his plans, the better."

"I agree," Liam stated firmly. "First, we need to make sure Liza is safe. The thing about the trigger word is that it can't be used remotely or over the phone. The omega has to be near the handler, otherwise it won't work. If Castro has it, he'll stop at nothing to get his hands on her."

"Then, we'll just have to make sure he doesn't succeed." I growled, my wolf itching to protect our mate. "We've stopped him before, and we'll do it again."

"Damn right we will," Liza said with more strength in her voice. Her resilience shone through as she declared, "I won't let him use me or anyone else like this ever again."

Liam sighed and rubbed a hand over his hair as he leaned back in the plush office chair. Then he groaned. "I have to admit, I'm a bit let down that you're not evil, scheming pieces of shit." He looked at each of us in turn, his gaze lingering on Liza. "From the second I discovered my sister was alive and with you, I've been preparing to take you all out."

I slowly turned from Liza to her brother. Seeing the similarities in their profiles was disconcerting, yet oddly reassuring. "Excuse me?"

He shrugged. "I thought you were using Liza, but listening to you all, I know the support she has here is genuine. You truly aren't a danger to her."

His words stung like a slap to the face. How could he even think we were capable of such things? I had to keep in mind that Liam's perception of us was built on assumptions and half-truths. The most important thing at this moment was his awareness of the full truth, which would allow us to move forward.

As we hashed out the details, a glimmer of hope sparked within me, fueled by our shared love of Liza. I wasn't a shortsighted man. The journey ahead would be difficult, filled with danger and uncertainty, but the thought of freeing Liza from the chains that bound her made it all worth it.

As I stole another glance at her, she seemed to sit taller, emboldened by courage, and I firmly trusted our love could conquer even the darkest shadows.

Chapter 8 - Liza

Listening to Ty and Liam go round in circles about what I was, how best to protect me, and *who* was better placed to protect me, drained all my energy.

"Enough!" I said, my exhaustion finally getting the better of me. "I'm not some science experiment for everyone to analyze. I just want some peace and quiet."

Their combined concern bore down on me, but I couldn't bring myself to care. All I wanted was a reprieve from the constant chatter about my safety, my powers, and whatever dangers lurked in the shadows.

"All right," Ty said gently, having felt my exhaustion and exasperation through our shared bond. "We'll give you some space."

"Thank you," I said, turning on my heel and marching back to my and Ty's room. The moment I closed the door behind me, glorious silence enveloped me. I exhaled in relief.

Peeling off my clothes, I stepped into the shower, letting the hot water cascade over my body. The heat soothed my tense muscles and washed away the grime and stress of the day.

As I lathered up my hair, the shower filling with the familiar scent of my shampoo, I pressed my fingers firmly into my scalp and allowed my thoughts to wander to the events of the past few days, to the uncertainty of what lay ahead, and to the love and support I'd received from Ty and my family.

Strong fingers joined mine, massaging my scalp.

"Ty." I gasped, my cheeks flushing with surprise. "What are you doing here? I was sure you and Liam would be talking for hours."

"I've been apart from you for almost four days. I couldn't stay away." He helped rinse my hair, then slid his hands around my waist as he pressed his body against mine. The water sluiced over us, and steam rose off our heated skin. His eyes bore into mine, dark and intense, leaving no doubt about the depth of his desire for me.

"Missed me?" I said, an attempt at a playful smile tugging at the corners of my lips. My pulse raced as the solid, reassuring weight of him pressed against me.

"More than you realize." Ty growled, low and rough. He bent his head, capturing my lips in a searing kiss that sent every nerve in my body aflutter. Our tongues tangled together, exploring each other's mouths with an urgency that spoke volumes about how much we needed one another.

As Ty's hands roamed my slick, wet skin, lust surged through me. It electrified my body, and I moaned softly. His strong, muscular frame pressed against mine was intoxicating, and I became lost in the heat of our passion.

"Touch me," I said, breathless with need. "Please..."

"Anything," Ty said, his fingers slipping between my legs to tease my sensitive flesh. He ran his finger along the seam, then plunged inside me. My hips bucked involuntarily as pleasure crashed over me.

"God, Liza... you're so beautiful like this," Ty said, drinking in the sight of me as he continued to stroke my most intimate places. His desire for me only made me more aroused.

"Ty, I need you." I moaned, digging my nails into his back as I pressed against him. "Now."

"Patience, love," Ty said, even as his free hand reached down to position himself at my entrance. The head of his cock pressed against me, and I whimpered in anticipation. It had been so long since I'd had a release like this. I craved it.

"Please, Ty..." My voice was thick with need.

He took my lips with his, then he thrust inside me with one smooth, powerful stroke. I cried out as pleasure exploded within me, arching beneath him as we moved in perfect harmony, urging each other on with whimpers and moans.

The shower became our sanctuary, a place where we could get lost in our love and forget the world outside. Our bodies moved in a primal dance. Ty drove into me, his hands gripping my hips to guide my movements. God, there was no place I would rather be than here in his arms.

"Ty... I'm so close." I gasped, my senses overwhelmed by the intensity of our lovemaking.

"Let go," Ty said roughly in my ear. "Come with me."

As he plunged in one last time, my climax shattered around me like a thousand shards of glass. Every nerve ending fired, my body quivered, and my vision went white as the force of my orgasm ripped through me. Ty followed me over the edge seconds later, his own release pulsing deep within me as we clung to each other, our breaths coming in ragged gasps.

The water continued to pour over us, washing away the sweat and desire from our bodies. I had never felt more alive or more loved. With Ty by my side, I was ready to face whatever awaited us.

He kissed me again, gently at first, then with more force, his cock hardening against me again.

"Already?" I arched an eyebrow in surprise as he pulled me close, his fingers dancing through my folds.

"Can't help it," he said, his lips moving along my jawline and brushing against the sensitive skin of my neck. "You drive me wild."

"Good," I said with a smirk, my fingers tangling in his thick, wet hair as I tilted my head back to give him better access. Ty took full advantage, his teeth nipping at my flesh before his tongue soothed the sting away. Desire coiled low in my belly as he continued his assault on my sensitive flesh.

"My turn. I want to find out just how wild I can make you." I dropped to my knees in front of him and looked up through my lashes, meeting Ty's heated gaze as I cupped his heavy balls. With a wicked grin, I rolled them together and watched the impressive length of his arousal.

"God," Ty groaned as I wrapped my fingers around him, giving him a slow, teasing stroke. His hips jerked forward involuntarily, and I giggled. He was so eager. I didn't make him wait long. Leaning forward, I flicked my tongue over the swollen head of his cock, tasting the salty-sweet pre-cum that beaded there.

"Please," he begged, betraying his desperate desire.

Who was I to deny my mate? Holding him steady at the base, I took him into my mouth inch by glorious inch until he hit the back of my throat. I maintained a steady grip with my free hand on his hips, firmly anchoring him in place as I moved my mouth along his length, bobbing my head up and down.

"Fuck," Ty gasped, his fingers tangling in my hair. The quivering muscles in his thighs told me he was fighting the urge to thrust into my mouth. Although I could handle the entire length of him, I liked to be in control in this position, and judging by the way his breath hitched and his hips twitched, he enjoyed it, too.

I let him slip from my mouth, blowing along his hard shaft. He shivered from the contrast of the heat from my mouth with the cold of the moving air.

One hand slid from his hip along his pelvis and under to cup his heavy balls, rolling them gently between my fingers as I took him into my mouth again. That was all it took. With a strangled cry, Ty's entire body tensed, and thick, hot streams of cum pulsed down my throat. I swallowed, not spilling a single drop, and released him with an audible *pop*.

"Your turn," Ty panted, hauling me to my feet before spinning me around and pressing me against the nearest wall. My hands were splayed out on the cool surface as I braced myself for what was to come. Ty dropped to his knees behind me, spreading my legs wide as his mouth found my already-soaked core.

"God, yes." I moaned, my head falling against the wall as Ty's tongue dipped between my folds, lapping at my clit with a fervent intensity that sent me soaring. He didn't tease me, didn't draw it out, didn't prolong the anticipation. Ty understood precisely what I needed, and he offered it without hesitation.

The intensity of my orgasm was like a freight train barreling through me, my entire body quivering with the force of it. Ty held me up, his grip on my hips leaving a firm and possessive mark.

"More," I gasped, pushing away from the wall to face him. "I need more."

The omega pheromones worked their magic, and Ty growled, lifting me off the floor and impaling me on his hard length. I wrapped my legs around his waist, clinging to him as he fucked me against the wall with a roughness that bordered on feral. Our bodies met with each resounding slap of skin against skin, our grunts and moans filling the room as we chased after another climax.

"*Ty!*" I screamed, my nails digging into his shoulders as my orgasm again tore through me, every nerve ending in my body lighting up like a firework. Ty followed suit seconds later, burying himself deep within me as his own release washed over us both.

"God, I love you," he panted, pressing his forehead against mine as we struggled to catch our breaths. "So much."

"Love you, too." I nuzzled his cheek before sliding down him to stand on shaky legs. The water sluicing down our bodies had started to cool, and we laughed as we stumbled out of the shower.

Ty wrapped my exhausted body in a soft, fluffy towel. My eyelids felt heavy, but when I left the bathroom and checked the time, it was only six in the evening.

Ty kissed me softly, sending a rush of warmth through me. Our kisses shifted from their wild and passionate nature in the shower to something gentler and more chaste, reflecting the love and intimacy we shared.

"As much as I'd love to continue this... I need to go see my mom."

"Of course," Ty said, helping me steady myself before wrapping an arm around my waist. "We'll go as soon as we're dressed."

As Ty and I pulled on our clothes, I inhaled deeply, capturing the lingering scent of our passion. My wolf's energy surged within me, vibrant and revitalized after our intense coupling. She was just as eager as I was to see my mom. We both needed the reassurance of seeing her ourselves, knowing that she was truly okay. Her blood on me was still vivid in my mind.

"You ready?" Ty asked, pulling me from my thoughts.

"Definitely." I nodded, mustering a confident smile that hid my inner doubts. My mind was consumed with worry as I considered how my dad and twin brothers would respond. It was time to face my family and deal with the aftermath.

"Actually, wait." I stopped him with a hand on his arm. "What about Liam? Where is he staying?"

"Ah... " Ty frowned slightly. "He's staying in the guesthouse for now. I didn't think it would be wise for him to leave just yet."

"Right." Liam had offered to help, to stand with us against Castro. "That makes sense."

As we stepped outside, the cool breeze brushed against my skin, sending familiar scents of the forest surrounding the Keller Estate my way. My wolf stirred, her excitement growing with every step, which I curtailed, reminding her we were going to my parents' house, not out for a leisurely run.

The ground beneath our feet on the verge outside was soft grass and hard-packed dirt, the sensations strangely comforting as we walked side by side.

"Your brothers are probably there," Ty said casually, though I didn't miss the tension in his voice. "Just a heads up."

"Thanks." I tried to prepare myself for the inevitable confrontation. Explaining Liam's actions wouldn't be easy. My brothers would be furious with him. They would also point fingers at Ty, holding him responsible. Despite the added security, my mom had been injured, and I'd been kidnapped. I understood that their anger stemmed from their love and concern for me. It was a delicate balance that needed to be maintained.

As we approached my parents' home, I could feel the nostalgia washing over me. Their voices drifted to my ears, laughter and serious undertones merging through the open windows. With each step closer, the sound became more familiar, evoking a sense of both joy and trepidation within me.

"Here goes nothing," I muttered, taking Ty's hand and giving it a reassuring squeeze. He returned the gesture, his grip strong and steady, anchoring me to him before we stepped through the front door, into the storm. "Thank you for coming with me."

"Of course." He gave my hand a gentle squeeze. "I'm here for you."

We stepped onto the porch, the wooden boards creaking under our feet. I raised my hand to knock but hesitated when I heard laughter and clinking glasses from inside. I didn't want to interrupt a joyous moment. Instead, I leaned out against the railing, the door to my back, watching as the last light of day faded away.

Ty nudged my shoulder. "Hey, you okay?"

"I am." I flashed him a smile. "It's just... strange being back here after everything that's happened. With Liam staying at the guesthouse..."

"Speaking of which," Ty said, his brow furrowing. "We have no idea where his estate is, do we? Where you were held?"

"No," I said. "It took us a while to get back to Presley Acres, so it must be quite a distance away. It's odd, though, Liam's adamant about sticking around. Maybe he wants to be part of a proper pack... or maybe he's just keeping an eye on things."

"Either way," Ty said, placing a reassuring hand on my back. "We'll figure it out. Now, come on. Let's go visit your family."

Nodding, I finally knocked on the door. A moment later, it swung open to reveal my mother. The sight of her pale skin and the bandage around her head had a sob rising in my throat.

"Liza!" She greeted me with such enthusiasm, shouting my name.

With hesitation, I slowly reached for the bandage, which was a stark contrast against her delicate complexion. Afraid I'd cause her more pain, I quickly withdrew my hand.

Guilt overwhelmed me, leaving me in a state of complete turmoil. It was selfish of me to be here when she was injured because of me. It would be best for everyone if I left before causing any more harm to my family.

When I made to leave, though, my mother pulled me into a tight embrace.

"I'm okay, sweetheart. I'm fine," she whispered, hugging me tightly as we stood in the hallway, then she held me at arm's length. "This was not your fault, Liza Mimms, do you hear me? Do you hear me?" Mom turned to Ty, filled with tenderness, and softly said, "Ty, dear. I understand things have been... difficult lately. But I want you to know we appreciate everything you've done for our daughter."

"Thank you, Rory. That means a lot," Ty said, his cheeks flushing.

When we walked into the living room, I was met with the sight of my father Scott engaged in a heated discussion with my brothers, Mason and Michael. Their conversation ceased the moment they became aware of our presence, their faces a combination of relief and concern.

The scent of my mother's homemade lasagna wafted through the air, making my stomach rumble loudly. The familiar comfort of our family home enveloped me as my mother ushered Ty and me inside. For all its warmth, a cloud of tension hung heavy in the room.

Mason and Michael stood near the fireplace, their expressions stormy, and their postures defensive.

"Little sis," Mason said, his face breaking into a grin before he strode over and wrapped me in a bear hug, lifting me off the floor.

"Hey there," Michael said, joining the embrace. His slender frame belied his strength, but it was still enough to make me feel small and protected between the two of them.

When they let me go, I noticed they scowled at Ty. My brother's had always been protective of me, but I couldn't let them blame my mate.

"Guys, I get that you're angry, but none of this was Ty's fault. He's done everything he can to keep me safe."

Mason's steely gaze met mine. After a moment, he sighed and nodded. "Liza. We trust your judgment. But Ty," he added, leveling a finger at my mate. "If something like this happens again, we won't be so understanding."

Ty swallowed audibly. "I understand, and I promise to do everything in my power to protect her."

"Good." Michael's lips curved into a wry smile. "Now we've got that out of the way, can we please enjoy some family time?"

"Absolutely," I said, feeling lighter.

My brothers led the way to the dining table, where Mom's lasagna sat steaming and inviting. The six of us settled into our chairs, and for a moment, it was like old times. I tried to forget the danger lurking outside and focused on my family.

As we ate, the conversation flowed easily, filled with laughter and teasing. Mason regaled us with tales of his latest football victories, while Michael shared anecdotes from his university classes. Ty chimed in here and there, and though he was still wary of my brothers, he was relaxing and becoming more comfortable around them.

I savored every bite of the delicious meal and every word spoken. Moments of normalcy were precious and rare. My thoughts strayed to Liam, wondering what he was doing at the guest house, but I quickly pushed those worries aside. Tonight was about my adoptive family—the family who had raised me—and I intended to enjoy it to the fullest.

"Here's to hoping for brighter days ahead," Mom said, lifting her glass of water in a toast. In that fleeting moment, the clinking of our glasses gave me a sense of reassurance and camaraderie, chasing away the doubt, and temporarily easing my worries.

As I looked around the table, my heart warmed with love for each person seated there, and I felt an overwhelming sense of gratitude for the bonds that held us together.

My father and I discussed my catering business and whether I'd continue working.

I caught sight of my mother standing in the doorway. She had been quiet throughout dinner, so I rushed to her side and wrapped her in a tight hug.

"Mom, I'm so sorry," I said with sincere remorse. "I never meant for any of this to happen."

"Shh, it's not your fault, sweetheart," she said, stroking my hair. "You're home now, and that's all that matters."

We held each other for a moment longer before pulling away. My father had joined us, and though he looked just as concerned as my mother, I could sense his curiosity.

"Tell us everything." He took a seat next to my mother. "What happened, and what exactly are we dealing with?"

Swallowing hard, I began to recount the events of the past few days—my abduction, discovering my captor was Liam. The truth behind my conception and Josef Wylde's plans to use me, and what impact that had on the threat of Castro and his goons. Ty chimed in occasionally, adding important details and clarifications.

As we spoke, my parents' expressions became more and more troubled, as did their outrage at Josef's plans to use me as a weapon to further his own murderous reputation. They were clearly worried about the danger that surrounded us, and their skepticism about Liam was evident.

"Are you sure you can trust him?" Dad asked, his brow furrowed in concern.

"His methods might be unorthodox," Ty said. "But I believe he will prove himself to be an ally. Right now, we need all the help we can get."

"Besides," I added, attempting to inject some levity. "He's got this weird soft spot for me. It's kind of hard to explain, but I think he genuinely wants to help."

"Still," Mom said, wringing her hands anxiously. "I don't like the idea of someone so unpredictable being around you."

"Neither do I," Ty added. "Right now, though, he's our best shot at taking down Castro and keeping Liza safe."

"Fine," Dad said, running a hand through his hair. "Just promise me one thing. You'll be careful, and you won't take any unnecessary risks."

"I promise," I said firmly, meeting his concern head-on. "We're going to get through this."

With that, we continued discussing our plan, weighing our options, and considering every possible scenario. Whatever lay ahead, as long as I had my family by my side, we'd face it with unwavering determination.

As Ty and I made our way out of my parents' house, it felt like a storm was threatening to break. In search of some solace, I twined my fingers with Ty's, and he gave my hand a gentle squeeze, his touch both comforting and protective.

"Everything's going to be okay," Ty murmured.

I wanted to believe him, but worry still sat heavily on my chest.

"Ty," I whispered. "Do you feel like we're being watched?"

He glanced around, his heightened awareness undoubtedly sharper than mine. "I have no idea, but I'll stay watchful," he replied, scanning the surroundings.

We climbed into Ty's truck, and as we pulled away from my parents' home, a sense of unease settled over me. My gut twisted into knots, making it difficult to breathe.

"Something's not right," I said. "Something's wrong."

"Wrong?" Ty asked, his attention on the road ahead. "What do you mean?"

"Look at that car." I gestured toward a black sedan in the rearview mirror that had been tailing us since we left my parents' place. "It's been following us for a while now."

"Stay calm," Ty said, his voice remaining steady, but his concern growing more apparent. "Just let me handle this."

His grip on the steering wheel tightened as he accelerated. The black sedan followed suit, its engine roaring to match our speed.

Fear coursed through me like electricity. "Ty, what are they doing?" I gasped as the car drew close, swerving dangerously behind us.

"Trying to run us off the road." Ty growled in a deep voice that told me his wolf was itching to get out. "Hold on, Liza."

He sped up again, expertly weaving through traffic as the sedan continued to tail us.

I gripped the door handle as the truck lurched and swayed. Ty's grasp on the steering wheel was so tight, his knuckles turned pale, his gaze flickering between the road ahead and the persistent black sedan chasing him. The realization hit me hard and fast. This wasn't just an aggressive driver. It was another kidnapping attempt.

When would this fucking end?

"Ty," I said, my throat tight with fear. "This is about me, isn't it?"

"Damn right it is." He floored the accelerator as we sped toward the estate. "But I won't let them take you."

"Can't we call for help?"

"Already did," Ty said through gritted teeth. "Backup's on its way."

"Are they going to make it in time?"

"Let's fucking hope so."

We raced down the winding road, and every twist and turn heightened my anxiety. My wolf paced restlessly within me, her instincts urging me to fight or flee. There was nowhere to run, and our enemy remained frustratingly out of reach.

The sensation of weightlessness gripped me as our vehicle careened off the road, my heart pounding wildly. Tires screeched, and the deafening noise of metal scraping against the road echoed in my ears as my body jolted.

I bit back a cry of pain.

"Are you okay?" Ty's voice was full of concern, but there was no time to dwell on injuries. We had bigger problems to deal with.

"Fine," I said through gritted teeth. "Just get us out of here."

Ty nodded, quickly assessing the situation. The black sedan that had been tailing us screeched to a halt not far from where we'd been forced off the road. Six large men emerged from the car, with masks obscuring their faces. The sight of them sent a chill through my veins, leaving no doubt in my mind they were after me.

"Stay close." Ty threw open the door and stepped out into the fray. I followed suit, adrenaline coursing through my veins, preparing me for the fight ahead.

Another vehicle pulled up, and more masked individuals spilled into the road.

"Who the hell are these guys?" I said under my breath, scanning the approaching figures. Their movements were precise, calculated. They were professionals.

"Doesn't matter," Ty hissed. "They won't lay a finger on you, I promise."

When the first attacker lunged toward us, Ty easily sidestepped the blow and delivered a brutal punch to the man's face. He crumpled to the ground. More were coming. We'd never be able to hold them off alone. Where was our backup?

"Ty, we can't do this on our own," I said, cold sweat breaking out over my body.

In response, he bared his teeth and snarled at the encroaching men—a primal warning that only appeared to spur them on.

The powerful roar of another engine had me tensing, expecting more attackers. The vehicle skidded to a stop beside us, and Liam jumped out. Over the chaos, I heard him shout to Ty, "Protect Liza!" before joining the fight.

His sudden presence caught me off guard. It was one thing to express a willingness to be involved, but it was a different matter entirely to actually show up and engage in the battle. That shock soon transformed into deep gratitude. Ty remained steadfast by my side, positioning himself as an impenetrable barrier between me and the remaining assailant, taking care of any who got too close.

"Stay behind me," he said, just as the sound of engines tore through the night. A fleet of cars and trucks skidded to a halt behind us, their headlights cutting through the darkness. Our pack members spilled out of the vehicles, ready for battle.

"About time!" Ty shouted. "Let's take these bastards down!"

Soon, the attackers were overwhelmed by the sheer force of our numbers. Even as they retreated, I had a gnawing fear that this was only the beginning. Who had sent these men after me? What would they try next?

Car doors slammed, and the vehicles sped off with a screech of tires. Two of the assailants were left behind, and they were quickly subdued. As our pack members started to leave, I sagged against Ty, my body shaking from the residual adrenaline. He put his arm around me and rubbed my waist.

"Thank you," I croaked, blinking back tears. He simply nodded, his fierce gaze never straying from the two men sprawled out before us. Whatever came next, we'd deal with it the same way, head-on.

Liam stalked toward us. "You two okay?" he asked, scanning Ty and me with concern. It was strange, seeing him worried about our wellbeing, but I couldn't deny the relief that flooded me at the sight of my newfound brother.

"Thanks to you and my pack," Ty said, his voice strained from the exertion of the fight. "We've got to interrogate these two and find out who sent them."

"Leave that to me." Liam's expression turned dangerously serious. Without waiting for a response, he turned away and strode toward the captives, radiating authority and menace.

"Be careful around him," I said to Ty, watching Liam with fear and fascination. "He's not like us."

"I can see that." Ty's face hardened. "Right now, we need him on our side."

As Liam approached the two men, his body began to shift and contort, fur sprouting from his skin, and his bones cracking with sickening sounds. A massive wolf emerged from the transformation, dwarfing even

Ty's formidable size. His fur was a deep black, streaked with silver that caught the moonlight, lending him an otherworldly air.

Liam towered over the men in his wolf form, his growl a low rumble that reverberated through the very ground beneath our feet. Their faces blanched with terror, and a thrill of satisfaction at their fear surged through me. I felt no compassion for them. They deserved it after what they'd tried to do to us.

The sight of Liam's massive wolf's form caused the two men to shrink back in fear, and they actually yelped when he snarled at them. The sheer force of his aura overwhelmed me, making it hard to breathe, and causing my knees to shake uncontrollably. It was as though I'd been transported to another realm, where the air buzzed with electricity, and thunder echoed around me.

"Stay put," Ty said, straining against his own shift. He took a step toward Liam, keeping the menacing wolf well within his sights. "I'll help him deal with these bastards."

"Ty, are you sure?" I asked, worry clawing at me. Even Ty was shaken by the immense presence of

Liam's wolf, and that scared me more than anything else.

"Trust me." He squeezed my hand reassuringly for a moment before releasing it, then he quickly shifted into his own powerful wolf form, still smaller than Liam but formidable, nonetheless.

"Please be careful." I watched as Ty joined Liam in stalking the terrified men. The two wolves moved with lethal grace, their muscles rippling beneath their fur as they closed in on their prey.

"Y-you don't have to do this," one of the men said, his attention darting between the enormous wolves and the remaining members of our pack who had formed a tight circle around them. "We were just following orders,"

Liam shifted back to his human form. "Save your pathetic excuses." He growled, as chilling as the wind that whipped around us. "You came after my family. There will be no mercy for the likes of you."

I couldn't tear my eyes away from the scene unfolding before me, my pulse pounding in my ears like a war drum. Mason and Michael stood beside me, their faces set in grim determination. They were ready to fight if necessary, but for now, we watched as Ty and Liam cornered the men.

"Who sent you?" Liam's wolfish snarl seemed at odds with his human body. "Tell us now, and we might spare your miserable lives."

"Please." I stepped forward, gaining the attention of one of the men. "Tell us why you did this."

For a moment, I was sure he'd ignore me. I noticed a fleeting expression of fear and something else crossing his face. Regret, maybe?

"Castro," he croaked.

I fought back the urge to be sick as my stomach churned violently.. How could anyone be so twisted, so consumed by their own desires, that they would go to such lengths to possess another person?

"He's obsessed with her." He pointed to me. "Said if we brought her to him, he'd pay us more than we could ever dream of."

Liam's cold demeanor bored into the captured men. "I don't care how high that bounty gets, you won't be collecting it."

He leaned in closer, so close the icy menace emanating from him was a physical manifestation. "Let this be a lesson to anyone who thinks they can come after my family. If they even try, they'll end up like you two, or worse."

It was strange for me to hear Liam refer to us as his family, but there was no denying his fierce, protective edge. The two battered men exchanged a frightened glance, their bodies tense with fear. Even though he was fighting on our side, Liam was undeniably terrifying.

Ty shifted back into his human form and came over to the three of us standing by our wrecked car. Mason moved to stand next to Michael. Ty looked back toward Liam, then spoke to my brothers. "I think you two should go." Before they could argue, Ty held up his hand. "This isn't a debate. Liza's been through enough tonight without watching a pissing contest over who's better placed to protect her. Please, go home. You don't need to be here for this."

As the twins faced each other, they communicated silently, their unspoken agreement evident when Mason nodded, and they both pulled me into a warm hug.

"Call us if you need us," Michael whispered, his warm breath tickling my ear, then they hurried over to their car, the smell of gasoline punching into the air as they made their hasty exit. I was so tired that my bones felt liquid. But as much as I wanted this to be over, I suspected things were only about to get worse.

I turned my face up to Ty. "What was that about? Why send them home?"

Ty indicated to where Liam stood over the two men. "I didn't think it fair to get them mixed up in this. They came when I needed them—when it mattered. I didn't want Liam to have any more of an audience. No witnesses."

"Listen carefully," Liam said, venom dripping from every word. "I'm going to let you go, and when I do, you're going to spread the word that Liza Mims is under my protection. Anyone who tries to harm her will answer to me. And take my fucking word for it, that's not a position anyone wants to be in." He grabbed the man who hadn't spoken by the arm, forcing him to stand. He moved so quickly, I barely comprehended what he was doing until I heard an audible pop. The attacker screamed in pain, his arm hanging strangely from the now-dislocated shoulder.

I stood by Ty's side, cold sweat drenching me as we watched Liam assert his dominance. Part of me was still reeling from the torture we had witnessed, but another part was relieved by Liam's intimidating presence. In the back of my mind, I knew he could very well take out the Kellers and any other threat that came our way if he truly wanted to. It was a frightening realization, but strangely, it comforted me.

The men nodded frantically, desperate to be released from Liam's wrath. As he turned to walk away, I reached out and touched his arm, my fingers fluttering against his skin.

"Thank you," I whispered. "That couldn't have been easy, but I appreciate your willingness to protect me."

His demeanor softened if only for a moment, and he gave me a curt nod. "No one messes with my family, Liza."

He walked away, leaving Ty and me alone with the two captives. I glanced over at Ty, who appeared to be completely absorbed in his own thoughts.

"Are you okay?"

Ty shook his head and blinked rapidly. "I'm fine. Liam may have crossed lines that I wouldn't, but he got results. Now our enemies will know we have an even stronger ally on our side."

I nodded. Liam's actions had been necessary, even if they had been difficult to witness. As we prepared to release the men, gratitude and unease toward my new protector warred within. In this dark and uncertain world, Liam's terrifying presence might just be what we needed to keep our enemies at bay, but at what cost?

My racing heartbeat filled my ears as I stood next to Ty, watching Liam with a terrifying ferocity. As much as I appreciated his protection, I wasn't sure we weren't playing with fire.

"Are we doing the right thing?" I questioned Ty, my fear slipping through. "Aligning ourselves with Liam?"

Before Ty could answer, his phone rang, and he glanced at the screen before taking the call. "Hello?"

"Put me on speaker," Castro's venomous demand radiated from the phone. Ty tapped the screen, and I instinctively moved closer to my mate and clutched his arm tightly.

"Who's with you? Who is that in the background?" Castro snapped with malice.

Sensing something was off, Liam jogged over, gestured toward the phone, and mouthed, "Castro?"

I nodded.

"None of your business," Ty said coolly.

"When it interferes with my plans, it most certainly is my business."

"Castro," Liam bit out. "It's Liam."

Tension crackled like a live wire in the air. My skin crawled. Castro's fury was palpable even through the phone. Liam, on the other hand, appeared entirely unruffled, his icy calmness contrasting sharply with Castro's seething rage.

"Traitor," Castro spat. "Why couldn't you do what was expected of you? All you had to do was take care of Ty. You were supposed to help me bring Liza back where she belongs."

"And where exactly is that, Castro? Where do you think Liza's rightful place is?" Liam questioned.

"By my side, of course," Castro answered quickly. "Just because you two have decided to become all buddy-buddy, it doesn't change anything for me. I'll get Liza. All you've done is made things a little bit harder."

"You're nothing but a psycho," Liam said coolly, a hint of disdain in his voice. "Your obsession with Liza is unnatural and twisted. You need to let go."

"Let go?" Castro snarled, making the hairs on the back of my neck stand up. "I'll never let go. Now you've shown your true colors, Liam, you've just made everything much more interesting."

"Is that a threat?" I interjected, my wolf's protective instincts kicking in. If Castro thought he could intimidate us, he had underestimated our resilience.

"No, Liza, you should know better than anyone that I don't make threats. This is a warning—your *only* warning," Castro said with a foreboding intensity. "I'll see you all soon when I bring a war to your doorstep. Enjoy the peace while it lasts."

The line went dead, and we stared at each other in stunned silence. His words draped over me like a heavy cloak on my shoulders that threatened to suffocate me. Beneath my fear, a raging fire ignited, fueling my need to protect my family and put an end to Castro's madness.

"Ty." I swallowed past the lump in my throat. "I'm scared."

"Me, too." He pulled me into his arms. We stood there on the dark road, embracing and drawing strength from each other. This battle was far from over.

My thoughts turned to Liam. Despite the dark, ruthless side he'd shown tonight, he had also proven his loyalty and protectiveness. In this dangerous game we were playing, we needed every ally we could get.

A mixture of fear and hope pulsated through my body. We were in for a fight, I had no doubt about that, but with Ty by my side, and now Liam as well, I believed we'd somehow find a way to keep our loved ones safe, and put an end to Castro's twisted plans.

Chapter 9 - Ty

The tension in the room was thick enough to choke on as Liam and I locked eyes, neither of us willing to back down. Our alpha egos were driving us both to take charge of the situation, and that never worked out well.

"Look." Liam's patronizing tone grated on my nerves, as if he thought he had all the answers. "I understand we have different opinions, but this isn't about us. It's about protecting Liza."

"Then, maybe you should listen to someone who knows her better than you do," I shot back, my nostrils flaring.

"Enough!" My father's voice broke through the stalemate, his authority silencing us both. "This bickering isn't going to help anyone. You two need to work with each other for Liza's sake, whether you like it or not."

"Castro is smart," Liam said. "He's not playing from the shadows anymore. We're waiting for his attack. He's playing 3D chess and he's going to make moves before we can predict them."

I couldn't shake the lingering suspicion that we were missing something crucial—a piece of the puzzle that would reveal Castro's intentions. We needed to be a step ahead, but how?

Suddenly, an idea struck me. "What if he starts to work with our enemies against us?"

Liam's eyes—so like Liza's—met mine, and for once, there was no hint of rivalry in them. "That's a good point, Ty. He could use their hatred for us to his advantage and gain allies in the process." He leaned forward, his arms resting on the table. "Castro will likely appeal to their individual desires for power, territory, or revenge. We need to get to them first and convince them not to join forces with him."

"Or at least make it explicit that siding with Castro will bring them more trouble than it's worth," I added.

"Exactly," Dominic said. "We'll need to approach each one differently and find the right leverage to keep them from betraying us."

"Remember, though," Liza added in her tranquil manner. "Liam carries a lot of weight in this world. His reputation alone might be enough to give some of these alphas pause before they consider crossing him."

I frowned, bristling at the idea of relying on Liam for anything. As much as I loathed admitting it, Liza was right. Liam's name held power and influence we could use to our advantage.

"Fine," I said grudgingly. "We'll utilize Liam's... reputation when necessary. But we can't assume everyone will back down just because they're afraid of him. We need to be prepared for anything."

"Agreed." Liam nodded, the seriousness on his face mirroring mine. "We'll divide and conquer, approach each of these alphas individually or in pairs if needed. We don't have time to waste, so we need a plan to approach them. Some may be willing to listen to reason, while others..." He shrugged. "We might have to get creative."

I raised an eyebrow. "Creative?"

"Subtle manipulation, bargaining, threats if necessary," Liam said, devoid of emotion. "Whatever it takes to secure their loyalty or, at the very least, keep them from aligning with Castro."

"Fine." The words tasted bitter in my mouth. "Let's be clear on one thing, though: Liza's safety is our priority. We're not starting a war here."

Dominic pulled out a notebook and set it on the table, ready to make a list. We spent the next hour discussing potential adversaries, becoming more urgent as we delved into old grudges and simmering feuds.

"Maximus Langston is one we need to watch out for," I said, tension strumming my nerves. "We've had a few business run-ins. He's a brute who attempted to take Liza. He let everyone know he wanted her, and he'd do anything to get what he wants."

"Then there's the Redwood pack," Liza added. "Didn't you mention their alpha, Malcolm, being jealous of our territory and resources? If Castro convinces him we're vulnerable, he could use him as a pawn in his game."

The list grew longer with every potential threat we added, but we were making progress. We needed to be prepared for any eventuality, and understanding our enemies was the first step.

With our list completed, Liza excused herself, leaving Liam, Dominic, and me to pore over our plan of action. While I didn't trust Liam completely, the shared objective of keeping Liza safe from harm bound us together.

That was enough for me for now.

"Excuse me," Liza murmured, with her head bowed as she stood up from the table. "I'm tired. Between last night and this long morning, I need to rest."

"Of course," my father said gently. "Take all the time you need."

As Liza left my office, worry settled in the pit of my stomach. She'd been through so much lately, and although she appeared to be holding up well, I could tell it was taking a toll on her. I wanted to be there for her, to comfort her, but there was still work to be done.

"Let's keep going over this list. We can't afford any mistakes," Liam said, snapping me back to the task at hand.

Time stretched on endlessly as the three of us hunched over our makeshift war table with a combination of files, hastily scribbled notes, and photos of the alphas we believed Castro might try to recruit in front of us. It was exhausting work, trying to predict the unpredictable, but we had no choice. We needed to stay one step ahead of him if we wanted to protect Liza and our packs.

"Ty," my father said after a while, placing a hand on my shoulder. "You need a break. Go check on Liza."

My muscles tensed, torn between my desire to be with her and my duty to protect our territory. But he was right. I would be useless if I couldn't focus.

Nodding reluctantly, I stood and stretched my stiff limbs. "I'll be back soon."

As I walked down the dim hallway, my senses heightened despite my weariness as I neared the gentle, rhythmic sound of Liza's tranquil breathing. I stopped outside our bedroom and listened, then pushed it open.

The sight that greeted me was one of such vulnerability, it nearly overwhelmed me with emotion. Liza lay curled up on the bed, her delicate frame half-hidden under a pile of blankets. Her breathing was slow and even, the rise and fall of her chest a comforting sight. I didn't want to disturb her rest—she needed it—but I wanted to get to the bottom of her lethargy. What if she was sick or something?

"Hey," I whispered, reaching out to brush my fingers against her cheek. "Time to wake up, babe."

Her eyelids fluttered open, revealing sleepy, fathomless blue eyes that warmed as they met mine. "Ty?" She stretched languidly, raising her arms over her head. "What's going on?"

"Nothing to worry about," I assured her, running my hand through her tangled hair. "I just... You've been so tired since you got back home. Are you okay?"

She sank into the mattress, the sheets pulling around her waist. "I didn't sleep too well at Liam's place. The nightmares were worse there."

I knew all too well the dread that could grip you during a nightmare, and the way it could leave you gasping for breath, your heart pounding like a jackhammer in your chest.

"I'm sorry." I brushed my thumb over her cheekbone. "I wish there was some way I could eliminate them for you."

Liza smiled weakly and covered her hand with mine. "Just being here with you... it helps. I feel so safe around you."

"Good," I said with a smile. "That's how it should be."

We sat in silence for a few moments, our shared pain hanging heavy between us. Then an idea struck me, a small way to brighten Liza's day and offer her some semblance of normalcy.

How about we go out for lunch? To take your mind off things. Just the two of us... and maybe some extra security," I added.

Liza's face broke into a radiant smile as she pushed herself into a sitting position. "That sounds wonderful." Her mood lifted. "I really could use a break from all this... intensity."

"Me, too." I stood up and offered her a hand. "Let's get ready and head out."

While Liza got ready, I tried my best to rid myself of the creeping awareness that something big was on the horizon—a storm brewing in the distance, threatening to tear apart everything we held dear. For now, though, I was going to focus on the present, on the woman I loved, and on the promise of a brief respite from the danger that surrounded us.

I would give her this day, this small taste of happiness, no matter what it took.

With a heavy hand on the doorknob, I hesitated for a moment before stepping out of the house. Extra security enveloped us like an oppressive fog, a constant reminder of the dangers we faced after the attempted kidnapping. I scanned the perimeter, taking in the familiar faces of my security team who'd been assigned to protect Liza. Jamie and Robin, her trusted guards, now led a team of six.

"Ready?" My whole body was on high alert.

Liza nodded, giving me a small smile as she slipped her hand into mine. "Let's go."

The hum of the car's engine provided a monotonous soundtrack to the mounting tension inside me as we drove toward town. As much as Liam had assured us that attaching his name with Liza's would effectively stop the manhunt, my gut told me I had a target with a bright red bullseye painted on my back.

Liza squeezed my hand gently. "You need to relax, Ty. We're going to be okay."

I sighed and forced a smile. "I'm trying. It's just… difficult to let go of the worry."

"Could you try? For me?" Her gentle plea tugged at my heartstrings.

The moment we parked, I went on high alert, scrutinizing our surroundings. The bustling streets and chatter of people all around us did nothing to lessen my anxiety.

"Ready?" Liza smiled warmly and gave my hand another reassuring squeeze.

Taking a steadying breath, I nodded. "Let's go." I did my best to muster confidence.

As we walked to the diner, every detail around us—footsteps echoing on the pavement, the scent of exhaust fumes mixed with the aroma of fresh bread from the bakery, the warmth of the sun on my skin—seemed amplified. My wolf's senses were both a blessing and a curse, and at times like these, they only served to fuel my paranoia.

"Ty, relax," Liza said when we entered the diner.

"Sorry, I'm just..." I didn't finish my sentence, but she nodded.

A bead of sweat rolled down my temple as we settled into our booth. I refused to let Liza out of my sight, even for a moment. My fingers tapped rhythmically against the table's edge, betraying the anxiety that churned within me.

"Ty," Liza said. "You're going to wear a hole in the table if you keep tapping like that."

I glanced at her and gave a tight smile. "Sorry. Just a little on edge."

"Clearly." She reached across the table and placed her hand over mine, stilling my anxious movements. Her touch was a warm balm over my frayed nerves, but it wasn't enough to dispel the unease that simmered inside me.

"Can you blame me? After everything that's happened, how can I not be worried?"

Liza sighed, her gaze penetrating mine as she sought to find understanding. "You're scared. Trust me... I am, too. But we can't let fear control our lives. We have to find a way to move forward, even if it means taking risks. And you suggested we do this to get a reprieve from all the chaos."

Her words stung because they were true. As much as I wanted to wrap Liza in an impenetrable cocoon and keep her safe from the dangers lurking around every corner, I had to accept that wasn't possible. Life was filled with risks, especially in our world, and I couldn't protect Liza from them all.

Reluctantly, I forced my muscles to loosen. "I'll try to relax, at least for now."

"Thank you." She patted my hand, then called over the waitress so we could order.

When our food arrived, I attempted to focus on the conversation and asked Liza about mundane things like work and her favorite hobbies. The normalcy of these topics should have provided some semblance of comfort, but I remained on high alert. My ears strained to pick up any unusual sounds, and my nose twitched at the slightest unfamiliar scent.

"Ty," Liza hissed. "You're not really here with me, are you? Your mind is elsewhere."

I winced, hating that I was causing her distress. "I'm sorry, Liza. It's just hard to let go of the worry, even for a little while."

"Then, maybe we should leave." She cast a furtive glance around the diner, also searching for potential threats. "If you can't relax, there's no point in trying to enjoy ourselves here."

"Maybe you're right." Relief and guilt washed over me at her statement. While I'd been hoping for an excuse to get Liza out of public and back to the safety of our home, I didn't want my paranoia to dictate our every move. God, I was the one who'd orchestrated this outing.

"Let's go," Liza pushed away her half-eaten meal, wiping her mouth with her napkin, leaving it on the table.

As we stood and prepared to leave, a sense of foreboding settled over me like a dark cloud. Though I desperately wanted to believe that Liam's protection would be enough to keep Liza safe, I couldn't shake the nagging doubt that it wouldn't be long before danger found us again.

"Let's head back to the estate." I guided Liza toward the exit. At least there, I was sure she'd be safe within the protected confines of our territory. The thought of having her out of harm's way was enough to put a small smile on my face.

She squeezed my hand. That one small gesture showed me she appreciated my concern, even if it made our outing less enjoyable.

Once we stepped out into the bright sunlight, we became exposed. My instincts were screaming to get us both to safety as quickly as possible. Once again, I surveyed the area, searching for anything out of place.

"Ty, don't worry so much," Liza said gently, pulling me from my thoughts. "You're making me nervous."

"Sorry," I said, regretting how my anxiety had affected what was supposed to be a nice lunch. I did my best to push my fears aside and focus on getting us home.

When we neared the car, the hairs on the back of my neck stood on end. Something wasn't right. The air was charged with tension, and the security team and I were on high alert. Before I could fully process what was happening, a series of loud cracks rang through the air.

The acrid stench of gunpowder burned my nostrils as the deafening echo of bullets bouncing off nearby cars pierced my ears. Instinctively, I lunged toward Liza, shielding her body with my own. The bitter metallic taste of fear filled my mouth, but I refused to let it show on my face. Protecting Liza was my only concern at that moment.

"Get down!" I shouted, yanking Liza behind a nearby vehicle for cover. Adrenaline ignited in my blood. Someone was shooting at us. More bullets zipped past us.

"Ty, what's happening?" Liza's knees buckled, and her body shook in sheer terror.

"Someone's trying to kill us," I said through gritted teeth. "Stay down and don't move."

Despite the fear that gripped her, she nodded. Who the fuck was behind this attack? Was it Castro or someone else entirely? Whoever it was, they'd made a grave mistake in targeting us.

"Ty, we need to get out of here!" Liza yelled. "We can't stay pinned down like this."

"Wait for a break in the gunfire, then make a run for it," I said. "I'll cover you, but you have to move fast."

She bit her lip and breathed heavily, then nodded with newfound conviction. As soon as the next pause in gunfire came, she sprinted toward safety, moving with surprising speed.

"Baby, you've got this." I looked at her with pride as she reached the car, a deep affection welling up inside me. My mate possessed a courage beyond measure.

Now it was my turn to make a break for it. I waited for another lull in the gunfire, then bolted toward the car, praying a stray bullet wouldn't strike me. The blood thumping in my ears made it difficult to hear my own footsteps.

Liza sagged in relief when I dived into the car. Her face was set with worry, but her eyes shone with fierce bravery. We had survived this attempt on our lives, but whoever was behind this wouldn't stop until they succeeded or were taken down themselves.

"Let's get out of here." I started the car and punched the gas, speeding away from the scene. As we left the chaos behind us, a renewed sense of purpose filled me. I would protect Liza at all costs, no matter who our enemy was or what they had planned for us.

We returned to the estate, the atmosphere in the car so thick it was like a physical weight pressing down on me. My body was still buzzing from the adrenaline of the attack, and my wolf pawed at the edge of my mind, seeking an outlet for its anger and protectiveness.

When we entered the house, a furious Liam met us in the foyer. His temper crackled dangerously close to the surface.

"What the fuck happened?" He growled, taking in our disheveled appearances.

"Someone took a shot at us," I said tersely, pacing. "In public, Liam. In the middle of the goddamn street. There were kids. Fucking kids!" I stopped and raked my hand through my hair, struggling to keep my own temper in check. "Nobody saw the shooter; they just saw the gun."

"Who was the target?" Liam's hands balled into fists, the tension evident in his clenched muscles. "Because if I discover someone was trying to kill my sister, I'll fucking tear them apart."

Liza had shrunk in on herself now she'd had time to process what had happened. She'd already been through so much, and I hated that this new threat had emerged just when she was starting to feel safe again.

"Regardless of who they were aiming for, Liza was in danger." I was calm but firm, desperately trying not to let my emotions get the best of me. "I shielded her with my body, and we made a run for the car when they were reloading."

Liam's jaw tightened, and he was barely holding back a snarl. Instead of lashing out, he inhaled deeply, filled his lungs with fresh air, and made a conscious effort to redirect his attention to the situation at hand.

"He strained with the effort of holding back his temper. "We need to figure out who did this and why. We can't afford to have any more attempts on either of your lives."

"Agreed," I said, my mind settling in a clear direction that centered me. "We'll go over the list of enemies again. There's got to be someone we overlooked or failed to consider."

Liam nodded, his intense focus never wavering from me. "I want to be involved in every step of this investigation. Whoever did this is going to pay."

The fierce protectiveness for Liza burned within him, radiating a strong and unwavering determination to keep her safe. In that moment, our differences and constant battles for dominance faded away, and we found ourselves united by a shared objective to protect the ones we loved.

As Liam, Liza, and I headed toward the study to strategize, a comforting warmth rose within me. For the first time since this entire mess began, we had a solid plan and allies who'd stand beside us no matter what. It didn't make the danger any less real or the fear any less potent, but it gave me hope that we could overcome whatever obstacles lay ahead.

No matter how dark things got, we'd make it to the other side bound by a love and loyalty stronger than any threat. To show that, I raised Liza's hand to my lips as walked down the hallway and brushed a kiss over her knuckles.

I stood in the study, my jaw clenched while Liam paced back and forth like a caged animal. His anger was a hum of energy that permeated the air. His fury didn't bother me—not really. Liam's concern was for Liza, not me, and that was fine. It wasn't his job to worry about my safety, it was mine.

I studied my mate. Dark smudges marred the delicate skin beneath her eyes. What was supposed to be a relaxing outing had only made her more exhausted.

"I'll be back in a minute or two. Liam, help yourself to a drink. I need to talk to Liza." Taking her hand, I walked alongside her to our bedroom. "I'm sorry, babe, I should have just let you sleep."

With all the grace she possessed, she reached up and kissed me softly, laying her palm over my cheek. "Did you shoot the gun? No. So, how is it your fault? I can hear Liam pacing from here. Why don't you go and answer his questions, because he won't settle until he has all the details. I'm going to read... maybe watch some television."

I covered her hand with mine, turning it and kissing her palm. "I'll be back soon." I watched as she lay down on the bed and picked up the book on her bedside table. She looked over the top of it and made a shooing motion.

With a deep sigh, I forced myself to return to my office and answer Liam's questions,

"Whoever did this is going to pay," he growled through clenched teeth. "This ends now."

Every time I closed my eyes, I was transported to the street outside the diner. I could picture Liza's face when we'd fled from the hail of bullets, her eyes wide with terror. The shooting had left her shaken to the core, and it tore at my wolf to admit that there was nothing I could have done to stop it. Now, more than ever, I needed to put an end to this threat, to find whoever was responsible, and to make sure they could never hurt her again.

My jaw clicked under the strain of the day. "Let's figure out who's after us, and why."

"Start with any recent enemies," Liam said curtly, filled with tension. "Anyone who might have a grudge or be looking for revenge."

"Castro is top of the list," I said. "But shooting isn't his style. This is more personal. I'm certain there's someone else involved. Someone closer to home."

"Then, we start digging," Liam said, his voice hard as steel. "And when we find out who's behind this, we make them regret ever turning their heads in Liza's direction."

"Agreed." I slammed my fists on the desk. My wolf rumbled within me, eager for the hunt, but my human side had to keep a grip on the reins, reminding him that we had to be smart about this. We couldn't afford to make any mistakes, not when Liza's life was at stake.

We spent hours poring over records and making calls, trying to piece together a list of potential suspects. As the shadows lengthened outside, casting long, eerie fingers across the floor, I became more and more uneasy. It wasn't enough to simply react to threats. We needed to be proactive, and to anticipate our enemies' moves before they could strike.

I stood at the window, staring out on the darkening woods beyond the estate. The scent of damp earth and fallen leaves filled my nostrils, a reminder that winter was fast approaching. I clenched my fists, my anger and frustration building within me.

"Ty," Liam said, drawing my attention to him. "We need to consider all possibilities."

I shifted my position so I was facing him directly. "I'm certain Castro is behind this. He must have somehow found someone who had a personal grudge against either you or me. He's been after Liza since the beginning."

"Maybe." Liam rubbed his chin thoughtfully, sounding doubtful. "Think about it, though. Castro is obsessed with Liza. Would he really risk her life?"

"You're right, and even if he thought she wasn't there, he can't kill me without killing her as we're fated," I added, my lungs constricting at the thought of what might have happened.

"So, maybe," Liam pondered aloud, "whoever attacked us wasn't following Castro's orders. When I put word out amongst the underground that Liza is under my protection, I may have inadvertently alerted enemies who don't care about shedding a little blood if it means getting my attention." He drummed a restless beat on the table with his fingers.

"Fuck." I rubbed my jaw. "So, we could be facing multiple threats here?"

"Looks like it." Liam sighed, and his expression filled with sorrow. "We need to act fast before they strike again."

"Agreed," I said, my mind racing with plans and strategies. "We need to focus on our enemies, who might be working with Castro, and who would be after you."

"Right." Liam nodded; his lips pursed. "To start off, let's examine all the facts again, cross reference everything. Perhaps we can uncover any links."

While we delved into the tangled web of our enemies, I thought of Liza. She was the reason we were all here, putting ourselves in danger. It didn't matter who we were up against. She was my mate, she completed my soul, and I would do whatever it took to keep her safe.

"Ty, what about this one? The Vipers are renowned for their ruthless tactics and willingness to take on anyone for the right price."

"Possible," I said, scanning the list of names of notorious gangs he held in front of me. "But we can't rule out any of them yet. We'll have to look into each one and determine which is the most likely threat."

"Fine," Liam said, his jaw set with resolve. "But time is not on our side."

I was fully aware that time was of the essence. As we continued our investigation, the taste of fear and desperation lingered on my tongue as a bitter reminder of what was at stake.

"Ty," Liza said from the doorway. She looked and sounded so vulnerable. "I... I can't sleep. Can you come sit with me for a while?"

"Of course," I said, my breath catching at the sight of her. I shot Liam a look that told him we'd continue this later, then followed Liza back to our bedroom, leaving the chaos of the day behind us for now.

As I settled into bed beside her and held her close, I made a silent vow to protect her from the lurking danger that threatened our peace. I would do whatever it took to keep Liza safe, even if it meant walking through the fires of Hell itself. Because she was my mate, my other half, and nothing would ever come between us again.

"Sleep now." I pressed a gentle kiss to her forehead. "I'm here, and I won't let anything happen to you."

While Liza drifted off to sleep in my arms, her breathing becoming slow and steady, I held on to that vow like a lifeline—a beacon of hope in the darkness.

Chapter 10 - Liza

Recent events pressed down on me, making it difficult to breathe. My wolf's anxiety bled into my bones, leaving me on edge and restless. I paced the living room, my footsteps echoing off the walls like a restless animal. The air inside the house was stagnant and oppressive. Another minute in the place, and I'd suffocate. I couldn't stay still any longer. I needed to run.

"Ty!" I called from our room, the sound of my voice echoing through the empty hallway.

Liam and Ty appeared in the doorway, wearing twin expressions of concern.

"I need to go for a run. Clear my head."

"I'm not sure that's such a good idea, Liza. Not right now," Ty said, rubbing his hand on my shoulder. The warmth of his touch was comforting, but it wasn't enough to chase away the dark thoughts swirling in my mind.

Liam turned to Ty. "I think she'll be safe enough. Between your guys and mine, no one is getting on the estate without us knowing."

"I don't know, Liam. What if—"

"You can't live with what ifs. You'll give yourself an ulcer. Either you trust the security we've set up or you don't." Turning my way, Liam gave me a wink.

Part of me wanted to laugh in his face. Wasn't he the one who had kidnapped me and kept me locked up? But I chose to ignore that part. My wolf really wanted that run, so if Liam could talk Ty down, then by all means.

"Promise me you'll take a guard with you? You won't go off without Robin or Jamie?" Ty stepped closer, worry lines creasing his forehead. As much as it frustrated me to have to take someone with me wherever I went, I knew he was only trying to keep me safe, so I nodded in agreement. After all, it was as much for my safety as it was for Ty's peace of mind.

"Thank you," he said, relief smoothing out some of the worry lines when he pulled me in for a quick hug. Even in that moment, with my brother standing right there, I was acutely aware of how well our bodies fit, and the warmth of his touch sent tingles through me, making my nipples erect.

When I stepped outside, the crisp fall air brushed against my skin, causing goosebumps to rise along my arms. The scent of damp earth and fallen leaves filled my nostrils, grounding me in the present. The gray sky overhead threatened rain, but I needed this run. I had to clear my head and let my wolf run free.

Robin was one of the guards who'd been assigned to accompany me. Normally, we had an easygoing relationship, but that was before. He was all business now as he waited at the edge of the woods, his posture rigid, and expression unreadable. It was clear he would rather be anywhere else, but I appreciated his dedication to duty.

"Ready?" I asked him, giving him a small smile as I approached.

"Always, Mrs. Keller," he said, a slight nod accompanying his words.

I took a deep breath and allowed the shift to embrace me. My bones cracked and rearranged themselves, fur sprouting from my skin as my body transformed into its lupine form. It was a sensation both foreign and familiar, and a reminder of the duality within me. My wolf emerged, her senses sharper, ready to explore the world around her.

I took off into the woods, my powerful legs propelling me forward as I darted between trees and leaped over fallen logs. My ears picked up the guard following behind me, his own wolf's form keeping a respectful distance, while still remaining within reach should danger arise. It was a delicate balance, and one I appreciated.

The wind carried the scent of pine and damp soil as my paws pounded against the ground in a rhythmic beat. My heart raced in sync with my stride, the adrenaline coursing through my veins amplifying every beat. The world became a mesmerizing blur, a kaleidoscope of colors, and a multitude of sensations that deepened my connection to everything around me.

Was this what it meant to be free? The rush of excitement set my thoughts in motion. The earth beneath my paws was incredibly intoxicating, especially when coupled with the way the trees gracefully swayed and bent around me as I moved. My past and fears had kept me trapped for such a long time that these moments of unbridled release felt like a healing elixir for my soul.

As my wolf reveled in our run, the burden of everything we had gone through eased a bit. There was still so much uncertainty hanging over us, and there was no getting away from the fact that I'd eventually have to face the challenges ahead. For now, I found solace in surrendering to the untamed allure of the forest, where my worries were momentarily cast aside, and I embraced the freedom of running with the wind at my back.

But even as I tried to concentrate on the sensations around me—the feel of the wind through my fur and the crisp scent of pine in the air—my thoughts persistently revolved around Liam. I desperately wanted to trust him, to believe that he truly loved me and would never betray me. But as I'd found out, life was rarely so simple.

Just as I wrestled with these thoughts, a familiar presence appeared in the woods ahead. Ty, in his massive wolf form, emerged from the shadows, his golden eyes blazing with understanding and concern. His presence alone was enough to put me at ease, bringing me comfort and reassurance.

Robin acknowledged Ty's arrival before gracefully disappearing into the trees, leaving us alone in the serenity of the forest. We ran beside each other through the forest that surrounded the estate. When we reached the clearing where I'd stashed my clothes,

I slowed to a stop. My chest rose and fell with each heavy breath, and my heart thumped wildly.

I shifted back to my human form. He did the same, standing before me, his handsome face clouded with worry.

"Hey." He gently reached out to touch my arm. "What's going on? You seem... troubled."

I hesitated, unsure how to express my fears without sounding paranoid or ungrateful for all that Liam had done for me so far. But Ty's patient, gentle smile encouraged me to speak my mind.

"Ty, do you think... Can we really trust Liam?" I wavered, hating how vulnerable I sounded. "I want to believe that he loves me and wouldn't betray me, but I'd be lying if I didn't admit it's a possibility. He's admitted he knows the trigger word. What if he activates me? From everything Liam shared, there wouldn't be a lot we could do about it. I'd be at his mercy."

Sympathy filled his eyes. "I can't even begin to imagine how you're feeling, but I do understand your concerns. It's natural to question things in a situation like this. But I've barely met the man, and I believe he truly loves you."

"Even if he does love me, that doesn't mean he wouldn't betray me. Power can make people do crazy things."

He nodded solemnly. "That's true. But everything Liam's done so far has proved to me he would do anything to protect you. I trust him to do the right thing when it comes down to it."

"Can you promise me that?" I asked, carefully studying him for any hint of doubt.

Ty hesitated. "I can promise you the support of me and the pack. As for Liam, based on his actions so far, all I can offer you is my faith."

I tried to absorb the unwavering conviction he offered, letting it seep into every fiber of my being. I wanted to believe him and trust that Liam wasn't a threat. Ty had always been able to read people well, especially other wolves, so if he believed in Liam, maybe I should, too.

"Thank you." I pulled him into a tight embrace. His muscular arms wrapped around me, giving me the security and warmth I desperately needed.

"Anytime. You are not alone in this," he murmured into my hair.

I gave him a weak smile. "I'll try to put my doubts aside."

"Good." Ty squeezed my waist reassuringly. "Because there's something else I need to tell you."

My stomach clenched with apprehension, and I braced myself.

"I could feel the energy of your aura levels while we were running. They're becoming stronger." Ty's brow furrowed with concern. "That can be both a blessing and a curse."

"Stronger?" I asked, struggling to process what he was saying, though pride surged through me. But was being powerful truly a positive attribute? Another part of me, the part that remembered the tales of destruction wrought by others who had lost control of their power, whispered a warning.

"Does that mean... I'm more dangerous?"

"Possibly," Ty said. "It also means you have the potential to do incredible things, to protect those you love. That's why we need to trust Liam. He can help you harness that power and use it for good."

If my power was growing, I needed to learn how to control it, not just for my own sake, but for the safety of those around me.

"We should go back," Ty insisted. "We have work to do."

As we resumed our trek through the woods, I concentrated on the sensation of Ty's hand in mine, the steady rhythm of our footsteps, and the crisp fall air against my skin. I tried to push away my lingering doubts about Liam, to trust in Ty's judgment, and the bond that connected us all.

"Family," I said under my breath, clinging to the word like a lifeline. For their sake, I would learn to control my powers. I would trust in Liam's intentions, despite the doubts clinging to the edges of my thoughts.

If it turned out he couldn't be trusted... well, I'd face that challenge if needed. With my family by my side, I could overcome anything.

As soon as we emerged from the forest, I heard my name being shouted. A familiar figure jumped up from the stone steps of the front door and rushed toward us.

Rosalie, my petite redhead assistant chef, ran over to meet me.

"Thank God you're safe," she said, hugging me tightly. Her relief radiated off her in waves.

"Hey." Sabrina joined the embrace. My best friend's short blonde hair was unkempt, hinting at her restless nights and exhaustion. "It took us a while to get here, but we made it."

"Surprised it took you this long." I stepped back from their warm embrace. "I half expected you to be here when I arrived home."

Sabrina slapped her hand on her chest dramatically. "You realize it's me we're talking about? I have a reputation for dramatic entrances to uphold. Can't have the people think I'm losing my touch." She grinned, but it did little to mask her obvious worry. "Seriously, we would have been here earlier, but when Ty texted to let me know you were on your way home, he asked me to give it a couple of days. Are you okay? We've been out of our minds with concern."

"Really, Liza," Rosalie added. "We couldn't just sit around worrying about you, now, could we?"

"Of course not." I wrapped my arms around her. "I'm really glad you're both here."

"Hey, what are best friends and cooking partners for?" Rosalie joked. The three of us laughed, and I could feel the bond between us strengthening.

I was relieved Sabrina had accepted the younger girl, and that they'd supported each other in my absence. Although I'd only recently hired Rosalie, I worried about her. She had an unmistakable aura of loneliness she tried to conceal, but there had been a couple of times in the kitchen I'd caught her off guard, lost in her thoughts, and looking terribly sad. I would have to make sure we included her whenever possible and encourage her to step out of her shell.

"Come on, let's get comfortable in the tearoom."

I led Sabrina and Rosalie down the hall. The familiar scent of chamomile and lavender wafted through the air, soothing my frayed nerves.

It didn't have the same effect on Sabrina. She was pacing in front of me, frustration building up on every pass. "I wish I could meet your kidnapper," she said, taking on a fierce edge. "Rory didn't deserve to be hurt like that, and Ty said the kidnapper is your brother. What the actual fuck, Liza?!"

Rosalie nodded in agreement from where she perched on the edge of her seat.

Sabrina stopped moving, but she still had plenty to say. "I mean it, that's a dick move. I'd love to give that fucker a piece of my mind. Hell, I'd kick his ass from here to kingdom come."

I opened my mouth to respond, but my eyes flicked to the doorway. Liam leaned against the doorframe with a bemused smile on his face. He must have been listening to Sabrina's rant, fully aware he was the subject of her ire.

"Speak of the Devil," I mumbled, mentally bracing myself for the impending clash.

I paid close attention to Liam to see how he would react to her threats, readying myself to jump in between them if need be, but something unexpected happened. He didn't do or say anything. He looked at Sabrina as if he was a man in the desert, and she was a glass of water.

"Apologies." He tore his attention away from her. "I was just... lost in thought," he confessed, a wistful smile playing on his lips. "Now, what was it you were saying about kicking my ass?" Liam's voice had taken on a luxurious, velvety quality.

"Liam." I pointed to Sabrina. "This is my *best friend* Sabrina Wells." I placed special emphasis on best friend. "Sabrina, this is my half-brother Liam Russell."

Sabrina's eyes roamed over his entire body, a seductive smile forming on her lips. "You know what?" She chuckled throatily. "I've changed my mind. You can kidnap me anytime you please."

"Yuck." I wrinkled my nose in distaste. I could practically taste the sexual tension in the room, and I suddenly felt extremely protective of Sabrina.

She was human. She didn't deserve to be caught up in this supernatural mess.

"Anyway," I remarked, trying to diffuse the tension. "Let's shift our focus to more pressing matters, like something to eat, and perhaps some upbeat gossip. We can discuss any... personal matters later." I shot a pointed look at Liam, hoping he understood.

"Of course." He nodded solemnly and left to go through to Ty's office, leaving us girls to chat, though I didn't miss the look he gave Sabrina.

The scent of freshly brewed tea and warm scones wafted through the air, embracing me like a comforting hug as I relaxed in the familiar surroundings of plush velvet chairs and delicate china teacups. It was good to be back in a space without talk of war plans or tactics and enemies, even if just for a little while.

"Ah, I've missed this place." Rosalie sighed and sank back into the chair, her face betraying the tension she carried.

"Don't worry," I said, reaching across the table and patting her arm "Once all the chaos has calmed down, we'll get back to work. Your job here is still secure. I'll keep paying your salary until this is all sorted."

"Thanks, Liza." The worry melted from her brow. "I wasn't sure what your plans would be, or if you were even going to continue." Her pale complexion did nothing to hide her embarrassment. "I've been contemplating asking for my old job back. I'm so glad I don't have to. I've learned more from you in the short time I've worked here than I ever did there."

"I'm glad you're happy here. Just remember that when we're rushed off our feet and you haven't had a day off." I laughed. I was so pleased it was working out the way I'd hoped. One of my goals in my business was to train an apprentice. She was a gifted cook, she just lacked confidence, but I'd soon change that.

As we sat drinking tea and spreading cream and jam onto scones, we chatted about the happenings in the town, and Sabrina shared stories of the outpouring of love she'd seen from our patrons since my disappearance.

"Seriously," Sabrina said between bites, catching the dripping jam with her napkin. "You wouldn't believe how many people were asking about you. There were cards, flowers, even a few teddy bears left at your office."

"Really?" I asked, genuinely touched. "That's incredibly sweet."

"I told you... you're loved." Sabrina winked. "Now you just have to make sure you stay safe so we can keep it that way."

"Speaking of..." Rosalie chewed on her thumbnail. "How are you holding up with all this craziness?"

"Truthfully?" The steam rose from my cup of tea as I took a sip, the familiar taste grounding me, helping me collect my scattered thoughts. "It's been... difficult, but I'm handling it. My parents have been amazing, and with Ty and Liam by my side, I feel even more empowered.

"Good." Sabrina was firm, leaving no room for doubt. "Just remember we're here for you too, okay?"

Rosalie echoed the sentiment.

"Thank you." Their unwavering support meant so much to me.

Just as Sabrina was about to entertain us with more gossip from the town, a commotion from downstairs interrupted our conversation. My wolf immediately tensed within me, sensing the disruption of the otherwise peaceful atmosphere.

I rose from my seat and headed toward the door. The instinct to protect my friends, both human and otherwise, surged within me like a powerful current, propelling me into action. As I hurried toward the source of the noise, my thoughts raced with possibilities, each one more unsettling than the last. What danger awaited me this time?

The house was a mess of chaos; the noise bouncing off the walls as I rushed down the stairs. My wolf's hackles were raised, fur bristling beneath my skin as we prepared for whatever threat was waiting for us. The scent of anger and fear hung heavy in the air, guiding me to the source.

"Stay here," I growled at Sabrina and Rosalie, who had followed me before racing down the remaining steps. I rounded the corner into the living room and skidded to a halt at the sight before me.

Liam had Nico pinned to the wall by his throat, and his razor-sharp claws were perilously close to the main artery. Nico's face was contorted with fear as he desperately clutched Liam's wrists, struggling to break free.

The memory of telling Liam about Castro and Nico's involvement in our father's death resurfaced like a tidal wave. I cursed inwardly, realizing my confession may have triggered this violent confrontation.

"Liam, let him go!" I rushed forward, grabbing his arm in an attempt to pull him away from Nico.

"Why should I?" Liam snarled. "He helped kill our father. He doesn't deserve your sympathy."

"Because he didn't know," I shot back, trying to appeal to Liam's rational side. "He was completely unaware of Castro's motives. He's not responsible for what happened."

Liam hesitated, his attention flicking between Nico and me as he weighed his options. My muscles burned with the effort of keeping my wolf in check. Liam's aura, so like my own, had every instinct in my body screaming to protect my family, to ensure their safety at any cost.

"Please," I begged. "He's not a threat, Liam. Let him go."

The tension in the room was so thick, it had the hair on the back of my neck standing on end. Liam's aura made the timber walls groan and heave beneath its power.

My wolf paced restlessly within me, gnashing her teeth, desperate to be released and eliminate this threat to our family. She strained against the confines of my skin, raring to shift and protect. To protect Liam and Ty, even though Nico wasn't a threat. It was a gut reaction. A primal instinct that clawed at my insides, urging me to act.

"Enough!" Ty's low rumble echoed around the walls as he strode in as every inch the alpha he was born to be. "Release him."

"Stay out of this, Ty," Liam snapped as he glared daggers at my mate, but Ty held his ground, his own aura rising to challenge Liam.

"Listen to yourself." Ty's eyes never left Liam, watching his every movement. He was poised and tensed, ready to jump in if Liam took it any further. "This isn't you. You're letting your emotions cloud your judgment."

"Maybe my judgment needs to be clouded." Liam tightened his grip on Nico's throat a fraction more. "Maybe I need justice."

"Justice?" Ty scoffed, taking another step closer. "You call this justice? Attacking someone who's already suffered enough."

The struggle between my human self and my wolf was reaching a breaking point. The atmosphere in the room was electric. The slightest spark would set off an explosion. I clenched my fists, with my nails biting into my palms, but it wasn't enough to keep the wolf at bay.

"Get away from him," I snarled, sounding rough and guttural to my own ears.

How could I control something so primal, so raw? It was like trying to tame a wildfire with a single bucket of water. My wolf's fierce desperation to protect our family—Liam, Ty, and even Nico—from any harm overwhelmed me.

"Please." I dropped to my knees as tears streamed down my cheeks. "I don't want to hurt anyone."

"Liza," Sabrina's voice cut through the chaos, drawing everyone's attention. She hurriedly made her way to my side and brushed my hair out of my face. "What's happening to you?"

Chapter 11 - Ty

My heart pounded as Liam's fingers dug into Nico's throat. I braced myself to intervene, but before I took another step toward them, the desperation in Sabrina's cry froze me in my tracks.

With just one word, she commanded my full attention.

"Liza!"

My focus went straight to my mate. She was pale, pained, and her face covered in sweat. Instinctively, I rushed toward her, my body moving before my mind had fully processed the situation. To my surprise, Liam reached her side at the same time, his worried look mirroring my own.

"What's happening Liza?" he asked calmly.

I grudgingly admired his ability to keep his cool under pressure. I had never been so completely powerless, and I hated it.

The powerful scent of fear surrounded all of us, and her muscles were taut. She was fighting against something inside her.

"I... don't know," she said through clenched teeth, her brows furrowed in confusion. "It's like I'm shifting... I can't... It's hard to fight her. I can't control it." Liza's mouth was clenched tight, her body tense and rigid. She was fighting an internal battle. Sweat beaded on her forehead, and her breaths came out in short pants. I hated seeing her like this, hated feeling helpless,

"Her wolf..." Realization dawned on me. "It's trying to take over and force the shift."

Liam's face paled, and he took hold of her hand. Leaning down, he said something to Liza I couldn't quite make out, but it sounded like he was talking directly to her wolf. I drew closer and watched intently. The tension in the air was like a ticking time bomb, waiting to explode.

"Easy there, girl," Liam said in a soothing, calm tone, apparently relaxed despite the dangerous situation we found ourselves in. "I get it. You want to protect your family, but I'm safe. Ty's safe. You need to trust Liza to handle this. She's strong enough to keep you both safe."

"Keep talking to her," I said out loud while silently praying that whatever connection he had with Liza's wolf would be enough to help her regain control. The thought of losing her to the beast within terrified me to my core.

I sent thoughts and memories through our mating bond to remind Liza of who she was.

The first time I saw her at the mating party, when she entered the room from the kitchen. How mesmerizing she was.

How glorious she looked when we were making love.

Reminding her of all who loved her and valued her: me, her parents, brothers, Liam, Sabrina— anyone I could think of to remind her of her importance in this life.

I marveled at her strength, and how she remained resilient despite all she had endured, and I told her she was the strongest person I knew and loved.

Something shifted in Liza, and the wildness in her eyes receded, her breathing slowing down just a fraction before she slid to the floor, and I went with her, holding her in my arms. Her muscles relaxed, leaving only exhaustion and vulnerability in its wake.

The tension in the room crackled like a live wire, the air heavy with the scent of fear and desperation. Liza's ragged breaths filled my ears as she struggled to contain her wolf, her body shivering violently in my arms.

"Stay with us." Liam's encouragement was soothing, like a calming breeze on a stormy day. "We need you here."

I watched as Liam recognized something within Liza's wild gaze—a flicker of understanding shared between siblings. A melancholic half-smile played on his lips, the corner of his mouth twitching ever so slightly.

"Your wolf... she was trying to come to my aid, wasn't she?" he asked, almost incredulously. Liza nodded slowly, the effort clearly taking its toll on her.

A heavy sigh escaped my lips as it all clicked into place. Of course. Her wolf was reacting to Liam's distress. He was her brother, and the aura he was emitting must have been unbearable for her sensitive instincts. Nevertheless, the danger for Liza remained just as potent.

"Damn it," I said, my voice hoarse with worry. "You need to keep your emotions in check, especially around Liza. She's already got enough to deal with."

"I realize that now," Liam admitted. "I'm sorry. It didn't even occur to me. I never imagined it would provoke such a strong reaction from her."

"Neither did I." I glanced down at Liza's drained face. "But we need to be more careful from now on. We can't afford to make any more mistakes."

Liam looked down at his sister, the stiffness in his posture softening. "I'm sorry," he whispered. "I didn't think my emotions would affect you so strongly. I'll do better, I promise."

I ached for both these siblings reunited after so long, trying to navigate their bond while still learning each other's strengths and weaknesses. It wouldn't be easy, but then again, nothing worth having ever was.

Liam moved to the other side of the room, away from Liza, but closer to the pale Sabrina. I'd forgotten she and Rosalie were still in the room. Sabrina was human, and although she knew about shifters, it had to have been frightening for her to see her friend like this. She was looking at Liam in an unusual way, but that was a mystery to unravel another time. Right now, Liza needed all my attention.

"Thank you." Liza tried to push herself out of my arms and up from the floor, but her muscles quivered.

"Let me help you." I stood and slid my arms under her, lifting her with as much care as I could muster. She leaned heavily against me, her breathing shallow and labored. She was so exhausted she didn't even protest when I scooped her into my arms and cradled her close to me. The soft scent of her shampoo filled my nostrils, mixing with the underlying aroma of her wolf.

"Thanks." Her words slurred with fatigue. "I'm not sure what happened. I've never struggled to control my wolf like that before."

"She was trying to protect Liam," I muttered softly, my voice a calm facade over the storm raging within me. "It's a natural instinct to want to protect your brother, especially considering how new your relationship is. Don't worry about it just now. We'll figure it out."

I practically felt the last ounce of energy leave Liza's body as she sagged against me, her breathing shallow, her face pale and drawn.

"This is why Liza needs to develop better control," Liam said in a hushed whisper. "I'll start working with her, training her. As an omega, she needs to learn discipline."

"Training? For an omega?" My brows furrowed. "How do you even know where to start?"

Liam sighed and ran a hand through his hair. "My father taught me when I was young. He wanted me to be prepared for anything."

"Your father?" I let out a dry chuckle. "I think that's the first time you've mentioned him without a hint of malice."

"Believe it or not, Ty, he did a few things right," Liam muttered. "He might have been an awful person, but he made sure I could handle myself, my wolf, and others, too."

The air became heavy, and I found I couldn't ignore the truth resonating in his words. Liam may have had a difficult past, but he had emerged from it stronger than ever, and if he could pass a fraction of that strength onto Liza, then perhaps she'd stand a better chance at overcoming her own demons.

I inclined my head. "You can train her. Remember, she's not just some random shifter you're dealing with. She's my mate, and if anything happens to her..."

"I get it. Protectiveness comes with the territory." Liam held up a hand. "Trust me, I have no intention of hurting Liza. I want her to be able to control her wolf, not fear it."

He was being sincere, and despite my reservations, I knew he was right. Liza needed guidance, and though it pained me to admit, Liam was better equipped to provide that than I was. For all my alpha instincts, I had never faced the same adversity he had. I certainly had no idea how to train an omega. If there was anyone who understood Liza's struggles, it was Liam.

"Fine." I clenched my jaw to suppress my growl. "But I'll be watching you. If anything goes wrong, don't think for a second I won't step in."

"Understood," Liam stated firmly, his penetrating stare searing straight into my soul. "I promise, Ty, I'll do everything I can to help her."

As much as the idea of entrusting Liza's safety to someone else made my blood boil, it would be wrong if I let my pride stand in the way of Liza's progress. If Liam could give her the tools she needed to master the skills her wolf needed as an omega, then it was a risk I had to take, because ultimately, all that mattered was keeping my mate safe, strong, and in control.

I exhaled deeply and let go of my lingering reservations. "We'll start her training as soon as she's well enough. In the meantime, we need to monitor her and make sure she doesn't push herself too hard."

"Agreed." Liam nodded, and when he looked down at the sleeping woman in my arms, I saw no trace of the hard mob boss so many shifters were terrified of. "She's stubborn, but that's part of what makes her so special."

"Tell me about it." I cracked a small smile despite myself. It was true. Liza's stubbornness could be maddening, but it was one of the many things I loved about her.

Liza stirred in my arms, her voice barely audible as she whispered, "Ty, I'm so tired."

I leaned down and nuzzled her hair with my nose. "Shh. You just need to rest, Liza. We'll take care of everything."

I cradled her limp form against my chest and carried her to our bedroom. It was a stark reminder of how much responsibility I held for her wellbeing not just as her alpha, but also as her fated mate. Each step brought me closer to the realization that this burden wasn't one I bore alone. Liam was now an integral part of our family, and his influence on Liza was undeniable.

In the doorway of our bedroom, I hesitated, overcome by a strange combination of protectiveness and vulnerability. I tightened my grip on Liza as a sense of security washed over me, yet deep in my heart, I had an unsettling feeling there was a deeper, unexplained power influencing our lives.

"Ty?" Liza must have sensed my inner turmoil because her voice quivered, and her wide-eyed expression met mine, pleading for reassurance.

"Everything will work out," I assured her, trying not to let my doubt show. "Just get some rest, okay?"

She nodded, and I laid her down on the bed, tucking the covers around her for added comfort. Her eyelids fluttered closed, and within moments, her breathing slowed and deepened as she fell asleep.

The room grew darker as I watched her, my concern for her safety overshadowing everything else. I wanted to stay by her side, to protect her from whatever invisible danger might be lurking in our midst, but there were others who needed me just as much. I had a business with hundreds of employees to run, and I was the alpha of the Keller pack. Liam was offering to help, and I had to take that gift. Not allowing him to train Liza to her full potential would only harm her.

A soft sigh escaped Liza's lips as she slept, her body finally at ease after the tumultuous events. I watched her for a moment, love swelling in me for this woman who had become my everything.

Her chest rose and fell in a slow, even rhythm, and her face relaxed in peaceful repose. All the tension and chaos from earlier faded away, leaving only the quiet beauty of this moment.

But I couldn't stay. Not when there were still so many questions left unanswered. With a lingering kiss to her forehead, I reluctantly tore myself away from Liza's bedside and closed the door behind me as quietly as possible before I made my way toward my office. My thoughts turned to Nico and the confrontation he'd had with Liam.

I harbored no ill will toward either of them. In fact, I'd figured something like it would happen eventually. I had thought if anyone was going to challenge Nico over the death of Josef Wylde and his pack, it would have been Liza. I couldn't blame Liam for being the one to do it. We all had our breaking points, especially when we were protecting those we cared about.

The tension in the room was like a tightrope, ready to snap at any moment. I stood in the doorway, observing Liam and Nico sitting on opposite sides of my office. Both wore stony expressions, their body language screaming animosity. The space between them felt dense with unspoken words and unresolved issues.

Forcing the two to talk it out was pointless. After their violent confrontation and Liza's reaction, I was confident it was over. If it flared up again, I would reevaluate my strategy and sit Liam and Nico down to talk. For now, I thought it best to continue as if nothing had transpired.

"Hey." I opted for a casual approach when I stepped into the room. "Nico, what brings you here?"

"I came with news about the shooting in town. Liam was right." Nico glanced at Liam, and I did the same to gauge his reaction. "We tracked down the car, and it's registered to a man named Benny Leopold."

All the oxygen in the room seemed to dissipate. Liam's face contorted into a mask of fury, and his clenched fists spoke of his readiness to tear something apart. As his power surged and his alpha instincts kicked into high gear, it felt like I was standing too close to a roaring fire.

"Benny," Liam seethed, his teeth grinding together as he struggled to keep his anger in check. "That bastard is one of my biggest rivals."

"Your rival?" I asked, my eyebrows knitting together in confusion. Obviously, I was aware Liam had enemies—any alpha worth his salt did—but this sounded much more personal. He spoke his name like it was poison on his tongue. It made me uneasy.

Just what exactly was Liam mixed up in?.

"Long story," Liam said with cold hostility. He glanced downward, his body language suggesting that he desperately wished the floor would swallow him up and spare him from saying any more. "He's bad news. If he's behind the shooting, we need to prepare for the worst."

"Agreed." I swallowed tightly. There was no telling what Liam's rival was capable of or how far he'd go to get what he wanted.

"Ty," Liam began, his shaky voice betraying his deep concern. "I'm sorry for bringing this danger to your doorstep. I never meant for my past to catch up with me like this."

With a quiet nod, Nico discreetly exited my office. I was grateful my father's informant had stuck around after his retirement. My own informant, Isaiah Culver, was currently doing a job for me that meant he couldn't stay close to the estate, so having Nico on hand was helpful.

Liam paced back and forth with his fists clenched at his sides. His infectious energy pulsed through the room, his footsteps creating a rhythmic pattern. The air seemed electric with anticipation. The scent of nervous energy hung in the air, mingling with the faint smell of sweat. I could feel the tension building like a coiled spring ready to explode.

"Hey." I was getting dizzy watching the man pace. "Have you thought about shifting? Letting off some steam?"

Liam stopped pacing and turned to face me, his eyes dark with barely restrained anger. He barked out a laugh, but it sounded harsh and bitter. "Shift? Hell, Ty, what I need right now is a good fuck, not a run through the woods."

"Jesus." I burst out laughing, taken aback by his crude remark, but understanding the sentiment behind it. The stress of the situation was getting to him, and he needed an outlet for his pent-up emotions.

"Sorry," Liam scrubbed a hand through his hair. "That was...uncalled for. I just—"

"Save it." I raised a hand to stop him. "We all deal with stress in our own way. Just... try not to take it out on anyone here, okay?"

"Right. Oh, by the way," he said, changing the subject abruptly. "Liza's friends are waiting in the tearoom. They wanted to make sure she's okay." He paused, then asked, "What can you tell me about Sabrina?"

I chewed the inside of my cheek. Why was he asking about Sabrina? "She's Liza's best friend, works with Liza in her catering business as a cook and as a waitress. She's pretty spunky, but she's been a good friend to Liza. Why? Is there something wrong?"

Liam hesitated, uncertainty flashing across his face, then he resolutely shook his head. "No, it's nothing. Just curious." There was a hint of something else hidden in his words, but he didn't elaborate.

I studied him, trying to gauge his thoughts, but his face remained an unreadable mask. Deciding not to pry, I shifted gears. "Well, if you're up for it, maybe you should take that offer of a run. It might help you release some of that pent-up energy."

For a moment, I caught a flicker of amusement in his eyes. "Yeah, maybe you're right. A good run might just do the trick." His lips quirked into a half-smile, the tension in his shoulders easing ever so slightly.

The moment Liam stepped out back, I turned my attention to the women in the tearoom. They needed reassurance that Liza was okay, and with everything that had happened, they'd been forgotten. They deserved some peace of mind.

Before I took a step toward the tearoom, footsteps approaching the front door stopped me in my tracks. I allowed a little of my wolf to bleed through so my senses sharpened, and caught the familiar scent of my best friend and business partner Bryce. Thank God. I certainly could use his support right now.

When I opened the door, Bryce's face broke into a grin. "Ty, my man." He clapped me on the shoulder before he entered. Although he carried himself with his usual confidence, I detected his tenseness.

"Hey, Bryce." I tried to smile despite the situation. "You're here to discuss some business, I assume?"

"Of course." He attempted a casual shrug. "But I also heard on the jungle drums about the recent events, and I just wanted to make sure everyone is okay."

"Thanks." There was no way I could hide my concern. Bryce had known me for too long. "We're managing." Something was up. I wasn't sure exactly why Bryce was here, but I was absolutely certain it wasn't just about business.

My stomach churned as he and I stood in my office and discussed our plans to expand the business. Liam's presence in the house still hung heavily in the air, but I couldn't let that distract me from the task at hand.

Bryce rubbed his hands together. "So, we've got a meeting with the investors next week. I think if we can present them with a solid plan for growth, they'll be on board."

"I like the sound of that." My wolf paced restlessly inside me, fixated on Liza's scent. He wanted to be by her side, to ensure she was getting the rest she needed. Honestly, that's what I wanted to do, too, but I needed to take care of other pressing matters.

"Ty." Bryce placed a hand on my shoulder, snapping me back to the present. "You need to focus. You're worried about Liza, but we have to make this work."

I took a deep breath to center myself. "You're right. Let's go over the numbers again."

We spent the next half hour immersed in spreadsheets and projections, trying to iron out every detail before we presented our expansion plan to the investors.

When we were done, Bryce sank back in his chair and stretched his legs out in front of, crossing his feet at the ankles. "Ty... I appreciate we've got a lot on our plates right now, but I can't help noticing the uneasy atmosphere in the house, and I'm guessing it has something to do with Liam."

I glanced at the door, wondering if it was possible for Liam to hear us even though he'd gone for a run.

Bryce continued. "His presence is almost overwhelming." I looked back at him and noticed the discomfort in his posture. "I've never experienced anything like it."

"You're not wrong." I rubbed the back of my neck. "Liam's strength is formidable. He's a powerful alpha, and he has me beat by a country mile."

"Is that why you're letting him stay here? Are you worried about what he might do if you turn him away?"

"Partly." I stared at the floor. "More than that, having him as an ally benefits us all. If things escalate, which they likely will, I'd rather have him with us than against us."

Bryce nodded slowly. "It's a good strategy. Just be cautious. Trusting another alpha, especially one that powerful? It can be dangerous."

"For the sake of the pack, and especially for Liza, I need to give it a shot." The situation settled heavily on my chest.

"Stay vigilant, Ty. Remember, you've got me and the rest of the pack behind you."

"Thanks, Bryce." I offered him a small smile. "Thanks a lot."

Our conversation was interrupted by the front door opening and closing—Liam returning from his run—and when he entered the house, I noticed a slight shift in the atmosphere.

"Guess your guest is back," Bryce said, his jaw set in determination.

"Let's go find out what he's up to," I said before I led the way out of my office.

As we entered the foyer, I could tell there was a visible transformation in Liam's demeanor. His earlier restlessness was gone, and he seemed calmer now.

"Hey, Liam. Good run?"

"Yes, thanks," he said with a nod. "I needed that."

I turned at the sound of footsteps on the stairs to see Sabrina and Rosalie were making their way down, concern etched on their faces. They must have gone up to our room to check on Liza, but it seemed she hadn't woken up yet.

"Hey," Sabrina said. "Liza's still asleep. We figured we'd head home and let her rest, but can you please tell her we'll be back soon to check on her?"

"God, I'm so sorry, Sabrina. I meant to come and tell you she was out for the count, but then Bryce dropped in, and I got caught up in a business meeting. I'll make sure she knows to call you when she wakes up."

I walked the ladies to the door, and as they stepped outside, Bryce followed closely behind, a smug grin plastered on his face. He'd always been drawn to beautiful women, and he and Sabrina had some history. Though it hadn't ended well, it was obvious he still had an interest in her.

"Hey there, gorgeous," Bryce said to Sabrina, trying to catch her attention. She glanced over her shoulder, rolled her eyes, and continued walking without acknowledging him any more than that.

"Ouch, that's cold," Bryce bit out under his breath. He couldn't stand being ignored, especially by someone he was into.

It was then that I saw Liam staring intently at Sabrina. His gaze was sharp and focused, as if he were trying to decipher some hidden meaning in her actions. I sifted through my memories, desperately seeking any thread of connection between them.

"Something wrong?" I asked Liam, trying to sound casual.

"Nothing." He sounded distant and never once stopped watching Sabrina's retreating figure.

Curiosity piqued, I closed my eyes and reached out with my wolf, focusing on the bond between wolves. It was a powerful and intimate connection, one that went far deeper than the superficial relationships most people experienced. It was only shared between true mates.

To my shock, there was a faint thread of that bond emanating from Liam, drawing him toward Sabrina like an invisible tether. I stifled my gasp. The bond was still weak, barely formed, but it was undoubtedly there.

"Wait, you and Sabrina?" I whispered in disbelief.

Liam stiffened, his eyes narrowing as he finally tore his attention away from Sabrina. "What are you talking about?" he growled.

"You must be able to feel that? It might be weak, but the fated bond between you two is there." I struggled to wrap my head around the revelation.

Bryce's gaze darted between Liam and Sabrina, the tension in the air straining like a taut bowstring. The gears were practically turning in Bryce's head as he tried to figure out what was happening. "A fated bond between a shifter and a human?" he exclaimed. "Who ever heard of such a thing?

"Then again," Bryce continued, a note of grudging acceptance entering his voice, "The Wylde family bloodline is definitely unique. Liza's your fated mate, after all."

I chose to ignore the dig.

Liam's gaze momentarily wandered elsewhere, lost in thought, before finding its way back to Sabrina. His expression was unreadable, but I already knew him well enough to recognize the unease simmering beneath the surface.

As Bryce's shoulders slumped in resignation, Liam reached out and patted him on the back. The gesture was awkward, almost tentative, but I recognized it for what it was—an attempt at reassurance.

Liam gave one last bittersweet gaze at Sabrina before heading inside without another word.

"Whatever was going on with you and Sabrina, it's over now, you know that right?" I told Bryce quietly. "She's clearly his mate."

Bryce stiffened further at my words, his jaw clenching, but he didn't argue. We both knew that challenging someone as dominant as an alpha like Liam would be a recipe for disaster.

"Let's just... focus on the task at hand, shall we?" I tried to defuse the situation before it could escalate. "We have more important things to worry about."

"Right," Bryce muttered, the muscles in his neck still corded with tension. He hurried to his car and left the estate, gravel crunching under his tires.

While I mulled over the implications of this presumed love triangle, I caught a whiff of Sabrina's scent in the air—a heady mix of jasmine and something uniquely her own. I wondered what it must be like for someone like Liam to experience that pull, that bone-deep connection to another being. I pushed the thought away, fully aware that at that moment, there was no time for such distractions.

I turned and made my way back up the steps and into the house, pulled by our bond to be near my mate.

Chapter 12 - Liza

The first rays of sunlight peeked through the curtains, warming my face. I stirred, my body buzzing with newfound energy, rejuvenated after yesterday's nightmare. Ty pulled me against him and pressed butterfly kisses against my cheeks, eyelids, and then my forehead.

"Good morning," he murmured, his voice gruff and thick with sleep.

"Morning." I wrapped my arms around him, tracing the contours of his back with my fingertips, relishing the taut muscles beneath my touch, and released a contented sigh.

Ty's stormy gray eyes fixed on me, and he brushed a stray strand of hair out of my face. "Are you feeling better today?"

I nodded and scooted away to sit up. "So much better. Thank you for taking care of me."

Ty frowned slightly, his fingers tracing invisible patterns on my arm. "I was worried about you. I've never seen you fight for control like that."

His concern couldn't be any clearer, and a lump of emotion formed in my throat. "I'm worried too. I'm not sure what's happening, but whatever it is, I need to get it under control."

"Did you hear any of the conversation Liam and I had yesterday while we were trying to calm you down?" His fingers never stopped tracing patterns on my skin, soothing me.

Memories flashed through my mind: Liam and Nico fighting, and my wolf trying to take control. I knew that if she'd gained the upper hand, she'd go after Nico. She saw him as a threat to her kin. I'd fought her desperately, trying to make her understand.

"I vaguely recall Liam speaking to my wolf, and I felt your worry through our bond, but the rest is a blur." Guilt gnawed at me, leaving a bitter taste in my mouth. "I'm sorry, Ty."

"Hey, hey, come on. This is not your fault." He caught my chin between his thumb and forefinger and tilted my face up. "You have nothing to be sorry for. Nothing. Understand? I'm not surprised you didn't hear anything. You were pretty out of it." Ty sighed. "Liam thinks he can help you."

"Help me, how?" I was skeptical, but I couldn't disregard the potential benefits without listening first.

The fear from yesterday's lack of control still haunted my thoughts.

"Part of the training your father gave Liam was how to work with an omega. Although he was young, Liam's confident he can help you gain control and work with your powers. He wants to start training with you this morning." He leaned in, pressing a tender kiss to my lips. "You are not alone in this, okay? I'm not going anywhere."

"Promise?" My voice came out barely above a whisper, and I hated how vulnerable I sounded.

"Promise." He sealed the promise with another soft kiss.

We stayed wrapped in the embrace, drawing strength from one another. Ty's unwavering belief in me was a life jacket in the stormy sea of self-doubt. I appreciated this man so much.

After weighing the options, I came to a conclusion. "Okay, I'll give it a try."

Ty pressed his lips to the top of my head, and he sounded relieved when he said, "That's all I ask. You have nothing to lose and everything to gain. However, before you go to Liam, I think I should make sure you're relaxed and in the right headspace for your training." Ty's fingers drifted under my nightshirt and along my side, his husky voice igniting a delicious heat within me.

"Really?" I quirked an eyebrow, trying to suppress the smile tugging at my lips. "How do you plan to do that?"

"Let me show you." He grinned wickedly as he rolled me onto my back. My pulse began to race as he climbed on top of me and straddled my waist. His hands slid under my shirt, fingertips dancing over my skin, making my nerve endings sing. Our gazes locked, and the love and desire I saw there left an indelible mark on my soul, intensifying my own needs.

"Are you sure about this?" I asked, my breath hitching as he leaned down and trailed soft kisses along my collarbone.

"Absolutely." The words vibrated against my skin. "You need to be centered and relaxed before facing whatever challenges Liam has in store for you. Let me help you with that."

"Okay." Giggling, I gave in to the sensations he was stirring within me.

Ty's lips met mine, and I eagerly welcomed him, our tongues tangling in a dance as old as time. His hands continued their exploration, drawing gasps and moans from deep within me. Heat pooled between my legs as my arousal grew.

He pulled away to remove my shirt and toss it aside, leaving me exposed to him. The intensity in his eyes made me shiver, but I didn't shy away. Instead, I reached up and pulled his shirt over his head, the sight of his muscular chest and toned abs causing my desire to flare even higher.

"God, Liza, you're so fucking beautiful," Ty said, lowering his head to capture one of my nipples between his lips. I moaned, arching my back, and threading my fingers through his hair as he teased the sensitive bud.

I gasped, my body on fire from his ministrations. "Ty, please…"

"Patience, love." He switched to the other nipple and gave it the same attention. I writhed, desperate for more, but he was relentless in his pursuit of pleasure, taking me to the edge and then back again.

Finally, when I was sure I couldn't take any more, Ty slipped a hand down between my legs, his fingers finding my wetness, where he began to stroke me with expert precision. My hips bucked against his touch, eager for the release he promised.

"Ty, I need you," I said, my breath hitching as he continued to tease and torment me with his fingers. With each touch, he awakened a hunger within me that I didn't know existed.

"Tell me what you want," he said against my skin, his lips trailing up my neck and nipping lightly at my earlobe.

"Please, I need you inside me." I moaned in desperation.

With a slow, wicked smile, Ty ceased his teasing and moved into position between my legs. "Your wish is my command." He aligned himself at my entrance and stared into my eyes, seeking confirmation.

I nodded, biting my lip in anticipation.

He pushed forward slowly, giving me time to adjust to him, and I gasped at the sensation of fullness and pleasure. We both moaned once he was finally buried completely within me, our bodies entwined and connected in the most intimate way possible.

"Are you okay?" Ty asked gently.

I smiled up at him, wrapping my arms around his neck, and urged him to move. "More than okay."

He began with slow, deliberate thrusts, each stroke sending shivers of pleasure through me. Our bodies moved in perfect harmony, our breaths mingling as we shared heated kisses.

"Touch yourself for me." Ty's voice was husky with arousal. The desire on his face emboldened me, and I slipped my hand between our bodies, my fingers finding my swollen clit and rubbing it in tight circles.

"Fuck, that's so hot." Ty groaned, his pace increasing as he drove in harder and deeper. The combination of his thrusts and my own touch brought me closer and closer to the edge until my orgasm built like a tsunami.

"I'm so close." I gasped, every muscle tensing as pleasure threatened to consume me. He anticipated my impending climax and intensified his thrusts, bringing himself nearer to his own release.

"Come for me." He gasped, too, straining with desire.

Those words were all it took. My orgasm exploded through me like a supernova. I clenched around Ty, drawing him over the edge. With a guttural cry, he spilled himself deep inside me, our bodies shuddering together in the throes of passion.

As we came down from our mutual high, Ty held me close, pressing tender kisses to my forehead and cheeks. "That was amazing, love."

"Absolutely incredible," I said, my heart pounding from the intensity of our lovemaking. We lay intertwined for a few moments longer, savoring the warmth and intimacy of our connection.

"Ready for your training?" Ty asked, running his fingers through my hair. As much as I wanted to stay in his arms forever, I had work to do.

Sighing, I nodded and reluctantly extricated myself from his embrace. "Time to face Liam, I suppose." I forced myself to smile as I dressed quickly.

We shared one final, lingering kiss before stepping out of the bedroom to face whatever challenges the day brought.

"Good luck." Ty squeezed my hand and kissed my temple when we finally approached Liam outside.

The cool, brisk morning air danced across my skin, leaving a trail of goosebumps in its wake. Liam stood a few feet away, his posture rigid and focused. He turned to face me with an intense gaze that felt like he was peering into the depths of my soul.

"Morning. I want you to understand that your training is going to be hard. I am not going to go easy on you just because you're my sister. There will be times where you will want to deck me, but I need you to understand that it's all for your own good."

My stomach twisted uncomfortably, and suddenly I wasn't sure I wanted to do this anymore. I glanced back at Ty, who gave me an encouraging nod before stepping away to give us space to work. I tried to quiet the nagging thoughts in my mind and focus on the task at hand.

"What do you have in store for me today?" I asked, mustering all my confidence.

"We're going to work on controlling your emotions." Liam's piercing gaze remained fixed on me. "When you get upset, you lose control of your wolf, and that's causing these earthquakes. If you don't get it under control, things will only get worse."

Each word emphasized the gravity of the situation. I had noticed that my emotions were tied to my wolf, but I'd underestimated just how dangerous that could be.

"Okay." I swallowed hard. "What do I need to do?"

"First, we must identify your triggers. Then we'll work on techniques to help you maintain control when those emotions rise to the surface."

This was going to be a painful process, but I had to trust that Liam would help me get this under control for the safety of my family and everyone around me.

"Let's do this." I hoped I sounded confident.

Liam nodded and began walking me through various scenarios, each designed to provoke a strong emotional response. With every trigger he pulled, my wolf stirred inside me, the ground quaking beneath my feet as she fought to break free.

"Focus," Liam urged me, never wavering. "Remember, if you're not in control, you're more of a danger to your loved ones than anyone else."

His words struck a nerve, and my throat tightened. If I couldn't control my emotions, I'd end up hurting the people I cared about most.

I closed myself off to everything going on around me and focused on my connection with my wolf. As much as she wanted to protect our family, we needed to find a balance. We had to learn to work with each other.

I steeled myself for the next round of challenges. "Let's try this again."

The sun had risen high in the sky, sending sharp shadows across the training grounds. Sweat trickled down my temples as I glared at Liam, who smirked at me from a few feet away. He'd been insufferable the whole morning, pushing all my buttons and doing everything he could to rile me up.

"Come on, Liza, is that really all you've got?" he taunted. "I was told you were supposed to be some sort of special omega, not just another weakling who can't control her emotions."

I clenched my fists and fought to keep my breathing steady. My wolf snarled inside me, ready to pounce at any moment. Liam was trying to provoke me, and it was getting harder and harder to ignore him.

"Shut up!" The quaking began again, and this time it was stronger as I fought to control my emotions.

"Ah, there it is," Liam said, his smirk widening. "That famous temper. Ty told me you were a bit of a hothead, but I didn't think it would be so easy to get under your skin."

"Ty said what?" I blazed with anger, and I took a step toward Liam, my wolf urging me forward. The ground shook even more violently, and I briefly wondered if it was possible for it to become a full-blown earthquake.

"Easy now." Liam held up his hands in mock surrender. "Don't want to lose control, do we?"

I gritted my teeth and forced myself to take a step back, trying to remember the techniques I'd learned in anger management classes years ago. Breathe in, count to ten, breathe out. Focus on something calming, like the way the sunlight filtered through the trees, forming dappled patterns on the ground.

"Is this what it takes to protect your family?" Liam snapped. "You're going to have to do a lot better than that if you want to stand a chance against your enemies."

"Stop it," I snarled, my control slipping away once more. Then in the midst of my anger, I remembered something else from those classes: that I had the power to choose how I reacted to situations. I could allow Liam's words to affect me, or I could make the choice that they didn't matter.

I closed myself off, blocking out Liam's taunts, and I imagined myself standing beside Ty, surrounded by our loved ones—the very people I was fighting to protect. A peaceful stillness settled within me, and my wolf settled down, appeased for the moment.

When I turned, Liam looked surprised. "Well, well," he said grudgingly. "Maybe there's hope for you yet."

"Thanks for the vote of confidence." I glared at him. Despite my annoyance, a small spark of pride flickered within me. I'd regained control over my emotions. It was a minor victory, but it was a start. With Liam's relentless training, I hoped I would only grow stronger.

It had been a long day. The cold of the morning had given way to the warmer afternoon sun as I stood on the uneven ground and faced Liam, my heart pounding. Sweat tracked down my back, making my clothes stick to my skin. Despite how much he'd already pushed me today, we were far from done.

Liam cracked his knuckles and gave me a sly grin. "Let's find out if you've been paying attention." He shifted his weight onto the balls of his feet, ready to spring into action at any moment.

"Bring it on," I said under my breath, steeling myself for whatever he had planned next. My muscles tensed, coiling like a spring, and I focused all my attention on him.

"Picture this." Liam's manner was smooth and mocking. "Someone has your precious family cornered. Poor Rory and Scott, they're terrified and helpless, completely at the mercy of their captor."

Anger flared within me, and my wolf snarled in response. I clenched my fists as I tried to keep control.

"Imagine Ty, beaten and bloody." Liam's face twisted into a cruel, sinister smile of satisfaction. "What would you do?"

"Stop it!" I shouted, rage boiling over. There was a brief movement of the ground beneath our feet, but I reined it in before it could escalate.

"Good." Liam nodded approvingly. "You managed to control it this time. You need to be prepared for situations like these. Your enemies will use anything they can against you, especially your loved ones."

Swallowing hard, I nodded. "I just can't bear the thought of something happening to them."

"Which is exactly why you need to learn control." Liam was more serious now. "I know I am repeating myself, but if you can't keep your emotions in check? You'll be more of a danger to them than anyone else."

My wolf's agitation and anger still simmered beneath the surface. She didn't like what he was saying.

Listen, I spoke silently, reaching out to her through our connection. *We have to stay in control. Losing ourselves to emotions will only put our loved ones in danger.*

My wolf hesitated, her growls echoing through my mind. Gradually, she understood what I was saying, and like flipping a switch, she calmed right down.

"Good job." Liam's lips lifted into a small smile. "That right there... that's what I want. You have powerful instincts, but you can't let them overwhelm you."

"Thank you," I said, still catching my breath from the emotional rollercoaster Liam had just put me through.

"Let's call it a day," he said. "You've made progress, but remember, this is just the beginning."

"Right." As I nodded, a mix of relief and resolve had me straightening my spine.

"Good. Go clean up and get some rest," Liam said. "We'll pick up where we left off tomorrow."

"Okay." I watched him walk away before heading inside to find Ty.

I found my mate sitting on a couch in the living room, flipping through a book. He looked up as I approached. "How did it go?" he asked, setting the book aside.

"Better than I expected, actually." I sank down next to him. "Liam really pushed me, but I managed to keep my emotions in check for the most part."

"Tell me everything," Ty said, twining his fingers through mine.

"It wasn't easy at first." Liam had taunted me mercilessly to provoke a reaction from my wolf. "But I learned that losing control would only put you and everyone else in danger, so when Liam started making cruel comments about you, they hurt, but I managed to stay calm."

"I'm proud of you, Liza."

"Thanks." I rested my head on his shoulder. "But we still have a long way to go. Liam says our lessons are far from over."

Ty wrapped his arm around me. "Don't worry. You're strong. You'll get through this."

"I hope so. I just want to be able to protect the people I love."

Ty pressed a gentle kiss to the top of my head. "You'll get there, and I'll be right by your side. No matter what it takes."

Buoyed by Ty's unwavering support, and the understanding that I had already made some headway, I held onto the belief that I would eventually gain control over my emotions and harness the power of my wolf, for the sake of my family, my pack, and myself.

"Your mom phoned while you were training with Liam. I told her and your dad what you were doing. Do you want to go see your parents?" Ty didn't need to ask twice. Seeing Mom and Dad was just what I needed to recharge.

We piled into the car with two members of my security team and left for my parents' home. Ty didn't let go of my hand for the entire drive.

The familiar scent of the woods surrounded us when we stood on the porch of my childhood porch, with a warm breeze caressing our skin. The weathered panels creaked underfoot as we, along with a couple of security guards, waited for my parents to answer the door.

The door eventually swung open, revealing my parents standing side by side. It was impossible not to be at ease in the presence of my mother, with her softly spoken and gentle demeanor. She opened her arms wide, and I stepped into her embrace. My father smiled at me, but it belied his worry.

"Sweetheart, it's so good to see you." My mother squeezed me tightly before letting go. Her attention flitted between Ty and me.

"Hey, Mom. Hey, Dad." I tried to sound upbeat despite the obvious tension in the air.

"Hello." My father gave me a quick hug, then nodded in Ty's direction. "Ty."

"Scott, Rory," Ty said respectfully with a smile.

"Come on in." My mother stepped aside to let us pass. As we entered, I spotted my older brothers sitting on the couch in the living room. They glanced up at our arrival, their eyes creasing in relief.

"Little sis." Mason rose from his seat to pull me into a bear hug.

Michael followed suit. "We're glad you're here."

"Guys, please." I extricated myself from their overbearing embraces. "I can breathe just fine, thank you."

"Sorry." Mason grinned, releasing me. "We're just worried about you, that's all."

"Speaking of which," my father said, glancing at Ty. "Ty told me you're doing omega training. How's that going?"

I fidgeted with the hem of my shirt. "It's been... challenging," I said, grateful for Ty's supportive hand on the small of my back. "But I'm making progress. Liam's helping me learn to control my emotions so I don't lose control of my wolf."

"Really?" my mother asked, hope shining in her eyes. "That's wonderful,"

Michael grimaced. "But what about Liam? Can we trust him?"

"His methods are harsh, but I think he genuinely wants to help me."

"Still, we can't forget what happened in the past." My father's haunted expression chilled me to the bone. "Just be careful, Liza."

"I will be. I promise." As I spoke those words, a surge of strength welled up inside me. I'd do whatever it took to regain control over my wolf and my life if I ever wanted things to go back to normal.

My mother smiled and patted my cheek. "We're proud of you, Liza. Just remember, we'll always be here for you, no matter what."

"Thanks, Mom," I said, tears pricking at the corners of my eyes. With my loved ones around me, and Ty's presence by my side, I was filled with a newfound strength. We'd make it through whatever challenges lay ahead.

A soft breeze drifted through the open window, carrying the scent of freshly cut grass and distant flowers. The sunlight danced across the living room floor, creating a warm and inviting atmosphere that somehow made me ache even more. I wished we could all just enjoy this rare moment of peace, but the events of late had marred any enjoyment.

"Listen," Ty said, addressing my brothers. "I understand your concerns, and I want you to know I'm taking them seriously. I've got someone keeping tabs on Liam when he's not with Liza or me."

Michael snorted, his expression unimpressed. "Oh, great. So while you're busy playing bodyguard, someone else is babysitting the real threat? That's supposed to make us feel better?"

"Michael!" I shot him a pointed look. He might have been my older brother, but I wasn't about to let him disrespect Ty like that.

"Sorry," he said, not sorry at all. Just as stubborn as ever, my brothers refused to budge on their opinions about Liam, even if it meant doubting Ty in the process.

"Look," Ty said, unfazed by Michael's outburst. "I get it. You don't trust Liam, and you have every right to be cautious. But I need you to trust me. I won't let anything happen to Liza, I promise."

Mason rubbed his chin thoughtfully as he studied Ty. "We want to believe you, man. We really do. But you can't blame us for being skeptical when he hurt our mother and kidnapped our sister."

"Of course not, but I swear to you I'm doing everything in my power to keep her safe."

As much as I wanted to be angry with my brothers for casting doubts over Ty's loyalty, I couldn't entirely fault them. Their fierce protectiveness were deeply ingrained in them, and they'd do anything to keep me from harm. Still, I wished they could look past their own prejudices and accept that Ty was on our side.

"Guys, please," I implored. "I need you to trust Ty. He's been nothing but supportive since this whole mess started, and I truly believe Liam has my best interests at heart."

Michael and Mason exchanged uneasy glances. Finally, Michael sighed and nodded reluctantly. "All right, Liza. We'll try to give him the benefit of the doubt. But know this," he added, fixing Ty with a steely stare. "If anything happens to her again because of Liam, we won't hesitate to hold you responsible."

"Understood. But I assure you, it won't come to that."

The conversation concluded, leaving me with a strange blend of gratitude and frustration. While I appreciated my brothers' unwavering commitment to my safety, I wished they could be more open-minded about the people in my life. Deep down, no matter how much they doubted Ty or Liam, they would never truly understand what it meant to be a part of this world of danger and hidden darkness lurking beneath the surface, because they had been sheltered from all of this before fate had intervened in my life.

As much as I loved them, sometimes I wondered if that ignorance would be our undoing.

The shrill ring of my phone interrupted the tense atmosphere, making everyone in the room jolt. Dread pooled in my stomach like molten lead, and my pulse quickened as I glanced at the screen. Unknown number.

My heart sank.

Castro.

"Should I take this?" I asked my brothers, Ty, and my parents. The last thing I wanted was to give him any more power over me or my family. But we were all aware that if his call went unanswered, it would likely lead to something bad. Something disastrous.

"Put it on speaker," Ty instructed.

With a sigh, I pressed the button and held the phone out so everyone could hear.

"Hello?"

"Ah." Castro's oily tone came over the tone, his words lingering in the air like a foul smell. "How nice of you to answer my call. How are you and your... family?"

"Cut the crap, Castro. What do you want?" I snapped.

"Feisty. I like that." He chuckled darkly. "I'm just checking in. I find myself enjoying keeping tabs on my favorite wolf and her wellbeing."

"Leave her alone." Michael growled, clenching his fists. "She doesn't belong to you,"

"Michael, let me handle this." I tried to remain calm despite the rage boiling beneath the surface.

"Very well," Castro said. "I simply wanted you to appreciate that I'm watching you, Liza. I must say, I'm not impressed with the company you're keeping these days."

"Are you talking about Liam?" I asked, my heart pounding. "What do you have against him?"

"Let's just say that I don't trust him, especially when it comes to you," Castro said cryptically. "But that's not why I called."

"Then, why did you call?" Mason hissed.

"Ah." Castro's voice oozed from the speaker like a snake's hiss. "I've left you a little gift outside your parents' home. You should go get it."

The line went dead, and I stared at the phone in disbelief. Blood rushed in my ears, drowning out the sudden burst of frantic conversation around me.

"Shit," Mason said, his face pale. "How did he get past our security?"

I rushed to the front porch, with Ty and my family right behind me, adrenaline dumping into my bloodstream. The dread that twisted through my gut was like a rope threatening to strangle me.

"Careful," Ty said as we reached the door. He opened it slowly, revealing a small, unassuming package wrapped in brown paper sitting innocently on the doorstep. "I smell blood. That doesn't bode well."

I was nervous when I bent to pick it up. In fact, I was terrified. There was no way of telling what it held until I unwrapped it, and with Castro, anything was possible. My family gathered around me, their expressions filled with a combination of fear and anger.

"We should check out what Castro left us." I tried to keep myself steady as I tore away the paper. My stomach clenched at the bloodstained cloth. With a shaky breath, I unfolded the cloth to reveal the horrifying gift within.

A man's severed head stared back at us, his lifeless eyes wide and mouth open in a silent scream. It was the man Liam had hired to abduct me. The man who had hurt my mother. The one who had caused so much pain to our family.

"Jesus Christ," Michael said, his face pale as he stepped back from the gruesome sight.

"Castro is trying to send a message," Dad said. "He wants us to know he can get to us, to anyone."

"Enough," I snarled, my wolf surging to the surface, desperate for vengeance. "This ends now. We find him, and we make him pay,"

As my emotions spiraled out of control, the ground quaked. The house moved on its foundations, with pictures falling from the walls as my family braced themselves against the sudden quake.

"Easy," Ty said soothingly, placing his hand on my arm. His touch sent a calming wave through me, helping to quell the storm raging inside. "Breathe. You need to get your wolf under control."

"Focus on us." Despite her own scare, my mom was clearly filled with concern. "Don't let Castro win by losing yourself."

I closed myself off to the room, forcing myself to take deep, steadying breaths as I worked to push my wolf down, reassuring her we were safe, suppressing the urge to shift and hunt down the man who had hurt so many people I loved. Slowly, the tremors subsided, leaving only our ragged breathing.

"We can't let him do this to us," I said when I opened my eyes. "We have to stay strong. That's how we'll beat him."

"Damn right," Ty said, his hand still gripping my arm reassuringly. "We're all here for each other, no matter what."

"Castro wants to play?" Mason growled, his eyes dark with anger. "Well, two can play that game. We won't stop until he's brought to justice."

"Agreed." Dad picked up some of the broken pictures in the room where we were standing. "He's made a terrible mistake in thinking he can tear our family apart. We will find him, and we will make him pay for everything he's done."

I couldn't stand to look at the gruesome sight any longer. Taking in my mother's pale and shocked face, I knew she'd seen as much as she needed to. Ty, my father, and my brothers dealt with the mess Castro had left on our doorstep. It was a sick reminder of the danger we were all in.

"Come on, let's go inside." I tugged my mom toward the door. She nodded, still too shaken to speak. As soon as we were inside, I grabbed the phone and dialed Liam's number. We needed answers.

"Hello?" Liam picked up after two rings.

"Get over to my parents' house, now," I said, unable to keep the fury down. "Castro left us a... a gift."

"Fuck," Liam said. "I'm on my way."

Mom and I waited in tense silence for Liam to arrive. When he did, his face was carefully schooled to reveal nothing. His presence made everything even more intense. But Liam was on our side, and right now, we needed him.

"What the hell is going on, Liam?" I said as soon as he stepped through the door. "I believed you'd already killed the bastard who hurt my mom,"

"Wait, what?" Liam looked genuinely confused, and it only fueled my anger. "I never said I killed him. I taught him a lesson, then I dismissed him from my services."

"Dismissed him?" I asked incredulously. "You should have ripped his throat out."

"Removing him from my pack should have been enough of a punishment." Liam was holding tightly to his restrained rage. "It left him vulnerable."

"Clearly." I paced the room. My wolf was restless inside me, desperate to take action, despite my efforts to keep her in check.

"Look," Liam said, running a hand through his hair. "I made a mistake. If I was able to go back and do things differently, I would, but we can't change what's happened. All we can do now is focus on finding Castro and making sure he pays for this."

"Damn right we will." I growled, my anger my own now that I'd calmed my wolf down. "We're going to make him regret ever crossing us."

"Agreed." Liam nodded; his expression grim. "First, let's make sure your family is safe. We need to be prepared for anything Castro might throw at us."

"Fine," I said. "After that, we're going hunting. I won't stop until we've found him and made him pay for everything he's done."

"Promise," Liam said, his expression meeting mine with a fierce intensity that left no doubt in my mind he meant every word.

As I looked around the room at the faces of my loved ones, I knew we were stronger than anything Castro could throw at us. He had made a terrible mistake in thinking he could tear our family apart, and we would make sure he paid for it dearly.

The front door slammed shut behind Ty and Scott, their tense expressions betraying the gravity of the situation. I heard my brothers' footsteps receding into the distance as they disposed of the grisly package.

"I don't want to know where you're taking it." I tried to shake off the dread that had settled.

"Found this in the box." Ty held up a crumpled piece of paper. The note read *I will make your enemies your footstool*. My blood ran cold as I realized Castro had left us a message. There was one other word scribbled on the paper—something written in Russian I didn't understand.

Liam blanched. "Castro has your trigger word, Liza.

The room was suffocating me, with Castro's threat bearing down on all of us. On cue, Michael and Mason burst back in through the front door, both looking ready for a fight.

"Are you okay, Liza?" Michael asked, laden with concern as he hovered protectively beside me.

Mason stood close by, his fists clenched and his attention flicking between Liam and Ty.

"Back off, guys," I snarled, more irritated than scared. "I can handle this."

"Like hell you can," Mason said, inching even closer. "You have no idea what kind of monster Castro is."

"I know better than the two of you do," I shot back, glaring at him. "But I'm not going to cower in fear just because he's out there."

Liam stepped forward. When he spoke, he was firm but somehow reassuring. "Listen, we're all on edge right now. But I swear to you, I will burn anyone to the ground who wants to hurt Liza. We're going to find Castro and make sure he can never threaten any of you again."

My brothers' reluctance was written all over their faces, but they appeared to accept Liam's words. Michael gave a curt nod while Mason said something under his breath.

"Thanks," I said quietly, sending Liam a grateful look. "We need to be united if we're going to face Castro."

"Absolutely," Liam replied, his gaze meeting mine with a determined intensity that gave me chills.

Ty emphasized the importance of ensuring everyone's safety and being prepared for whatever lay ahead, his firm stare encompassing the room.

"Right." I punched my fists at my sides. "We'll stop him, and when we find him, he'll wish he'd never crossed us."

Chapter 13 - Ty

While I stood by the window, staring out into the night, I rubbed my temples, trying to ease the headache that refused to go away. The head situation at Liza's parent's place was finally handled, and we'd returned home, only for Liza to say she needed space. Neither Liam nor I blamed her, because pain and fear clung to her like a second skin. She'd been so shaken up she'd shook the house—literally.

The door opened. "Ty, we need to talk about what happened," Liam said, leaning against the frame, his arms crossed beneath his chest, and his face set grimly. This conversation was inevitable, but part of me had hoped to avoid it for just a little while longer.

I gestured for him to come inside. "What's on your mind?"

"Look, you're angry. Hell, I'm fucking pissed off." He rubbed a hand through his hair in frustration. "Blaming my father isn't going to help anyone."

"Your father is the one who turned Liza into... into this." I let my emotions get the better of me. "Who has a child just to basically turn them into a sleeper agent? Who literally turns their child into a weapon to 'activate' at their word? He brainwashed a kid. She didn't deserve any of this."

"Of course she didn't," Liam said. "My father wasn't some heartless monster, Ty. He did what he thought was necessary to protect our family and our pack."

"By turning an innocent child into a pawn?" I shot back, slamming my fist on the desk. "Liza never asked for any of this. She deserved better."

"Damn it, do you think I'm unaware of that?" Liam said, his whole body blazing with fury. "I wish there was a way to undo what was done, but I can't do it. Yes, Liza was a kid, but this was fed into her subconscious even as a newborn. It's who she is."

"Who she is?" I laughed humorlessly. "You're really going to stand there and tell me that the woman we both care about, the woman you call your sister, is nothing more than a tool for your father's twisted games?"

"Fine, you want to understand why my father did what he did?" Liam asked, his voice tight with frustration. "Because sometimes you have to do whatever it takes to win, especially when you're dealing with treacherous people like your family."

It was like he'd punched me in the gut, but I held my ground, refusing to let his accusations shake me. "My father did what needed to be done," I hissed. "Your father was a toxic poison who had to be eradicated for the good of everyone involved."

"Is that what you tell yourself?" Liam sneered, taking a step closer. "To justify the blood on your family's hands?"

My own blood boiled as I glared at Liam. A storm brewed between us, and I clenched my jaw to keep my wolf in check.

"Say that again." I growled low in my throat.

"Your family is no better than mine," Liam spat. "You act all high and mighty, but you're just as ruthless and cutthroat when it comes to getting what you want."

"Enough!" I roared, unable to hold back any longer. My fury exploded like a dam breaking, and I lunged at Liam with every ounce of strength I had.

We collided with a bone-jarring impact and crashed to the floor, grappling and snarling like wild animals. Liam's teeth snapped at my throat, his hands clawing at my face and chest.

"Stop this," my father barked the moment he and Isaiah rushed into the room. They grabbed hold of us, trying to pry us apart as we continued to struggle against each other.

"Let go of me," I snarled, fighting against Dominic's iron grip.

"Both of you, stand down." Isaiah sounded thunderous in the now silent room as he held Liam back. "What the hell are you two doing? You're supposed to be allies."

I broke free from Dominic's hold, my breaths coming in ragged gasps as I glared at Liam. "He thinks he can insult my family and get away with it?"

"Is this how you plan on keeping Liza safe?" Dominic's words were laced with disappointment. "By tearing each other apart?"

Liam scoffed, his eyes never leaving mine. "I'm no ally to you, Dominic," he said. "I'm only here to protect and help my sister. As far as I'm concerned, the Kellers can all still go to Hell."

Liam's words echoed in my ears once he'd stormed out of the room, slamming the door behind him with enough force to rattle the walls.

My father turned to me. "Ty, getting on Liam's bad side is not what we need right now. You need to fix this."

I gritted my teeth, feeling the bitter sting of truth to his words. Deep down, I knew he was right. We couldn't afford to let our personal issues distract us from the task at hand: protecting Liza.

"Fine," I said, frustration simmering beneath the surface. "I'll try."

"Good." Dominic nodded firmly. "We can't afford to waste any more time bickering. We need to be united if we want to keep Liza safe."

I went up to our room to change my ripped shirt. Thankfully, Liza was asleep. I took a moment to watch her. A small lock of hair had fallen over her face, and every time she exhaled, it fluttered. I moved across the room and gently tucked the stray lock behind her ear, admiring her beauty up close, but she never stirred.

I moved to the closet and picked out a fresh shirt, tugging the ripped one over my head and throwing it in the trash before I quickly buttoned the fresh shirt. With a final glance at Liza, I returned to my office to have a look at Bryce's proposal,

I was nose deep in financial progress reports when one of my guards knocked on the door and entered the room with Isaiah. The guard's posture was tense and alert. "Alpha Keller," he said. "We've received word that Liam has checked into a hotel in town."

I frowned. How had things escalated to this point? It felt like everything was spiraling out of control, and I needed to regain some semblance of order before it was too late.

"Thank you for letting me know," I told the guard, trying to keep my voice steady. "Alert the security team to keep tabs on him, but don't engage unless absolutely necessary."

"Understood, Alpha." The guard gave me a curt nod before leaving the room.

As soon as the door clicked shut, I sank into my chair, and rested my forehead in my hands. My mind was a chaotic whirlwind of guilt, anger, and fear. This wasn't how things were supposed to go.

"We were supposed to be coming together, to be stronger as a united front. Instead, our alliance was crumbling before it had even taken off."

Isaiah placed a hand on my shoulder. "You can't blame yourself for this."

"Can't I?" I asked, lifting my head to look at him. "I'm the one who provoked him, who pushed him to this point."

"Maybe." He shrugged. "But Liam's not entirely blameless. He's the one who chose to walk away when we need him most."

"Still, I should've handled it better," I said. "We need him on our side now more than ever."

"Then, you have to do what you have to do," Isaiah said in that wise tone of his that reminded me why I hired him in the first place. "Go talk to him. Settle your differences and find a way to move forward together. It won't be easy, but it's necessary."

I stared out the window, watching the raindrops splatter against the glass and slide down in rivulets. Liam checking into a hotel didn't surprise me in the least. Tensions were high, and we all needed some space. It didn't make things any easier, though.

"Ty?" Liza's tentative voice pulled me from my thoughts, and I turned to find her standing in the doorway, her hair tousled from sleep.

"Hey," I said gently, trying to offer her a reassuring smile. "You should be resting."

"Where's Liam?"

I sighed. There was no point in sugarcoating the truth.

"Your brother and I... had a disagreement." I rubbed the back of my neck. "He checked into a hotel. It's probably for the best for now. We both need to cool off."

Liza frowned and pursed her lips. "What happened?"

I reached for her hand. "It doesn't matter. What matters is that we're going to fix this. I'm going to fix this." I squeezed her hand, the warmth of her skin against mine reassuring. "I promise."

"Just tell me, Ty."

"We argued about what your father did to you," I said, my own anger flaring up again at the thought. "I couldn't understand how anyone could do that to their own child, and Liam... well, he sort of defended him. Things got heated, and he left."

As I spoke, I watched the hurt and confusion play across Liza's face. She looked away, swallowing hard, and I knew she was fighting back tears.

"I can't believe he didn't tell me," she whispered.

"Maybe he didn't want to wake you or hurt your feelings. Or maybe he's just as conflicted about it as we are."

"Still..." Liza trailed off, and her eyes were bright with unshed tears. "I just don't know what to think anymore."

I cupped her face in my hands and tilted her head up until our eyes met. "We're going to get through this. We'll figure out the truth, no matter how hard it is."

The fire crackled in the hearth as Liza and I settled on the couch. The warmth of her body pressed against mine was a comforting presence—one that I needed more than ever with everything going on. Her fingers traced the contours of my face, stopping to examine where Liam had struck me earlier.

"Looks like you made it out alive," she said softly. "There aren't that many bruises, but it's still going to hurt for a bit."

I thought it was because Liam hadn't wanted to hurt me too badly, but I kept that to myself. Instead, I offered her a wry smile. "Guess I'm lucky."

"Or he was holding back," she said, narrowing her eyes slightly. "I'm not happy with either of you right now. This whole situation is just messed up."

"Believe me, I know," I said, staring at the dancing flames in the hearth. "But we can't let our focus slip. We need to figure out how Castro keeps getting his hands on all this information about us."

Liza sighed and nestled her head in the curve of my shoulder. "You're right. It's like he's aware of our every move. It's unnerving. How does he do it?"

"Your guess is as good as mine," I said, my mind racing with possibilities. Was there another mole within our ranks? Had someone else betrayed us? Or was Castro simply that good at gathering intel?

"Maybe he has someone on the inside?" Liza said hesitantly, voicing my own concerns. "Another traitor, like before, with Cecily?"

I shook my head. "No. I refuse to believe that. We've been so careful, and I trust my people. There must be another explanation."

"Like what, though?" she pressed, her brow furrowing in frustration. "There's no way it's a coincidence he has all that knowledge."

"Maybe he's been spying on us himself." I tried to come up with a plausible scenario. "Or maybe he has some sort of magical means of gathering information. It wouldn't be the first time we've encountered something like that in our world."

"Magical or not, it's dangerous," Liza said, her grip on my hand tightening. "We need to find out how he's doing it before he causes any more damage."

I stared at the crackling fire, with its warmth licking at my face. Where did Castro get his information? It was a problem we couldn't ignore any longer, and I felt a chill down to the bone despite the heat from the flames.

I sighed, rubbing my temples as I considered the idea that there might be another mole in our midst. My pack had already been betrayed once, and that wound was still raw. The thought of another traitor among us made my stomach churn with anger and disappointment.

"I shouldn't dismiss that we might have another mole in our ranks so quickly. Anything's possible." I gritted my teeth. "But I'm praying it's not true. One mole in our ranks was bad enough. Believing someone else has betrayed us would be... unbearable."

Liza leaned against me, seeking comfort in my presence. I wrapped my arm around her, drawing strength from her body pressed against mine, and we faced the flickering flames, searching for answers in them.

"Maybe we should investigate your staff more thoroughly," she said hesitantly. "I mean, I don't want to cast suspicion on anyone, but we have to be sure."

I nodded, responsibility settling heavily over me. "You're right. We need to be certain no one else is working against us."

"Ty, are you okay?" Liza asked softly,

"Of course." I forced a smile, even though I was anything but. The possibility of another betrayal ate at me, threatening to consume me like the fire before us. I needed to protect my pack and Liza from harm, and that meant rooting out any treachery, no matter how painful it might be.

"Let's make a list of everyone who could have access to sensitive information," I said, determined to take action. "We'll look into their backgrounds, their connections—anything that might give us a clue as to their loyalty."

I checked over the list of names we'd compiled, each one a potential mole and potential knife in our backs. The thought sent an icy finger down my spine, but I tried to shake it off. *Focus, Ty.* We needed answers, not baseless suspicions. Yet, as much as I wanted to trust those around me, the doubt lingered like a dark cloud.

"Ty," Liza said gently, laying a hand on my arm. Her touch was warm, grounding, but I felt her concern through our bond. "You're overthinking this."

"Maybe." I rubbed the back of my neck. "But I can't help it. It's just... no one should be aware of the existence of a trigger word for you. Liam would never put you in that position. But if Castro was as astute as I give him credit for, would he care who had the word?"

"True," she said, her brow furrowed. "Liam is fiercely protective of me. He wouldn't risk my safety, even if he disliked your pack. I don't think Castro would want to share. He would want the trigger word and the power over me all to himself."

"Right." I couldn't shake the nagging thought that Liam had been planning to take us out at one point. Could he be conspiring against us? No, I couldn't allow myself to think like that. Not when we still had so many unanswered questions.

"Let's keep digging." I tried to push my doubts aside. "There has to be something we're missing. A connection, a clue—anything."

Liza nodded. "We'll find it, Ty. We'll get to the truth and protect our pack."

While we continued to search for any shred of evidence, my unease only increased. The shadows in the room appeared larger, and my instincts screamed that something was amiss. But what? My thoughts raced, struggling to piece the puzzle before us.

"Ty, what if it's not someone on this list? What if we're missing something important?"

"It's possible," I said. "But we have to start somewhere. If there is another mole, they're likely hiding in plain sight."

"Then, we'll keep looking," she said firmly. "We won't give up until we've found the truth and ensured the safety of our pack."

Eventually, sleep chased us to bed. Liza had been trying to hide her yawns, but she lost the battle. Between training with Liam and Castro's *gift*, she was exhausted. The minute she was nestled under the covers in our bed, she was asleep.

I lay back and watched the clock. "Damn it," I muttered to myself. I needed to talk to Liam face to face and hash this out once and for all. No more bad blood between us, especially when it came to our mutual love for Liza.

The moon hung low in the night sky, casting its eerie glow over the world below. I couldn't sleep. My mind was a whirlwind of thoughts about Liam and his possible betrayal. I needed answers, and I needed them now. Clad in my favorite leather jacket, I slipped out of the house, careful not to wake Liza.

The engine of my car roared to life, echoing through the quiet streets as I drove into town. My knuckles turned white on the steering wheel, my tension coiling. What if Liam was the one conspiring against us? Would he betray Liza like that?

I pulled up to the hotel. Its neon sign flickered in the darkness, casting an ominous glow over the entrance. After taking a moment to compose myself, I stepped out of the car and walked toward the building, steeling myself for the impending confrontation.

As I approached, Liam emerged from the shadows, his expression guarded. "Ty," he questioned me coldly "What the fuck do you want?"

"Look, we need to talk," I said, striding forward. "You and I are both aware there's still some bitterness between us, but we can't let that interfere with protecting Liza."

Liam crossed his arms under his chest, his eyes narrowing. "Yeah, you're right. We have to put aside our differences for her sake. Don't forget, she's my sister. I'd do anything for her, even if it means crossing you or your family."

"Let's clear the air, then," I said. "Tell me straight up... are you working with Castro? Are you trying to bring my pack down from the inside?"

The silence that followed was stifling. I watched as Liam's face contorted with anger and hurt before he finally spoke. "I can't believe you'd even ask me that. After everything we've been through, after everything Liza's been through, do you really think I'd betray her like that?"

"Believe me, I don't want to think it," I answered honestly. "There are too many unanswered questions. Too many coincidences. The trigger word, the relentless attacks… I need to be sure where your loyalties lie."

"My loyalty is to Liza," he said firmly. "Always. End of story."

"We have to come to some agreement, Liam. We can't go like this. It's Liza who's suffering."

He winced when I mentioned her name, as if he'd just realized how much his attitude would hurt her.

"Fine," Liam said. "A sparring match. We'll settle this like wolves."

"Agreed." I nodded, already going over strategies in my mind. "But we do it at the estate, not here. When it's over, whatever grudges you have will be let go."

"Deal." He reached out a hand to shake, a hard glint in his eyes.

As Liam had shifted and ran to the motel, we drove back to the estate in my car in silence, the tension between us thick enough to cut with a knife. When we approached the grounds, I caught a whiff of the night air, crisp and cool against my skin. The scent of the surrounding woods, earthy and alive, helped calm my nerves.

"Wait here," I told Liam as we got out of the car. "I need to find witnesses for the match."

I found two guards at the door and took them to the field.

The moon illuminated the estate, casting eerie shadows as Liam and I stood facing each other in the open field. Adrenaline coursed through my veins. The scent of damp earth filled my nostrils as I steadied my breathing and prepared for battle.

"Ready?" Liam's icy blue eyes never left mine.

"Let's do this." I clenched my fists at my sides.

With a swift movement, Liam lunged, his fist connecting with my jaw. Pain exploded through my face, but I shoved it away and countered with a punch to his gut that forced the air from his lungs. He doubled over but quickly recovered and aimed a kick at my side.

"Is that all you've got?" I taunted, dodging his attack, and landing a solid hit to his ribs.

"Hardly," he said, retaliating with a swift kick to my thigh.

Our fists flew, an intricate dance of violence fueled by years of bitterness and mistrust. As we traded blows, I thought about Liza. This match wasn't just about settling old grudges, it was about proving that I was fit to protect her, no matter what threats came our way. If that meant putting my own pride on the line, so be it.

"Enough of this," Liam growled, his breathing ragged as he wiped blood from his split lip. "We're getting nowhere."

"Then, let's take this to the next level," I said, my voice hoarse from exertion.

With a nod of agreement, we both stepped back, our bodies shifting effortlessly into our wolf forms.

As my vision sharpened and my senses heightened, I charged at Liam, my powerful jaws snapping at his throat. He twisted out of my reach, his lean body agile and quick. We circled each other, our growls echoing in the night air as we searched for an opening.

Suddenly, Liam lunged, his sharp teeth sinking into my shoulder. I yelped in pain but managed to shake him off, my own teeth finding purchase on his hind leg soon after. He snarled and twisted away, limping slightly while he regained his footing.

Come on, I thought to myself, pushing through the pain and fatigue that threatened to overtake me. *You can't back down now.*

Liza's frantic footsteps drew my attention away from the exhausted satisfaction that had settled over me after the fight. Her shout rang out, sharp with anger and worry as she sprinted toward us. "What the fuck are you two doing?"

Liam and I exchanged a glance before we shifted back into our human forms, sitting on the grass, still panting heavily from the fight.

Liza glared at us, punching her fists onto her hips. "Ty. Liam." She ground out our names like curses. "I can't believe you would be so reckless and stupid. You could've seriously hurt each other,"

"Baby, relax." I tried to soothe her concern, struggling to hold back my chuckle. The adrenaline was still coursing through my veins, making it hard to keep my laughter in check. "We were just working some things out."

"Working things out?" Liza's volume rose, and her tone became unbearably high-pitched. "By trying to tear each other apart?"

"Sometimes, that's what it takes," Liam said, his chest still heaving from exertion. He shot me a knowing look, a small smile tugging at the corners of his mouth, too. "Isn't that right, Ty?"

"Exactly." Laughter spilled from me as I lay back on the grass, feeling lighter than I had in days. "We needed this. Trust me."

Liza stared down at us in disbelief, clearly not amused. "You're both idiots."

"Come on," I said, catching my breath and pushing myself up onto my elbows. "Forgive us for being... well, men. We just needed to clear the air. It's done now."

"Fine," she said, her anger slowly dissipating, even as she maintained her stern expression. "Don't expect me to patch you up if you ever go at it again like this."

"Deal." Liam chuckled softly, then he got to his feet and extended a hand to help me up.

"Well, then, fine." Liza crossed her arms. "Now that you two have 'cleared the air,' can we focus on what really matters? We still have a lot to figure out."

I hesitated for only a moment before following Liza, the relief from the dissolved tension between Liam and me propelling me forward. I caught up to her as she reached the front door and grabbed her arm.

She whipped around, her eyes still flashing. "Are you both insane?" she hissed, yanking her arm free. "What was the point of all that?"

"Look, Liza." I tried to choose my words carefully. "Liam and I needed to work through our differences. We had to find a way to trust each other."

"By beating the crap out of each other?" she scoffed, holding the door open but not stepping inside. Her intense stare bore into me, demanding an explanation.

"Sometimes, that's how it works with male shifters." I rubbed the back of my neck sheepishly. "It's a part of who we are, and now we can move forward with a clean slate."

"Fine," she said, though she wasn't entirely convinced. "Don't expect me to be thrilled about it, Ty. I've been around enough fighting and violence lately."

"Understandable." I nodded, knowing full well the emotional toll recent events had taken on her. "We'll do our best to avoid any more conflicts, especially in front of you."

"Good," she said, finally stepping inside the house.

I followed her, hoping to ease her frustrations further. "Listen," I said softly as we walked down the hallway toward the living room. "We're here for you. All of us. You're not alone in this fight."

"I know," she said, her anger dissipating slightly. "I just... I need some time to process everything, okay? And my brother and my mate fighting each other like idiots is not helping."

"Sorry." I offered her a small smile. "Take all the time you need. We're here for you when you're ready."

"Thank you," she said, and I noticed a subtle change in her posture as some of her burden eased.

When we entered the living room, I felt a renewed sense of purpose and unity. The tension between Liam and me had been a hindrance, but now it was gone, replaced by a mutual understanding, and a shared goal: to protect Liza at all costs and find Castro so we could put an end to the threats against her.

Liza sank into one of the plush armchairs and stared into the fireplace while I took a seat across from her, giving her the space she needed.

Chapter 14 - Liza

The cold, damp air in the basement clung to my skin like a shroud. The roughness of the concrete walls scraped my skin as I tried to push away, but my body refused to cooperate. My wrists, bound above my head, burned, and I gagged at the metallic tang of blood fouling the air.

"Please," I rasped. "Please don't do this."

"Ah, Liza, you still don't understand." Josef Wylde's voice echoed through the room, colder than the frigid air that seeped into my bones. He stepped out of the shadows with a cruel smile twisted on his lips. "I'm doing this for you. It's for your own good, my dear. It's time you learned to control yourself."

I wanted to scream, to tell him he was wrong, but all that came out was a choked sob. I shivered when his fingers traced my cheek, the icy sensation lingering long after his touch had faded.

"Let's begin, shall we?"

My heart pounded as he raised his hand, and then pain exploded across my body, ripping through every nerve. He was tearing me apart. I tried to cry out but no sound escaped my lips. Through it all, my father's laughter filled the room, mocking me, tormenting me.

Then just as suddenly as it had started, the pain stopped, and I was hanging by my arms, gasping for breath, the ground trembling with the aftershocks. I looked up at my father's face looming over me, the cold smile still etched onto his features.

"Again," he said simply.

"No!" I screamed, finally finding my voice. It made no difference. The pain returned, and my consciousness slipped away, falling into darkness...

I jolted awake, my heart racing, and a cold sweat covering my body. The remnants of the dream—or was it a memory?—clung like cobwebs. I shook my head, trying to rid myself of the images. No matter how hard I tried, I couldn't escape the haunting memory of my father's twisted smile.

"Are you okay?" Liam asked warily as I stumbled into the kitchen the next morning. His eyes widened and intensified as he took in my disheveled appearance. God, I must have looked a mess.

"Did my old house at Heather Falls have a basement?" I asked, shaking with barely suppressed emotion.

Liam's brow wrinkled at the question, and he appeared to be searching his memories. "Yes," he said after a moment. "Why do you ask?"

"Last night... I had this dream." I took a breath to steady myself, the memories threatening to overwhelm me. "I was in a basement, and Josef was... he was torturing me. It was so real, but I don't remember anything like that actually happening."

Liam's face drained of color, and his eyes held a haunted look I hadn't seen in them before. It was as if he was looking at something far away, something horrifying. My gut clenched at the realization that it wasn't just a dream but a twisted memory of something that had actually happened.

"Tell me," I said, my body shaking with fear and uncertainty. "What really happened?"

"You were so young," he said softly, the pain in his words cutting through me like a knife. "You were just a toddler. Our father... he used to take you down to the basement for training."

"Training?" I asked, barely able to get the word out past the bile in my throat. "What kind of training?"

"Brainwashing," Liam spat out the word with a thick layer of disgust. "He wanted to mold you into the perfect weapon, to bend your will to his own, and he thought that by subjecting you to physical and emotional torment, he could achieve that. It was sick, Liza. Wrong on every level."

My nails dug into my palms as I struggled to process this new information. The air around me thickened, making it difficult to breathe as the truth settled onto my chest.

"Did you know?" I snapped. "Were you aware of what he was doing?" My stomach revolted, and I squeezed my mouth shut, swallowing hard to keep the contents of my stomach where it belonged.

"Hey," Liam said gently. "I'm sorry you had to remember that, Liza. I'd hoped you were too young."

"Too young to recall being tortured by my own father?" I spat out bitterly, glaring at him. There was no anger in his expression, only sadness and regret.

"Listen," he said hesitantly, rubbing the back of his neck. "I was gone by the time your... training started. Remember I told you Dad left me a book, though." He grimaced as if the mere memory left a foul taste in his mouth. "It had all his twisted ideas about how to 'train' you."

"Train me for what? To be his perfect little weapon?"

"Something like that. He believed that because of your unique abilities, you needed to be molded and controlled. It was sick, Liza. I couldn't let anyone hurt you like that."

My chest tightened as I tried to process all of this, to reconcile the man in my memories, the one I thought I knew, with the monster Liam was describing. The pain and fear from the dream—no, the memory—still lingered, forming a tight band around my neck, making it difficult to breathe.

"Is there anything else I should be aware of?" I asked. "Any other horrors lurking in my past?"

"Nothing I know of," Liam said softly, placing a reassuring hand on my shoulder. "That book... I want you to know something."

I looked at him, my body tense with anticipation.

"I ripped out the pages detailing what he did to you. I burned them," he said, his blue eyes filled with emotion. "I'd never hurt you like that, Liza. I swore to protect you and be there for you, no matter what, and I meant it."

A wave of relief flooded through me, causing me to release a shaky breath. "Thank you, Liam. That means more than you could ever possibly appreciate."

Outside, the wind sighed through the trees, carrying with it the scent of damp earth and pine. I focused on that, trying to keep myself in the present instead of being swallowed by the darkness of my past. Liam's hand on my shoulder was both comforting and heavy. A reminder of the complex bond we shared.

As the day wore on, I couldn't shake my unease. My mind kept replaying the nightmare-turned-memory, the sensation of cold metal against my skin, and the insidious whispers of my father. Even the laughter of the staff in the house as they went about their daily routine grated on my nerves. I decided to move my pity party to the kitchen, where I could at least try to do something productive.

With my hands buried in a mound of dough, I tried to push the unsettling thoughts from my mind. The kitchen was my sanctuary, and losing myself in the rhythmic kneading of bread usually soothed my frayed nerves. Today, however, the ghosts of my past clung like a second skin, refusing to be cast off so easily.

"I've added rosemary. What to add next?" I murmured to myself, scanning the shelves for inspiration. My gaze landed on a jar of sundried tomatoes. "Hmm, a little Mediterranean twist might be just the thing." I moved some jars and congratulated myself when I found one full of olives.

As I chopped the tomatoes and olives, the rich, earthy scent grounded me in the present. For a brief instant, I allowed myself to forget the darkness lingering on the edges of my consciousness and lost myself in the vibrant colors and flavors before me.

"Hey Liza," Rosalie said as she walked into the kitchen, the tall shelves that lined the wall dwarfing her frame. Her red hair was pulled back into a tight bun, emphasizing the slight flush that colored her cheeks. She seemed off, hesitant, her eyes darting about the room as if searching for an escape route.

"Rosalie, hey. What brings you here?" I asked, keeping my face down, trying to sound casual despite the turmoil churning inside me. If she picked up on it, she didn't comment.

"Uh... I just wanted to check in and make sure you're doing all right. You were so out of it last time." Even her voice sounded odd.

"I'm fine, honestly. I'm working on some new recipes right now, but we can chat while I do that."

After a moment of silence, she cleared her throat awkwardly. "So... how are things with Liam? You two have been spending a lot of time together lately."

"Uh, yeah, we have." Heat crept up my neck. "He's been helping me with my training, trying to teach me how to control my power and stuff."

"Is it going well?" she asked, fidgeting with the hem of her sweater.

"It's not easy, but I'm getting there."

"Good," she murmured, and I detected the relief in her tone. "I'm glad you're making progress." She stared down into the bowl. "What are you making?"

"Sun-dried tomato and olive bread." My hands worked deftly as I folded the chopped ingredients into the dough. "I figured it might be a nice addition to our next pack dinner."

"Sounds delicious." Rosalie watched me knead the dough as if it held the answers to all her questions.

Unsure of why the girl was acting so uptight, I decided to give her something to do. Maybe she just needed to have busy hands. I'd promised I'd keep paying her till things settled down, but maybe it was worrying her more than she was letting on.

"Why don't you put on an apron and make some of those tomato and mushroom souffles you made for Mrs. Henderson? They were so delicious. Ty and I can have them for dinner." I moved along the worktop so she could work beside me.

"I'd love to, Liza." For the first time since she'd arrived, her stiff demeanor relaxed, and we began our food prep in a companionable silence.

It didn't last. I watched Rosalie's eyes glaze over for the third time in as many minutes. "Earth to Rosalie," I said, waving a hand in front of her face. "What's going on with you today?"

"Sorry." She blinked rapidly and grinned sheepishly. "I just... have something on my mind, I guess."

"Clearly." I nudged her with my hip. "So, are you going to tell me what's bothering you, or do I have to guess?"

Rosalie worried her lower lip with her teeth. Finally, she sighed and said, "Okay, so you know how Liam is really hot, right?"

"Uh, sure," I said, startled by the sudden change in topic. "I mean, he's my brother, but objectively speaking, I can understand why someone would think that."

"Right, well," she said, her cheeks flushing a pretty shade of pink. "The thing is, I think I saw some kind of... bond between him and Sabrina."

"Wait, what?" My lower jaw dropped, and I stared at her in disbelief. "Rosalie, are you sure about this? I mean, Sabrina's human, and humans don't form bonds with shifters." I thought back to the way Liam had looked at Sabrina, and her flirting, but surely that was just sexual chemistry.

She shrugged, her shoulders rising and falling with indifference. "I'm just telling you what was there. There was definitely some kind of thread connecting them. I wouldn't have mentioned it if I wasn't sure."

Clearly, arguing would be pointless. Rosalie had made up her mind. "I'll talk to Ty about it. If anyone can confirm whether or not there's a bond between Liam and Sabrina, it's him."

"Thanks," she said, and she seemed relieved that I'd taken the matter out of her hands.

As we returned to our tasks, my thoughts were anything but focused on the food in front of me. A bond between my brother and my best friend should be impossible, and yet Rosalie had been so certain of it. If she was right, everything could change, and I wasn't sure how to feel about that.

"Hey," Rosalie said. "I wasn't gossiping. You know I wouldn't say anything if I didn't think it was important, right?" She opened the oven and placed in her souffles.

"I know." I gave her a reassuring smile. "You're just looking out for everyone involved, and I appreciate that."

"I just don't want anyone to get hurt."

Rosalie let out a forlorn sigh and stared out the window once she had the souffles prepped . "I see everyone around me settling down, and I get that I'm still young, but I can't help thinking about it. I want a life where I'm secure and loved. God, I want a family of my own. If I'm being honest, I'd be willing to do anything to secure that happiness."

As I studied her face, I couldn't ignore the intensity emanating from her. It was a side of Rosalie I hadn't experienced before, and it both surprised and impressed me. "I think it's natural to want those things," I reasoned. "And I have no doubt that one day, you'll find someone who will give you all of that and more."

"Thanks, Liza. I truly appreciate hearing that from you."

"Anytime," I said with a grin, patting her on the shoulder.

"I should get going. We'll talk more later, okay?" Rosalie grabbed her coat and waved goodbye, leaving me alone in the kitchen.

The moment the door closed behind her, I sighed and shook the heaviness out of my limbs. The conversation I'd just had with Rosalie and the unresolved issue of Liam and Sabrina's bond cluttered up my mind.

There was only one way to clear my head, and that was to train.

***

"Ready for another session?" Liam asked as I approached him, the corners of his lips twitching.

The two of us stood in the middle of the small clearing, the towering trees around us seeming to close in on our bodies. The sky was overcast, casting an eerie gray light over our makeshift training ground.

Liam circled me. "I want to be honest with you, Liza. There were some methods in that book on how to help you channel your energy and use it at will. But they were borderline torture. I can't bring myself to even consider using those methods on you."

His words sent an involuntary shiver through my body as I recalled some of the memories of the cellar. The thought of enduring such pain made me sick. I was glad Liam was being honest with me, and the fact he valued our relationship enough to come up with his own ideas was admirable.

"Thank you." The memories of the cellar had affected me more than I liked admitting, and I clasped my hands tightly to keep them from trembling. "I trust you."

"Good." He smiled reassuringly at me. "Now, let's try something different. We're going to try to find the thread where your magic rests. It might be difficult at first, but don't get discouraged."

I took a step back to steady myself, feeling the ground beneath my feet. Finding the source of my magic sounded like an insurmountable challenge, but if anyone could help me do it, it was Liam.

We started off by sitting cross-legged in the grass, facing each other.

"Close your eyes and focus on your breathing. Listen to the sounds around you," he said softly. "The wind rustling through the trees, the birds singing, the distant hum of cars on the highway. Let your mind wander, but don't let any single thought take hold. Just allow them to pass through your awareness like clouds floating across the sky."

I did as he suggested, my body gradually relaxing more and more as I let go of the tension I'd been holding onto. My thoughts came and went, but I didn't dwell on any of them, I simply let them be, trusting that they would lead me to the thread of my magic.

The sun was beginning to set, turning the sky rose-gold as Liam and I continued the training session.

Sweat trickled down my back, but I ignored it, determined to find the source of my magic.

"Think of it like this," Liam said. "Your brain is made up of different areas, each responsible for a specific function. The same goes for your magic. It's somewhere inside you, fueling your abilities, and helping you function. You just need to locate it."

I nodded, yet still struggled to find that elusive thread of power within myself. My frustration grew with each passing second, and my wolf began pacing restlessly beneath my skin, equally eager to uncover the mystery.

"Take a long slow breath, in for two, out for three," Liam said. "Relax, and remember that you are not alone in this. Your wolf is here to help you, and so am I."

I closed my eyes and breathed in and out, trying to relax my mind and focus on the sensation emanating from deep within my body. The overwhelming energy danced just beyond my reach, teasing me with its raw power. My wolf was eager, encouraging me to push past the uncertainty and take hold of this newfound force.

"Remember, you're in control. Your magic is a part of you, waiting to be harnessed."

"Okay." I took another breath, held it, then let it go. "I'll try."

As I reached inward once more, my fingers brushed against the energy. The magic resting in my heart was like a dormant volcano waiting to erupt. It was intoxicating, and for a moment, I reveled in its untamed beauty.

"Did you find it?" Liam asked excitedly.

"Yes," I said, awe washing over me. "It's there inside my heart."

"Good, that's brilliant. Now, let's work on controlling it."

"Right." Determined to master the unpredictable force within me, I pushed on. As we continued practicing, I found that summoning the magic was far more exhausting than I had anticipated. My body grew heavier, and my thoughts slowed.

"Liza, are you okay?" Liam's worried voice penetrated my mind.

"Fine." I opened my eyes and dragged a hand over my face. "Just... tired."

"Yes, connecting with your magic can be draining. We should stop for the day."

"Are you sure?" Dedication and exhaustion waged a war inside me. "I don't want to give up so easily."

"Resting is important, too," he said, placing his hand on my shoulder. "You've made incredible progress today, and I'm proud of you."

"Thank you." His unwavering support meant a lot to me.

"Come on." Liam helped me up and ushered me toward a nearby bench. "Let's get you something to eat."

The sun dipped low in the sky as we walked back to the house. Exhaustion seeped into my bones, but it was accompanied by a surge of accomplishment that had been absent from my life for far too long.

"You should be proud of yourself, Liza," Liam said. "Today was just the beginning, and you found the seat of your magic so much faster than I expected. You've already come so far."

"Thanks." A small smile tugged at my lips. "I couldn't have done it without you."

Our camaraderie comforted me, like being wrapped in a warm blanket made of love and security.

I glanced over at Liam and decided to broach the subject Rosalie had brought up.

"Hey," I said tentatively. "So, uhm, Rosalie, my sous chef, mentioned the craziest thing to me this afternoon. About... Sabrina. That you two might be fated. I mean, it shouldn't be possible for a shifter to be fated to a human, right?"

Liam's eyebrows shot to his hairline, then he sighed deeply and ran a hand through his hair as he pondered my question. "To be honest, I'm not sure what to make of it. To my knowledge, it's never happened before. Sabrina's human, and humans aren't supposed to be fated to shifters."

"Are you just going to ignore it, then?"

"Even if I wanted to," he said, running a hand through his hair, "my wolf wouldn't let me. This is something we'll have to deal with head-on."

I sighed, knowing he was right. Our wolves were a part of us. Their instincts and desires often guided our actions. I did not like the thought of Sabrina being pulled into this world, but we couldn't simply sweep it under the rug when it involved one of our own.

"Let's just take it one step at a time, okay, Liam?"

Before he could respond, the front door creaked open, and Ty stepped out onto the porch, his face drawn.

"Hey, you two." He walked down the steps to meet us. "I've got something to report, and I'm not too happy about it."

Chapter 15 - Ty

I stood in my office, the recent discovery a heavy weight bearing down on my shoulders. Liza's theory that there might be another mole in the pack had haunted me all night long. Despite having already dealt with one traitor in the pack and another on my security detail, there was still something nagging at the back of my mind, urging me to dig deeper into the people around us.

"Everyone checked out, even Isaiah," I said, more to reassure myself than Liam and Isaiah, who were in the room with me, as well as Liza. The unease lingered, though, like an itch I couldn't quite reach.

Isaiah spoke up from where he stood in the corner of my office. "I did a thorough background check on every staff member. I was up all night trying to find anyone who could have any connection to Castro. No one on your team had any links to him." Though he spoke with conviction, the bags under his eyes belied his exhaustion.

The tension in the air was palpable as Liam's narrowed focus bore into Isaiah and me. "What did you find out?"

I hesitated. This was going to hurt Liza more than anything else we'd faced so far, and it killed me that I had to be the one to break the news.

"Ty?" Liza said, frowning. She hadn't caught on yet, and every second that passed made it harder for me to speak up.

"Isaiah." I motioned to the man standing behind me. "Give her the papers."

As Isaiah handed over the documents to Liza, I tried to brace myself for the inevitable fallout. The scent of her confusion and fear mingled with the lingering traces of coffee and ink in the air, creating a dissonant symphony that set my nerves on edge.

Liza's fingers shook as she flipped through the papers and scanned the contents quickly, then went back over them with more detail. Her heart raced so loudly I could hear it, each beat pounding like a drum in my ears.

"No." She closed the papers and slapped the top sheet. "This can't be true."

I desperately wanted to pull her into my arms, but she needed space—time to process this devastating revelation.

Instead, I thrust my hands into my pockets and swallowed the lump in my throat. "We should have looked deeper into her background." The words tasted bitter on my tongue, heavy with guilt. "I should've thought about it."

Liza's fury was a storm about to break. Her hands clenched and unclenched, an unconscious movement that betrayed her struggle for control.

"Who are you talking about?" Liam asked.

"Rosalie. She was getting weekly calls from an unknown number." Liza scanned through the documents again. "Shortly after each call, money would be deposited into her account."

"Could be coincidental." Liam shrugged half-heartedly. He was well aware our situation was far from ordinary.

"Except the calls were traced to a VOIP number." I pulled a copy of the file from the pile in front of me and passed it to him. "A fake number."

Liza's expression flashed with hurt then confusion as she read on. "This isn't right. It says Rosalie's father is in prison, but Rosalie told me she doesn't know her father. He was a married man who had an affair with her mom, and when her mom got pregnant he didn't want anything to do with either of them. Her grandmother raised her."

"I'm sorry, love, but she lied to you. Isaiah double-checked. Rosalie's father and sister raised her. He owes a lot of money to a loan shark. She changed their names and got a new identity when he went to prison to distance themselves and escape his past," I said bitterly, my protective instincts warring with the need to give her space. "Either way, it's all caught up to her in the end."

"Her father's debts must be astronomical," Liam said, glancing up from the file. "I know the shark. The guy's a nasty piece of work. Rosalie's job as a chef's assistant wouldn't come close to paying off a fraction of what will be owed."

"Which means Castro could've easily planted her," I finished, my gut twisting. Why hadn't I looked closer at Rosalie when Liza hired her?

"Fuck it," Liza cursed, slamming her fist down on the table, making me, Liam, and Isaiah jump.

"Easy, love." I went to her side. The ache in my chest mirrored the anguish I was sure she was feeling.

"Everything we've been through, and it's one of our own who betrays us... *again*." The room rumbled beneath our feet, but Liza quickly controlled the rage. Her training was helping her. "How could we have missed this?"

"None of us are infallible," I said gently, placing a hand on her shoulder. "Now we've discovered the truth, we can deal with it."

"Deal with it?" She shrugged off my hand. "How do we even begin to fix this? We thought we were safe, and now? Now we're back to square one. I want to confront Rosalie." Her lips twisted into a sneer. "If she betrayed us, I need to understand why."

"Absolutely not." Isaiah and Liam echoed my sentiments, their expressions hardening as well.

"None of you have any right to deny me this," Liza said, her anger exploding like a volcano. I went to reach over and take her hand, but my body was frozen, not from the cold, but from what I could only assume was Liza's newfound ability to paralyze us with her powers. I couldn't move anything except my mouth. It seemed Isaiah and Liam were in the same predicament.

This was new.

This was terrifying.

Panic shot through me. "Liza, stop this."

"None of you will prevent me from confronting Rosalie." Her fury was evident in the way her words scraped against the walls, making the air itself quiver.

"Okay, Liza," I spoke through gritted teeth, forcing my voice to remain steady. "We'll do this your way, but you won't go alone. If Rosalie is a threat, I couldn't live with myself if you were hurt."

"Fine," she snapped, her chest heaving.

As her anger dissipated, her grip on us loosened, and my muscles instantly regained their strength. She slapped her hand over her mouth, her eyes wide and terrified as she looked at the three of us.

"Shit, I'm so sorry." She was visibly shaking. "I had no idea I was able to do that. I didn't mean to hurt you."

"It's okay," I assured her. "We're not hurt, just surprised. We're learning new things about your abilities every day. Now we've discovered another one."

"Let's just... be careful, okay?" Liam said. "We'll be there with you when you confront Rosalie, but we won't interfere unless it's necessary."

"Agreed." I tried to quell the dread in the pit of my stomach. Liza had every right to face Rosalie, but the thought of her putting herself in danger made me want to wrap her in a protective embrace.

"Thank you." Her eyes met mine for a moment before she turned away, steeling herself for the confrontation to come.

I needed to give Liza some room to take everything on board and prepare herself for facing Rosalie. It was time to make my parents aware of the situation. I walked across to their place, with the heady scent of my mother's roses thick in the air. The warm sun on my skin did little to alleviate my nerves.

"Mother, Dad." I entered their living room, finding them seated on the plush couch. Their faces instantly morphed to twin expressions of worry. I very rarely surprised them with a visit. "I need to tell you something."

My mother scrutinized my face. "What's wrong?"

Dad simply leaned forward, his silence amplifying the need for an explanation.

"Rosalie, Liza's assistant chef, is more than likely another mole." I recounted the details of the phone calls, the deposits, and her father's debt.

"Shit." Dad rubbed his chin thoughtfully. "I suppose it was only a matter of time before we found the person responsible for all this chaos."

"How has Liza taken the news?" my mother asked gently.

"Surprisingly, better than expected. She's angry, of course, but she's holding up well. We did discover something else today," I added, hesitating for a moment before continuing. "We still don't know the full extent of Liza's powers yet. Liam is working with her, but when her emotions got the better of her, she accidentally paralyzed us."

"Paralyzed?" My mother's eyes nearly bugged out of her head. "You mean, she can control people's movements?"

"Seems that way." I rubbed a hand over my jaw. "It took us by surprise, but we managed to calm her down. We'll have to figure out how to help her control it later."

"Indeed, we'll need to be careful moving forward," Dad agreed. "For now, focus on keeping Liza safe and getting to the bottom of this Rosalie situation. We'll handle the rest."

My mom stood and placed a hand on my shoulder. "I'll come over and visit with her soon. I can only imagine the blow this has dealt her."

"Thank you."

My mother's gaze narrowed in on my bruises. "What the hell happened to your face? Why are you all bruised up?"

"Ah." I winced. There was no escaping the wrath of mother. "It's nothing, Mother. Liam and I had a little... disagreement."

"Disagreement?" she scoffed. "You call this a disagreement? Look at your face." She gestured wildly at my battered visage. "Liam must be so much stronger than we thought if he managed to do this to you."

"Actually, I let him hit me. It was part of a... plan."

"Part of a plan?" Her voice rose dangerously. "You willingly damaged your face? Ty, have you lost your mind?"

"Mother, please." I patted her hand. "It was necessary. We needed to establish trust."

"Trust? By letting him beat you up. I swear, sometimes I don't understand you." She shook her head in disbelief.

"Persephone," Dad cut in, placing a comforting hand on her arm. "Calm down. It might appear unorthodox, but if Ty thought it was the right call, we should trust his judgment."

"Alphas," Mom said with a huff. "I'll never understand why you all insist on making things so difficult for yourselves." She shot me a disapproving glance before stalking out of the room, leaving only my father and me behind.

"Son," Dad began. "How do you plan to handle this situation with Rosalie?"

"I'm leaving it up to Liza," I said firmly. My mate needed to confront the betrayal herself. It was important for her to regain some control after everything that had happened.

"Are you sure that's wise?" Dad asked.

"Trust me, Dad, she needs this." My gut told me it was the right choice. "Besides, we'll be there for support if she needs us."

"Very well," he acquiesced, nodding slowly. "Just make sure you're vigilant. We can't afford any more surprises."

"Of course," I said, just as a low rumble echoed through the house, followed by shattering glass. The ground shook beneath our feet, and I exchanged a wide-eyed glance with my father.

"Wha—" I started, but my phone rang in my pocket, cutting me off. I pulled it out and answered, my breathing quickening.

"Ty." The panicked voice on the other end belonged to one of my guards. "There was an explosion at the gate at the rear entrance. Three of our men are down, and the gateway is destroyed."

"Fuck," I cursed. Before my rage could fully take hold, fear gripped me, making my heart beat a staccato rhythm against the confines of my ribcage. "Liza?"

"She's safe."

I breathed a sigh of relief. "Stay put, and secure the area. I'm on my way."

"Understood," the guard said before ending the call.

"An explosion?" Dad said, gaping at me. "What the hell is going on?"

"Castro," I growled as the scent of smoke wafted into the room. "He's escalating things, trying to send another message."

"Well, he's definitely got our attention now." Dad's expression hardened with resolve. "Let's go assess the damage and make sure everyone's safe."

"Right behind you." Whoever had done this—be it Castro or someone else—would pay dearly for attacking my family.

Liam met us on the way. The scent of burned wood and acrid smoke filled my nostrils as I walked through the carnage, the metallic tang of blood barely detectable beneath the overpowering stench. The destroyed gate loomed before me. The battle had come to our doorstep.

This was more than just a simple act of aggression. It was an outright declaration of war. If there was one thing I knew for certain, it was that no one would come after my family without facing the full wrath of the alpha wolf within me.

The once grand entrance to our home had been reduced to rubble and twisted wreckage. Within that destruction lay the lifeless bodies of three of my guards.

"Goddamn it," I said under my breath, my fists clenched so tightly my knuckles cracked. How dare they attack my family like this?

"Ty." Dad's voice was strained as he surveyed the devastation. "Help me move this debris so we can get to the bodies."

Nodding, I pushed aside my anger. Working together, we began clearing away the charred remains of the gate, uncovering what was left of the men who had been on duty.

"Son of a bitch." I growled when we finally uncovered the third guard, his body mangled beyond recognition. These were my men, under my protection, and I had failed them.

"Don't blame yourself," Liam said. "We'll find whoever did this, and we'll make them pay."

"Damn right we will," I said, my resolve hardening. No one attacked my family and got away with it.

"Officer Martinez," I heard my dad say to the approaching policeman. "What did you find?"

The officer's face was grim. "I can't be certain it's just a preliminary investigation, but the blast patterns indicate the explosion originated from inside the guards' office, sir. Judging from the debris, it appears one of the guards opened something containing a bomb."

I worked my jaw from side to side. Someone had managed to plant a bomb right under our noses, and three of our own had paid the ultimate price for it. A low growl escaped my throat, my inner wolf demanding retribution.

"Thank you, Officer." Dad nodded solemnly. "Please keep us updated on any new information."

"Will do, sir," the officer said before returning to his duties.

My phone vibrated in my pocket, drawing my attention away from the wreckage. Pulling it out, I frowned at the unknown number displayed on the screen. Hesitating only for a moment, I answered the call.

"Ty." The familiar voice made my blood run cold. Fucking Castro. "What do you think to my little gift?"

"Castro, you bastard," I snarled, barely able to contain my rage. "Three innocent lives were lost because of your sick and twisted games."

"Ah, but that's the risk you take when you dance with the Devil," he taunted. "You've been poking around, asking questions. Now it's time for you to make a move, or are you too afraid to face me when I have the upper hand?"

"Your threats don't scare me," I spat. "I promise you this, when we find you—and we will find you—there will be hell to pay."

"Bold words," he sneered. "Remember, Ty, I'm not the only player in this game." The line went dead, and the silence it left behind echoed in the stillness.

"What did he say?" Liam asked, the muscles in his jaw ticking.

"Castro wants us to make a move." I put my phone back in my pocket. "He insinuated he's teamed up with someone. I figure it's Benny, since he's behind the shooting in town."

"Fuck." Liam ran a hand through his hair, leaving a streak of ash behind. "This just keeps getting worse and worse."

Chapter 16 - Liza

The faint odor of burned wood and singed metal still lingered in the air as we stood in Ty's office with the aftermath of the bombing fresh in our minds. My fingers twitched nervously. I felt like a sitting duck as I stood gazing out the window. My attention was fixed on the construction workers outside, the cacophony of hammers and drills disrupting the usual peace as the crew hurried to repair the damaged gate. The bombing had shaken all of us to our core and reminded us that Castro was deadly serious about this war and getting his hands on me.

Ty and Liam stood behind me, watching the scene unfolding outside. One of them sighed, and I tasted the bitterness of worry on my tongue.

"Castro will stop at nothing," Ty said, and his words did nothing to calm anyone. "We have to be prepared for anything he throws at us."

I turned around to watch my brother and mate.

"Agreed." Liam rubbed the back of his neck. "But what else can he do? He already tried to take Liza by force, and it didn't work."

"There's a lot he could do." I had to stop my imagination from running through one awful plot after another. "He won't give up until he's got me. He could try to kill anyone in the family next."

"Castro can't just kill Ty," Liam said. "If he does, it'll kill you, too, Liza. Since you're his end goal, he must have other plans for Ty. But what?"

His words sent a jolt of fear through me that had my lungs constricting. The idea of Castro having any control over Ty's life, even indirectly, made me sick to my stomach.

"Maybe Rosalie knows something," I suggested quietly. "She's been working with him, after all."

"Rosalie?" Ty scoffed, his eyes narrowing with distrust. "How much do you think she really knows? If she's just a pawn then Castro is blackmailing her into doing his bidding. I doubt she'd be of use to us as an informant. He didn't give Cecily any knowledge of his plans. I can't see Rosalie being any different."

"Maybe not." Liam shrugged one shoulder. "It's worth a shot, isn't it? If she has any information, anything that can help us figure out his plans or where he's hiding, it's better than going in blind."

I nodded and looked at my watch. My resolve strengthened when I saw the time. "She's due here any minute. I'll find out if there's anything she can tell us."

I went downstairs to wait for her in the kitchen. I'd asked her to come in for the morning to help get some meals together for a regular order. It had been hard to keep my usual pleasant manner and not rip her head off, but I'd done it, and she was on her way in.

"Good morning, Rosalie."

"Morning." She appeared oblivious to my inner turmoil, so I forced a smile in return, hoping it didn't look strained.

Her gaze drifted through the window toward the damaged rear gate, and genuine shock registered across her features. "Oh, my God, what happened?"

"An explosion," I said tersely, hating that I had to question her sincerity. "Castro's people."

"Castro?" She gasped, and her face paled, which was an achievement for a redhead with such a pale complexion. "That's... that's terrifying. Are you all okay?"

"Everyone's fine," I assured her, gripping the countertop to keep my emotions in check. "We've got a lot of work to do, so we should get started on today's orders."

Now that she was actually in front of me, I struggled to hide my true feelings and treat Rosalie as I normally would. I found concentrating on the work and completing the checklists for the menus made it easier. I had two separate households to cook for. Mrs. Martinez held a charity board meeting every three months and always ordered a cold buffet lunch for forty people, which Sabrina would deliver and set up. Mr. and Mrs. Chalmers were long-standing customers who had ordered a three-course, sit-down meal for eight people, which would be delivered to their house. Thankfully, Mrs. Chalmers had arranged her own servers.

I was finding it increasingly hard not to blurt out what I knew. It took everything in me to focus on our checklist so I wouldn't lose control of my temper and let slip some of my abilities, and what I could and couldn't control. The last thing I wanted was to give this poisonous viper any more information she could pass on to Castro. There were a few moments when I caught her giving me a thoughtful look, and I figured she was on to me, but then she'd shake her head and carry on with her checklist.

Eventually, we had the tasks split between us, and we moved to our separate cooking stations.

"Rosalie." Now was the time to confront her, and I found myself trembling. Taking a deep breath to steady myself, I said "I've been thinking... You've been working for me for a while now, but I've just now realized that apart from one conversation, I haven't learned much more about you outside of this job."

Her hands paused over the vegetables she was chopping, and I watched her shoulders tense ever so slightly. "There's not much more to tell, really," she said with a forced laugh, resuming her chopping with a little too much enthusiasm. "I'm just a simple girl who loves cooking, you know?"

"Of course," I said, my blood pounding against my skin as I weighed my next words carefully. "You must have some hobbies, goals, or something outside of cooking, though."

"Uh, well." Her eyes flickered nervously around the kitchen, looking for an escape. "I like reading and taking long walks, I guess. And I've always wanted to travel more, see more of the world."

"Sounds lovely." I tried to keep my tone light. "What about family? I know about your grandmother, but do you have any siblings?"

She bit her lip, still chopping vegetables with practiced precision. "My family... Well, there's not much to tell. My grandmother is gone. I have a half-sister. It's just the two of us now." She definitely hadn't mentioned any siblings before when she'd told me the story of how she came to live with her grandmother, only that her "sperm donor" was married. Her story was changing.

"Where did you grow up?" I asked, acting as if I were merely making conversation while we worked. Inwardly, my anger intensified as she told me lie after lie. If she'd only told me the truth in the first place, I might have been able to help her. Now, it was too late. I gripped the knife handle so tight, my fingers hurt.

"Here and there," she said evasively, her movements becoming slightly more tense. "We moved around a lot when we were younger."

"Must've been tough moving all the time." I watched her closely. "Did your mother have to travel for work?"

"Something like that." Rosalie avoided eye contact, and I caught the scent of her anxiety over the caramelizing onions.

"What about your sister?"

"Her name's Lily." She swallowed audibly. "She's twenty-two."

"Must be nice to have a sister," I said wistfully, studying her face for any signs of deceit. "You didn't mention her before. Are you two close?"

"We used to be," she said softly. "Things... changed."

"What do you mean?" Despite myself, I found myself feeling guilty for prying, but it was quickly followed by determination as I continued to question her.

"Can we just not talk about this right now?" Rosalie's voice cracked with emotion. "I'm sorry, Liza, but it's just too painful."

Too painful? What about the way she'd double-crossed me? Something about her reaction made my stomach twist. The more questions I asked, the cagier she became, her anxiety and fear heightening. It broke my heart. I'd held out some hope Isaiah was wrong, and that the initial story she'd told me was the truth, but everything pointed to them being right about her working with Castro.

"Rosalie." I glanced around to ensure that no one could overhear us. "Whatever it is you're going through, I want to help, but you need to be honest with me."

"Please," she begged, fear flashing over her face. "Don't make me do this."

"Make you do what? Rosalie." I tried to keep myself steady despite the emotions raging inside of me. "You can trust me. Tell me what's going on."

Again, her eyes darted around the kitchen before settling back on me, filled with anguish. "Liza, I... I can't. You don't understand."

"Make me understand." I took a step closer to her. "We can work this out."

For a moment, I thought she might relent and finally reveal the truth. Then her expression hardened, and she shook her head. "No. I won't drag you into this mess."

She swallowed hard, her tears welling up. Instead of answering me, she bit her lip, a subtle sign that she was bracing herself for a tough decision. Before I was able to react, she spun on her heel and bolted toward the door.

"Rosalie!" I sprinted after her. She was fast, but anger fueled my muscles, giving me the strength to catch up. I lunged forward, grabbing her arm just as she reached the door. "Stop."

"Let me go!" she shouted, struggling against my grip. "Please, just let me go."

"Tell me the truth, Rosalie," I said, digging my fingers into her arm. "Tell me why you're working with Castro. Ty!" I shouted as Rosalie tried to wrench free from my grasp. "She's trying to escape!"

Right on cue, Ty and Liam appeared in the doorway. Their faces were hard and unyielding, but I saw their concern for me in their eyes. Ty rushed forward, quickly grabbing hold of Rosalie's other arm while Liam moved to block her only exit.

"Why, Rosalie? Why lie?" I fought to keep my composure, but her tears made it difficult, and a lump grew in my throat as my resolve faltered.

"Please, don't hurt me." Rosalie was barely audible through her sobs. "I'll tell you everything."

She wiped her face with the back of her hand, and I braced myself for whatever she was about to reveal.

"My dad left his wife and moved in with my mom. They had Lily two years after I was born. Moving was normal for us as kids, and Lily was the one constant in my life. I love my sister. She's everything to me." As she spoke about her sister, her whole face calmed, and her voice softened. "When my mother died ten years ago, my father did the one good thing he'd ever done for us: he left Lily and me with my grandmother. When he heard she'd passed away, he came back, and I found out the sorry truth that he couldn't keep a dollar in his pocket, and that was why we'd always moved around. He liked to gamble. He was in debt. A lot of debt." Although her voice shook, it took on a harder tone. "He ended up in prison, and while he was there, someone working for his loan shark tried to kill him. He promised he'd get the money and pay off the debts."

The room appeared to grow colder as she spoke, the shadows creeping closer. The pain in her face was raw and vulnerable, and I felt a pang of sympathy for her.

"I changed my name and my sister's name, and we tried to run away from the loan sharks," she said, her eyes fixed on the floor. "They still caught up to us. Lily was kidnapped, and they still have her. They won't let her go until I pay off our father's debts."

"Is that why you didn't mention her when we talked before?" I asked gently.

Rosalie nodded. "I knew you would want me to bring her over and make her feel a part of things, but I struggled to find the right explanation for her absence. So I thought it better to just not mention her at all."

"Rosalie," Ty said softly.

Liam's grip on her arm had gentled, but he still didn't let her go.

"That's when Castro found out about my situation." Rosalie sniffled, but her voice never wavered. "He offered to help me if I would be his ear in the Keller Estate. He said he'd pay my debts if I did a few tasks for him. He was the one who sent me the ad you posted looking for an assistant, Liza. He had my background check altered so you wouldn't find out about my secrets."

"What has Castro told you about his plans?" Ty asked when she stopped speaking.

"Castro doesn't tell me anything," Rosalie admitted. "I'm only meant to hide the microphones and pass back anything I hear."

I reeled from that revelation. She might have just punched me in the gut.

"Rosalie." I was shaking with anger and disbelief. "Where are the mics? Show us. Now."

She blanched. She'd been caught, and now it was time to face the consequences.

"Okay," she squeaked. "I'll show you where they are."

We followed her as she led us through the house, stopping every few steps to point out the tiny listening devices hidden in plain sight. In the living room, one was nestled between the pages of a book on the shelf. In the kitchen, another was concealed under the fruit bowl. Each discovery made the betrayal that much worse, and I struggled not to let my emotions get the better of me.

Rosalie reached up to pluck a mic from behind a painting in the hallway. As she handed it to Ty, I glared at her, my heart pounding.

"Is that all of them?" I asked with barely suppressed fury.

"Th-there's one more," she said, leading us into my bedroom. My breath hitched, and I felt sick to my stomach as she walked over to my vanity and pulled out the final mic, hidden within the delicate petals of a decorative flower.

Rosalie's chest heaved as she sobbed uncontrollably. "I'm so sorry," she said, wiping at the tears streaming down her face. "I never wanted to hurt you or your family. I just... I had to save my sister."

My heart ached for her, despite the anger still simmering beneath the surface. The betrayal stung like a fresh wound, but Rosalie's desperation had me tamping down my emotions. Her fear and the love for her sibling had driven her to make such terrible choices.

"Rosalie," I said softly, wavering despite my best efforts to stay strong. "How much do you need to save your sister?"

She sniffed, her eyes red-rimmed and swollen from crying. "I... I don't know," she said, on the verge of fresh tears. "The debt is huge, and the interest keeps piling up. Castro sends me money to pay off the loan shark each month, but it only pays the interest.

I've been trying to pay extra off, little by little, but it's like I'm drowning."

"Give me a number. How much would it take to get your sister back and put an end to this nightmare for both of you?"

"Seventy-five thousand," Rosalie whispered. She looked up at me with a desperate expression, clearly expecting me to balk at the sum.

My heart dropped, then I steeled myself. "I'll give you the full amount."

Rosalie's eyes went wide, her shock and disbelief evident on her face. "You... you will?"

"Only if you promise to take it and never show your face here again," I said, heavy with anger and sorrow. I'd been betrayed by someone I had considered a friend, but I knew that her sister was in danger through no fault of her own, and I couldn't just stand by and do nothing. At the same time, though, I couldn't allow Rosalie to stay, not after everything she'd done.

Rosalie only nodded.

"Good," I said, my own voice more unsteady than I cared to admit. I turned away from her, blinking back tears of my own. My heart felt like it was being torn in two. I wanted to help Rosalie save her sister, but I couldn't forgive her for betraying our trust. It was a conflicting whirlwind of emotions that left me drained and hollow.

Rosalie's face crumpled, and she looked at me with such raw vulnerability, it was almost unbearable. "I never meant to hurt you, Liza, I swear," she said between sobs.

I wanted to believe her, truly I did, but the betrayal cut too deep. The pain squeezed my lungs, making it hard to breathe. "You were working for him," I hissed. "You put us all in danger."

"Only because I had no choice," she cried in desperation. "If I didn't do what he asked, my sister would have died."

As much as I understood her plight, it was hard to accept her explanation when there was a knife twisting in my chest. Regardless of the hurt, I couldn't leave her sister to suffer the same fate.

I turned to Liam, who stood silently at the edge of the room, his arms crossed below his broad chest. "I want you to make sure Rosalie uses the money to get her sister back. After that, escort her out of town."

"You're sure about this?" Liam asked, searching my eyes for any doubt or hesitation.

"Positive." I tried to sound more confident than I was. "We can't just let her sister be another pawn in Castro's sick game."

Liam nodded solemnly. "I'll take care of it."

"Thank you." Rosalie wiped her tears away with the back of her hand, her shoulders shaking with suppressed sobs.

"Don't thank me," I spat. "Just remember, once you get your sister back, I never want to see your face again. Got it?"

Rosalie nodded. "I understand."

"Good." I turned away from her, my breaths coming in short pants. This whole ordeal had left me emotionally drained and desperate for some semblance of control.

"Goodbye, Liza," Rosalie said as I stormed away from her, my heart hardening against her voice. I refused to look back, no matter how desperate she sounded. I couldn't bring myself to feel any compassion for her when she had betrayed us.

I barely made it outside before the dam broke, my chest shaking with the force of my sobs. Cold wind bit at my cheeks as I stood on the porch, staring into the vast wilderness that surrounded our home. It was a cruel reminder of how vulnerable we truly were, and how much I'd allowed myself to trust someone who had been working against us all along.

"Damn you," I hissed through clenched teeth, balling my fists at my side. My anger surged, overwhelming the pain, and I needed to let it out before it consumed me completely.

I shifted without a second thought, my human form giving way to the powerful wolf within. My senses sharpened, the world around me coming alive in a way it never did when I was human. The scent of damp earth and pine needles was a calming balm, while leaves rustling in the breeze reached my ears like the whispers of conspirators.

I sprinted into the forest, my paws pounding against the ground, relishing the freedom and strength my lupine form provided. As I ran, I tasted the cool, crisp air on my tongue, and the dampness of the soil beneath my feet. Each stride brought a momentary reprieve from the turmoil inside me, and for a short time, I was invincible.

My paws thundered against the damp forest floor, sending dirt and leaves flying behind me. I pushed myself to run faster, harder. My heart ached with every beat, but I couldn't stop—not yet. The wind whipped through my fur, stinging my eyes, making them water, but I barely noticed the discomfort. All I focused on was the pounding of my paws on the ground, and the fury that burned like wildfire beneath my skin.

I tore through the underbrush, branches snapping and cracking beneath my powerful paws. The once-familiar woods had become a blur of green and brown, the world around me reduced to nothing but a backdrop for my rage. The blood roaring in my ears and my labored breathing drowned out the birdsong and rustling leaves.

"*Where are you?*" Ty echoed in my mind.

"*Deep in the woods,*" I replied, slowing my pace when I felt his approach. "*Just... keep following my scent.*"

While I waited for him, I took stock of my surroundings. I'd run so far and so fast, I didn't recognize this part of the forest anymore. It didn't matter. All that mattered was that I was away from the house, and away from the betrayal that had broken my heart.

When Ty finally appeared, his massive wolf form materializing from the shadows, relief shuddered through our mating bond. His golden orbs met mine, filled with an unspoken understanding of the pain I was experiencing. He stepped closer and rubbed his head against my shoulder, offering comfort in the only way he knew how.

"*Thank you.*" I leaned into his touch. It wasn't enough to erase the hurt, but it was a balm for my battered soul.

We shifted back to our human forms in an unspoken agreement. The forest floor was soggy and cold beneath my feet, but I barely acknowledged it. Ty studied me with concern, his eyes searching mine for some sign of reassurance. I wasn't sure I'd even be able to give him that, but I knew what I had to do.

"Ty, I want to learn to fight. I can't let Castro or anyone else hurt our family again, and I need to be able to defend myself."

He frowned, his mouth twisting into a grimace. "Liza, I'm here to protect you. I don't want you to put yourself in danger."

"Exactly," I argued. "Everyone is putting their lives on the line to protect me, and look where it's gotten us. Castro is still out there, plotting against us. I need to be able to defend myself and our family."

"Even if you learn to fight, it doesn't mean you'll be able to stop him."

"No, but it means I'll have a better chance." I stared him down. "I'm not weak. If anything, I'm stronger than all of you."

His gaze never wavered from mine, but I saw the flicker of understanding in his eyes. He didn't like it, but he knew I was right. I couldn't just stand by and let others fight my battles for me when the stakes were so high.

"Hey, guys," Liam's echoed through the forest, drawing our attention. He kept his distance. "Can we talk for a minute?"

"Of course," I said, catching my breath. "What's up?"

"Look," Liam said hesitantly. "I don't want Liza fighting, either, but she should be able to defend herself should Castro get too close. I fear he will try to activate her."

"Over my fucking dead body," I snapped. "I won't let him manipulate me like that."

The wind rustled through the trees as we stood in the fading light. A sudden, tangible energy crackled like electricity between us.

"Maybe I should activate you," Liam suddenly said uncertainly. "Take that power away from Castro."

Chapter 17 - Ty

The moment Liam mentioned activating Liza, my wolf surged to the surface, its claws itching to rip apart the man who dared suggest such a thing. Teeth bared, I lunged at him, only to be restrained by Liza's unexpectedly strong grip on my chest.

"Ty, stop!" Her panicked cry pierced the air. "Let him explain."

My thoughts spun like a tornado, caught between the fierce desire to shield Liza and the desire to listen to her plea. My breaths came in ragged gasps as I fought to control my wolf, forcing it back beneath the surface. Eventually, I managed to calm down enough to speak.

"Fine." The word was no more than a low growl as I glared at Liam. "Explain."

"Look, Ty, I get why that set you off." Liam's voice was steady despite the fact that he'd just narrowly avoided being mauled. "But, please, hear me out. If I activate Liza and then immediately deactivate her as her handler, Castro loses his leverage over her. She won't be a weapon for him to use against us."

I curled and uncurled my fists, trying to process what Liam was saying. It sounded too simple, too easy. What if something went wrong? Liza was more than just a weapon. She was my mate. Hell, she was entire life. The thought of putting her in any danger nearly stopped my heart.

"Is that really all there is to it?" I asked skeptically. "What if you can't control her once she's activated? What if she becomes... a monster?"

Liam shook his head. "Trust me, Ty, I know what I'm doing. With me as her handler, she'll be safe. Ultimately, it's Liza's call."

I turned to Liza, who was looking blankly at the ground. Finally, she raised her head and said, "We should wait. We have no idea what Castro is bringing to our door, and it might come down to using me as a last resort."

"For fuck's sake, Liza! You're not a weapon for us to use."

"Ty." She reached out and stroked my arm. "When it comes to protecting our pack, I'll do whatever it takes."

I hated the idea, but I had to admit that she was right. We needed every advantage we could get against Castro, but what would be the cost to Liza if we utilized her abilities?

A tense silence hung in the air between us. Liza's eyes, filled with longing and uncertainty, bore into mine, silently begging for reassurance and guidance. My wolf paced restlessly within, snarling at the thought of Castro having any sort of control over our mate.

"Fine," I said reluctantly, though every fiber of my being screamed in protest. "But only as a last resort." The words were laced with a growl, my inner wolf's protective nature bleeding into them. "Until then, Liza shouldn't answer any calls that could be from Castro."

Liam nodded. His serious expression showed that he understood just how much this decision cost me. "We have to be prepared for every possibility. We can't afford any more surprises."

But if sacrifices had to be made, then we would face them head-on.

Liza's spine straightened. "I get it, Ty. I don't want to be used as a weapon, but I will if it means protecting our pack."

Despite my pride in her fearless courage, the thought of her being forced into becoming something she wasn't continued to trouble me. If Castro got his hands on her and manipulated her like some expendable pawn, I'd tear his fucking head off his body and stick it up his ass.

If Castro was intent on bringing war, this was the reality we were now facing, and we had to adapt if we wanted to survive. "We need to strengthen our defenses and make sure everyone is ready for whatever Castro has planned. Most importantly, we need to remain united. We're stronger as a pack."

***

Later, I stood near the living room window, watching the darkening sky outside. The somber clouds above seemed to reflect the brewing tempest swirling inside me. As much as I wanted to rip Castro apart for everything he'd done, I had to be patient and wait for the right moment to strike.

Liam ended his call and walked over to join me at the window. "I have news about Rosalie."

I turned to face him, my breath hitching in anticipation. "Well? What happened?"

"She was telling the truth," Liam said. "The loan shark has been holding her sister captive. When I showed up, that bastard nearly pissed himself when he saw who he was dealing with."

A small, satisfied grin found its way to my face at the thought of the loan shark's terror. Despite my dislike for Rosalie betraying us, there was a sense of satisfaction knowing that her association with Liam had provided her with a degree of security.

"Did you get her sister back?" Liza rose from her chair and joined us at the window.

Liam nodded, his eyes warming when he looked at his sister. "Yes, we got her back. She appeared physically unharmed. Mentally? Who can say? I escorted them to Rosalie's place and followed them as they drove out of town."

"Good," I said, a weight lifting off me now that I knew Rosalie's sister was out of harm's way. Despite everything, I couldn't bring myself to hate her. She'd only been trying to protect her family, just as I was trying to protect mine.

"Is there any chance she'll return?" Liza's voice carried a tinge of sorrow as she reflected on her deceitful friend.

"I doubt it," Liam said, his piercing gaze meeting mine. "She's very much aware that coming back would only put her family in more danger."

"Then, I hope she finds the safety and peace she's looking for," Liza said somberly.

I reached out and wrapped my arm around her, drawing her close. "We all do, Liza. We all do." She glanced up through her long eyelashes at me. "Why did you let Rosalie go? She betrayed us."

"Rosalie was just trying to protect her family." She sighed and brushed her fingers over my cheek. "She made a mistake, but her intentions were never selfish."

Liam nodded in agreement. "She was caught between a rock and a hard place. I can't blame her for wanting to save her family."

"Neither can I." Liza's tear-streaked cheeks betrayed her emotions as she softly confessed, "It still hurts, though."

"Of course it does." I pulled her into a tight embrace. "Sometimes, we have to put ourselves in other people's shoes and try to understand their actions."

"Grace," Liza said against me. "That's what it is, isn't it? Showing grace even when it's difficult."

"Exactly." I pressed a soft kiss to her forehead, and she sagged against me. "Come on," I said, gently guiding her toward our bedroom. "You need to get some sleep."

"Right." She tried to stifle a yawn. "Tomorrow's going to be a long day."

"Especially if you're going to learn how to fight," Liam said with a grimace.

"Yeah"—Liza managed a small smile—"but I hope I won't have to use what I'm being taught."

"So do I." Liam's expression was somber. "It's better to be prepared than caught off guard."

"Goodnight," I said as we reached the bedroom door. "I'll be in soon."

"Goodnight." She pressed a chaste kiss to my lips before going into our room.

I made my way down the stairs and stepped outside into the cool night air, my attention drawn to the newly fortified gate that marked the entrance to the estate. My team had worked tirelessly since dawn, and their efforts showed. The reinforced structure gleamed under the moonlight as a testament to both their dedication and the threat that loomed over us.

The sorrow of the lives lost because of Castro was like an elephant sitting on my chest. Three good wolves would never return to their families. I pounded the side of my fist against the wall. This couldn't continue. I needed to address the pack soon to reassure them that we were doing everything in our power to protect them.

"Ty," Liam said softly from behind me. "You should get some rest, too. Tomorrow's going to be a long day."

"I'll just toss and turn all night," I admitted, unable to look away from the forbidding gate. "Too much weighing on my mind."

He leaned against the wall. "Liza's safe, Rosalie's situation is resolved, and we've strengthened our defenses. You're doing everything you can."

"It's not enough. I need to make sure everyone's safe."

"Understandable," Liam answered. "But you need to take care of yourself. If you're a mess, you won't be able to look after yourself, never mind the pack. You won't be able to look after your mate. Go to bed. Get some sleep. We can figure out what we're going to do in the morning."

"Thanks." Patting him on the back, I turned and walked back into the house. "Night."

"See you in the morning."

The next morning we gathered around the breakfast table, the platters heaped with bacon and eggs sitting in front of us. Liza looked more rested than she had the night before, though there were still shadows clouding her eyes. Liam sat across from her, nursing a mug of black coffee while we discussed our plans for the day.

I glanced at Liza. "Today's your first lesson in fighting. We're going to start with the basics and build from there."

"Sounds good. I'm ready for whatever you have in store."

"Let's finish breakfast first, then we'll head outside."

As I took a bite of buttered toast, my mom arrived. Her soft footsteps echoed through the kitchen as she approached Liza and wrapped her in a warm embrace.

"Good morning, dear," she cooed, planting a tender kiss on Liza's cheek. "I wanted to come by and check on you."

"Thank you, Persephone," Liza said, returning the embrace with a smile. "I'm doing better."

Better was an understatement. Liza looked focused and ready for whatever challenges lay ahead. It was there in the way she held herself, and in the fire that burned behind her eyes. My wolf was proud, even as he bristled at the thought of her putting herself in harm's way.

Dad strolled into the room not long after, his stomach growling at the sight of the table filled with food Liza had prepared, which had my mate giggling.

"Dominic, Persephone, would you like to join us for breakfast?" Liza gracefully glided across the kitchen to fetch extra plates and cups.

"Thank you, Liza. This looks wonderful," my father said as he joined us at the table. His presence anchored the room, his natural leadership qualities shining through even in this casual setting.

"So?" Liam asked Liza, his eyes gleaming mischievously. "You think you're ready for Ty's training?"

Liza hesitated for a moment before responding, her brow furrowed in thought. "I don't doubt Ty's abilities," she said. "But I can't help but wonder if he might be too emotionally attached to train me properly."

"Hey," I muttered. Deep down, I thought she had a point. My wolf's need to keep Liza unharmed could hinder my ability to push her to her limits.

"I agree with Liza," my father said.

"Really, Dad?" I asked, annoyed. "You think I can't handle training her?"

"It's not a matter of whether you can handle it," he answered patiently. "It's a matter of whether you can do so objectively. And I believe that, given your feelings for Liza, it may be difficult."

I groaned to hide the sting to my pride. "Fine. Liam, you'll train her, then."

"Me?" Liam gaped at me. "Are you sure?"

"Positive." I forced a smile. "You'll push her to be her best."

My mother shook her head. "I don't understand why Liza should train to fight at all. As the lady of the pack, she shouldn't be concerned about learning to fight."

"Persephone, my love," Dominic said. "I understand your concerns, but we must face the reality that times are changing. We can't expect Liza to sit idly by while danger threatens our pack."

My mother sighed as her delicate features creased with worry. "I understand. I simply wish it weren't necessary for her to be involved in such matters. She deserves a life of peace and happiness, not one filled with war and fighting."

"Believe me, I wish the same," my father assured her, taking her hand in his. "But we must do everything we can to protect this family, including ensuring Liza has the skills she needs to defend herself."

"Very well." My mother patted her mouth delicately with her napkin. "I will support her and trust that you all have her best interests at heart."

"Thank you, Mom," I said.

"Let's get started, then." Liam pushed his chair back and rose from the table. "Liza, meet me out back in ten minutes."

My wolf growled in frustration, his instincts still urging me to protect Liza at all costs. I berated him and told him to calm the hell down.

With each step away from the kitchen, my jealousy and frustration grew stronger. My wolf snarled. He didn't understand why I wasn't the one training her. As much as it pained me to admit it, they were right. I had to put my emotions aside and trust Liam to do what was best for Liza and our pack.

Ten minutes later, I stood on the edge of the training field, watching as Liam and Liza squared off against each other. I put hand up to shield my eyes from the sun, keeping the other firmly tucked in my pocket as I willed myself to stay put and not interfere.

Liam slipped into a fighting stance. "The most important thing to remember is to keep your center of gravity low and maintain your balance. That way, you're less likely to be knocked off your feet."

"Got it," she said, mimicking his posture.

"Good," he praised, then lunged at her without warning.

Liza barely had time to react, but she managed to sidestep his attack. Liam immediately followed up with another strike, forcing her to jump back to avoid being hit.

"Stay focused," he coached. "Anticipate my movements and counter them accordingly."

"Right," she panted, ducking under a sweeping kick, and attempting to retaliate with a punch.

Liam easily blocked her attack and pushed her away, grinning at her. "Not bad, but you need to be faster."

I watched her closely, my wolf struggling to stay still as Liam roughed her up during the sparring match. The sound of flesh hitting flesh echoed in my ears, making it almost impossible to hold back the protective instinct that threatened to take over.

"Let's try that again." Liam circled Liza like a predator stalking its prey. "Remember, keep your weight on your back foot, and don't let yourself be thrown off balance."

Liza wiped sweat from her brow with the back of her hand. In one swift motion, she lunged toward Liam, directing a forceful punch at his chest. He sidestepped easily, grabbed her arm, and pulled her into a chokehold. She gasped for air, clawing at his forearm, but he didn't relent.

"Focus, Liza! Use your legs!" Liam barked.

With a sudden burst of understanding, she lashed out, landing a swift kick behind his knee, and forcing him to release his grip on her throat. She spun away, coughing and wheezing as she tried to catch her breath.

"Better," Liam said, rubbing his leg where she'd struck him. "You need to be faster. If this were a real fight, you might not get a second chance."

I bit down on the inside of my cheek, trying to block out the image of Liza struggling against an enemy. It went against every fiber of my being—both man and wolf—to watch her in such a vulnerable state. I had to keep reminding myself that this was for her own good.

"Come on," Liam said, beckoning her forward for another round. "You can do this. Just remember what we've been practicing."

As she squared her shoulders, her expression hardened with resolve, propelling her forward to attack him again. This time, she managed to land a solid hit on his jaw before he could react, but it didn't deter him for long. He retaliated with a swift kick to her midsection, sending her sprawling onto the ground with a pained grunt.

"Look at that, you're dead," Liam taunted, standing over her.

My wolf couldn't take it anymore. A low growl escaped my lips, and I bared my teeth at Liam, ready to tear into him for hurting our mate. But Liza cut through the haze of rage, stopping me in my tracks.

"Stop it," she admonished, pushing herself up from the ground. "I'm fine. This is what I need to do to protect our pack."

Her words stung, but she was right. Swallowing down the bitterness, I forced myself to step back. As much as I hated seeing her hurt, I had to trust that she was strong enough to handle whatever fate had in store for her.

One thing was certain: if Castro or anyone else ever dared to lay a hand on Liza in a real fight, they'd have to get through me first, and I would make sure they regretted it for the rest of their very short lives.

My phone buzzed in my pocket, interrupting my tense scrutiny of Liza's training. I glanced at the screen and scowled at Hiram's name on the screen.

"It's Hiram," I said to Liam.

"Put it on speaker," he said.

"Ty, we need to talk," Hiram said, not bothering with the niceties of a greeting. "ASAP. I'm sending you a location."

The text came through just as he finished speaking, and I stared at the address he'd provided. It was a couple of hours away. It pissed me off to no end that he dared to summon me, but it must have been important.

"I'll be there," I said, swiping the screen to end the call.

"Let me come with you," Liam said. "We'll leave some extra security here for Liza while she continues her training."

I chewed on that, my gaze drifting back to Liza as she squared off against one of our pack's trainers. Despite her heavy panting and sweat-soaked face, her eyes blazed with intensity. The thought of leaving her behind, even with extra protection, had my wolf snapping his jaws at the edges of my mind.

"Ty, I get you don't want to leave Liza, but we have to find out what Hiram has to say," Liam said quietly.

"Fine," I replied reluctantly. "But we're not taking any chances with her safety."

"Agreed."

Once we had everything arranged, and the security were told they'd be out on their asses if they so much as blinked and took their eyes off Liza, Liam and I set off for the meeting point.

While we drove, my mind raced with possibilities. What could be so urgent that Hiram needed to speak with us immediately? Why hadn't he given us any hint of what was going on?

"Any idea what this is about?" Liam asked, echoing my thoughts.

"None." I gripped the steering wheel tighter. "But knowing Hiram, it can't be good."

The wind whipped through the open windows of the car as Liam and I sped down the highway, pushing away the lingering scent of sweat from the training session. My thoughts were consumed with worry for Liza and the impending showdown with Castro.

"Tell me more about your connection to Hiram," Liam said, breaking the silence. His voice was steady, but there was a note of curiosity that couldn't be ignored.

I hesitated for a moment, then determined there was no point in hiding it any longer. "Hiram had Sylas when his gambling addiction was at its worst. He helped us out of a tight spot, and we've been on good terms ever since."

"Your father attacked my father's pack because he believed we were connected to mob bosses," Liam said, surprise evident in his statement. "Now you're telling me you have connections to Hiram, who is a mob boss?"

"Wait a minute, Hiram is a mob boss?" I asked, shocked by the revelation. "I was aware he was into some shady stuff, but I had no idea he was that deep in crime." I laughed at the irony of how things had turned out. We had spent years hating each other for the very same reason we were now working together.

"Life has a funny way of surprising us," Liam said.

After a couple of hours, we arrived at a restaurant tucked away in a small town. This was way more impressive than the last place I'd met Hiram at.

"Business must be booming," I said, taking in the grandeur.

We cautiously approached the door, scanning for any potential dangers. As soon as we entered, we could practically taste the aura of affluence and supremacy in the air: plush carpets, gleaming hardwood floors, expensive artwork adorning the walls. This was a place where deals were made, and lives were changed.

Hiram's eyes widened when the hostess showed us into a private room. "So, the rumors are true." A slow grin stretching across his face. "You *are* in cahoots with Liam."

Hiram's reaction was priceless. He hadn't expected me to show up with one of the most dangerous men in the country.

"Yeah, you could say that."

It was strange. The more time I spent with Liam, the less he came over like the ruthless mob boss everyone made him out to be. In fact, he acted more like a brother-in-law than anything else.

"Didn't think I'd ever see the day." Hiram leaned back in his chair and examined us closely. "But I guess stranger things have happened."

"Indeed, they have." Liam's voice was cool and collected. He wasn't fazed by Hiram's surprise. If anything, he looked almost amused.

Standing there, I took in the grandeur of Hiram's new place of business, noticing every intricate detail. The scent of expensive cigars wafted through the air, mixing with the rich aroma of leather and polished wood. It was a far cry from the dingy warehouse where I'd last met him.

"Anyway," Hiram continued, his hands coming together with a resounding clap as he shifted his focus to the task at hand. "Now that we've gotten that little revelation out of the way, let's talk about why you're here: Castro. He's causing quite a stir, isn't he? And I'm afraid he's not alone. There are plenty of others who'd love nothing more than to take you down—both of you."

"Which is why we need your help." Liam's eyes locked on Hiram. "We can't do this alone."

"Of course not," Hiram said, a sly smile creeping onto his face. "Fortunately for you, I'm always happy to lend a hand, especially when it means taking out the competition."

The dim light from the chandelier above highlighted the lines of age and experience on Hiram's face. He exuded the air of authority of a man well-versed in the workings of the criminal underworld. I was relieved he was on our side. It was like having an ace up my sleeve.

Hiram clasped his hands as he leaned forward in his chair. "The whispers in the underground are becoming more persistent. There are many who want a piece of Liam's empire, and they're considering teaming up with Benny to take you both out. But I don't think you need to worry about Benny for the moment."

My jaw clenched as I listened, a growl threatening to escape my throat. "What happened with Benny?"

Hiram shook his head. "He's been roughed up a bit after that shooting attempt. Nothing to do with me, I might add. Whoever is financing him made it abundantly clear that neither you nor Liza were meant to be harmed."

"Castro," I spat out, the name leaving a bitter taste in my mouth. "He's the one pulling the strings behind Benny."

Hiram sighed, rubbing his temples. "I can't say I'm surprised. You're going to have to shake hands with some devils, Ty. Liam has a lot of enemies, and they're all itching for a chance to get in on this war just to claim a share of his fortune. This whole mess is only getting worse."

My insides churned. I did not want to make deals with criminals, but we needed all the help we could get if we were going to protect our pack and keep Liza safe.

"Remember," Hiram continued, fixing me with a steely gaze. "I'm on your side. You need to take this war seriously. You can't afford to let your guard down even for a second."

"Trust me, Hiram, I have no intention of letting anyone hurt my family. I'll do whatever it takes to keep them safe."

"Good." He nodded, the faintest hint of a smile playing on his lips. "Now, let's talk strategy."

As we delved deeper into our discussion, I marveled at how complex and treacherous this web we'd found ourselves in had become. It was a precarious dance of alliances and betrayals, with lives hanging in the balance.

Hiram's eyes gleamed with a cunning glint as he leaned in closer. "I have someone who could be of help, Ty." My wolf bristled at the thought of trusting another stranger.

"Who?" I asked carefully, filled with caution.

"His name is Sven Richardson, alpha of the Summers pack," Hiram said, gesturing for someone to come forward. A tall, imposing man with an air of quiet menace stepped out of the shadows, his icy blue stare assessing me carefully before he extended a hand.

"Ty." He met me with a firm handshake, his grip strong enough to make it clear that he was not a man to be trifled with. "I've been watching your situation closely. I believe I can assist you."

"Really?" Skepticism crossed my face as I raised an eyebrow. "Why should we trust you?" I knew of the Summers pack. They had a reputation for their ruthless attitude.

"Because, my dear Alpha Keller," Sven said smoothly. "I want Benny's territory. If you can help me get it, I'll offer you my resources in return."

I glanced at Liam, who nodded imperceptibly. The idea of striking bargains with additional devils didn't sit right with me. However, given our current state, we didn't have much of a choice.

"Tell me, Sven." Despite the growing unease in my gut, I tried to maintain my composure and asked, "What exactly do you bring to the table?"

Sven's lips curled into a sly smile. "As it turns out, I'm quite skilled in the art of war. I've been hired out for many conflicts, and my strategies have proven effective time and time again."

"Are you suggesting we wage war against Castro?" I asked, my skin crawling. We were alphas— protectors. War was not in our nature.

Liam's face was hard to read as he spoke. "You don't like the idea, but we need any advantage we can get. Sven's expertise could be invaluable."

Sven's smile was unnerving, a thin slash across his pale face, as he extended his hand to Liam. "Thank you for your trust."

"Trust has nothing to do with it," Liam said coolly, shaking Sven's hand briefly. "It's business."

I clenched my jaw and tried to push down the unease bubbling up inside me. I didn't like this one bit, but Liam was right. We needed all the help we could get.

I locked eyes with Sven and nodded. "We'll work together. You help us protect our pack, and we'll help you gain Benny's territory."

"Excellent," Sven said, his smile widening a fraction, though it didn't reach his cold, calculating eyes.

The scent of rain and gasoline filled my nostrils when we exited the cabin. The storm clouds overhead threatened to unleash their fury at any moment, mirroring the turmoil in my soul. My decision pressed down on me, making my wolf pace restlessly in the back of my mind. We were playing a dangerous game, and the stakes were higher than they'd ever been.

As we moved back toward our car, a truck crept into view, its engine growling ominously. My heart rate spiked, and adrenaline surged through my veins as fear gripped me. Hiram's men reacted instantly, their guns drawn, ready to defend us against any potential threat.

"Wait," I barked, holding up a hand to signal them to stand down. My instincts screamed to be cautious, but I needed to identify who was behind the wheel.

The window of the truck rolled down slowly, the sound grating on my frayed nerves. Then a face emerged from the shadows within, causing a chilling sensation to travel down my back and sending a wave of icy fear through my veins.

Castro.

His grin was smug and sinister, full of malice and arrogance. He raised his hand in a mocking salute before the truck sped off, disappearing into the stormy night.

"Son of a bitch." I growled, my fists clenching at my sides. My wolf snarled at me, desperate to give chase and tear Castro limb from limb.

"Let him go," Liam said quietly. "We'll deal with him soon enough."

As we climbed into our car, my gut told me we were heading down a dark and treacherous path—one that would test our resolve and force us to confront our deepest fears. No matter what lay ahead, I swore I would do whatever it took to keep Liza and my pack safe. Even if it meant making deals with devils and strategists like Sven.

If Castro thought he could intimidate us with his little drive-by stunt? Well, he had another think coming.

Chapter 18 - Liza

The moment we stepped into my parents' house, the atmosphere turned tense as Liam, Ty, and I, along with some guards, stood in my parents' living room. Even the delectable scent of Mom's homemade apple pie couldn't mask the uneasiness that hung over us like a dark cloud.

My brothers eyed Liam with contempt and wariness, and they moved in front of my mother to shield her. The news of Castro's stunt had brought a cold sweat to my body, and the fact that he was so close only made the situation even more alarming.

"Are you kidding me? This is absurd," Michael spat, throwing his hands up in the air.

"Easy, Michael," I said, trying to keep the peace. "We're all on edge and need to stay calm."

"Look," Ty cut in. "We came here to talk about the Castro sighting and the additional security measures we want to put in place for the house."

Mason stepped forward with his shoulders squared. "I don't trust him, Liza." He jerked his head toward Liam, and narrowed his eyes. "Neither should you."

"Guys, can we just focus on what's important here?" I said in exasperation. "There's a psychopath out there, and we need to protect our family,"

It was one thing when we had no idea where Castro was, but now that he was so close...

I swallowed hard, trying to keep my composure.

"Damn it," Mason said under his breath. "What are we supposed to do now?"

"First things first, we're going to put extra security on this house," Liam said. "With this war coming, no one is safe, especially your family, Liza."

My brothers stared at Liam with their jaws clenched. Whatever anger they'd been holding back suddenly exploded.

"Who the hell do you think you are?" Michael growled, taking a step toward Liam.

"Mike, don't!" I grabbed for his arm, but he shook me off.

"Your little stunt with Liza wasn't enough? Now you're dragging our entire family into this mess?" Mason added, his low, menacing growl resonating through the room.

"Enough," Ty barked, stepping between them and Liam to create a physical barrier. "This isn't helping anyone. We need to focus on protecting our family and stopping Castro."

I held my breath and watched the scene unfold, then silently thanked Ty for intervening before things turned ugly. My brothers' faces were red, their gazes locked on Liam. Liam, however, seemed unperturbed. His expression was cool and impassive, betraying no emotion. In a physical fight, my brothers stood no chance against Liam. Still, I was glad it didn't get that far. We had enough problems without adding family feuds into the mix.

"Look, we're all on edge here, but attacking each other won't solve anything," Ty said, his alpha authority ringing through his voice.

"Fine," Michael said and stepped back, though his posture remained stiff.

Mason mirrored his actions, still glaring at Liam.

"Let's focus on what needs to be done," Ty said, ever the voice of reason. "Liza's safety is our priority, and we have to work together."

Liam nodded, the slightest hint of a frown on his brow. "Agreed," he said, voice barely above a whisper.

"Good." Ty exhaled, visibly relieved.

While we discussed our next steps, I glanced over at my mother, who was standing near the kitchen counter. Her hands were clasped tightly together, her fingers digging into her skin. She wasn't comfortable with Liam's presence, considering what had happened to her. Well, more because of the man whose head had been delivered to us.

My father wrapped an arm around her, offering her comfort and reassurance. "Rory, I promise we'll do everything in our power to keep Liza and our family safe."

"I know, honey," my mother said. She glanced up, giving me a weak but encouraging smile.

"Okay, so what's our next move?" Mason asked, the anger from before forgotten.

The air was suffocating as we gathered in the living room. I could taste everyone's fear—a bitter, acrid tang that clung to the back of my throat. Ty stood beside me, his body radiating warmth and strength. It was a comfort, but it wasn't enough to erase my worry.

"Extra security?" My father's voice was edged with disbelief, his eyes darting between Ty and Liam. "You're telling us Castro is out there, planning some kind of war, and you want to put more guards around our house?"

"Exactly." Ty was unyielding. "This isn't just about protecting Liza anymore. Your entire family could be at risk."

"War?" My mother's hand was shaking as she reached for my father. "A real war? What does this mean for all the men in our pack?"

"Mom, I..." Words failed me. How could I explain the gravity of the situation without scaring her even more?

"It means we need to be prepared." Ty's gaze never left my father's face. "I'll be holding a pack meeting soon to discuss what's happening and how we can protect ourselves. If a war is coming, we'll need every able-bodied man to step up and fight."

My father sighed heavily. I watched my mother's hands shake as she clutched at her husband's arm. "There hasn't been a pack war in centuries." He shook his head. "It seems history is coming full circle." My dad turned, his face etched with years of wisdom and experience. "I'll fight, Liza. Not just for the pack, but for you." He sounded firm, and unwavering, and pride surged in me.

"Us, too." Michael crossed his arms while Mason nodded, his face set in a grim expression. They might have had opposite personalities, but when it came down to protecting their little sister, they were always united.

The last thing I wanted was for my family to be swept up in this brewing storm. My insides twisted painfully at the thought of losing any one of them. "I don't want this to come to war," I began, cracking under my emotion. "There has to be a way to stop it."

"The only way we can stop it is by being prepared," Ty answered firmly, his analytical mind already working through possible strategies. "We'll do everything in our power to protect our home and the ones we love. We'll face whatever comes head-on."

Despite his reassuring words, a shroud of unease settled over me. Would we be able to protect everyone we cared about? Or would this war tear us apart, leaving nothing but shattered hearts and broken dreams in its wake?

I looked around the room, studying the familiar faces of my family members. They were all willing to risk everything for me, for the pack. It was both humbling and terrifying. Somehow, I had to find the strength within myself to face whatever lay ahead.

***

The sun blazed overhead, casting its unforgiving heat upon us as we continued our training. Sweat trickled down my back, and my muscles screamed for a break, but I couldn't afford to stop. Not when Castro was out there, waiting for his next move. Exhaustion weighed heavily on me, yet the thought of my family and of Ty pushed me forward.

"Come on," Liam barked as he lunged, his fist swinging at my face. I barely dodged in time, feeling the rush of air as it whizzed past my cheek. "This isn't a game. You need to tighten up."

"Damn it, Liam," I grumbled because he was right. My movements were sluggish, my focus scattered. "I'm trying."

"Trying isn't good enough." His eyes narrowed as he circled me. His voice was harsh, cutting me like a knife. "You're not some porcelain doll, Liza. You're a goddamn Wylde. Start acting like it."

His words ignited a fire within me. I couldn't cower in fear or let my insecurities hold me back. I needed to be strong for myself and for those I loved.

With renewed conviction, I charged at Liam with my fists clenched and my pulse pounding in my ears. Our blows connected, the sound echoing through the yard as we traded hit after hit. He didn't pull any punches, and neither did I.

"Is that all you got?" he taunted, smirking while I struggled to catch my breath. Anger bubbled up inside me, fueled by both exhaustion and frustration.

"Shut up," I snarled, driving my fist toward his face. He dodged it, but I was ready and followed up with a swift kick to his gut that sent him stumbling back. "How's that for all I've got?"

"Better," he said, catching himself and grinning through the pain. "Still not enough."

"Enough for now." I wiped the sweat from my brow.

We continued our back-and-forth until we were both panting and covered in dirt. Finally, we collapsed onto the ground, laughing as we lay there.

"Sorry I'm being so tough on you," Liam choked out between laughs, his eyes meeting mine. "I just don't want anything happening to you. If you're serious about learning to fight, you have to stop holding back and being afraid of your own strength."

His words struck a chord within me. The fear that had been gnawing since Castro's appearance had grown into something bigger—something paralyzing—but I couldn't let it control me. I needed to face it head-on and embrace the power that coursed through my veins.

"Thank you." I was almost hoarse from exertion. "You're just trying to help. I promise I'll keep pushing myself."

"Good," he said, offering me a hand to help me up. "Because we're not done yet. We've still got a lot of work to do."

With his hand in mine, I effortlessly stood up, feeling a sense of security and support.

The sun began to dip below the horizon, and the dim light of dusk fell over the training grounds. With each passing moment, my fear started to fade, giving way to a newfound sense of confidence. Liam was right. The only way to overcome my fear was to face it and embrace the power that coursed through my veins.

"Promise me something," I said, turning to Liam. "Promise me you won't let me give in to the fear."

"Of course." His words were full of sincerity. "I'll always have your back, Liza. You're not alone in this."

"Thank you," I said, grateful for his unwavering support. With that, we parted ways for the evening, and I hurried into the house, eager to share my progress with Ty.

When I got upstairs, I heard water running from the bathroom. I followed the noise, finding Ty emerging from the shower with beads of water glistening on his skin. My heart skipped a beat as I took in the sight before me, and desire flared through me.

"Hey." Ty's voice was husky when he saw me ogling his sculpted muscles. "How was training?"

"Intense," I said, tracking a bead of water that dripped down his abs. "Liam was really tough on me today, but... I think it's actually helping."

"Good." He grinned. "You're so strong. You'll be able to overcome anything."

His words were like a balm to my frayed nerves, soothing the raw edges of my emotions. The desire I held for him grew stronger, fueled by the connection between us. I stepped closer to him, the heat of his bare skin radiating onto mine.

"I couldn't do it without you," I said, my hands finding their way to his waist.

"Neither could I." He gave me a searing kiss that ignited a fire inside me. In that moment, I needed him more than anything, not just for the physical pleasure he provided, but for the emotional support that helped keep me grounded.

Chapter 19 - Ty

My heart raced with anticipation as I listened to howls of wolves in the forest. Slowly, my pack began to gather in the clearing.

I had never been more nervous in my life.

"Are you ready, Ty?" My father stood beside me, his sharp eyes quickly moving from one pack member to another."

I blew out a breath and nodded. "As ready as I'll ever be."

Dad clapped a hand on my shoulder. "You're going to do great, son. Just tell them the truth. They'll understand."

I gathered my courage and took a step forward to address the crowd. "Thank you all for coming at such short notice. I'm aware there are a lot of rumors and whispers about what's been happening lately, and it's time to clear the air." I wavered slightly but pushed through the nerves. Since I'd taken over as alpha, it had just been one blow after the other, and all because of Castro.

"We've done our best to keep this under wraps, but we can't hide it any longer. A war is coming."

Murmurs rippled through the crowd. I glanced over at my father, and he gave me an encouraging nod. It was time to reveal the secrets that had been plaguing our family for so long.

"The cause of this war is tied to actions my father took many years ago." The words hung heavily in the air, and the pack's unease grew palpable. "In his efforts to protect the pack, he made choices that have now come back to haunt us all."

My father stepped forward, his spine straight and head held high. "It's true." His words came out steady. "I made decisions that I believed were for the good of our pack. Years ago, I gave the order to eliminate the Wylde pack in Heather Falls. The pack my daughter-in-law was born into."

Gasps resonated around us, creating a backdrop for the escalating clamor of voices shouting their outrage and betrayal. My wolf was desperate to be let out, to defend my father. As much as I wanted to do that, though, he had to face this on his own.

"Quiet down!" I roared, punctuating it by slamming my fist against the nearest tree trunk. As if someone had pressed a mute button, they all shut up. "Let him explain."

Dominic looked into the sea of angry faces, his posture tense but unyielding. "It was a mistake." The remorse in his words was undeniable. "I believed the pack at Heather Falls posed a threat to our way of life, but I was wrong."

"Wrong?" a burly man near the front spat. "You wiped out an entire pack, and all you can say is you were wrong? How many innocent lives did you end?"

"Enough." I stepped forward. "We're all aware of what happened, and we're facing the consequences now. Tearing ourselves apart won't undo the past or help us face what's coming."

The man glared at me but said nothing, his chest heaving with barely restrained fury. I turned back to my father, silently urging him to continue.

"I am truly sorry for what I've done," my father said in a cracked voice.

The pack grew silent as they exchanged nervous glances with each other, their gazes darting back to me and my father every so often. Their outrage was a wildfire that threatened to consume us all. It was then that Liam, one of our strongest warriors, stepped forward, his measured and deliberate words breaking through the heavy air.

"I get it. You're angry at Dominic. Hell, I've been angry at him my entire life. He ordered the death of my family—my pack. But we can't forget who the real enemy is."

The pressure in the air dissipated as the crowd listened intently. I kept a close eye on Liza as she stood and moved over next to Liam. She inhaled deeply, then started to speak.

"I understand why people might think Castro has a right to be angry. After all, he lost his pack that night, too." Her voice quivered, but it carried enough power to be heard by everyone. "Despite what Dominic may have been planning, Castro is the one who killed my and Liam's father. He is the one terrorizing our pack when Liam and I have put the past behind us."

The pack's attention were riveted on her. With every word she spoke, the weight on my chest lessened. She was right. We needed to focus our anger on the true enemy. Castro.

Her vibrant blue eyes held a power that instantly drew me in when they met mine. If I had ever doubted that she stood by my side, those doubts vanished. Together, we would do whatever it took to protect our pack.

"Castro is the focus," she said. "Castro is the enemy."

Liam stepped forward. "If Liza and I can find it in ourselves to forgive, then surely the rest of you have no reason to be so angry?"

The question challenged each pack member to look inward and confront their own concerns. Through my bond to each of them as their alpha, I felt their renewed dedication and unity. It was clear most of the pack members were willing to follow Liam and Liza's example, letting go of their anger and resentment to focus on the real threat at hand.

"We need each other now more than ever," I said. "We must stand together as a pack."

One by one, the members of the Presley Acres pack nodded their agreement, their expressions resolute. They understood the gravity of the situation and the importance of standing united against our common foe.

"From this moment on, we train, prepare, and fight as one. We are the Presley Acres pack, and we will not let that scum Castro destroy us."

The clearing exploded with shouts of agreement, their voices merging into a powerful symphony that resonated throughout the forest.

When the pack dispersed to begin their preparations, pride swelled within me. We were strong, fierce, and unstoppable.

"Thank you," I said to Liza as I pulled her close, relishing the warmth of her body against mine. Her blue eyes blazed with love and dedication.

She rested her head on my shoulder. "We're a team, Ty. Always."

Her words resonated within me, a reminder of our unbreakable bond. As long as we had each other, there was nothing we couldn't overcome. Yes, Castro was a formidable enemy, but he had underestimated one crucial factor—the strength of the Presley Acres pack, united as one.

***

As I stood on the front porch, watching the twilight sky, I rolled back my shoulders. My muscles ached gloriously from the pack run the night before, but it was a good ache. I'd needed the exertion. I had taken on so many emotions from my pack during our run—their fear, their anger, their grief—that I had been on the brink of collapsing.

Now, I closed my eyes and breathed deeply, trying to find that elusive place of calm.

My muscles remained taut, though, refusing to relax, even after the pack meeting. My father's confession had been a hurricane erupting within our ranks, but it was necessary. With the truth laid bare, we could face Castro as a unit.

"Can't sleep?" Liza asked as she stepped up beside me and stroked my back.

"Too much going on inside my head," I said, flexing my hands to try push away the memories of the meeting.

Liza reached up and lay her palm against my cheek. "If you like, I can give you a massage. Maybe it'll get rid of some of that tension."

"Are you sure? You don't have to—"

"Of course I'm sure." She led me over to one of the cushioned chair. "Now, sit back and let me work my magic."

I exhaled deeply as I sank into the chair. Liza's warm hands found their way to the muscles in my shoulders, her fingers digging into the knots that had formed from stress. The initial pressure had me wincing, but soon, I sank into her tender, caring touch, and the soothing scent of jasmine that clung to her skin.

My thoughts began to drift as Liza's worked her hands down my back, each stroke easing away the tightness. The world beyond the porch faded away until all I noticed was the rhythmic kneading of her fingers, and the gentle whisper of her breath mingling with mine. I never fully grasped the way her touch could bring me solace and fulfillment.

She pressed harder on my muscles, and I found it impossible to ignore the heat building in my belly. Her hands possessed a magic I had never experienced before, and my cock stiffened, straining against my pants.

"Ty." Liza breath was hot against my ear. "I can feel how tense you still are. Let me help you relax."

Her words were like a catalyst, and I pulled her around and onto my lap, our lips colliding in a whirlwind of passion and hunger, and it was as if a dam broke. We were all hands and mouths, our kisses hungry and desperate. I pulled her closer, and tilted my erection against her while I tasted her.

Our passionate exploration continued, my hands wandering beneath her shirt over the smooth skin of her back. She scooted back a bit and unfastened my pants, reaching inside. I stifled a moan as she wrapped her fingers around me.

"God, Liza... I want you." I groaned as I buried my free hand in the soft waves of her hair, reveling in the silky texture. My other hand traced a path along the delicate curve of her neck, and the quick beat of her pulse betrayed her own need.

"I want you, too, " she murmured into my mouth, her hands eagerly exploring my chest and tugging at the fabric of my shirt. She slid down off my lap and freed my cock, then took me into her mouth.

She took slow, deliberate control of my body, captivating me completely in the sensation. I needed to lavish her with pleasure. Touching her shoulder, I pulled her off and onto my lap, lifting her nightdress to caress her thighs, relishing the sweet sounds that fell from her lips.

"Please," she said, and I couldn't deny her anything. With one hand holding her tightly against me, and the other exploring her most intimate secrets, I slowly brought her closer to the edge, our bodies entwined in a dance as old as time itself.

As I continued to pleasure Liza, I remembered we were on the front porch, exposed and vulnerable to anyone passing by or peering from a neighbor's window. The realization sent a thrill through my veins and only made my cock that much harder.

"Ty," Liza panted against my ear, her breath hot and heavy with desire. "What if someone sees us?"

Her words aligned perfectly with my thoughts, igniting a wicked excitement within me at the thrill of the risk. "Doesn't it excite you?" The intensity of my desire made my voice husky with lust. "The idea that we could be caught at any moment?"

Liza hesitated before responding, her fingers gripping my shoulders tightly as she pondered the possibility. "Yes, but maybe we should move inside."

"Inside?" I said, momentarily disappointed by the suggestion.

"Come on." Liza's eyes burned with a fiery intensity as she broke free from my grasp. "We can continue this without worrying about prying eyes."

Even though the adrenaline rush of being potentially spotted thrilled me, my mate's privacy and protection came first. Reluctantly, I agreed, and the two of us rushed inside.

I locked the door behind us, ensuring any uninvited guests would be kept at bay. I turned back to Liza, where she was leaning against the wall, her face flushed and lips swollen from our fervent kisses.

"Where were we?" I asked, closing the distance between us, and capturing her mouth once more.

"Here," Liza's breathless voice whispered in my ear after she broke the kiss before she pulled me into the nearest room—a spacious walk-in coat closet. Darkness wrapped around us, providing an intimate cocoon for our heated desires.

"God, Liza, I need you." I groaned, grabbing her around her waist and picking her up. Our lips crashed together again, our tongues twining in a frenzy as I pressed her back against the wall.

"Please," she pleaded, wrapping her legs around my waist, searching for friction. The urge to be inside her surged through my veins like wildfire, burning up all the self-control I possessed.

"Are you sure?" With the weight of the moment pressing upon us, I managed to ask, fully aware that once we passed this threshold, there was no return. Her answer came in the form of a passionate kiss full of promise and unspoken emotion that somehow still spoke volumes.

As Liza clung to the bar holding the coats above us, I guided myself into her, both of us sighing in unison. With every shared touch, the world around us blurred, leaving only the intoxicating sensation of our bodies merging, and the overwhelming ecstasy of finally giving in to the long-awaited passion.

"Ty! Oh, fuck, Ty," Liza moaned, her nails digging into my shoulders as we moved faster, more urgently. Her body felt like heaven, the heat and wetness of her arousal driving me wild with need.

I buried my face in her neck, inhaling her scent as a primal growl rumbled through my chest. This was what I had been missing. This electric connection with Liza that overwhelmed my senses and filled me with a newfound vitality.

"Tell me what you want," I panted, eager to please her in every way possible.

Her breath hitched, and her body quivered with anticipation.

"Harder... Please, Ty..." she begged, and I hungrily obliged, thrusting into her with a renewed fervor. The scent of our arousal clouded the small space, and we both moaned loudly. Liza scraped her teeth against my throat as I slammed into her again and again.

My heart thundered, the intensity of our passion driving us both closer and closer to that precipice. Liza's breaths came in short, ragged gasps, her nails surely leaving half-moons in my shoulders.

"God, I'm so close..." She strained with the effort of holding back her climax.

"Let go," I growled against her skin. "Let go and come with me."

On cue, her walls clenched around me, and I shuddered as I spilled myself inside her. Liza's cries of ecstasy filled my ears, her legs tightening around me as she rode out the aftershocks of her own release.

We clung to each other, out of breath, our hearts racing. The world outside ceased to exist. There was only us, our bodies entwined, and the love we'd allowed ourselves to express.

As our breathing began to return to normal, I reluctantly disentangled myself from her, carefully setting her down on her feet, even though her body still trembled.

"Are you okay, love?" I asked, my tone laced with worry.

"More than okay." She grinned. "A little overwhelmed."

I pulled my pants back up and fastened my belt. "A good kind of overwhelmed, right?"

"The best kind," Liza said as she straightened her own clothing. Her eyes met mine, captivating me with the love and tenderness radiating from them.

"Let's get out of here before someone wonders what we're up to." Our fingers twined together as we stepped out of the closet.

The world outside appeared brighter, more radiant somehow. We shared one final, lingering kiss before heading to the bathroom to clean up, with our hands linked, and our bond stronger than ever before.

Chapter 20 - Liza

I leaned against one of the pillars on the front porch as the sun beat down on me while I waited for the pack members to arrive for training.

When Mason and Michael arrived, they sauntered over to join me.

"Big day, huh?" Mason sounded eager to get started. With his athletic frame and infectious grin, he naturally drew people toward him. The man was charming and magnetic.

"Massive." I couldn't help but tease him, and with a grin, I playfully poked his side. "You sure you're ready for this? Because I don't think you can handle it."

He nudged me with his shoulder and grinned back at me. "Don't worry, little sis. We're gonna kick some serious ass."

"Ready as we'll ever be." Michael adjusted his glasses. Unlike Mason, he had a reserved nature and preferred to resolve conflicts through words and debates rather than physical force. But like many others in the pack, he was here to train, preparing for a war not of his own creation. "We're here to support you, Liza."

"Have you been practicing?" I asked them, searching their faces for any sign of doubt or fear.

"Of course," Michael said, more somber than our brother. "This isn't going to be easy. The reality of war means we understand that some of us may not make it out alive, but we must be ready, nonetheless."

"Hey," Mason cut in, his jovial tone gone. "Don't talk like that. We're gonna get through this together."

"Right." I swallowed the lump in my throat. "We'll protect each other, no matter what."

At that, Liam's words from our last training session echoed in my mind: *stop fearing what's inside of you.* He was right. I needed to face my own power if I wanted to keep my family safe. As I looked at my brothers—two men who meant the world to me—I knew I couldn't let them down.

"Thanks, guys." I was grateful for the constant support and love of my brothers. We might have our differences, but we were family.

As we watched from afar, boots crunching on gravel caught my attention. Hiram Loveska was an intimidating alpha. He arrived with a horde of men from his pack, their hardened expressions and battle-ready appearances alluding to their combat skills.

The tall blond man that accompanied him was probably Sven. He had an air of menace that unsettled me, and he wasn't a man I would want to be alone with. Ty had told me they would arrive today to train with our pack, but dread still twisted in my gut at the sight of them now, though I couldn't allow fear to rule me.

Startled by the sound of the door opening behind me, I quickly turned and saw Persephone making her way out to join us on the porch. We watched as the three packs gathered on the grounds of the estate.

"Look at them." Persephone nodded toward the assembled shifters. "Three alphas, three different packs," she said thoughtfully. "This could either work out amazingly or end very badly."

I glanced at her, taking in her concerned expression. "Do you think they'll be able to trust each other?"

"Eventually, yes," she said, her expression narrowing as she studied the shifters' interactions on the training field. "It's going to take some time. There's a lot of tension between them."

When Ty stepped forward to address the combined forces, I could feel his responsibility bearing down on him through our mating bond. He was meant to lead these packs during this fight, but he wasn't a strategist like Hiram, and my heart ached for my mate.

Hiram nodded, offering silent support while Sven looked on blankly. It would be Ty leading us through Hiram's plan, and I hoped their combined efforts would be enough to bring us victory.

"Let's get started!" Ty shouted, and the packs moved into action, forming groups to practice various combat techniques.

There were more than a few heated exchanges, accompanied by aggressive posturing and snarls.

"Are you sure this is going to work?" I asked Persephone.

Her lips were pursed as she studied the groups. "Give them time. They're all strong-willed individuals, and they need to learn how to work together."

I sighed, watching as Ty tried to defuse yet another disagreement between two burly wolves—one from Sven's pack, the other from Hiram's. It seemed like we were making little progress, and time was not on our side.

Ty jogged up to stand with Hiram, Sven, and Liam before he spoke to the men standing in their separate packs. "Attention everyone." A strong command emanated from him. "I wanted to extend my thanks to all of you who have gathered here today. We're all united in our pursuit of a common objective: to stand up to Castro. Remember, this is about safeguarding our loved ones and our very way of existence. Now, that was a good try, but we can do better. Let's resume."

He ordered the men into groups again but was struggling to assert his authority. It wasn't surprising as he wasn't the alpha of Hiram's or Sven's packs, and they were reluctant to follow him. The lack of cohesion made my stomach twist with anxiety.

Two men took things a little too far, and Ty had to jump in between one of their pack members and one of our own. He ordered them to do ten rounds of burpees, then stepped back and watched the others.

By the end of the practice session, things looked anything but promising. The packs retreated, and a sense of unease settled deep within me. This wasn't going well, and Ty knew it.

Later that night, Ty and I sat on the balcony overlooking the moonlit estate, and the scent of blooming jasmine carried on the warm breeze. Ty's shoulders were hunched, and every other minute he sighed deeply. I was certain he was mentally reliving the events of the day.

"Hey," I said softly, snuggling into his lap. "It wasn't all bad today. They'll figure it out."

He stroked a hand down my arm. "It was a fucking disaster. I'm letting everyone down."

I turned and flattened my palms on his cheeks. "You're doing the best you can. So are they. It's going to take time for everyone to adjust and learn to trust each other, but you'll get there."

He nodded, but his jaw clenched as he stared out into the night.

"This is uncharted territory for everyone. Three packs coming together to fight a war none of us ever expected. It's no wonder tensions are high."

He finally nodded in understanding. "You're right. It'll work out. God, I just wish we had more time."

I rubbed my thumb along his cheekbone.

His worried gaze bore down on me, and I could sense the weight of his concern. Despite my reassurances, time was a relentless, looming shadow. Time we might not have.

I heard a cough, and Isaiah appeared from the shadows like a wraith. He scanned our surroundings before settling on us.

"Sven is in your office. He says he has some concerns he wishes to discuss with you." Isaiah kept himself carefully neutral.

Grumbling, Ty and I got up and went to his office to find Liam leaning against a bookshelf, his arms loosely crossed. Sven stood by the window, his tall, imposing figure casting an eerie shadow in the moonlight. My skin prickled, and I decided to keep my distance, finding solace behind Ty's broad shoulder.

"Sven." Ty held his hand out for a handshake with the other alpha. "I understand you have concerns about today's training."

"Concerns?" Sven scoffed, turning to face us. His icy blue eyes pierced right through me. "Your pack is weak, Ty. They'll be slaughtered if we go into battle like this."

I bristled at his blunt assessment, my fingers curling into fists. Though I couldn't deny the truth in his words, it hurt to hear our pack disparaged so callously.

"I'm aware that our pack isn't used to fighting," Ty said, seeming perfectly calm. "But we're doing everything we can to prepare them."

"Everything you can?" Sven sneered, stepping closer. Even though Ty had assured me he hadn't picked up on any malice coming from Sven, I couldn't shake off the bad vibes emanating from him. "You're going to get them all killed. Your pack is full of wimps."

My pulse raced, anger flaring hot in my veins. I wanted to lash out to defend Ty and our pack, but I had to keep my emotions in check. Ty was the alpha, and the last thing he needed was me losing control or undermining him in front of another alpha.

Bitterness churned in my stomach at Sven's harsh assessment, though. Our pack was inexperienced in combat, and it left us vulnerable. As much as I hated to admit it, Sven and Hiram's packs were far better prepared for battle.

"Your pack *is* weak, Ty," Liam agreed, his tone level and unemotional.

I glanced over at Ty, whose jaw clenched so tightly I feared he might crack a tooth. His eyes blazed, but there was something else, too. Fear. Fear that his pack and his family wouldn't survive this war.

"Perhaps you should let Sven and Hiram take the lead at training." Liam's unwavering attention focused on Ty. "Yes, this is your war, but with the way things are going, we're all going to end up dead."

"Fine," Ty bit out before he paced a few steps away, raking a hand through his hair. His frustration, his desperation to protect our pack, radiated off him like heat from a fire.

***

The following morning, I awoke to shattering glass. Adrenaline flooded me as I stumbled out of bed and followed the noise to the kitchen. There, among the shards of a broken coffee mug, stood Ty, glaring down at the floor.

"Ty," I said cautiously, not moving from the doorway. "What happened?"

"Nothing." He refused to even look at me. "Just... go away, Liza."

I swallowed hard, my insides twisting into knots. Ty's mood had not improved overnight after Liam had suggested Sven and Hiram take over the training. If anything, it had worsened.

"Talk to me, baby." I stepped closer to him. "Please. We need to get through this. We can only do that by working together."

He finally looked up, his face contorted with pain and frustration. "I'm not sure there is a 'together' anymore," he said, turning away from me once more.

"Don't say that," I said, my voice cracking. "You know that's bullshit. Look, you weren't trained for any of this." I tried to find the right words. "I think that's partly because your father coddled you. That doesn't mean you're weak. It just means you have some catching up to do."

"Thanks for the pep talk," he snarled sarcastically. "I feel so much better now."

"Ty, please." My eyes stung with unshed tears. "We can do this."

"Or we can just die," he said darkly.

I was appalled by his words. "Don't talk like that. We're going to get through this. We have to. Maybe..." I hesitated, knowing what I had to say next would hurt. "Maybe you really should let Hiram and Sven take the lead during training. For now, at least. They have experience we don't have."

Ty whirled on me. "Are you saying you don't trust me to protect you and the pack?"

"That's not what I meant," I said, my heart aching. I hated hurting him, but our pack needed help, and Ty needed to accept it.

"Maybe I am weak," he spat, pulling away from me.

"You're not weak," I said firmly, grabbing his hand. "You're just out of your element. Please, take the advice being offered to you."

He didn't respond—just stared out the window. The muscles in his back tensed under his shirt. I had pushed too far.

"Leave me alone," he said, his words cutting through the air like shards of ice.

My heart pounded in my chest as I stormed out of the room, fresh rage fueling my every step.

Needing to clear my head, I made my way to the training area, where Liam was waiting for me, his piercing blue eyes locked onto mine as I approached.

"Ready for some practice?" He sounded upbeat, but the lines around his eyes were tight as he studied me.

"Let's do this." I tried to push thoughts of Ty to the back of my mind.

I couldn't focus on the training, though. My mind kept drifting back to Ty and how he'd reacted to our conversation. Every time my concentration slipped, Liam took advantage, easily knocking me off balance and sending me sprawling to the ground.

"Fuck," I cursed, gritting my teeth as I picked myself up off the ground and brushed the sand off my clothes before I got ready to go again.

"Focus! You have to learn this, Liza. You need to learn what you're capable of. You're relying on everyone else to protect you when you're probably stronger than anyone here. Stop worrying about Ty and his fucking pity party, and stop being afraid of yourself."

I stared at my brother, hating that I was doubting Ty, but Liam was right. I needed to protect myself.

I centered myself, then found my wolf inside more than willing to guide me. In a flurry of movement, I had Liam pinned to the ground. When I looked down at him, he was grinning up at me proudly.

Chapter 21 - Ty

I was sitting at a small table in one of the spare bedrooms, bathed in a gentle, warm glow as the morning sun made its way through the curtains, highlighting the emptiness that lingered from not spending the night with Liza. My foul mood had kept me pacing the halls instead of seeking solace in her arms.

I ran a hand through my disheveled hair and grunted in frustration.

"Ty." My mother's voice was right beside me, and I jerked, slapping a hand to my chest. I hadn't even heard or scented her entering the room. "You can't keep moping around like this. It doesn't suit you or your position as alpha."

"Mom," I growled, irritated by her intrusion, but I still looked up at her with a plea. "Dad didn't prepare me for this. I'm flying blind here."

She put her hand on my shoulder and squeezed softly. Her presence was always accompanied by the soothing scent of lavender. "He didn't, but you're not alone in this fight, Ty. You have people here who want to help you, even if they come from dubious backgrounds. They're still risking their lives and those of their packs to take down Castro. For the sake of the pack and Liza's life, you need to get your head out of your ass and accept their help."

Her words pierced through the fog of my self-pity and reignited the fire within me. I met her gaze and immediately sensed the strength of her determination.

"You're right, Mother. I'm sorry." I inhaled deeply, allowing my mother's scent to wash over me and give me strength.

"Good. Now, go out there and show them what a Keller alpha is made of." She patted my shoulder.

Once I stepped outside, the crisp morning air invigorated me. The world pulsated with energy, as if it could hardly contain the anticipation of the battles ahead. As I ventured through the pack's territory, my heightened senses allowed me to fully immerse myself in the surrounding sounds and scents.

I stood at the edge of the training field, the grass clammy beneath my feet. The morning mist clung to my skin, and the scent of dew mixed with earth filled my nostrils. My mother's pep talk resonated in my heart. The truth awaited, ready to sting, and it was time to face it like the alpha I was.

"Everyone, gather 'round!" My voice echoed through the field. The pack members paused in their sparring, turning their attention toward me, some looking with suspicion, others with overflowing curiosity. On the sidelines, Sven fixed his gaze on me, his smile impossible to decipher.

I wavered slightly, then pushed my shoulders back. "First, I owe you all an apology. I've been in a foul mood. I've been letting my ego get in the way of what's best for all of us. That stops now." I swallowed hard, and the weight of vulnerability settled heavily in my stomach. "I'm out of my element here." I looked at each of them. "As your alpha, I don't want to lead you down a path of destruction. There's a situation ahead of us that surpasses our individual abilities, and we must be prepared. That's why I'm asking Sven Richardson of the Summers pack"—I turned to face him—"to take over the training."

My words caused an outbreak of low murmurs as my pack processed the information.

Sven's smile broadened, and his eyes locked with mine. I watched his expression transform from surprise to respect, the change playing across his features. He had fully expected me to remain stubborn, but this was about more than me. Lives were on the line, and if I stood in the way of the packs' unity, I would bear the blame for those deaths.

Sven moved to my side, shook my hand, and with the other, clasped my shoulder. He nodded his head solemnly. "I'll do everything I can to get us prepared for what lies ahead."

"Thank you." Relief flooded my being. "I trust you'll do what's best for the pack."

"All right, everyone." Sven clapped his hands. "Let's get to work. We've got a lot to learn, and not much time to do it."

I watched from the sidelines, observing the pack as they moved with newfound purpose. They were quick, agile, and focused, their bodies moving in tandem like a well-oiled machine. Under Sven's guidance, they would soon be prepared for the war.

I'd made the right choice. Swallowing my pride and putting Sven in charge of training hadn't been easy, but it was what our pack needed. The sight of them training and integrating with the other packs gave me greater confidence than I'd had the day before.

"Nice move." Hiram caught me off guard by approaching from behind. "Turning leadership over to Sven like that. Acknowledging your weaknesses doesn't mean you're incapable. Quite the opposite, in fact. It shows growth. Understanding the importance of knowing when to step aside and let someone else take the reins is key to real leadership, Ty."

"Thanks, Hiram." Strangely, a warmth spread through me at his encouragement. "It wasn't an easy decision, but I believe it's the right one."

"Sometimes, the hardest choices are the ones that need to be made," he said, patting me on the back. "You're proving yourself to be a worthy alpha. We're all behind you."

***

The sun dipped below the horizon, and I called a halt with my sparring partner. My muscles ached, but it was a satisfying kind of pain—a reminder of the progress we had made. I glanced around at my pack and saw their faces flushed and sweaty, but they were rejuvenated by a new fire in their bellies and a motivation that hadn't been there before.

Sven called everyone over. "That's enough for today. You've all done well, but remember, this is just the beginning. We need to keep pushing ourselves if we want to be ready for anything."

A chorus of affirmative grunts and nods rippled through the group, and pride swelled within me. My pack was strong, resilient, and loyal—qualities I admired and respected. Under Sven's guidance, we would only grow stronger.

Sven, Hiram, and I stayed back, discussing our plans for tomorrow's practice. My muscles protested, begging for the heat of the shower to cascade over me, but there was no time for rest.

"Let's concentrate on strategy tomorrow," Sven commanded respectfully. "We need to be smart about how we approach Castro."

"Agreed," I said, my thoughts drifting to Liza. Her absence during practice had been a constant reminder that I'd royally fucked up that morning. "Let's get some rest and regroup tomorrow morning."

With a nod to both Sven and Hiram, I turned and made my way toward the house, determined to find

Liza and make things right. Guilt niggled at me for not being more understanding, supportive, and receptive to her advice. Now, more than ever, we needed each other.

I headed toward one of the flower gardens I knew Liza preferred. The space was an oasis of calm in the chaos of our lives. Jasmine and lavender wrapped around me like a soothing embrace, and there, among the vibrant blooms and verdant greenery, sat my mate.

"Hey," I murmured, hesitant to disturb the peaceful scene she'd created.

She smiled up at me, surprising me with her warmth and understanding. "Hi, Ty," she said, gesturing to the blanket spread out before her, laden with sandwiches, fruit, and a bottle of homemade lemonade. A wistful sigh escaped her as she patted the spot beside her. "Come, sit with me. I figured you might need a break."

"Thank you," I said, settling down beside her. "I'm sorry, Liza. For everything. But mostly for being such an asshole this morning. I just don't like feeling weak. I've been so caught up in my own issues, I haven't been there for you like I should have been."

Her hand found mine, and she intertwined our fingers. "We're all struggling right now. It's okay to be overwhelmed."

My guilt lifted at her easy forgiveness. We shared a quiet moment of understanding, and a silent promise to face whatever challenges lay ahead as one. Then we enjoyed our impromptu picnic, surrounded by the garden's beauty, and the gentle sounds of nature. Despite the chaos surrounding us, I found solace in the fact that we still had one another.

I pressed a tender kiss on Liza's lips, my apology mingling with the taste of the lemonade she'd been sipping. "I apologize for being such a grumpy dick," I whispered, my lips softly brushing against hers, with the warmth of her skin on my fingers as I tenderly caressed her cheek. "You didn't deserve that."

"Neither did the rest of the pack," she replied, her eyes scanning my face for the sincerity she knew would be reflected there. "But I understand why you've been tense."

Sighing, I settled back onto the blanket, my hand still loosely entwined with hers. "Training was different today." I squeezed her fingers, taking in the idyllic scene unfolding around us: bees hovering around vibrant blossoms, butterflies dancing on the gentle breeze. "I let Sven take over, and it turned out better than I expected."

"Really?" Witnessing the relief on Liza's face, I could tell that the news had eased some of the concern I had unintentionally imposed on her. "That's great, Ty. I'm glad you're learning to trust others with some of the responsibility."

"Me, too." I really was proud of how my pack had responded to Sven's guidance. They were strong, united, and soon, they'd be ready to face whatever came at us, and it was all because I'd finally swallowed my pride and admitted that I couldn't do it alone.

Liza picked up our joined hands and kissed the back of mine. "I believe in you. Never think otherwise. But we both realized that this was out of your wheelhouse. I do trust you to always do what's best for the pack."

Her words warmed me from within like a shot of fine whiskey, burning away the lingering doubts and insecurities that had plagued me since this whole mess began. Although I'd acknowledged my shortcomings, having Liza beside me made me feel invincible. With her in my life, by my side, I could conquer the world, or at least protect our pack from whatever threats might come our way.

Liza's trust in me settled both heavy and light on my chest; an anchor and a buoy all at once. "It isn't just for the pack," I said quietly, our shared breaths warm between us. "I'll do whatever it takes, including putting my ego aside, if it means keeping you safe."

Her eyes shimmered, and she nodded, understanding the depth of my promise. We sat there for a moment, wrapped up in each other, before life resumed its course, and we had to part ways.

Later, as I sat in my office, I mulled over the day's events. The worn desk beneath my fingertips bore the scars of generations of use, grounding me in the present while connecting me to my family's past. Outside, the wind sailed through the trees, their leaves rustling in a timeless dance, the melody of nature that had always brought me peace.

"Ty." I blinked and looked up to see my father standing in the doorway. Dominic Keller, the man who had been alpha before me, made the large space of my office somehow cozier by his mere existence.

"Hey, Dad." I straightened in my chair, my instincts urging me to show the respect he deserved. "What brings you here?"

He stepped into the room, shutting the door behind him before perching on the edge of my desk. "How are things progressing?." His face creased, eyes tightening at the corners. "How are you holding up?"

I looked up at the ceiling, considering how much to reveal. This was my father. The man who had guided me every step of the way, even when I stumbled. "To be honest," I said. "I've been struggling. Mom gave me a much-needed reality check."

"Your mother has always had a way of cutting through the noise." He grinned. "What did she say?"

"She reminded me that I needed to face the truth, no matter how difficult it may be." I paused, my fingers gripping the edge of the desk. "I told her that I was flying blind because you didn't prepare for this sort of thing. But then she told me there are people here who want to help, even if they seem sketchy. They're risking their lives to take down Castro, and I need to accept that help for the sake of the pack, and Liza's life."

"I feel like I owe you an apology," Dominic said, pausing to face me. He appeared to struggle with his words as several emotions flickered across his face. "I didn't raise you to be a fighter. I wanted you to lead the pack with your mind, your heart, and your ability to bring people together."

"Being a fighter isn't inherently bad, Dad." I tried to understand where he was going with this. "But I understand. You wanted more for me."

"Exactly." He sighed and rubbed a hand over his face. "I focused so much on helping you become the alpha I envisioned, I didn't prepare you for the harsh realities of leading a pack in times of conflict."

"Times like these, you mean?" I asked with a wry chuckle.

"Yes, Ty. I never thought my mistakes would come back to haunt you. I should've understood that no matter how hard I tried to protect you, there will always be battles that need to be fought, even if they're not the ones I anticipated."

"I don't blame you, Dad," I said. "You did the best you could."

"Thank you, son." He smiled weakly. "But I need you to know that I'm sorry for putting this burden on you. No matter what, I am so incredibly proud of the man and alpha you've become."

I hadn't realized how much I'd needed to hear those words from my father. It eased my doubts and fears. I knew he held on to a great deal of regret. It was in his eyes, but so was the love and pride that shone through.

"Thanks, Dad," I said. "I'll do whatever it takes to protect our pack, and Liza."

"I know you will, son." Dominic nodded, steady and unwavering. "Remember, you're not alone. You have your family, your pack, and the strength inside you. Trust in that, and you'll find the way forward."

As if wanting to show that strength I had inside me, my wolf stirred beneath my skin, eager for the freedom of the run. My father nodded when he felt his alpha call out to him.

"What do you say we go for a run?" he suggested. "It's been too long since we've done this."

I nodded, anticipation building within me. The bond between us was stronger than ever after our honest conversation, and I wanted nothing more than to go for a run and spend some quality time with him. We quickly went outside, where we undressed and stood side by side, our muscles tensing as we prepared to transform.

In unison, we let our wolves take over, our bodies morphing and contorting until we stood on four legs, and our fur bristled in the cool evening breeze. My father's wolf was as regal and powerful as the man himself, his silver fur gleaming, and his eyes filled with wisdom and strength. Beside him, my own wolf was a darker shade of gray, and I saw the fire that burned within me in the reflection of my father's eyes.

We exchanged a look, acknowledging the connection between us, before launching ourselves into the forest. The world around us blurred as we sprinted through the trees, our paws thudding against the soft earth and leaves crunching beneath our weight. The scents of the forest, and the musk of the countless animals that called it home invigorated me.

Running in unison, a powerful bond of camaraderie and understanding became apparent, revealing a void I hadn't recognized. Throughout my life, my father had been my constant pillar of support, guiding and shaping me into the alpha I had become. Yet, running alongside him added an extra layer of significance to everything we had discussed earlier.

I glanced over at him, watching his wolf moving gracefully and effortlessly through the undergrowth, and felt an upsurge of gratitude. He had been honest with me about his regrets and fears, and in doing so, he had shown me that even the strongest leaders have their weaknesses. It was a lesson I would carry with me in the coming war.

As we returned to the house, we slowed to a trot, panting, and exhilarated from the run. My muscles thrummed with energy, and my mind was clearer than it had been in days. We paused for a moment, catching our breath before shifting back into our human forms, with the cool air now biting against our bare skin.

"Thank you, Dad." I was raw with emotion. "For everything."

Dominic looked over at me, filled with pride and love, and placed a hand on my shoulder. "You're my son, Ty. I'll always be there for you, no matter what."

Chapter 22 - Liza

A peculiar heaviness weighed down my steps as I approached Liam. When I finally reached him, I discovered he was not alone. A man stood beside my brother, who was as tall as he was wide—that is to say he was massive. He had to be at least six foot six, with broad shoulders that stretched the fabric of his shirt. His eyes were cold and calculating as he sized me up like a predator would its prey.

"Who's this?" I asked, trying to sound calm as I gestured at the stranger. My pulse quickened, and an uneasy sensation settled in the pit of my stomach. This was not part of our usual training routine.

"Meet your sparring partner for today," Liam said, inclining his head at the hulking man.

"Are you serious?" I raised an eyebrow at my brother, trying to gauge whether he was joking. There was no way this guy was supposed to be my sparring partner. He looked like he could crush me with one hand. "Does Ty know about this?"

Liam's smirk told me all I needed to know—Ty had absolutely no idea about any of it. I'd learned enough about my older brother to understand that if there was even the slightest chance that Ty would get in the way of his training methods, he just wouldn't tell him. Better to ask forgiveness and all that shit. If Ty knew anything about this, it wouldn't be happening. But Liam seemed to relish pushing boundaries and testing limits, especially when it came to me.

I squared off against the mountain if a man, his muscular frame towering over me like an imposing shadow. I felt a fleeting flicker of unease as I stared up at him, but I quickly pushed it aside. I'd faced greater challenges before. I could handle this.

"Ready, little girl?" The gravelly timbre of the stranger's voice turned my blood to ice.

Swallowing hard, I bobbed my head in confirmation. "Whenever you are." I tried to inject some confidence into my tone, though it wasn't entirely convincing, but it would have to do.

Without warning, the man lunged, his movements swift, powerful, and surprisingly graceful for his size. Caught off-guard, I barely managed to dodge out of the way, the air rushing past me as his fist connected with nothing but empty space. My heart hammered as it hit me that he wasn't holding anything back. He was coming at me like he really wanted to hurt me.

"Keep moving," Liam called from the sidelines, offering no assistance beyond his verbal encouragement.

I gritted my teeth. I didn't need a goddamn cheerleader. I needed my brother to step in and put a stop to this madness.

But Liam remained steadfast, observing the fight with an intensity that told me he wasn't going to interfere. I had to find a way to stand my ground, to prove to him, and myself, that I was trained to handle whatever was thrown at me, including this giant of a man who wanted to hurt me.

"Think, Liza, think," I said under my breath as I dodged another blow, wiping the sweat from my brow with the back of my hand. My opponent was relentless, his attacks growing more aggressive with each passing second. I had to find a weakness— something to exploit and turn the tide in my favor.

As I ducked and weaved, I tried to remember everything Liam had taught me: how to read an opponent's body language, how to predict their next move, how to counterattack with precision and force. It wasn't easy, especially with adrenaline thrumming through my veins, and fear gnawing at the edges of my focus. But if I wanted to survive this, I had to dig deep and call upon every ounce of strength and skill I possessed.

My muscles ached, and my breath came in ragged gasps, but I couldn't afford to falter now. Sweat dripped down my forehead, the saltiness stinging my eyes, and the scent of nature mixed with blood permeated my senses.

"During a battle, there won't always be protection for you," Liam said from the sidelines. He was barely audible over the sounds of our grueling fight. "Worst-case scenario, we are all fighting off someone else, leaving you unprotected. What will you do to stay alive?"

I gritted my teeth as adrenaline surged through my veins, and I dodged another blow. Every inch of the man radiated menace. The heat of his anger felt like the embers of a dying fire threatening to roar back to life at any moment.

My heart pounded as Liam's words sunk in. There *would* be times when I'd have to face danger alone without the protection of my family. The thought terrified me, but it also fueled my need to master my abilities.

"Focus!" Liam's presence was reassuring, even if he was encouraging the mountain man to maim me. "Remember what I've taught you."

I centered myself, calling upon the magic within me, and recalling the countless hours Liam and I had spent training. He had shown me how to channel my power, how to cause earthquakes and paralyze others with just a flick of my wrist. It hadn't been easy, but I had come a long way since those first shaky attempts.

Drawing upon those lessons, I expertly evaded the man's attacks, then waited for the perfect moment to strike. When it came, I didn't hesitate.

"Gotcha," I cried, thrusting my hand forward and directing my magic at the man. He froze mid-lunge, and I pumped my fist into the air. "I did it!".

"Good," Liam praised. "Now, finish it."

A strange, frenzied sensation coursed through me. It was like a bloodlust had taken hold of my very being, and I reveled in it. The man beneath me looked terrified, his eyes darting around frantically. His pulse pounded against the tip of my finger, my claw a hair's breadth away. Just one swift slice and I'd end him. The thought was intoxicating, and for a moment, I forgot that this was only a sparring match.

"Enough," Liam cut through the haze, jolting me back to reality. "You've won. Let him go."

I blinked, suddenly aware of my actions. "Shit," I said, retracting my claws and releasing my power on him. My breathing was ragged as I stared at the petrified man on the ground, the bloodlust slowly dissipating from my veins. A thin stream of blood oozed from a small cut on his neck, and I gasped, stumbling back with my hands shaking.

"Shit," I said, my breath hitching. "I didn't mean to... "

The man's aura had been menacing, but that was his role for today, to make me believe I was in real danger. He'd done his job well. Perhaps too well. My heart hammered as I thought about how close I'd come to seriously hurting him, even killing him.

"Listen, Liza." Liam stepped closer and gripped my upper arms, refusing to let me run. "You're safe. He was never a real threat, and you handled yourself brilliantly. You need to learn to control that bloodlust. It's powerful, and it can be dangerous if you let it take over."

Ty burst into the training area, and his eyes were wild. He took in the scene before him—the man on the ground, the blood, and me standing there, shaking.

"Are you okay?" he asked urgently, checking me over for injuries.

"I-I'm fine." The words felt like lead on my tongue. "It was just... it got out of control for a second."

"Out of control? I felt your distress through our bond. Now, does someone want to tell me what is going on?" Ty's attention flicked between Liam and me. "What the fuck happened?"

Liam sighed and ran a hand through his hair. "We were practicing her abilities, and she let the power get to her head a bit. She pulled back in time."

"Are you seriously telling me you thought this was a good idea?" Ty's words were now a low, menacing growl as he glared at Liam. His handsome face contorted into something terrifying. With the heat emanating from him, I was surprised his clothes didn't combust.

Liam crossed his arms defensively. "Not only did I think it was a good idea, but it was also necessary. She needs to learn how to protect herself in a real-life situation. We can't always be around to save her."

"By putting her in danger? By making her think she might actually kill someone?" Ty shot back, taking a step toward Liam. Their faces were inches apart now, their bodies tensed for a fight.

"Look, it worked, didn't it?" Liam was not backing down. "She managed to get the upper hand, even when she was scared. She can do this, Ty. With more practice, she'll only get better."

Ty's jaw clenched, and the muscles in his neck corded as he tried to rein in his anger. There was something incredibly enticing about the way his raw emotions played across his face, sending a pulse of desire right to my core. My clit throbbed, and I did my best to control it. This was so not the time or place to start feeling horny.

"Yuck," Liam muttered, casting a sideways glance at me. He must have sensed the shift in my emotions, instantly killing my mood.

I flushed with embarrassment, looking away from both of them.

"Fine." Ty forced the word out through gritted teeth. "Next time you pull something like this, I'm here, too. We both make sure Liza is ready for it. Understood?"

"Understood," Liam grumbled, stepping back from Ty, and the tension between them slowly faded.

"Let's clean up this mess and get our heads back in the game," Ty said, gesturing to the training area littered with broken branches and the injured sparring partner. "We have bigger things to worry about than our own in-fighting."

I replayed the scene in my mind, the fear coursing through me as I fought for my life, and the strange thrill of power that had overtaken me when I'd gained the upper hand. I still had a long way to go before I had all the skills and could protect myself without a cheerleader on the sidelines, but today's events had proven that I wasn't entirely helpless.

"Hey," Liam said when he came to stand next to me. "I'm sorry if I pushed you too hard today. I just wanted you to know that you're stronger than you think."

"Thanks." I gave him a small smile. "I get it. You were just trying to help, and in a way you did. I have more confidence in my abilities. Maybe next time, a little less bloodshed?"

"Deal." He grinned, rubbing my shoulder gently. "Now, let's get back to it. We've got a lot to do."

***

The rest of the day, I couldn't shake the image of my claws at that man's throat. Every time I blinked, it flashed before me: his eyes wide with fear, the blood welling up beneath my claw, and that raging fire inside me, urging me to finish what I'd started. It terrified the fuck out of me.

I paced around the kitchen, my heart hammering as I tried to shake the thought that I'd been inches away from becoming a killer. Liam had told me stories about our father's grandmother, whose bloodlust had consumed her. Her handler had murdered her when they couldn't control her anymore. Was that what I'd felt today? That same darkness lurking just beneath the surface, waiting for the perfect moment to strike?

"Hey," Sabrina's voice echoed through the hallway, cutting through my racing thoughts like a lifeline.

I took a ragged breath, trying to shove my fears aside as I went down the stairs to see her. "Hey, Sabrina." I smiled, but it felt fake even to me. "What brings you here?"

"I wanted to check in with you and make sure you're doing okay." She pulled me into her arms for a hug. When we sat at the table in the kitchen, she frowned. "I've been looking for Rosalie everywhere. Didn't she come in today?"

A pit formed in my stomach. With everything that had happened, I'd forgotten to tell Sabrina about Rosalie's betrayal. She deserved to hear the truth, but how could I tell her without hurting her?

"About Rosalie..." I swallowed hard and dragged in a breath. "She... She betrayed us, Sabrina."

"What?" Sabrina paled, shock and hurt flashing across her face. "How? What did she do?"

I sighed, my hands shaking as I recounted the story. "She was working with Castro this whole time, feeding him information about us, about our family. We found out when Ty and Isaiah did a deep dive into all the employees, and I confronted her. She had no choice but to admit everything."

Sabrina jumped up from the table, suddenly blazing with fury. She paced back and forth in front of me, her fists clenched at her sides. "I can't believe this, Liza! We trusted her. We let her into our lives, and she just... stabbed you in the back."

"Believe me, I know." Recounting the story of Rosalie's betrayal had brought my own rage back to boiling from where it had been a steady simmer. The bitter taste of betrayal still lingered in my mouth as a harsh reminder of Rosalie's deception. While I watched Sabrina pace around, I felt a surge of protectiveness toward my best friend. We didn't often let others into our close-knit circle, and to have one of them turn on us stung deeply.

The door swung open suddenly, and Liam stepped inside. He scanned the room, one eyebrow raised, until he finally settled on me. "Liza, I—"

He spotted Sabrina, and his entire demeanor changed. His whole face softened, and he lost all sense of purpose, as if he'd forgotten why he'd come looking for me in the first place.

"Uh... hi, Sabrina," Liam said, smoothing down his hair.

"Hey." The word was little more than a breath. It was as if the anger that had been consuming her had suddenly evaporated, replaced by an entirely different emotion.

I sighed. I hadn't yet found the courage to deal with the elephant in the room—that my brother was fated to a human. It wasn't that I cared about Sabrina being human, it was the fact that she was my best friend and had no idea what destiny had in store for her.

"Damn it," I said under my breath, rubbing my temples as I tried to focus on the present instead of the tangled mess of emotions swirling inside me.

Before I even began to process it all, the atmosphere shifted, and an ominous feeling of dread settled over me. My instincts screamed to act, to protect those I loved most, but I couldn't pinpoint the source of the danger.

"Get down!" Liam screamed suddenly, but it was too late.

The world exploded around us in a deafening blast, glass shattering and raining down like deadly hail. As the shockwave slammed into us, Liam's arms wrapped around Sabrina and me, shielding us from the worst of the impact.

Time passed in slow motion for a few seconds. Liam's mouth moved, and I had to blink several times before his words registered.

"Are you both okay?" Liam's voice broke through the ringing in my ears. The chaos had subsided, leaving us surrounded by shattered glass and debris. I gasped for breath, trying to ignore the sharp pain in my side where the force of the explosion had thrown me against the wall.

"Y-yeah." I was shaking, and breathing hurt, but otherwise, I couldn't identify any other injuries. "I think so. What about you, Sabrina?"

"I'm fine, thanks to Liam." She was equally unsteady. She looked up at him with gratitude shining in her eyes. She may not know about their connection yet, but what would happen when she did? What changes would it bring about?

"Thanks for saving us," I said.

I lifted my hand from Liam's shoulder and froze, staring at the red fluid staining my fingers. The metallic tang filled my nostrils, making my stomach twist with nausea. My breath hitched in my throat.

Liam was hurt, and badly.

Blood coated everything; a macabre painting splashed across the room. Dark crimson flowed from Liam's neck. It seemed to pulse out from the artery in his neck and made my breathing hitch in terror. Every time his heart beat, it sent more of his life's blood down his chest. My hands shook as I tried to hold back the panic.

Sabrina began shouting. "Liam! No, no. Liam!" I wasn't even sure she was aware of what she was doing or why. The bond strengthened between them even though neither had acknowledged it. *Fuck*, Sabrina wasn't even aware of its existence.

She looked up at me. "Liza, what do we do?" She grabbed the nearest thing to her—the tablecloth—and tried to staunch the bleeding.

"Stay with me." I desperately tried to stop my voice from cracking. "You're going to be okay." I had to stay calm. *Think, Liza. Come on, think*!

"Li-Liza..." Liam gasped weakly, a gut-wrenching gurgle coming from his throat.

I needed to focus. I couldn't let my fear take over. I inhaled deeply, forcing myself to remain calm. Tears streamed down my cheeks. Tears... My tears could heal! I had to act quickly, otherwise I'd lose him.

"Please, Liza..." His voice was becoming weaker, the pristine white tablecloth Sabrina was holding to his neck now saturated red, soaked with my brother's blood. I pulled it out of the way, and had to physically push a sobbing Sabrina back.

"Shh, Liam. Save your strength." I wiped my face with my hands and placed them on the jagged wound in his neck. The warmth of his blood contrasted sharply with the cold, clammy skin beneath my fingers, then I kneeled over him, and with my tears falling onto the wound, I willed my healing power to flow through me and into him.

"Come on," I said, more to myself than to Liam. "Work."

Sabrina held his hand, her eyes never leaving his face as she mumbled over and over, "Please, Liam, please."

I bit my lip, shutting out everything else and concentrating on the flow of energy between my hands and Liam's neck. The air around us became electrified, charged with the strength of my magic as it worked on his torn flesh. At first, I didn't think it was working. Blood continued to ooze from between my fingers, slick and warm against my skin. Then, a subtle change. The ragged cut began to close, the flesh knitting itself like two pieces of fabric stitched by an invisible hand.

"Damn." Sabrina eyes flitted between Liam's face, me, and his healing wound, then back to me, her words coming between sobs. "Liza, it's working."

I let out a choked laugh. My brother's life had teetered on the edge, and somehow, miraculously, I'd been able to pull him back. It was a feeling unlike anything I'd ever experienced before: raw, powerful, terrifying.

Beneath it all, a fierce pride burned bright, stoking the flames of my newfound confidence.

"Of course it's working." I tried to inject some levity into the situation. "It's me you're speaking to."

With Liam's worst injury now healed, I allowed myself a moment to take in the rest of his battered body. Cuts and bruises marred his once flawless skin, but he was alive. As I looked down at him, I swelled with a fierce protectiveness that threatened to consume me.

"Let's get you cleaned up." Sabrina and I helped move him across the room where there was no glass. He winced, but at least he was moving. It was nothing short of miraculous, and it was all because of me. Sabrina rushed to find an unbroken bowl and a clean cloth before she began cleaning the blood from his skin.

Eventually, he felt strong enough to stand, so Sabrina and I helped him up, and with one of us on either side, we supported him and slowly shuffled out of the house.

Burning rubber and gasoline assaulted my nostrils once we stepped outside, with Liam leaning heavily on us for support. The remains of an SUV smoldered in the driveway, reduced to a twisted heap of metal and shattered glass. The explosion had come so suddenly, so violently, that my head was still spinning.

"Ty!" I scanned the chaos for any sign of my mate. "Where are you?" Panic coiled inside me. "Ty!"

"Over here," came his terse reply, and I spotted him kneeling by the wreckage. His eyes flickered toward us for a moment, and when he registered the sight of us, he came running toward me. "Whose blood is this? Are you okay, Liza? Sabrina?"

"It's Liam's blood. He was—" I began to explain, but Sabrina cut me off.

"Oh, my God, Ty, you've never seen anything like it. Well, maybe you have, but it was fucking mind-blowing. Liam was bleeding, he had a great big wound on his neck, Liza... Liza fixed him." The adrenaline must still have been coursing through her system as her words came out in one long rush and ended on a sob. "He could have died, but he saved me, Ty. He saved me and Liza."

Ty turned his worried gaze to Liam, then me. "Are you sure you're not injured, love?"

"I'm fine," I reassured him. "Just tired from healing Liam. I think he needs to go to the hospital. He lost a lot of blood."

Liam, who'd said nothing—which was a testament to how hurt he was—finally spoke up, though he sounded weak. "I'm fine. A couple of good steaks, an early night, and I'll be fine."

I cocked an eyebrow at him. "So, if Sabrina and I were to walk away now, you could stand on your own?"

Reluctantly, he shook his head. "Probably not."

"Right, which is exactly why you need to go to the hospital." Ty's concern for my brother was a far cry from the distrust of their initial meeting. "You should get checked, Liam. Liza's never healed a wound like that before. What if she missed something or it's only temporary? We don't know the extent of her healing powers. Just let the ladies take you to hospital so the nurses can fuss over you."

To all our surprise, Sabrina growled at Ty's last statement. I wasn't even sure she was aware she'd done it, but it certainly meant a conversation was in the cards from my brother and me about their bond and what he planned to do about it.

Ty handed me a set of keys, then gave me a kiss that rumbled down to my toes. "You're certain you're not injured?"

"I'm fine. Liam pushed me out of the way of the glass. I'll phone you from the hospital." Although I'd managed to heal Liam's most serious injury, I couldn't shake the nagging worry that it wasn't enough. As Ty said, I'd never healed an injury like that before. He'd lost a lot of blood, and still bore countless cuts and bruises.

"Okay. Be careful."

More people were arriving—pack members from the training area, and the police. .

"Isaiah, follow them to the hospital. Make sure everything's all right." Ty's command rang in my ears as Sabrina, Liam, and I headed for the car. Through our bond, I felt Ty's concern as well as his pride in me.

"Got it, boss," Isaiah said smoothly, a stark contrast to Ty's rougher tone. The handsome informant nodded, though his face remained solemn. He was worried about Liam, but there was something deeper: a responsibility for our safety. It wasn't just because he worked for Ty. It was personal.

"Let's go."

We got Liam comfortable in the car. The explosion had been sudden, unexpected, and terrifying. My hands shook slightly as I recalled the glass shattering around us, and the feeling of Liam's hand shoving me out of the way. God, we'd come so close to losing him.

Once we pulled up to the hospital, Isaiah parked nearby, keeping a watchful eye on the entrance. He gave me a reassuring nod before turning his attention to the surrounding area and scanning for any potential threats.

"Stay safe," I said to him, knowing his wolf's hearing would mean he'd catch my words, despite the distance between us. He offered a small smile in response, and I felt immensely grateful for his presence.

Inside the hospital, Sabrina and I stayed by Liam's side while doctors and nurses worked tirelessly to stitch up his remaining wounds. The antiseptic burned my nose, and the constant beeping of machines, and the murmurs of worried families pierced my ears. As frightening as it all was, I was thankful I'd been there for my brother in his time of need.

"Almost done," one of the nurses said gently as she finished stitching Liam's arm.

Sabrina watched her with a hawk's eye. She never questioned the need to be by Liam's side, and instead made casual conversation with me, but her attention was on the nurses and making sure they behaved appropriately. If any got too personal, she made a point of going to Liam and standing next to him.

"Thank you," she said earnestly once the nurse finished stitching Liam's arm.

"Who needs telepathy?" I said, my lips curving into a small, defiant smile. "I can save lives. That's what really matters." And I meant it. In that moment, when I'd been able to heal Liam's wounds and save his life, I'd felt more powerful than ever before. More connected to my true self.

Chapter 23 - Ty

Sven and Hiram arrived with their pack while I stood among the wreckage, somehow keeping my anger simmering beneath the surface. I clenched my fists, the tension coiling within me like a tightly wound spring as anger and shame bubbled up inside me. Castro had made a mockery of me yet again.

"Ty!" Sven's cold, calculated shout cut through the air. "What the fuck happened here?" Their expressions mirrored my own frustration, and their rage emanated off them.

I recounted the events, watching the same thought forming in both Sven and Hiram's minds. It was clear Benny and Castro thought of me as the weak link, and that thought gnawed at my pride like a relentless beast.

"You can't keep letting them walk all over you like this. You need to send them a message they won't forget," Sven said. "Show both that you're not to be trifled with."

"Agreed," Hiram said. "You've got to show them you're not a pushover, Ty, because, right now, Castro is making you look like a little bitch."

As much as I hated to admit it, they were right. Castro was playing me for a fool, and I needed to show him that I wasn't about to roll over and submit. But what kind of message would make an impression on someone like him? My father hadn't raised me to be ruthless or vengeful, only to lead with compassion and understanding. But the time for diplomacy had passed. My pack was suffering, and it was my duty as their alpha to protect them.

I nodded, swallowing the lump that had formed in my throat. My phone buzzed, interrupting my thoughts.

"Ty?" Liza's strained voice echoed through the line, and my stomach clenched at the realization that she shouldn't have to sound like that, ever.

"Is Liam okay?" I asked, hoarse and uneven as concern for my mate's brother bore down on me like a physical force.

"He's going to be fine," she said shakily, her breath hitching. "They're stitching him up now. But... Ty, it was so close."

Her words sent a fresh wave of anger flooding through me, hot and fierce. Sven and Hiram were right. I couldn't let this go unchallenged any longer.

"Thank God," I said, relief momentarily washing over me. "Liza, stay with him until he's stable."

"Of course." She sniffled. "I love you, Ty."

"Love you, too."

I turned back to Sven and Hiram, steeling myself for the difficult conversation ahead. "Liza says Liam will be fine, but she's clearly distressed. What do you suggest we do? This isn't in my nature. I've never had to deal with anything like this." My chest tightened with anxiety. "But I have to do something to prove I have a chance in this war."

"Remember," Sven said, his whole demeanor carrying a predatory edge. "This isn't about being cruel or ruthless. This is about protecting our own. Sometimes, you have to fight fire with fire. We need to send a message they can't ignore."

Hiram scratched his chin thoughtfully. "We need to hit them where it hurts most," he said, his eyes flashing dangerously. "Show them that they've underestimated you, and make it clear that you're not to be trifled with."

A predatory grin played over Sven's lips. "I have just the thing in mind. It's going to push you out of your comfort zone, Ty."

His expression reminded me, once again, why I was glad he was on my side. "Tell me." I wouldn't let Benny and Castro threaten my pack any longer. It was time to prove that I was every bit the alpha they'd underestimated, and they would soon learn just how much they'd miscalculated.

"Castro is using Benny as a resource. Since I'm planning on taking over Benny's territory, I don't want to destroy anything that will be useful once I'm in charge." Sven paused and began to outline his plan. "Benny imports a lot of his material from one main supplier. We cut that off, and we cut off a lot of his resources: drugs, weapons, you name it. By destroying this shipment, Benny and Castro will both take a big hit, and that should send the right message."

My nostrils flared as I tried to wrap my mind around the idea of plunging into mob territory. It was brutal, calculated, and undeniably effective. Could I bring myself to go that far and become something I'd always fought against? It went against everything I believed in, but desperate times called for desperate measures.

"Ty, listen." Sven's tone was deadly serious. "This isn't your style, but you need to understand that these people don't care about honor or loyalty. They will stop at nothing to destroy everything you hold dear. If you want to protect your pack, you have to be prepared to do what it takes."

As we began to plan our assault on Benny's operation, my wolf snarled in anticipation, eager to finally strike back at those who'd dared to threaten our family. The road ahead was dark and uncertain, but one thing was clear: Benny and Castro would soon learn they'd messed with the wrong alpha.

"How are we going to do this?"

"Leave that to me, Ty. I'll handle the details." Sven's menacing grin was a reflection of the ruthless strategist Hiram had promised him to be.

I wasn't sure how I felt about handing control over to someone else, even someone as capable as Sven. There was no denying he had more experience with these matters than I did, and my pack needed me to make the best decisions for them. Swallowing my pride, I nodded curtly.

***

My nose twitched at the sterile smell of antiseptic as I entered Liam's hospital room, and the beeping monitors created a steady rhythm in the background. Liza had done an excellent job convincing him to stay overnight, despite his protests that he was fine and needed to get back to the pack. As alpha, it was my responsibility to make sure my pack was safe, but seeing the man I now considered to be my brother-in-law lying on that crisp, white bed, bandaged and bruised, I felt utterly powerless.

"Hey," Liam greeted me with a tired smile, his voice hoarse from the painkillers. "Where's Liza? How's everything at the house?"

"Cleanup is underway, and Sven and Hiram have been helping out." I forced a smile of my own as I took a seat by his bedside. "I sent Liza to the cafeteria— don't worry, Isaiah is with her. I need to talk to you about something else, and I don't want Liza to know just yet."

Liam shifted slightly in his bed and winced at the movement. His injuries weren't as severe as we'd feared. Yes, he'd been sliced up pretty badly, but the doctors had stitched him up within hours. Still, the sight of him, injured and vulnerable like this, filled me with urgency. We couldn't afford to let our enemies keep attacking us like this.

Taking a cleansing breath, I plunged into the details of Sven's plan. I explained how we were going to hit Benny where it hurt by destroying his shipment and cutting off his resources. It was a risky move, stepping into mob territory like this, but I wasn't sure we had any other choice.

Liam listened intently, his expression unreadable. Then slowly, he sighed. "It will definitely send a message, but you know it'll only antagonize Castro more, right?"

"I figured," I grumbled, my heart heavy with my decision. "But we can't afford to look weak anymore, Liam. They've already caused too much damage, and I can't let them take anything else from us."

"I get it." Liam strained from the pain of his injuries. "You've been passive for too long. Castro has been walking all over you and thinks he's better than you. It shows, man." He grimaced as he tried to find a comfortable position in the hospital bed. "Just be careful. This isn't like you, but sometimes we have to do things we don't like to protect our pack."

"Thanks," I said, placing a hand on his shoulder, feeling the solid muscle beneath my fingertips. "I appreciate your support."

"Of course," Liam said, offering a small smile despite his pain. "Promise me one thing."

"Anything."

"Keep this from Liza," he said, his expression serious. "If she finds out you're stepping into mob territory, she'll freak the fuck out. We can't afford for her to go off the deep end, with everything else going on."

I hesitated, guilt twisting in my gut at the thought of keeping something so important from my mate. But I understood Liam's concern and the logic of his words. Liza was already under enough stress with Castro's constant threats. Putting this weight on her shoulders wouldn't do her any favors.

Liza wouldn't want me to embrace this darker path, but there was no other choice. Castro had pushed me too far, and the decision I'd made pressed heavily, like the suffocating grip of an unseen force, as I considered the path I was about to tread. A path that would lead me far from the man I wanted to be.

***

A few days later, the plan hatched into motion. The cold wind whistled through the trees as we stood outside the abandoned warehouse, our breaths fogging in the air. Eerie shadows crawled across the rusted metal walls, setting the stage for a tense confrontation.

"Remember." Hiram checked me over, nodding at me, his eyes sharp and calculating. "You're playing the traitor. Benny needs to believe you've turned your back on Liam."

I nodded, my stomach roiling with unease, but I steeled myself. The stakes were too high to back down now.

"Let's do this." I pounded my fists on the sides of my thighs, then forced myself to relax. This had to look natural, not forced.

We entered the warehouse, with the door creaking loudly behind us. Inside, the darkness was oppressive, broken only by the dim glow of an overhead light. Benny sat at a makeshift table surrounded by armed guards who tracked our every movement.

As I walked farther into the dimly lit warehouse, my skin prickled. Damp rust tinged the air, and dripping water echoed off the walls. Hiram walked beside me, his confidence a comforting presence, though the pressure was more intense than anything I'd ever felt.

My breathing must have increased because Hiram hissed, "Remember, play your part."

I nodded, and set my jaw. This meeting was crucial, a chance to sway Benny from Castro's side, but I couldn't help the knot of anxiety that coiled in my stomach. I had to be convincing to play a role utterly contrary to my nature. If Benny saw through the façade… well, there was no turning back.

Benny rose to stand by his makeshift table and turned to face me as we approached. His arrogant sneer had my hackles raising, but I forced myself to calm, reminding myself of the game at hand.

"Ty." His voice dripped with false warmth. "What a pleasant surprise."

"Cut the crap, Benny." I struggled to maintain an even tone. "You know why we're here."

"Of course," he said, flashing his teeth in a grin. "You're going to help me get to Liam, is that it? You've finally seen the light?"

"Something like that." A pang of guilt thrummed through me for even pretending to turn my back on my friend.

Benny laughed, and the sound grated on my nerves. "I never thought I'd see the day when Ty Keller, the great alpha wolf, would cower before Castro. He must have you pretty scared, huh?"

My fists clenched at my sides as I fought to control my temper. "This isn't about fear, Benny. It's about survival."

"Survival?" He scoffed, shaking his head. "You're weak, Ty. That's why Castro targeted you in the first place. He was sure you'd fold under pressure."

"Is that what you think?" Venom dripped from every word. "Do you really believe I'm just going to roll over and let Castro destroy everything I've built?"

"From where I'm standing, it looks that way," Benny said smugly. "Honestly, you're no threat to Castro. You're nothing but a pathetic little bitch."

"Keep pushing me, Benny. You'll find out just how much of a threat I can be."

"Ooh, big words from the little wolf," he taunted, clearly not taking me seriously.

"Enough." Hiram stepped forward. "We didn't come here to argue. Ty is offering you a chance to break free from Castro's grasp, to save yourself before it's too late. It's your choice whether you take it or not."

Benny's gaze flicked between us, considering. Then with a dismissive snort, he said, "I'll stick with my plan with Castro. We'll take you all out, one by one. Starting with Liam."

"I wouldn't be so sure, Benny, boy. Watch this." My finger hovered over the phone's screen. I pressed the send button, and the text message went flying off into the ether.

Moments later, on cue, Benny's phone rang. He glanced down at the screen and paled, his expression going from shock to anger and confusion. "What did you do?"

"Let's just say your world is about to change," I said cryptically, my pulse thundering.

"Enough of this shit," one of Benny's men barked, drawing his gun and aiming it our way. Time slowed then as everyone present reached for their weapons.

But Hiram was faster. In a fluid motion, he whipped out his own gun and pressed it to Benny's temple. The room held its breath, the tension thick enough to choke on.

"Everyone stand down," Hiram said, cold and steady. "Or old Benny here gets a bullet through his skull."

Benny's men hesitated, glancing between their boss and us. Ultimately, they lowered their guns, not wanting to risk Benny's life.

"Smart choice," I said, smirking at the fear that flickered across Benny's eyes. It wasn't often that the tables were turned on him, and I relished the power it gave me. "Now, listen closely. If you don't cut your ties with Castro right now, there'll be more where this came from. A lot more."

"You think you're some sort of mob boss now?" Benny spat, his bravado returning, despite the barrel of the gun still pressed to his head. "You're out of your league, wolf boy."

I smiled at that. "No, I'm not a mob boss. But I have three of them in my corner, and they're more than happy to help me make your life a living hell."

"Three?" Benny scoffed, his brow furrowing as he tried to call my bluff. "Liam, Hiram, and who else?"

"You'll find out soon enough," I said, keeping my cards close. Let him wonder and worry about who was backing me. It would only serve to weaken his resolve.

Benny's fury radiated off of him like heat from a bonfire. His nostrils flared as he bared his teeth. "Fine," he spat, the word like a poisonous dart aimed straight at my chest. "I'll pull out of my deal with Castro. Don't think that's going to change anything. I'm one of many who'd love the chance to take Liam out. I promise you that you'll regret it."

"Thanks for the warning." I forced a smile onto my face. "If you think we're going to back down, you're sorely mistaken."

"It's your funeral," Benny sneered, and the room crackled with tension as our gazes locked.

"Let's go," Hiram said, barely audible. He still had his gun trained on Benny, but he was just as eager to put some distance between us and the volatile mobster as I was.

Before we turned to leave, I took one last look at Benny. He was full of hatred, but it held an undertone of fear. Though I hated to admit it, that fear was contagious. I worried about what lay ahead for my pack, for Liam, and for myself.

We'd won this round, and I had to believe we had the strength to keep fighting, no matter how long the war dragged on. My pack was my family, and there was nothing I wouldn't do to protect them, even if it meant stepping into the dark world of mobsters and criminals.

As we walked away from Benny and his seething anger, a strange mixture of relief and apprehension washed over me. Relief that we'd managed to sever a key alliance between Castro and Benny, and apprehension because our problems were far from over.

"Ty," Hiram muttered. "You did what you had to do."

I nodded, trying to push aside my doubts and focus on the positive outcome. "Yeah, but Benny's right. There's still a war coming for us."

Chapter 24 - Liza

The atmosphere in the house was like a thick fog that clung to my skin and refused to let go. Liam had been released from the hospital and was in the house instead of the hotel he'd been staying at, but still, there was a nagging whisper in the back of my mind that something was wrong. I just couldn't put my finger on what it was. I assumed it had to be because of the bombing, but something told me there was more to it than that.

I needed to find Ty and get some answers. I wandered the hallways, with my footsteps echoing off the floor against the ornate walls adorned with family portraits. When I turned a corner, I picked up on the muffled voices of Ty, Hiram, and Sven. They were having an intense, hushed conversation, like they didn't want anyone to overhear.

"Really took matters into his own hands, didn't he?" I identified Hiram's gravelly voice. "Never thought I'd see Ty dive headfirst into mob tactics."

"Me neither." Sven's tone equally somber. "You have to admit, it was effective. Benny's defenses are weakened now, and we've sent a clear message to Castro that we're not to be trifled with."

My stomach twisted into knots at their words. What had Ty done? My blood boiled at the thought of Ty getting involved in their mob-like activities. I'd always known Ty to be a kind and gentle soul— nothing like Liam who apparently reveled in this sort of life. Bursting into Ty's office, I planted my feet, with my hands on my hips, and glared at my mate.

"Ty, what the fuck have you gotten yourself involved in?" I snapped.

"Hey, now," Ty started, clearly taken aback by my sudden entrance. "We did what we had to do."

"Really? Mob tactics? That's the solution?" I said, my focus darting between Hiram and Sven, who only appeared amused by my outburst.

I studied Sven and Hiram, their expressions making my skin crawl. They stood behind Ty like shadows, their influence creeping into his decisions and actions. I couldn't shake the idea that they were changing him right before me, and with this war closing in on us, I wasn't their biggest fan.

"Benny's out." I tried to remain steady despite my growing frustration. "But what about the others

Castro has in his corner? Are we just going to go around shooting them down and blowing up shit over there, too? Is that who we are now? No better than Castro, not caring about the lives of innocent people? Like our guards who are dead?" My gut twisted with emotion, and tears pricked at the corners of my eyes.

Ty slammed his palms on his desk as he rose out of his chair. "I made the choice I thought was best, and I stand by that decision. Benny was a heavy hitter, and with him out, we've weakened Castro's forces. You need to understand that everything I'm doing is to protect our pack... and you." As he moved out from behind his desk, his eyes never left mine, and I saw the anger simmering in his eyes.

"Protect me?" I scoffed, a flare of anger in my response. "You think involving yourself in mob activities, risking innocent lives, and tarnishing your own reputation as an alpha is protecting me?"

He took a step closer, his towering frame momentarily making me feel small, but I refused to back down. "Yes, Liza. If it means winning this war and taking Castro out once and for all, then yes." He softened slightly. "It's also to keep you from losing control and going berserk. From being manipulated and used by Castro. You have to be mindful of the true enemy here."

My chest constricted at the mention of my potential loss of control, but I couldn't let that sway me. I met his gaze, unyielding. "I understand the stakes, Ty, but there has to be a better way. Some way that doesn't compromise who we are."

"Who we are?" he snapped. "I am the alpha, Liza. I made a choice, and I expect you to respect it."

I was shaking with rage. "I get that you're the alpha, and I understand that this is a war we need to fight, but don't you dare think for one second that I'm just going to blindly follow you off a cliff."

With those words, I allowed the fury within me to manifest physically, and the room began to shake with purpose. The floor trembled, and the windows rattled in their frames.

Sven and Hiram, who had been watching the exchange with interest, now looked around in shock, clearly unprepared for this display of power from me. Neither of them had ever witnessed my abilities first-hand, and I wanted everyone present to know exactly what I was capable of when pushed too far.

"Let's make one thing perfectly clear," I said, my voice steady and strong through the cacophony surrounding us. "I am not some submissive little bitch who'll cower at your feet and do whatever you say without question. I am your mate, your partner, and you'd do well to remember that. Now that Benny's territory is wide open, thanks to you, Sven has no reason to stick around anymore. How can you trust him to follow through on his promises?" I spat, glaring at Sven.

Sven smirked in response. "You're smart, Liza. I'll give you that." He leaned back in his chair, arms crossed over his chest. "But I'm a man of my word. I still plan on taking Benny out completely. However, I will admit that this situation worked in my favor." He paused for a moment, studying me intently. "I offered to lend my men, and I'm not backing out, but I'm impressed by your thinking."

I reined in my power and locked eyes with Ty, willing him to see reason. He looked away first, running a hand through his hair in frustration. Then I turned on my heel and stomped out of the office without another word. This was not the life I wanted, and not the person I wanted my mate to become. How could I make him understand that?

Frustration coursed through me as I entered the kitchen, and my hands itched to do something, anything, to take my mind off the stress that clung to every fiber of my being. It was then that I spotted the dough on the counter, waiting to be kneaded into submission. I grabbed a fistful of it and began working my fingers into its pliable mass with an intensity that bordered on aggression.

"Goodness." Persephone startled me out of my focused rage. "I'm glad that's dough and not my son's head."

I looked up to see Ty's mother leaning against the doorframe, looking amused. At that moment, I was a little embarrassed at how lost I'd become in my own anger.

"Sorry." I tried to force a smile. "It's just been... a lot lately." Understatement of the century.

Persephone nodded. "Why don't you take a break?" she said gently. "Come for a walk with me, away from all this noise and chaos."

I hesitated, glancing back at the dough that still had my fingerprints embedded in it. After a moment, I concluded that I needed the fresh air and the chance to clear my head. So, with a sigh, I covered the dough, wiped my hands on a nearby towel, and followed Persephone out of the kitchen.

We walked in silence for a while, away from the sounds of sparring and training, with the cool breeze kissing my skin. The scent of wildflowers wafted through the air, creating a stark contrast to the tension that had been suffocating me inside the house. For a moment, I allowed myself to breathe in the serenity of our surroundings, letting it wash over me like a soothing balm.

Persephone broke the silence between us. "I'm on your side with all of this."

I glanced at her, surprise flickering across my face. "You are?"

"Of course," she said firmly, her eyes meeting mine with unwavering conviction. "I don't like what's happening any more than you do."

I blew out a heavy breath as I looked out over the surrounding landscape. "I just don't understand how we got here," I whispered.

"Sometimes," Persephone said gently, "we find ourselves in situations we never anticipated simply because we didn't speak up when we should have."

I turned my attention back to her. "What are you saying?"

"Perhaps if I'd been half as brave as you are, if I'd questioned Dominic's decisions instead of just blindly following him, things might be different now," she said, an edge of regret tinging her words "Instead, I followed the traditional upbringing I'd had."

I stared at Persephone as we walked side by side, bewildered but grateful for her support. The fierce woman I'd always known her to be was revealing a softer, more vulnerable side I'd never imagined she possessed.

"Persephone, I have to admit, I'm surprised." I glanced at her curiously. "You've always come across so strong and unyielding. I never would have thought you were raised to be a traditional lady of the pack."

She chuckled, shaking her head. "Oh, Liza, appearances can be deceiving. Yes, I was raised to be the perfect mate, to look pretty, and stand by my man's side without question. That doesn't mean I didn't have my own thoughts and opinions on things."

"Then, why didn't you ever say anything? Why did you let Dominic make all the decisions without any input from you?"

"Because that's what I was taught to do." A hint of sadness crept into her words. "It was ingrained in me from a young age. That's just how things were done. And I suppose, in some ways, I was afraid of what might happen if I went against tradition."

"Isn't it better to fight for what you believe in, though?" I said, my own convictions strengthening with each word. "Isn't it worth risking the wrath of tradition if it means creating a better world for ourselves and our loved ones?"

"Absolutely," Persephone's gaze remained steady and determined. "That's why I commend you, Liza. You're doing something I wish I'd had the courage to do when I was younger. You're standing up for yourself and your beliefs, and you're refusing to let anyone, even your own mate, dictate your life for you."

"Thank you," I said, my cheeks flushing with pride. "I just... I don't want history to repeat itself. I don't want us to lose everything we hold dear because we were too afraid to fight for it."

"Nor do I," she said. "That's why I believe in you. You are challenging the status quo, and that might be exactly what we need to ensure our survival. The world is changing, and we can either adapt or die. I, for one, would rather adapt."

"Me, too," I said, a renewed sense of purpose filling me. I was certain the road ahead wouldn't be easy, and there would be plenty of obstacles to overcome, but with the support of people like Persephone, I was more confident than ever that we could get through this. Persephone and I would make sure that history didn't repeat itself. Not on our watch.

***

The door to our bedroom creaked open, and I glanced up from the suitcase spread out on the bed. Ty stood in the doorway, his panicked eyes darting between me and the clothing strewn across the room.

"What are you doing?"

I continued folding a sweater, my heartbeat quickening at the alarm in his voice. "Packing."

"Why are you packing? Where are you going?" he took a hesitant step into the room.

"Because, Ty, it's obvious you'd rather have a mate who's just in the background." My anger bubbled beneath the surface, but I fought to keep it in check. We needed to have this conservation, and I wouldn't let my emotions derail it.

"What. No? That's not true," he protested. "I never said that."

"Actions speak louder than words." I paused to look him straight in the eye. "You made a huge decision about this war without even consulting me. You dismissed my concerns when I confronted you about it." I shook my head. "You don't care about my opinion at all." He needed to understand that I wasn't just some fragile flower who would wilt under the pressure of our situation.

Despite the tremor of emotion threatening to break through, I remained steady and calm. "I don't want to leave, but you have to understand that we're a team. We're supposed to be in this together, and that means making decisions as a couple, especially when those decisions put all our lives on the line."

I paced the floor of our bedroom, my thoughts racing as I considered what Ty's newfound alliance with Hiram, Sven, and even Liam could mean for our future. The air around me was heavy and stifling. The decisions that had been made were physically pressing down on me. My chest ached with worry, not just for Ty, but for all of us. We were walking a dangerous path, and I couldn't shake the notion that we might be heading toward a point of no return.

"Ty." I stopped in front of him as he sat on the edge of the bed and cradled his head in his hands. "I need you to listen."

He looked up, exhausted, and there was a small part of me that didn't like that I was adding to it. "What is it, Liza?"

"There's something else we need to address." I tried to find the right words to convey my concerns without sounding accusatory. "You're not a mob boss like my brother. He was built for that life, and he thrives in it. You? I don't think you're capable of living that life, and you're getting too close to a line you won't be able to come back from."

Ty's expression shifted to one of defensiveness. "Liza, I did what I had to do. We needed their help, and they were willing to give it."

"I understand that," I said. "You need to remember that Hiram, Sven, and even Liam are still mob bosses, though. They have their own agendas, their own goals. Eventually, they may want something from you now they think you're willing to play dirty."

Ty's gaze dropped to the floor, but the conflict played out inside him—I could feel the warring emotions through our bond. He was a good man, an honorable leader, but in his desperation to protect our pack and me, he'd ventured into dangerous territory.

"Maybe you're right," Ty said quietly. "But what do you suggest we do about it now? We can't just walk away from the alliance."

"I know we can't." I sat down beside him on the bed. "But we can be cautious. We can keep our eyes open and make sure we don't get pulled deeper into their world than we absolutely have to be. Most importantly, we need to remember who we are, not just as individuals, but as a pack... and as mates."

I studied the worry lines etched into his forehead and the tiredness in his face. He'd been carrying so much pressure on himself, trying to protect our pack, and maintain alliances with people like Hiram and Sven, who were more dangerous than we'd ever imagined.

I rubbed his arm. "I understand that you needed to send a message. Please, don't lose sight of who you are in the process. You're not like them, and you shouldn't be."

He looked at me as if he was trying to find reassurance in my words. Slowly, he nodded. "You're right. I've let myself get caught up in all of this, and it's not who I am or who I want to be."

"Good." I smiled softly at him. "We need to find our own way through this mess, not just follow in their footsteps."

"Thank you for reminding me of that." Ty pulled me into a tight hug, his warm breath ruffling my hair as he said, "I'm sorry for the way I spoke to you earlier. I've just been so stressed out, and it came out wrong. I promise I'll never leave you out of the loop again."

"Apology accepted," I murmured against his chest, feeling his heartbeat slow and beat steadily beneath my ear. "Just remember that we need to support each other and make decisions as a team."

"Absolutely. Now, I think I need to go for a run. Clear my head a bit. Would you like to join me?"

"Maybe later." I knew he needed some time alone to sort through his emotions. "You go ahead, and we'll talk more when you get back."

"When I get back? So, you'll be here? You're not leaving?"

I nodded, and he pressed a tender kiss to my forehead before releasing me from his embrace. "I love you, Liza."

"Love you, too, Ty."

I sighed, allowing a rare moment to bask in the quiet that settled around me. Ty's scent still lingered in the air, but it was fading as he distanced himself from the house on his run. I appreciated the solitude, even if just for a few minutes.

My phone rang, shattering the silence. Glancing at the screen, I saw Sabrina's name and immediately answered, expecting her usual upbeat greeting. Instead, I was met with a gut-wrenching sob, my best friend's voice cracking under the strain of her pain. Instinctively, my hand clenched around the phone.

"Sa-Sabrina? What's wrong?" I said, fear slamming into me.

"Please..." she said between sobs, and my stomach clenched painfully. I wanted nothing more than to wrap her in my arms and protect her from whatever was causing her this agony.

"Shh, don't say anything," a low, menacing, familiar voice cut in.

The hairs on the back of my neck stood on end, and ice replaced the blood in my veins.

Castro.

"Your friend is in a rather precarious situation, and I'd hate for things to get... messy."

"Castro," I snarled. "What have you done to her?"

"Nothing. Yet," he replied calmly, though the threat was clear. "That depends on you, doesn't it?"

A cold sweat broke out on my forehead. "What do you want?"

"Isn't it obvious?" There was an edge to his voice that sent shivers down my back. He sounded completely unhinged. "I'll call off this little war, Liza. Nobody else has to get hurt. All you have to do is come to me."

"Or what?" I was shaking, betrayed by my fear, despite my best efforts to remain strong.

"Or I'll kill Sabrina, then every member of your family, and every other person you love. If that's not enough, I'll move on to your precious Keller pack, and take them out one by one."

My knees buckled, and I sagged against the wall, my legs too weak to support me.

He paused for a moment, as if savoring the torment he was inflicting upon me. "I'm giving you the choice to come to me, Liza. That being said, if you refuse, I won't hesitate to activate you. And I'm sure you are aware what that means."

The dormant power within me stirred restlessly. If Castro activated me, I would become a weapon of destruction capable of annihilating everything I loved.

I clutched the phone in my hand, Castro's ultimatum bearing down on me. The threat of Sabrina's death hung in the air, and beneath it all was the unspoken menace...

He would take me against my will if necessary.

"Two days," Castro drawled. "I'll text you an address. If you don't show up, Sabrina is dead, and your pack will share her fate."

"Fine." I tried to remain steady. "Just... just don't hurt her."

"Tick tock, Liza." With those chilling words, he ended the call.

Chapter 25 - Ty

We gathered in my office to discuss our next steps. Uncertainty pressed down on us like a heavy cloud. My eyes darted around the room, taking in the faces: Liza, Hiram, Sven, Liam. They were all focused and determined, but something was off.

"Everyone's here." I turned to face them. "Let's get down to business."

"First off," Hiram said gleefully. "Benny's gone underground. That leaves Sven here with the opportunity to take over his territory."

Sven was leaning against the wall, his hands tucked in his pockets. Despite the heavy atmosphere, Sven's self-assured expression was obvious. "I'll have control of Benny's territory soon."

"Good," I said tersely, my mind racing with the potential implications of this development. Gaining control of Benny's territory was a significant advantage for us, but it also raised the question that had been gnawing since our meeting began. "What will Castro do now?

"Anyone got any ideas?" Liam asked, rubbing the back of his neck as he paced around the room, searching for a spark of inspiration, or a nugget of information that might lead us to our next move.

I looked over at Liza, who was usually full of energy and ideas, but she was withdrawn. There was an eerie calmness about her that set me on edge. It was like she was holding back a storm within herself. The sensation nagged, but I couldn't quite put my finger on it.

"Without Benny, Castro's options are limited," Hiram said, scratching his beard thoughtfully. "He's gonna be desperate, and desperate men are unpredictable."

"Unpredictable, yes," I said, my nostrils flaring as I took in the scent of unease wafting through the room. "Not invincible. We need to find him before he finds another way to strengthen his position."

"Perhaps we should gather more intel on his connections and resources," Hiram said. "That way, we can cut him off before he has a chance to strike."

"Good idea," Sven said. "If we can weaken more of his support, we can make it easier to bring him down."

As the conversation carried on, I continued to steal glances at Liza, trying to gauge her emotions. Her blank expression and lack of input only intensified my concern. I knew her well enough to be sure that something was definitely bothering her.

The scent of unease lingered in the air, making my wolf pace restlessly within me. Liza's forced calmness bothered me.

"Listen." Liam leaned forward and placed his palms on the table. "We should take the fight to Castro."

"Easy for you to say," Hiram said. "But we haven't seen a single sign of him since that day outside my restaurant."

"True," Liam said. "Now that Benny's gone, one of the other bosses Castro managed to wrangle in might be hiding him."

"Taking the fight to him would be reckless," Sven said with a shake of his head. "We need more information before we make any moves."

My attention kept drifting back to Liza. Waves of tension emanated from her, making it hard to ignore her unease.

The door suddenly burst open, and Isaiah strode into the room, commanding everyone's attention. "I've got news. Castro has no one else in his corner."

"Are you serious?" Hiram exclaimed. "No one's backing Castro anymore?"

"Exactly what the hell are you talking about, Isaiah?" Suspicion flickered across Sven's face as his eyes narrowed.

I glanced at Liza, but my attention was quickly drawn back to Isaiah when he began to explain himself. The confidence radiated from him as he spoke, leaving no doubt that he believed what he was saying.

"I've been working with moles from other packs for the past few weeks, gathering information," Isaiah explained. "My main goal was to compile a list of everyone who was backing Castro—all the bosses, enforcers, anyone with even a hint of loyalty to that bastard." He paused, gathering his thoughts before continuing, "What I found was that Benny was pretty much the linchpin holding everything together. With him out of the picture, the other bosses have backed out. They think Castro's cause is lost and don't want to risk their own necks over it."

We stared at Isaiah in shock, none of us saying a word as we tried to comprehend what he'd just said.

My heart raced, each beat echoing the building hope within me that maybe, just maybe, the end of this nightmare was in sight. But I couldn't let myself get too carried away until we had more concrete evidence to support Isaiah's claims.

"Can you confirm this, Isaiah?" I asked, trying not to sound too hopeful. "Is there any chance some of them might still be loyal to Castro?"

"From what I gathered, it's highly unlikely." Isaiah's dark eyes met mine. "Of course, there's always a chance some could be hiding their true intentions, but the general consensus among the bosses is that Castro's finished."

The energy in the room shifted, crackling with anticipation and hope. Each face around me brightened at the prospect of Castro's vulnerability. I felt it, too—that sudden spark of exhilaration, knowing we had a real chance at victory.

"Well, goddamn." Hiram smirked, leaning back in his chair as he looked around the room. "I never thought our plan would do this much damage. Good job, everyone."

My pack mates and our allies couldn't contain their excitement, grinning and slapping each other on the back as they celebrated the unexpected turn of events. We may have stopped the war before it had even started.

I should have been celebrating, too, but I kept drifting back to Liza.

She stood apart from the others, her arms crossed and expression distant. The news about Castro's dwindling army had barely registered with her. As I watched her, dread settled in the pit of my stomach. Was there something she wasn't telling me? After all that crap the other day about teamwork, too. Something that might put her or the rest of us in danger?

Hiram cut through the excited chatter. "Let's not get ahead of ourselves. I'm going to confirm what Isaiah told us, speak to the other mob bosses, and find out if they really have backed out. Until I can verify it myself, we need to stay sharp and be ready for anything."

"Of course." I tore my attention away from Liza and met his stern expression. "We'll keep our guard up."

Isaiah huffed. "I'm a reliable source."

"Hey, I know." I chuckled as I patted him on the shoulder. I silently hoped Isaiah knew how much I valued him for all he had done. "You've done amazing work. I'm glad to have you as my informant."

"Thanks," he said, finally cracking a small smile. "I want to help end this as much as any of you. For all our sakes."

"Your efforts haven't gone unnoticed." I slapped his back before turning my attention to the group gathered around the table. Everyone was discussing plans and possibilities,

Liam's hand on my shoulder caught my attention, and I turned to face him, sensing both urgency and resolve in his touch.

"Ty, there's something I need to tell you," he said somberly.

"Sure, what's up?" I asked, my curiosity piqued by his demeanor.

"Once all this is over, I'm going into hiding." The declaration hit me like a punch to the gut, making it hard for me to breathe for a moment. I stared at him, trying to process what he was saying. "I've got things to handle. Things that don't involve Liza. While I'm doing that, I can't be her brother, I need to be the mob boss."

"You sure about that?" Liza would be devastated if her brother just disappeared without a word.

"Positive." Liam's determination was etched into his features. "I can't be around Liza while I'm the mob boss. It'll only put her in danger."

He made a valid point, but it didn't make the situation any easier to swallow.

The thought of Liza losing her brother without knowing why tore at me. I couldn't let him just slip away from her life without a word. She deserved better than that.

I sighed, running a hand through my hair. "You can't just disappear on her. You have to tell Liza what's going on. She needs to understand why you're doing this."

"Ty—"

I held my hand up. "Disappearing is not fair to her. She's your sister, and she loves you. She deserves to be told the truth."

Liam stared for a long moment, his jaw tense and eyes flickering with indecision. Finally, he exhaled heavily, his shoulders slumping in defeat. "Fine. I'll speak to her, but I need to handle one last thing."

"Thank you. It won't be easy, but she needs to hear it from you."

I watched him go. He had promised to talk to Liza, but there was something else hidden beneath the surface. A secret he didn't want to share. I had a feeling our conversation wasn't quite finished.

"Wait."

He stopped and looked over his shoulder.

"You said you have one more thing to handle." Comprehension dawned on me. "Sabrina?" I stared at Liam, concern and disbelief swirling.

He sighed heavily, his expression clouded with uncertainty. "Yeah, it's Sabrina." He rolled his shoulders back. "I'm going to have to break our bond. I'm not even sure how it happened, but I need to reject her. That's how it works with us wolves, so I'm hoping it'll be as easy as that for a human, too."

"Are you sure about this?" From what I'd heard, breaking a bond was painful, like tearing apart one's own soul.

Liam nodded. "I'm a mob boss, Ty. The last thing I need is a mate just so people can put a target on her back." His words were heavy with a sense of duty, but I detected the pain lurking beneath them. Losing a mate was not something anyone took lightly, especially not an alpha wolf like Liam.

As much as I wanted to support him, I worried about Sabrina's wellbeing. She was Liza's best friend. My mate saw her as a sister. I had to ask the question that had been nagging me ever since I'd learned about their bond. "What if rejecting her causes more harm than good?"

"Then, I'll deal with it," Liam answered firmly. "But I can't risk her life by staying connected to her. Not when the stakes are this high."

I understood the logic in his decision, but I still ached for both him and Sabrina. It wasn't a choice being made out of love or desire but rather cold necessity. "I trust you, Liam. Just be careful. Sabrina's important to Liza, and I don't want either of them hurt."

Liam nodded, his face grave. "I'll do everything I can to make this as painless as possible for her. For both of them."

***

I found Liza in the dimly lit kitchen, staring blankly at a row of gleaming knives on the wall. Even from several feet away, I could sense that her usual strong aura had evaporated.

"Hey," I said softly, making my way over to her. "Everyone's gone now. You okay?"

Liza blinked, snapping back to reality, and gave me a smile that didn't quite reach her eyes. "Yeah, I'm fine. Just... exhausted, I guess."

I frowned. There was more to it than that. Her exhaustion wasn't just physical, it wore on her emotionally as well, as if she were trying to hold back a storm within her—one that threatened to break free at any moment.

"Hey," I said softly, putting my arm around her waist. "You should get some rest. We've all been pushing ourselves too hard lately."

She gave me a wan smile. "It's just been a lot, you know? Everything that's happened, everything we're still dealing with..." She trailed off, but I understood what she meant. The constant battles and threats, the looming specter of Castro... it was enough to break anyone down. Through it all, Liza had shown a strength and resilience that awed me.

"I get it," I squeezed her hand gently. "But we've come a long way, and things are starting to look up. The pack is safe, and that's what matters most."

Liza shrugged out of my grasp and drifted to the wall. Her eyes were distant and her body language guarded. She had said she was relieved, but something about her didn't sit right with me. It was as if a veil had been drawn over her emotions, and I couldn't quite see through it.

"You sure you're okay?"

"Yes, Ty, I'm fine. You should focus on finding Castro. Like you said, this won't be over until he's dead."

Her words gave me pause. There was an undercurrent of something in her tone. Fear? Dread? I couldn't quite put my finger on it. My wolf stirred within me, urging me to find out what was wrong with our mate. I trusted Liza, but she sometimes kept things to herself when she thought it would protect others.

I watched her muscles tense as she crossed the room, her slender fingers drumming against her thigh in a nervous rhythm. "I need to keep up with my training," she declared, her voice steady, despite the unease that vibrated beneath the surface. "I'll go find Liam and arrange a time we can spar."

"Actually," I said hesitantly. "Liam left to speak with Sabrina."

Her steps faltered, and she whirled around to face me, the color draining from her face. "What? When?"

"Right after our meeting." I tried to gauge her reaction. "He wanted to talk to her about something."

The tremor of panic that rippled through Liza hit me like a tidal wave, and I instinctively braced myself for whatever was coming next. Instead of an outburst or a flood of tears, the room itself responded to her distress. The faint sound of glass tinkling filled the air as the windows quivered in their frames.

"What's going on, Liza?" I said, my own anxiety heightening as I stepped closer to her, desperate to help in any way I could.

Her eyes locked onto mine, but I wasn't sure she saw me through the shadows of fear. "Castro called me," she whispered so softly I barely heard her, as if saying his name any louder might summon him. "He has Sabrina."

The air around us thickened, choking me as I tried to process what she was telling me. Castro had been one step ahead of us all along.

"Fuck," I hissed, my anger flaring at the thought of him laying a hand on Sabrina or anyone else from our pack. "We need to find her, and fast."

Liza's fingers twisted around themselves nervously. "There's more," she said, her eyes downcast. "Castro told me that if I agreed to meet with him, he would let Sabrina go. He's going to send me a time and a place, but I didn't tell anyone because I was afraid it was a trap. I was going to figure out how to handle it on my own."

"Damn it, Liza." I growled. "You should have told me. You don't have to face him alone."

Looking up, she tried to hide the shimmer of tears in her eyes. "I know," she said, her breath hitching like she was hyperventilating. "I didn't want to put you or anyone else in danger."

Chapter 26 - Liza

Shattering glass had me jolting at the sudden explosion of noise. Ty's face was a storm of fury as he glared at the broken remnants of the vase he'd hurled against the wall.

"Fuck! You were going to just walk right into Castro's hands? Sacrifice yourself for everyone?"

I swallowed hard, guilt and fear knotting in my stomach. My plan had been reckless, but with Sabrina's life hanging in the balance, I hadn't seen any other way. "I had to do something,"

"Something?" He threw his hands up in exasperation. "Risking your own life is not just 'something.'" His nostrils flared as he pulled out his phone, his fingers flying over the screen. "Liam," he nearly snarled into the receiver. "Get your ass back here. Now." He didn't wait for a response before slamming the phone onto the table.

I stood, frozen, as Ty paced the room like a caged animal. My lungs wouldn't take in any more air, and his betrayal and hurt bore down on me.

He was justifiably angry, but I'd had my reasons, damn it.

"I'm sorry. I didn't want to put you or anyone else in danger, but I couldn't just sit by and do nothing while Castro has Sabrina."

"Nothing?" Ty's voice was incredulous, his eyes wild as he typed something in on his phone. Probably ratting me out to Liam. "You don't have to carry this burden alone. You're the one who got upset when I made decisions without you. You told me we need to be a team, work things out as mates. How is this any different?"

I turned away. He'd never understand.

***

The ticking of the grandfather clock in the corner of the room grew louder and louder as we waited for Liam to return. Its relentless rhythm was like a hammer pounding against my skull. Ty's jaw was clenched tight as he paced back and forth in front of the fireplace. I sat on the edge of the sofa, wringing my hands anxiously in my lap.

Ty's anger rolled off him in waves. It wasn't only directed at me, but at himself for not realizing sooner what I had been planning. Even though I understood his concern, I held the firm belief that I had been right to try and go to Castro alone. My best friend's life was hanging in the balance, and I would do anything to save her, even if it meant risking myself.

The front door slammed shut with such force that it made me jump, and I looked up when Liam strode into the room. His face was flushed, his breaths coming in short, sharp pants as though he'd run all the way back to the house. He didn't say a word, but the fury in his eyes spoke volumes.

"Have you lost your goddamn mind?" Liam's words boomed through the room, his usually easygoing demeanor now one of deep-seated fury.

Yep. Ty had texted him. Great.

"Putting yourself in that kind of danger? How could you even think about doing something like that?"

"Because Sabrina is in trouble!" I snapped. "Don't you get it? A complete psychopath is holding her hostage, and I'm supposed to just sit here and do nothing?"

"Look, we're all worried about Sabrina," Liam said softly as he tried to reason with me. The struggle was written in the lines of his face. His wolf had to have been going nuts. "You can't let your emotions cloud your judgment. We need to handle this carefully, strategically. You walking into Castro's clutches isn't going to help anyone."

"Especially not Sabrina," Ty added, his face pleading with me to see reason. *His* reason.

I forced myself to calm down, even though every fiber of my being screamed to act and do something, anything, to save my best friend. "Fine." I threw up my hands. "But we need to act fast. I won't let that monster hurt her any longer than he already has."

The scent of dread hung thick in the air, threatening to choke me as I paced back and forth in the living room. Every heartbeat was a relentless reminder that Sabrina's life hung in the balance. Liam and Ty stood nearby, their expressions grim.

"Castro isn't above murder," Ty said with disgust. "We know what he did to Cecily just to keep her quiet."

"Let's not forget what he sent Liza," Liam added. "He's more than capable of hurting people."

I shuddered. The image of the severed head he had delivered still haunted me in my nightmares. That had been Castro's message. He had wanted me to know just how far he was willing to go to get what he wanted.

I bit hard into the side of my thumb as I struggled to keep my emotions in check. Now he had my best friend in his grasp, ready to inflict whatever twisted horrors he could imagine upon her.

"He'll hurt Sabrina if I don't do what he wants," I whispered. "That's why I was going to..."

"Give yourself up to him," Liam finished for me, his tone heavy with understanding. He locked his gaze onto mine, searching for something. Hope, perhaps? Or maybe just a trace of sanity.

I nodded, swallowing hard. "I thought it was the only way to save her."

"We'll come up with a better plane." Ty stepped closer, finding my hand, and giving it a reassuring squeeze. "We'll find a way to save Sabrina without putting you in danger."

"Ty's right," Liam said. "We can't let Castro win. Not like this."

I drew in a shaky breath. I wanted so badly to believe them, but the cold tendrils of doubt wrapped around my insides, threatening to strangle what little hope remained inside me.

"Remember," Ty said. "You are not a sacrifice. We will not let you walk willingly into Castro's clutches."

The air in the room buzzed with tension as Ty picked up his phone and punched in a number. I rubbed my sweaty palms on my jeans, trying to keep my thoughts from spiraling out of control.

"Isaiah," Ty said curtly. "We need you here. Now."

Within minutes, Isaiah appeared at the front door, concern marring his handsome face.

He stepped into the living room and scanned our faces, taking in the serious expressions before settling on me. "Talk."

"Castro's taken Sabrina," I said shakily. "He wants me to give myself up in exchange for her."

Isaiah's nostrils flared, but his expression otherwise remained calm. "Let's see if we can find her first." He pulled out his laptop, his fingers flying over the keys. "We can try tracking her phone." Isaiah's words were clipped and precise, his attention fully on the screen.

While he worked, I let my mind drift back to Sabrina, her infectious laugh, her vibrant energy, and the way she could always lift my spirits. The thought of her at the mercy of someone like Castro made me sick to my stomach.

"Damn it," Isaiah said under his breath. "Her location services are turned off. All I've got is her last location, right outside Presley Acres."

"Let's break this down," Ty commanded as he leaned over the table. "We need to come up with a plan that takes Castro by surprise."

Liam's fingers thrummed on the table as he considered our options. "If we can catch him off guard, it'll give us the advantage."

Isaiah nodded, rubbing his chin thoughtfully. "So, first things first. We need to make him think Liza hasn't told anyone about Sabrina. If he believes she's acting alone, he won't be prepared for the rest of us."

"Okay, so what's the plan?" I asked, folding my arms, trying to steady my nerves. At least we were going to do something. Action. I needed to take action.

"Here's what I'm thinking," Ty said. "When Castro calls for you, we'll have you agree to meet him, but we'll be hidden nearby, ready to ambush him when he shows up."

"Sounds risky." I bit my lip as I studied the map, my stomach churning at the thought of facing Castro alone. "What if he figures it out?"

"We'll be close," Liam asked, placing a hand on my shoulder, and giving it a gentle squeeze. "We won't let anything happen to you or Sabrina."

"Besides," Isaiah added. "Castro won't be expecting it. He won't expect you to have asked for help if he told you not to. He expects to be obeyed. He'll think he has the upper hand, and that's when we'll strike."

"Something about this still feels off. I can't quite put my finger on it, but... I don't know. I just have a feeling that Castro is smarter than we're giving him credit for."

I tapped my fingers on the table, watching as Liam, Ty, and Isaiah pored over maps and notes, trying to finalize our plan. I couldn't quite get enough air into my lungs. Something felt off. We were missing a vital piece of the puzzle.

"Guys," I said, interrupting their intense discussion. "I don't think this is going to work."

They all turned to me, but Ty spoke first. "Liza, we've been over this a dozen times. We'll be there with you every step of the way, and we won't let anything happen to you or Sabrina."

I shook my head, frustration bubbling up inside me. "That's not what I mean. It's just... I have this gut feeling that Castro is expecting us to try something like this. He's too smart to not have a backup plan in place."

"Your instincts have been right before," Isaiah said, scanning the map as though willing it to reveal some hidden truth. "But we can't just sit here and do nothing while Sabrina's in danger."

"Of course not," I said, agitated by their lack of understanding. "I'm not saying we should give up. I'm saying we need to be smarter about this."

"Maybe you're just worrying too much because of Sabrina," Ty said gently, reaching across the table to squeeze my hand. His touch did little to alleviate my unease.

"Of course, I'm worried about Sabrina," I shot back, my words edged with desperation. "That's why we need to be sure we're doing everything we can to outsmart Castro and get her back safely." I lowered my gaze to the table. "I need to go see my parents." I had a plan, but they couldn't know about it at all. "I just... I need to see them before we move forward with this." My voice wavered slightly as the guilt settled in. I hated this deception.

"Of course," Ty said immediately. "You should spend some time with your family."

"Take a guard with you." Liam's brow furrowed with worry. "We can't be too careful, even though Castro's preoccupied now."

After finding a free guard, I drove straight to my parents' house.

The moment I stepped into my childhood home, a wave of nostalgia hit me. The familiar scent of my mother's cooking filled the air, blending with the comforting creaks and groans of the old house. Just for a second, the world lifted from my shoulders.

"Hey," Mason said, all boisterous and booming as he emerged from the living room, followed closely by Michael.

The sight of my older brothers brought a genuine smile to my face, even as the shadows of fear and uncertainty lingered in my mind.

"Hi, guys," I said, embracing each of them in turn. Mason hugged me tightly, nearly lifting me off the floor, while Michael's embrace was gentler yet no less protective.

"Mom and Dad are in the kitchen," Michael said, his quiet manner contrasting sharply with Mason's exuberance.

"Thanks." I headed toward the warm, inviting glow that spilled from the kitchen doorway. When I entered, I found my parents fussing over a pot of stew on the stove.

"Sweetheart," my mother said, rushing over to hug me. "We were so worried about you."

"Everything's going to be okay." I hugged her tighter, taking comfort in the familiar embrace. It felt like a lifetime since I'd been here, surrounded by the love and support of my family.

"Sit down." My father pulled out a chair for me at the kitchen table. "You must be exhausted."

I sank into the seat. For a few precious moments, I allowed myself to forget the dark path that lay ahead, focusing instead on the laughter and love that filled the room.

While we ate, we chatted about everything and nothing, reminiscing about the past, and sharing updates on our lives. As the evening wore on, the concern etched deeper in my parents' faces, and my brothers watched me with furrowed brows.

"Are you sure you're okay?" Mason asked.

"Really, I'm just glad this will all be over soon." I forced a smile onto my face. The lie tasted bitter on my tongue, but I couldn't bear to burden them with the truth.

"Promise us you'll be careful," Michael said in a soft voice.

"Of course," I assured him, reaching across the table to squeeze his hand. "I promise."

Once the night drew to a close, I hugged each of them tightly. This might be our last moment together. My heart ached with the secret I carried, but I held fast to the belief that my sacrifice would keep them safe.

"Take care of yourself, little sister," Mason said into my ear as he hugged me goodbye.

"Always," I said, tears pricking at the corners of my eyes. With one final glance at the home that had been my sanctuary for so long, I turned away, steeling myself for the battle that lay ahead.

I left my parents' home with my decision settled on me like a shroud, threatening to suffocate me beneath its crushing burden. Ty and Liam were oblivious to my true intentions, and that knowledge tore at me like razor-sharp talons. They couldn't know—not when so much was at risk.

"Are you ready to head back?" the guard asked, breaking through my tumultuous thoughts.

"Let's go." I blew out a breath.

Castro was cunning, but I would not let him win. For Sabrina, for my family, and for myself, I was going to end this.

As I approached the estate, the sight of it filled me with bittersweet emotions. It was a haven in the midst of chaos, and yet tonight, it might become a symbol of loss. The soft glow of the porch light beckoned me inside, and I braced myself.

"Hey," Ty said as I entered, clearly relieved to have me back in his sight. "How was your time with your family?"

"Good," I said softly, trying to act as normal as possible. "I needed that." How should someone act when they were lying to their mate before a big, dangerous rescue mission?

"Come here," he said, opening his arms.

I melted into his embrace, savoring his strength around me.

This was the calm before the storm. It swirled around us as we sat together in our bedroom. Knowing what I had planned and that I'd be going into danger fueled the fire that burned between us.

I leaned up and kissed him greedily. "Fuck me, Ty."

"Are you sure? Now?" Ty breathed.

I nodded, not trusting myself to speak. There was no turning back now. As I stepped closer to him, the scent of him wrapped around me, intoxicating me even more. "I need you," I whispered, my voice trembling. "Now, more than ever."

His lips found mine, and it was as if a dam had burst inside me, unleashing a torrent of passion and longing.

Our mouths moved hungrily against each other, tongues tangling, and teeth nipping, as if we couldn't get enough. Ty's hands roamed over my body, leaving a trail of heat in their wake. I clawed at his shirt, desperate to feel the hard planes of his chest beneath my palms.

"Off," I gasped, pulling away from him just long enough to yank his shirt up and over his head.

He complied without hesitation, revealing the muscular expanse of his torso. I let out a shaky breath, drinking in the sight of him. His broad shoulders, chiseled pecs, and rippling abs were a testament to his strength and power, and I wanted all of it.

Without waiting for permission, I pressed my lips to his collarbone, trailing warm kisses along the curve of his neck before working my way down his chest. He shuddered beneath me, his hands tangling in my hair, urging me on.

"Please," he whispered, his voice strained with need. "Liza, please."

I couldn't deny him anything. Lowering myself to my knees, I unbuttoned and unzipped his jeans, tugging them down along with his boxers, until he stood before me, fully exposed. My eyes widened at the sight of his impressive length, but I didn't hesitate. I wanted to taste him.

Taking him into my mouth, I savored his taste on my tongue, the velvety smoothness of his flesh contrasting with the hard steel beneath. Ty groaned, his fingers tightening in my hair as I began to move, taking him deeper with each stroke. His breathing grew ragged as I increased my pace, and soon he was thrusting in and out of my mouth.

"Fuck." He gasped, his hips bucking involuntarily. "You're going to be the death of me."

"I want you to taste me, too," I panted, feeling a desperate need for more of him. He hesitated for only a moment before his eyes darkened with desire.

He pushed me back and crawled onto the bed, settling his head between my legs. His fingers teased the sensitive skin of my inner thighs before he lowered his mouth to me, his tongue darting out to lap at the folds of my sex. I gasped, arching into him as pleasure coiled in my belly, then spread through my veins like wildfire.

Ty's tongue explored every inch of me until I was writhing beneath him. He teased and tantalized with each stroke, driving me further and further over the edge until I was hanging on tightly, desperate for release.

When I could take no more, I shattered into a million pieces as a wave of sheer ecstasy crashed over me.

It wasn't enough.

"Ty," I whispered. I couldn't muster my voice any louder. "I need you inside me."

He pulled away from me, his eyes blazing with lust and something deeper—a bond that went beyond the physical, tying us together on a primal level. Wordlessly, he positioned himself at my entrance, his gaze never leaving mine as he thrust into me.

The sensation was indescribable. It was if all my senses were heightened, and every nerve ending was alive with pleasure. Ty moved slowly yet deeply, filling me completely as we joined in a rhythm as old as time itself.

My breaths came out in rasps as my body responded to his every thrust, the intensity escalating with each passing second. Ty groaned against me, his hands gripping my hips as I tightened around him. Suddenly, I was soaring, my whole being consumed by a wave of pleasure that left me trembling and gasping for more.

My body was alive, and my heart stopped as Ty moved. He trembled, his control slipping as we built toward something beautiful and divine. His eyes never left mine, the intensity of his gaze only adding to the intensity of the moment.

"Ty!" I cried out, feeling myself on the brink of something extraordinary. "Please, don't stop!"

"Never," he panted, his voice strained with desire. He drove himself into me one final time, pushing us both over the brink and into oblivion.

The force of my orgasm sent shockwaves through my entire body.

Our cries of ecstasy rang out in unison, our bodies shaking with the force of our release.

As the world slowly came back into focus, Ty's arms were around me again, holding me close as we fought to catch our breaths.

"Whatever happens tomorrow," he whispered, pressing a gentle kiss to my forehead, "know that I love you, Liza."

"Always," I murmured back, guilt niggling at my gut.

When Ty finally fell asleep, his body satiated and relaxed against mine, I gently disentangled myself from his embrace, careful not to wake him, and I silently climbed out of bed and began to move. With my resolve steeled, I took one last look at Ty's sleeping form. He looked so peaceful in slumber, his chest rising and falling with each steady breath. I pushed down the guilt at keeping my true intentions from him. As much as it hurt me, involving them would only put everyone at greater risk.

"Please let this work," I whispered, praying to whatever divine force might be listening. "Keep him safe."

Though Castro was cunning and ruthless, he could also be predictable. Every move he'd made so far had been calculated, every step planned in advance. If there was one thing I knew about him, it was that he loved poetic justice. It was both his greatest strength and his Achilles' heel.

My gut told me exactly where he was holding Sabrina—the place where everything had started all those years ago. The very location that had set the course for our lives, intertwining them in a twisted dance of fate and vengeance.

As I crept quietly through the house, my footsteps light against the wooden floors, my decision settled heavily. Was I making the right choice? Would my actions ultimately save Sabrina and protect my pack, or would they lead us all to ruin?

I couldn't afford to doubt myself now. I had come too far and lost too much to turn back. This was the only way, the only path that led to any hope of saving my best friend and securing our future.

***

The cool night air stung my skin as I stepped out of the house, closing the door softly behind me, and creeping into the ethereal, moonlit landscape. The urgency of my mission pushed any discomfort to the back of my mind. I glanced around, ensuring that I was alone before I shifted. My bones cracked and rearranged themselves, fur sprouting from my pores until I stood on all fours as a sleek, powerful wolf.

I hesitated for a moment, taking one last look back at the house that had become my sanctuary. Memories of laughter and love filled my thoughts, threatening to overwhelm me with their intensity. But I couldn't dwell on those now. I had a mission to complete.

I lifted my snout to the sky, inhaling deeply. The scents of the forest, fallen leaves, and the faint traces of nocturnal creatures stirred something inside me. This was a part of who I was, both as a human and a wolf. All spoke to a part of me that was wild and free.

My heart pounded as I pushed aside my fears and doubts. Sabrina needed me, and I would not let her down.

As I began to move through the woods, my instincts guiding me toward my destination, I knew my life would never be the same. If it meant saving the ones I loved, then I would face whatever came my way without hesitation or regret.

With a sudden burst of energy, I lunged forward, my paws finding purchase on the soft ground as I raced through the shadows. The wind whipped past me, tugging at my fur, and I reveled in the sensation of freedom that came with running through the woods. Even as I embraced the wildness within me, my gut twisted and turned.

Please let this work, I thought like a mantra, each beat of my heart echoing the sentiment. *Please let this work.*

When I neared Heather Falls, the sound of rushing water became more pronounced, growing louder with each stride I took. I sensed Castro's presence nearby, like an insidious darkness lurking just beyond my reach. Though I tried to focus, his twisted grin and cold eyes haunted my thoughts, reminding me of the danger I was about to face.

But I couldn't let fear hold me back when Sabrina's life was on the line.

I growled, shaking off the tendrils of doubt that threatened to ensnare me. I could do this.

My ears flicked back and forth, straining to catch any sound beyond the thunderous roar of the waterfall. It was more than just my senses that told me he was near. I could *feel* that heavy, malevolent presence. Castro was here, and he knew I was coming.

A cold laugh echoed through the night. "I must admit, I wondered if you'd figure it out," Castro taunted from the shadows.

I snarled, my sides heaving, and my anger burning like wildfire, fueled by the image of Sabrina in pain, and the knowledge that Castro was the cause.

As if on cue, he emerged from the trees with a sinister grin plastered across his face.

I fought to steady my breath and calm my racing heart. It was too late to turn back now. I had made my choice, and I could only hope it was the right one.

"Ah," Castro said, smugly satisfied. "I must admit, I'm impressed that you chose to come on your own. It shows a certain... *courage*."

His words sickened me, but I refused to let him see how much they affected me, so I bared my teeth at him.

He chuckled darkly, taking in my tense posture and narrowed eyes. "You always were a feisty one, weren't you? Don't worry. I'll make this easy for you."

Castro gestured to the shadows behind him, and my stomach leaped into my throat when Sabrina emerged, her face pale and bloodied, her arms bound tightly behind her back.

"Come here," he said, his tone deceptively gentle. "And I'll release your friend."

My entire body trembled with fear and relief. Sabrina was alive. Battered and bruised, but alive. If all I had to do to save her was walk a few steps closer to Castro, then so be it.

As I moved toward him, a slew of emotions rushed through me. Anger at Castro for putting us in this position. Guilt for betraying Ty and Liam by coming here alone. Underneath it all, a simmering promise that no matter what happened next, I would make sure Sabrina walked away from this nightmare unscathed.

I shifted and simply pretended I wasn't stark naked. "Very well," I said through a tight mouth, stopping just a few feet in front of Castro. "Now, let her go."

His eyes glittered with amusement as he studied me, clearly enjoying the power he held over us. For a moment, I was afraid he'd change his mind and that he'd decide Sabrina's life wasn't worth sparing after all. Then, with a cruel smile, he released her.

"Please, Liza, don't." Sabrina sobbed. "There has to be another way."

My gaze flicked between Sabrina and Castro, his smug grin only fueling my resolve.

"Stay strong, Sabrina," I said, my voice barely audible. "I promise you everything will be okay."

With that, I took a determined step toward Castro. The ground shifted beneath my feet as though acknowledging the gravity of my decision.

His evil eyes gleamed with satisfaction, but I refused to let him see how much he affected me. I was doing this for Sabrina, and no one else.

"Good girl," Castro purred, sickeningly sweet. "Now, come closer."

"Let her go first," I said, my tone unwavering. If he thought I was going to blindly follow his orders without securing Sabrina's safety, he was sorely mistaken.

"Fine," he reluctantly said, pushing Sabrina savagely toward a broken tree stump as she screamed.

Castro reached out and grabbed me, holding me tightly to him, the lecherous look in his eyes making me sick to my stomach.

I had to trust my plan.

Chapter 27 - Ty

A sudden jolt tore me from my sleep, and an inexplicable sense of dread washed over me. My ears strained for any sound as my heart hammered. The first thing I noticed was the cold, empty space beside me.

"Liza?" I called out. Even as I said her name, I realized I couldn't sense her presence in the house.

I bolted upright, my instincts screaming that something was wrong. The sheets tangled around my legs as I stumbled out of bed, my senses sharpening, trying to pick up any trace of her. Instead, the silence felt oppressive, like a soundproof dome had been placed over the room. With each inhale, I tasted the stale air. It held no scent of her.

"Damn it," I muttered, my frustration mounting. Liza's disappearance didn't make sense. I pushed open the bedroom door, my footsteps echoing through the empty hallways. The wooden floorboards creaked beneath me, but I barely heard them over the blood pounding in my ears. When I reached the stairs, I caught a glimpse of moonlight filtering through the windows.

"Where are you, Liza?" I whispered, more to myself than anyone else. I needed to find her. The thought of anything happening to her had fear stampeding through me, but I couldn't do this alone. I needed Liam.

"Liam!" I hollered, the sound echoing through the house. "Wake the hell up!"

In mere seconds, Liam appeared in the doorway, his eyes wide and alert, his chest heaving as though he'd just awoken from a nightmare. "What's wrong?"

"Liza's gone."

"Shit." Liam cursed again, running his fingers through his disheveled hair. "We have to find her."

"Damn right we do." I paced back and forth, my body as taut as a bowstring. "She must've gotten a message from Castro and went to him instead of telling us. Why the hell would she do that when we had such a solid plan?"

"Maybe we're missing something." Liam rubbed at his stubbled jaw, his expression troubled. "Either way, we have to find her. Now."

"Agreed." We shared a look of determination before setting off through the house. The air was thick with tension, making it hard for me to breathe, or maybe that was just the fear. Whatever the cause, I couldn't shake the feeling that Liza was in grave danger, and it was up to us to save her.

"Any ideas on where she could be?" Liam asked, his voice tight as we raced down the hallway.

I glanced at the clock, my heart pounding. It had only been an hour since we'd gone to bed. Liza couldn't have gone far. I tried to shove down the panic and took a deep breath.

"Let's check the house first," I said.

Liam nodded, but his expression remained grim as we hurried through the darkened hallways.

We searched every room, calling out Liza's name over and over, but there was no sign of her. My frustration mounted with each passing second, and I felt like a caged animal desperate to escape. With every fiber of my being, I wanted to find Liza, to keep her safe from the monster who had haunted us for so long.

"Nothing," Liam muttered when we met up in the hallway again. "She's not here."

"Then, let's check the garage," I suggested, my mind racing with possibilities. We jogged down the stairs, our footfalls echoing through the empty house.

The garage was just as silent, and all the cars were accounted for. I cursed under my breath, slamming my fist against the wall. Where the fuck could she have gone?

"Maybe she didn't leave by car," Liam said, trying to think logically despite our mounting desperation. "Let's talk to the guards at the gate."

We sprinted toward the entrance, the cold night air biting at our skin as we rushed to the gates. The guards looked startled when they saw us approaching, their eyes wide with concern.

"Did Liza leave through here?" I demanded, my patience wearing thin.

"No," one of the guards answered, shaking his head. "We haven't seen her."

"Fuck!" I growled, raking my fingers through my hair. Helplessness was a bitter pill I refused to swallow.

"Wait," Liam said suddenly, his eyes narrowing in thought. "Castro... he's a creature of habit, right? This all started because of what happened at Heather Falls."

I blinked at him, then realization dawned on me. How could we have been so blind?

"Let's go," I said. "We're not wasting another second."

Liam and I locked eyes, a silent understanding passing between us. With an almost imperceptible nod, we bolted out of the house and shifted into our wolf forms, the transformation swift and familiar. Our powerful paws pounded against the ground as we raced toward Heather Falls at full speed. The sensation of wind whipping through my fur and the earth trembling beneath me was both exhilarating and anxiety-inducing. Castro was going to pay for what he'd done.

The woods were a blur of shadows and moonlight, a haunting déjà vu of that fateful night when everything had changed. As we ran, the world around us seemed both foreign and intimately familiar. My heightened senses picked up every rustle of leaves and distant snap of twigs, each sound feeding the fire of determination burning within me. I would not let Liza down again. I would make sure she was safe.

Come on, Liam, I urged internally, knowing he couldn't hear me in our wolf forms, but hoping somehow that my thoughts would reach him. *We have to save her.*

Liam responded by picking up speed, his sleek form effortlessly gliding alongside mine. We were a team, bound together by blood and a shared purpose. Together, we would put an end to Castro's reign of terror.

As we neared our destination, the familiar roar of rushing water filled my ears. Heather Falls loomed ahead, its cascading waters a veil of silver in the moonlight. My heart hammered, anticipation and fear warring within me as we closed the distance.

And then, piercing through the night, we heard it. Sabrina's voice, sharp with terror, crying out, "No, Liza!"

In that instant, adrenaline surged through my veins, lending strength to my already powerful limbs. We burst through the tree line, coming upon the scene that would forever be etched into my memory.

No! The word echoed through my mind, reverberating with the force of a thousand screams. I couldn't let this happen. Not again.

The moment we broke through the trees, my heart clenched at the sight before me. Castro's powerful arm tossed Sabrina to the side with alarming force. Her body slammed into a nearby tree and crumpled to the ground like a discarded ragdoll.

My voice echoed, raw and guttural, as I shifted back into human form. *"Stop!"*

Liam did the same, his snarl fierce and eyes blazing with fury. We would not let this monster take our family from us. Not without a fight.

"Ah, Ty and Liam," Castro sneered, looking utterly deranged. His fingers clawed into Liza's arm as she struggled against him, her face contorted with pain and determination. "I've been waiting for you."

"Let her go!" Liam growled, taking a step forward, fury snapping in the air around him.

Castro smirked, pure evil radiating from his twisted gaze. "You know, I'd love nothing more than to rip your throat out, Ty, but I need you alive to keep Liza breathing." He paused, his eyes narrowing thoughtfully. "I think I'll just keep you as a slave so you can live to see me making her mine over and over again."

"Over my dead body," I spat, my entire being focused on protecting Liza and stopping Castro. The air crackled with tension, the scent of blood and fear heavy in the night.

My chest tightened at the sight of Liza struggling in Castro's grip, and a growl rumbled through me. Her eyes met mine, pleading with me to understand something I couldn't yet grasp.

"Ty," she murmured, shaking her head slightly. "Trust me."

I snarled, my body tensing as if preparing for an attack. Whatever plan Liza had in mind, I needed to be ready, but seeing her held captive by that monster made it difficult. I wouldn't let him take her from me.

Liam crouched next to Sabrina, who lay crumpled against a tree trunk. He gently touched her face. The scent of her blood made my stomach churn.

"Get her out of here," I told Liam, not taking my eyes off Castro. "She needs help."

Liam shook his head. "I'm not leaving Liza, Ty. Not again."

"I know, but you're Sabrina's mate. She needs you, too." My heart ached for Liam, torn between protecting his sister and the woman he was destined to be with.

A cold sweat broke out on my skin as Castro's threat hung in the air, heavy and suffocating. Liam stood his ground, his eyes flicking between Liza and Sabrina.

"Aw, how noble of you," Castro sneered, tightening his grip on a now-still Liza. "But remember, if you don't let me leave with her, I'll activate her. She'll kill her brother and best friend without a second thought."

My jaw clenched, the muscles there twitching with barely contained rage. How could he do this? Use Liza against us like that? My vision blurred red. We needed a plan, and fast.

"Handle me," Liza suddenly said, her voice calm and steady despite the situation.

"Wh—" I began, but stopped myself, realizing her words were meant for Liam. My heart pounded, my mind racing to catch up with what Liza was saying. She had a plan, and she needed Liam to trust her.

Liam glared at Castro. "You want to play this sick game? Let's play."

My heart raced in anticipation, wondering how this would play out. Liam's smirk widened as he understood Liza's plan. Castro gritted his teeth and raised his hand, attempting to activate her. But before he could utter the word, Liam beat him to it.

"*Nachinat*," Liam said confidently, a glint of triumph in his eyes.

Castro's eyes widened, and he screamed with rage. "No! You can't do that!"

I remained as still as stone, watching the scene unfold before me. Liza's head dropped, her body going limp. It was as if she'd suddenly become a puppet, waiting for someone to pull her strings. Castro hesitated, slowly stepping away from her. Liza's movements were slow and mechanical as she turned to face Liam.

"Give me my mission," she requested, her voice void of emotion.

Chapter 28 - Liza

I blinked, trying to focus as my world swirled around me. I felt like a stranger in my own body, as if something had come undone. To my left, someone was yelling, their voice strained and desperate. I turned my head slightly, my vision hazy as I tried to make out the face that should have been familiar, but it was like grasping at a memory that kept slipping through my fingers.

"Get away from her!"

My gaze shifted to my handler. He, too, seemed oddly familiar, yet distant at the same time. His eyes locked onto mine, and his lips curled into a smile.

"Remember what I told you, Liza," he said. "I promised I'd never use you, and I meant it."

I stared at him, confusion flooding my mind. What was he talking about? And why did his words hold such weight?

"Listen carefully," he continued, his eyes never leaving mine. "You're free from your shackles, but I need you to do me a favor. Help me end the life of the man who took our father from us."

"What?" My voice trembled as I fought to make sense of his words. My heart pounded, and the blood rushed through my veins.

"Once Castro is dead, you'll deactivate forever."

A shock of lightning tore through my head, the pain so intense I was certain death would claim me. Just as suddenly as the agony had arrived, it vanished, leaving me gasping for breath and clinging to consciousness. As I became aware of my surroundings once more, I found Ty at my side, his gray eyes wide with concern.

"Are you okay?" he asked, gripping my arm tightly.

I nodded, still trying to catch my breath. "Yeah, I'm fine," I managed, although I wasn't entirely sure that was true. A niggling sensation tugged at the back of my mind, like a command I had to fulfill. My gaze darted around, searching for Castro, but he was nowhere to be seen.

"Castro took off for the trees." Ty followed my line of sight.

The urgency of the command in my brain grew stronger. I tried to rise, but Ty held me back.

"Wait. We need to come up with a plan first."

"I can't," I told him, my whole body straining with the effort of resisting the compulsion. "I was given a command, and I have to follow it. I can't ignore it."

"For fuck's sake, Liam," Ty muttered under his breath, his anger palpable, but there was also an understanding in his eyes. We both knew it was better for Liam to have given the command than Castro. At least now I had the freedom to choose when to deactivate. And for the moment, I was buzzing with energy—an energy I needed to use to take Castro out.

"I know you wanted to be the one to do this, but it has to be me." I stood, wincing slightly as my body protested. "I have to be the one to take him down."

Ty hesitated for only a moment before nodding grimly. "Fine, but I'm coming with you."

"Thank you," I whispered, my heart swelling with love.

Liam stayed with Sabrina, ensuring she was safe as Ty and I took off toward the woods. We raced through the underbrush, our senses heightening as we tracked Castro's scent. My muscles ached from the strain of pushing myself to my limits, but the adrenaline coursing through my veins kept me going. The cool night air stung my nostrils as I breathed heavily, the earthy forest scents mingling with the coppery tang of blood spilled earlier.

"Stay alert," Ty warned as we moved deeper into the woods. "Castro won't go down without a fight."

As we made our way deeper into the forest, my senses sharpened, and I caught the smell of worms in the ground, termites in the trees, while the sound of rustling branches and distant growls echoed around us. My skin prickled with awareness, and I could almost taste the electricity in the air.

Every molecule of air brushed against my skin, and I sniffed, picking up on Castro's scent among the crisp pine needles. He reeked of sweat and something darker, more sinister.

"Can you feel that?" I murmured to Ty, my eyes darting around the shadows cast by the towering trees.

"Feel what?" he asked, his voice tense and alert.

"Castro. He's close." My muscles itched, eager to take action.

"Wait," Ty whispered, stopping in his tracks.

I paused as well, realizing he'd picked up on something. Our surroundings seemed to come alive with movement. We weren't alone.

"An ambush?" I growled, baring my teeth as I searched for the source of the threat.

Ty stiffened, his body language mirroring my own wariness. "Looks like it."

From behind us, Sven appeared, his expression grim. "Did you really think we'd be the only ones here?"

For a moment, I bared my teeth instinctively, thinking he had betrayed us. But Sven held up his hands in a placating gesture. "Relax. There's still a battle happening. Castro has men all over, waiting to attack. I've got my own guys placed, though. Tonight's fight won't be as big as it would've been if Benny had stayed involved. We got word of this and arrived as quickly as we could, but I sensed you two were already here. Go on, find Castro," Sven urged. "My men will handle the rest."

"Thank you," I said, though it was difficult to convey true gratitude when I was so focused on the mission Liam had given me.

As Ty and I made our way through the trees, men materialized out of nowhere and made to grab me, but I was on another level now, activated and driven by a single-minded determination to fulfill my command.

"Get back!" I snarled, kicking one attacker in the chest with enough force to send him flying into a tree trunk. Another came at me from behind, but Ty intercepted him, landing a vicious punch that left the assailant's face bloody and broken.

"Nicely done," Ty grunted as he scanned the surroundings.

"Thanks," I replied. "You're not too bad yourself."

Sven's men appeared just in time to handle the remaining attackers, allowing Ty and me to continue our hunt for Castro. We came across more of his henchmen, but they were no match for our combined strength.

My heart pounded while we pressed on. The cool night air felt almost electric on my skin, and the forest seemed alive with the sounds of our pursuit—the crunch of leaves underfoot, the distant echoes of Sven's men fighting, and the steady beat of our hearts as we closed in on our prey.

The forest's shadows seemed to reach out and claw at us as Ty and I moved cautiously through the trees. The ground beneath my feet felt strangely comforting, grounding me despite the chaos unfolding around us.

"Almost there," Ty muttered under his breath, his eyes scanning the darkness for any sign of our target.

My heart raced with a mixture of dread and determination. We had to end this not just for ourselves, but for everyone affected by Castro's twisted machinations.

When we rounded a bend and emerged into a small clearing, the sight that greeted us sent shivers down my spine. Castro stood at the center of it all, his entire body practically vibrating with rage. His snarl was feral, his eyes cold and deadly as they locked onto mine.

"You!" he spat, his voice dripping with venom. "Traitor!" He bared his teeth at us. "How could you betray your own pack?"

"You were never part of our pack. You killed my father, and now you'll pay for what you've done."

The moment our eyes locked, I knew there would be no mercy or remorse. This was a battle to the death, and only one of us would walk away alive.

As I charged forward, I thought of the family Castro had taken from me, the love and warmth I'd been denied for so long, and it gave me strength.

"Let's end this," I whispered, closing the gap between us.

With a final surge of energy, Ty and I lunged at Castro, the world narrowing down to this one moment, and this one fight for justice and revenge.

Then, there was only the fight.

Chapter 29 - Ty

The air crackled with tension as Liza and I circled Castro, our wolf forms lean and powerful. My ears twitched at the distant howls from the other packs, and the scent of blood spurred me on. My heart thudded as I fought the urge to leap forward and tear into Castro, but this was Liza's fight.

I growled, and she responded with a low snarl that sent goosebumps down my spine. She was ready. We charged together, our paws pounding against the earth, and leaped at Castro. He twisted away with a snarl, swiping a paw across Liza's flank. She yelped, but her eyes burned with fierce determination.

Before I could land a blow on Castro, his backup arrived. Men in various stages of shifting burst out of the trees, lunging for me with claws and teeth bared. Their attacks came fast and relentless, forcing me to dodge and weave between them.

I snarled and snapped at the wolves attacking me, feeling the sting of their claws tearing into my fur.

Despite the pain, my instincts took over, painting the world in red and black as I ripped through my attackers. Their numbers dwindled, but each time one went down, another seemed to take its place.

Where were they all coming from?

I couldn't keep up with what was happening with Liza and Castro. My building rage had my heart nearly tearing out of chest.

"Ty!"

Liam's yell cut through my thoughts like a bullet. He burst through the trees, shifting into his own wolf form, larger and stronger than any I'd seen before. Together, we made short work of the remaining wolves attacking me.

The injured wolves lay scattered around us, their whimpers filling the air. The vibrations of their pain resonated within me as my attention was drawn back to Liza and Castro. The fur along my spine bristled at the sight of them locked in battle. A surge of protectiveness coursed through me, urging me to aid Liza, but a firm grip on my shoulder stopped me in my tracks.

I glanced over, watching as Liam shifted back into his human form, his expression serious. "You have to let Liza do this."

I shifted back to human form, too, snarling, yearning to rip Castro apart. "Are you insane? She could be killed!"

"Trust her," Liam insisted, his eyes unwavering. "This is her mission, Ty. Once it's done, she'll be free of what our father did. She needs this."

I stared at him, my heart pounding against my ribs like a caged animal. The taste of fear lingered on my tongue, mixed with the scent of blood and sweat. Liam was right. Liza needed this victory for her own revenge, for her peace, but it felt like a thousand needles were drilling into my chest as I forced myself to stay put.

"Stay with me," Liam murmured. "We'll be here if she needs us."

"Of course," I replied through gritted teeth, watching as Liza dodged another swipe from Castro.

My senses were on high alert: the metallic tang of blood in the air, the sound of their snarls and growls, the sight of Liza's graceful movements, the taste of dirt and sweat on my tongue, and the feel of Liam's calming presence beside me.

"Come on, Liza," I muttered under my breath, my eyes never leaving her as she circled Castro.

"Ty," Liam's voice was a low growl in my ear. "Remember who she is."

My gaze flicked to him for a moment, his determined expression mirroring my own. "I know," I whispered, turning back to the fight. "But it doesn't make this any easier."

"Nothing worth fighting for ever is," he replied softly, and I couldn't help but agree.

Chapter 30 - Liza

I lunged at Castro, my claws slashing through the air. He dodged with surprising agility for someone his size, and I could feel the weight of his stare—a dangerous mix of fury and obsession. Sweat trickled down my brow, mingling with the coppery taste of blood on my tongue.

He growled, circling me like a predator. The air was thick with tension as I faced Castro, my heart pounding. No longer the object of his twisted obsession, I was now his enemy. He lunged at me with a roar.

Our battle began in earnest, a deadly dance of snarls, snapping teeth, and claws sinking into flesh. I could taste blood in my mouth—mine and his—as we fought with everything we had. Though my parents hadn't been perfect, they were still my family, and Castro had torn them from me. He'd destroyed any chance I had at a normal life, and I couldn't let him win.

It was during one particularly brutal exchange that I realized how close I was to committing murder. I didn't know if I was capable of it, but as I looked into Castro's hate-filled eyes, I knew there could be no peace for me, for Ty, unless he was dead. That realization both terrified and strengthened me.

He raked his claws across my side. Pain flared through me, and for a moment, I feared he might have the upper hand.

But then, echoing through the night, I heard Ty's howl. It pierced the darkness like a beacon, and I knew that if I died here, he would die, too. I couldn't—wouldn't—let Castro have that power over us.

My heart thundered, a wild rhythm that matched the chaos unfolding around me. I leaped forward, my wolf form propelling me through the air, and landed on top of Castro, our snarls and growls echoing through the night. His eyes blazed with rage, but underneath it all, I could sense his shock.

For a moment, something like fear flickered in his eyes, and then he surged forward with one last desperate attempt to break free. But I was ready for him, and I used his own momentum against him, slamming him into the ground with a force that rattled my bones.

I howled, pressing my paw down on his chest and pinning him beneath me, letting him know it was over.

The look in his eyes changed then, from anger and defiance to a sort of resignation, and with a shudder, he shifted back into his human form.

"Please," he rasped, blood staining his lips. "Don't kill me. I swear, I'll leave you and your family alone. You'll never see me again."

I stared down at him, still in my wolf form, my ears twitching as I listened to the distant howls of Ty and the others. Was it really possible that I could just let him go? That he would disappear from my life forever? The old Liza, the one who hadn't been tormented by him, wanted to believe him and consider his plea, to give him grace and trust that this nightmare could finally be over.

The new me, though? She knew better. This wasn't just about me anymore. It was about all the lives he'd ruined, and all the pain he'd caused. If I let him go now, who was to say he wouldn't come back someday seeking revenge?

"Please," he said again, tears streaming down his face. "I'll do anything."

I shifted, looking the man in the face. He smiled, an evil, victorious smile, believing he'd appealed to my humanity. No more. I had a mission, and I wanted it over. A growl rumbled deep within me, and before I knew what I was doing, I shifted my hand and drove my claw into his chest, piercing his heart. His eyes widened in shock, and as the life drained from his body, the realization of what I'd done hit me like a tidal wave.

Castro was dead. I was free.

The second his heart stopped beating, and the last breath gurgled out of him, a second sharp charge ripped through my head, forcing a pained howl from my lips. My vision blurred, with darkness creeping in around the edges as I struggled to maintain consciousness.

"Stay with me," a distant voice urged, barely audible over the ringing in my ears. "You can't give up now."

But it was too late. The darkness swallowed me whole, and I blacked out.

The sterile scent of the hospital room greeted me when I stirred back to consciousness. The steady beeping of a heart monitor was a comforting reminder that I was alive, and I blinked my eyes open, taking in the unfamiliar surroundings.

"Thank God." Ty sounded all choked with emotion as he wiped tears from his cheeks, his relief evident. "You're awake."

"What happened?" I asked groggily, struggling to sit up. My body ached all over, but the pain was bearable.

"You were screaming in pain and then you blacked out," he explained, concern etched on his face. "We got you here as fast as we could."

"Is Castro..." I trailed off, unsure if I wanted to know the answer.

Liam stepped forward, a somber look in his eyes. "He's dead. You killed him."

I shuddered at the thought, memories of the brutal fight replaying in my mind. Before I could dwell on it, Liam uttered the dreaded word, "*Nachinat.*"

Ty snarled at him, but nothing happened. There was no overwhelming urge to submit, no uncontrollable wolf instincts—just me, blinking at the men in confusion.

Liam sagged in relief. "You never have to worry about being controlled anymore. You're free."

"Will I still go berserk one day?" I asked cautiously, afraid of what freedom might mean for an omega like me.

Liam shook his head. "Omegas only went crazy because their brains were being messed with every time they were activated. You won't have that problem anymore."

Relief washed over me, and I found myself grinning. "I do feel lighter," I admitted. "And my wolf seems more relaxed than she's ever been."

"Good," Liam said, embracing me in a tight hug. "I promised I'd save you, and I'm glad I could keep that promise."

His words were bittersweet, almost like a goodbye. "Liam, what's going on?"

"Being a faceless mob boss for so many years has its consequences," he explained, avoiding my gaze.

"There are people who want me dead. I'll still be around, but I have to return to my world."

"What about Sabrina?" I questioned. "Are you just going to leave her?"

He sighed, pain clouding his eyes. "She's not meant to be part of my world, Liza. I won't be claiming her. Promise me you'll never tell her what she is to me."

"Is that really the best choice? She deserves to know."

"Please. It's the only way I can keep her safe. If my enemies find out what she means to me, she'll become a target." It cost him a lot to ask this of me.

Finally, with tears streaming down my face, I whispered, "I promise." Even as I said the words, I knew I'd end up breaking them. Liam and Sabrina deserved to know the love a mating bond could bring.

"Thank you," he breathed, kissing the top of my head. "I'll see you soon." Turning to Ty, he instructed, "Take care of my sister." And with those final words, Liam left the room.

When the door closed behind him, I was left with a mixture of relief, sadness, and newfound freedom, all tangled up in an uncertain future.

Chapter 31 - Liza

I sat beside Sabrina's hospital bed, picking at the edge of the rough blanket draped across my legs. Sabrina fiddled with the cast on her broken arm, which was the only evidence remaining of her collision with a tree. She stared blankly at the ceiling, still trying to process everything that had happened. The rhythmic beep of the heart monitor played like a metronome, punctuating the silence.

"Hey," I said softly, nudging her with my elbow. "You're going to be okay, you know."

Sabrina blinked and slowly turned to me, her eyes glassy but slowly brightening. She forced a small smile and shook her head. "I can't believe we made it out alive, Liza."

"Neither can I," I admitted, rubbing my hands together nervously. "But we're here, and that's what matters."

Her smile grew slightly, and she exhaled. "Yeah, you're right. We're alive, and that's enough for now."

"Exactly." I placed a reassuring hand on her shoulder, trying to convey all the strength and support I could muster. She needed it.

We lapsed into silence again, listening to the soft whispers of the nurses outside the door. The eerie shadows on the walls played tricks on my eyes.

"Hey," Sabrina began tentatively as she broached the subject. "Do you know where Liam is? I haven't seen him since..."

I swallowed hard, a knot forming in my throat. Though Liam had said he'd be back, I feared he might go underground again and leave us all behind. "He's taking care of some things," I managed to choke out.

Sabrina studied me for a moment, then sighed. "When I was almost unconscious, I could have sworn he called me his mate, but I must have imagined it, right?" She shook her head and chuckled, trying to brush it off.

My heart raced, and I bit my lip, struggling to hold back the truth. I was terrible at secrets, and this one felt like an unbearable weight. The words tumbled from my mouth before I could stop them. "Actually, he did call you his mate."

"What?" Sabrina's eyes widened, and she sat up straighter. "You're serious? He really said that?"

"Uh-huh."

"Damn..." She shook her head and laughed. "That guy. He better not run off like a wimp after saying something like that."

"Trust me, I'll make sure he doesn't," I replied, trying to sound far more confident than I was.

We shared a look of understanding, a camaraderie forged in the fires we'd faced together. It wasn't enough to erase all the trauma, but it was a start. Our conversation trailed off, and we sat in silence for a while, each lost in our thoughts. I tried to focus on the antiseptic scent in the air to ground myself in the present moment. Sabrina tapped her fingers against her cast, creating a soft rhythm that almost drowned out the beeping of the machines around us.

We were survivors, and no matter what happened next, I knew we'd face it together. But as I stared at the sterile white walls of the hospital room, I wondered where Liam was, when he'd return, and what our lives would look like now that this nightmare was finally over.

The door creaked open, and Ty entered the room with a soft smile on his face. "Ready to get out of here?" he asked, his voice soothing like warm honey.

"More than ready," Sabrina replied, her eyes brightening at the prospect of leaving the hospital. I shared her sentiment. The sterile walls were starting to close in on me.

A nurse followed Ty inside, wheeling in a chair for me. "Hospital policy," she explained when my eyes narrowed at the wheelchair. "Just until you're safely in the car."

"Fine," I said, and eased myself into the seat. My body still ached from the battle with Castro, but I was eager to put it all behind me.

Ty and Sabrina helped me adjust, their hands gentle and caring. The scent of lavender drifted from Sabrina's hair, mingling with Ty's earthy aroma. It reminded me of home.

We made our way through the maze of hallways, the steady hum of fluorescent lights above us punctuated by the occasional beeping of a monitor or murmured conversation between medical staff.

Once outside, the crisp autumn air nipped at my cheeks—a stark contrast to the stale atmosphere of the hospital. I breathed it in deeply, letting it fill my lungs and chase away the lingering unease. Leaves rustled in the wind, their colors a vibrant tapestry of reds, oranges, and yellows. The world felt alive, and so did I.

Ty helped me into the car, making sure I was comfortable before sliding into the driver's seat. Sabrina chatted excitedly about her plans once she was fully healed. Listening to her, I couldn't help but find some hope of my own.

Ty pulled us away from the hospital, and we drove in companionable silence for a while, but as we neared Sabrina's house, I couldn't contain my curiosity any longer.

"Ty," I said. "I need to see Castro's body."

He hesitated, his grip on the steering wheel tightening. "Are you sure? It's not a pretty sight."

"Please," I pressed. "We thought we'd killed him once, and I have to know for certain. I need closure."

"All right." He relented with a sigh, his eyes meeting mine in the rearview mirror. "But give me some time to make arrangements. We'll take Sabrina home first."

"Thank you," I whispered.

As much as I wanted to forget about Castro and move on, I couldn't until I faced the reality of his death. The truth, no matter how gruesome, would finally set me free.

Twenty minutes later, I stood near the edge of a clearing in the woods. A huge funeral pyre had been constructed for Castro and his dead wolves, their bodies piled high with dry branches and leaves. Ty's pack members moved about, making final preparations for the grim ritual.

"Are you ready?" Ty asked softly, standing beside me, his lips in a tight line.

I nodded, swallowing tightly. "Yes."

My heart pounded as I stared at Castro's lifeless body atop the mound. I'd been sure I'd killed him, but after his last stunt, I wasn't taking any chances. As morbid as it seemed, I wouldn't feel real peace until I witnessed him turn to ash.

"Goodbye, Castro," I whispered, clenching my fists at my sides. "You'll never hurt anyone again."

Somebody lit the pyre beneath the bodies, and I waited until the fire roared, its heat growing more intense by the second. My skin tightened and prickled as the flames flared, reducing the bodies to ashes and smoke. The air grew thick with the acrid stench of burning flesh, and I covered my mouth and nose with my hand.

"Let's step back," Ty suggested, his voice barely audible over the crackling blaze. He gently took my arm, guiding me away from the inferno.

As we retreated, I thought of how different life would be now that Castro was gone. My past, once shrouded in darkness, was finally coming into the light. And though the road ahead wouldn't be easy, I knew I could face it with the love and support of my newfound family.

"Your nightmare is over," Ty said softly, his eyes filled with understanding. "You're free now."

Relief washed over me, so powerful it left me weak in the knees. Tears leaked from the corners of my eyes as the reality of those words sank in. My nightmare was indeed over, and for the first time in what felt like an eternity, I was truly free.

"Thank you," I whispered, leaning into him for support as we watched the flames reach their peak. "For everything."

He wrapped a protective arm around me, pulling me close. "You're welcome. Now let's go home."

The crunch of gravel under the tires signaled our arrival at the estate. I glanced over at Ty, who offered me a reassuring smile as he parked the car. My heart raced in anticipation of seeing my family again, but there was also a nagging sense of apprehension. Everything had changed since we last met.

"Ready?" Ty asked, his hand resting on my knee.

I took a deep breath and nodded. "Let's do it."

We stepped out of the car, and the front door swung open, revealing a flurry of familiar faces. My parents rushed out to greet me with open arms, and I fell into their warm, loving embrace. The scent of my mother's lavender perfume calmed my nerves while my father's strong grip grounded me.

"Sweetheart, we're so glad you're safe," Mom whispered into my ear.

"Me, too," I replied, holding back tears.

My brothers waited their turn before engulfing me in a bear hug. Their unique scents—two different colognes tinged with sweat—brought back memories of our childhood, when we'd bicker and tease each other mercilessly. Despite their differences, they'd always been fiercely protective of me.

"Little sis, you sure know how to give us a scare," Mason teased, ruffling my hair.

"Like you've never done that to me before," I retorted with a grin.

"All right, all right," Michael intervened, chuckling. "Enough with the sibling rivalry for now."

Ty's parents approached me next, their expressions warm and welcoming. Persephone hugged me tightly, her long black hair brushing against my cheek. Her embrace felt like a protective shield. She genuinely cared for me.

"Welcome home," she said softly, pulling away and studying my face. "You've been through so much."

"Thank you," I replied, touched by her concern.

Dominic stepped forward, his eyes filled with regret as he wrapped his arms around me. "Liza," he began, his voice thick with emotion. "I know I've apologized before, but I need you to understand how truly sorry I am for the pain my actions have caused you. It was never my intention to bring you harm."

I looked into his eyes, seeing genuine remorse there. Though his past actions had set off a chain of events that had led us down this dark path, holding onto resentment wouldn't help anyone.

"Thank you for saying that, Dominic," I said quietly. "I appreciate your apology, and I'm ready to move forward."

The remaining weight that had been bearing down on my shoulders lifted. We stood there for a moment, united by our love and determination to heal as a family, while the sun peeked through the clouds, casting warm rays upon our faces. Perhaps we'd finally found our way out of the darkness and into the light.

***

The sun was setting when Ty called the pack together in the clearing behind the estate. I stood beside him, the cool evening breeze sweeping across my skin. The rustling leaves above us whispered a promise of new beginnings.

"Keller pack," Ty began, his voice strong and commanding. "Today, we celebrate our victory. Though we didn't have to fight on our end, this ordeal has taught us that we cannot afford to grow complacent. We must continue to strengthen ourselves, and ensure that any enemy who dares threaten our pack will think twice."

He paused, allowing his words to sink in, and I felt a surge of pride at the determination in his eyes. My mate, a true leader.

"Let it be known," he continued, "that we are not weak. We are the Keller pack, and we will stand united against any challenges that come our way."

A chorus of approving howls and barks erupted from the assembled wolves. I grinned, sharing in their enthusiasm, and glanced up at Ty. He caught my eye and winked, making my heart flutter despite the gravity of the situation.

"Tonight," he announced, "we run as one!"

And with that, the transformation began. Clothes were shed as fur sprouted and bones shifted. The air was filled with the sound of snarls and growls as each member of the pack embraced their inner wolf.

I closed my eyes, welcoming the familiar sensation of my body morphing as the powerful muscles of my wolf form emerged. When the change was complete, I opened my eyes to find Ty's wolf—a magnificent beast, with a coat as black as midnight—waiting for me. With a playful nudge, he urged me forward, and together we led the pack through the forest.

Our paws pounded the earth, sending up a spray of dirt and leaves as we sped through the densely wooded terrain. The world was a blur of green and brown, lit by the soft glow of twilight filtering through the canopy above. I relished the feeling of freedom, and of unity with my pack and my mate, as we raced side by side.

The damp moss, decaying leaves, and the musk of hidden creatures inundated my senses as we ran. My ears pricked at the distant hoot of an owl, and I let out a joyful howl in response. It was an affirmation of our victory. A declaration that we were finally free from the darkness that had plagued us.

We had survived, and together we would thrive. For we were the Keller pack, and nothing could stand in our way.

In the quiet hours before dawn, I found myself drawn to the edge of Heather Falls, my old home. A chill wind whispered through the trees, carrying memories of laughter and heartache, love, and loss. The full moon shone like a silver coin against the inky sky, shining like a beacon on the battered remains of what had once been my sanctuary.

I shifted and considered my old home. "Goodbye," I whispered, the word catching in my throat as I touched the twisted gate that marked the entrance to the ruins. The metal was cold beneath my fingertips, clammy with the dew that clung to every surface. In the distance, I could hear the faint roar of the water as it cascaded down the falls as an eternal reminder of the passage of time.

"Leaving it behind for good?" Ty's voice came from behind me, startling me out of my reverie, making me jump a bit. I felt his warm breath on my neck as he approached, the familiar scent of him comforting and grounding amidst the tendrils of overwhelming memories.

"Finally," I whispered. "I can't live in the past any longer. I need to move forward, with you and our pack."

"Then, say your goodbyes," he murmured gently, pressing his body against mine in a gesture of support. His warmth enveloped me, fortifying me against the ghosts that still haunted this place.

I closed my eyes and took a deep breath, letting the scents of the decaying wood fill my lungs. I allowed the memories to wash over me one last time, both the beautiful and the painful, embracing them all, but refusing to let them hold me captive any longer.

"Goodbye," I whispered again, more firmly this time, as I released the past and embraced the future that awaited us.

Opening my eyes, I turned to face Ty, his amber eyes alive with understanding and love. He rubbed his cheek against mine in a tender gesture that spoke volumes without the need for words.

"Let's go home," I said, stronger now as I took his hand and led him away from Heather Falls.

We walked together through the moonlit forest, leaving the past behind us as we stepped into our new life—one filled with promise, growth, and endless possibilities. For we were the Keller pack, and no matter what lay ahead, we would face it together.

Chapter 32 - Ty

The scent of vanilla and chocolate wafted through the air, a comforting and sweet reminder of Liza's loving touch in every pastry she baked. I stood in the kitchen doorway, watching as Sabrina helped my heavily pregnant mate finish up the last of their orders for the bakery. Their laughter rang like music in the cozy space, bringing warmth to my heart despite my ever-present concern for Liza.

"Careful with that one." Liza balanced a tray of cupcakes over her swollen belly. "It's a little wobbly."

"Got it," Sabrina said, gingerly setting the tray on the counter. "I don't know how you do it, Liza. You're about to pop, and you're still running around here like it's nothing."

"Hey, I'm just trying to keep busy until he decides to make his grand entrance." Liza chuckled, rubbing her belly affectionately.

My protective instincts flared at the sight of Liza's discomfort, but I knew better than to try and smother her with help. She was so damn strong, and I was filled with admiration and love for her every day. Our son would be arriving any day now, and though I was full of joy, I couldn't shake the worry that lingered in the back of my mind.

I wanted our son to have a better life than either of us had known, free from the dark legacy of Liza's father, and the burden of being an omega.

Ten months had passed since the day Castro died. We'd been overjoyed when we found out she was pregnant, but the worry that our child might be born an omega like Liza haunted us. The last thing we wanted was for our child to suffer as Liza had at the hands of her father. Thank the heavens it was a boy.

"Careful, love," I said, trying not to sound too controlling. "Don't push yourself too hard."

Liza flashed me a smile, clearly reading my thoughts. "I can still handle myself, Ty. Besides, Sabrina's here to help."

Sabrina, always cheerful and energetic, buzzed around the kitchen. Her short blonde hair bounced as she darted from one task to another. She glanced over and grinned. "Trust me, Ty. She's in good hands."

I held up my hands in surrender, unable to resist a grin. "Just making sure."

At Liza's four-month ultrasound, the doctor had confirmed that we were having a son., which had relaxed us. Our son would be an alpha, not an omega. Now all that remained was the anticipation of his arrival.

"Ty," Liza called, jolting me from my thoughts. "Can you grab the powdered sugar from the top shelf, please?"

"Sure thing." I moved quickly, handing her the sugar while casting a protective glance at her belly.

"Thanks." Liza's warm gaze met mine. She was more than aware how much she and our unborn son meant to me.

"Any time." I leaned in to give her a quick kiss.

"Fun time's over, you two," Sabrina said playfully. "Let's finish these orders before Liza's maternity leave officially starts tonight."

"Right." I nodded, getting out of their way. We weren't sure how much longer Liza would last before our son arrived, so it was best to get everything done now.

My phone buzzed, and the caller ID said unknown. A knot tightened in my stomach. I had an idea who it was.

"Excuse me, ladies." I stepped out of the kitchen to answer the call. "Hey, Liam."

"Ty," he said, low and cautious. "Is Liza doing all right?"

"Better than ever, actually. Our son will be here soon." I cracked with emotion but quickly composed myself. "We still miss you, though."

"Good to hear." Liam sighed. "I wish I could be there, but you know how it is. Too many enemies."

"Believe me, I understand. Promise me you'll come meet your nephew as soon as it's safe."

There was a pause on the other end of the line, and for a moment, I worried that I had said too much. Then Liam sighed, the sound heavy with emotion. "I promise I'll visit when I can. I'd be there now if I could."

"I know," I said, understanding the danger he faced but still wishing things could be different. "Just... don't stay away too long."

"Believe me, I don't want to." His voice softened, almost wistful. "But I have to lay low for a while longer. There are still too many people after me."

"Speaking of which," I started, curiosity getting the better of me. "What exactly are you up to? You've been pretty elusive lately."

"Let's just say I'm working on something big," Liam answered cryptically. "I need you to be with Liza, though. You're her rock, and when the news breaks that I'm dead, she's going to need you."

"Wait, what?" My stomach dropped, my mind racing to understand his words. Then it clicked, and I grinned. "You're getting out of the business, aren't you?"

"Something like that," he said with a hint of amusement in his voice. "Let's just say it's time for me to start over, and I can't do that with a target on my back."

"Really?" Liam had always been a bit of a lone wolf, but he cared about those close to him. "That's great news, man."

"Thanks. I just wanted you to know so you wouldn't be alarmed when news is out."

"Of course. We understand." He deserved all the love and support he could get.

"Take care of Liza, and make sure you get word to me when my nephew is born."

"Will do," I said, grinning in spite of the situation. "Take care of yourself, too."

"Always." With that, the line went dead, leaving me with emotions I couldn't quite deal with right now. There was no time to dwell on them, though, because at that very moment, Liza shouted from the kitchen.

"Ty!" She sounded strained, panicked, and I rushed back into the kitchen, looking for the danger.

"What happened?" I asked, skidding to a stop as I took in the sight before me. There was a puddle of water at Liza's feet, and her face was now pale as she clutched the edge of the counter.

"Either I just had a very unfortunate accident, or my water just broke." She panted, trying to catch her breath.

"Shit." A grin spread across my face as I stared at the puddle of water at Liza's feet. This was really happening. Our baby was on his way.

"Ty," Liza whimpered as she clutched her belly. "We need to get to the hospital."

"Right." I sprang into action. "Sabrina, can you finish the orders?"

"Of course. You two just go and have that baby," Sabrina said with a wide smile, her spunky personality shining through even in this intense moment. She waved us off while I helped Liza gather her things and picked up the pre-packed hospital bags.

"Stay safe, guys," Sabrina said as we headed for the door.

"Thanks, Sabrina," Liza said between breaths, gripping my arm tightly as another contraction hit. We had been through so much together, and now this journey was about to reach its peak.

The summer sun warmed our skin as we stepped outside, but it did little to dampen my excitement. Liza leaned heavily against me, each step toward the car a feat of strength.

"Almost there, love," I said into her ear, my warm breath mingling with the cool breeze. "Just a little farther."

"I can't wait to meet him," Liza panted, her eyes glossy with tears from the effort. It was a sentiment I shared wholeheartedly. After months of waiting and preparing, it was finally time to welcome our son into the world.

Once we reached the car, I carefully helped Liza into the passenger seat and strapped her in securely. Her labored breathing filled the otherwise silent vehicle, each gasp a testament to her strength.

"Ready?" I asked, my hand hovering over the ignition as I glanced at her one last time.

"Let's go have our baby." A weak smile played on her lips despite the pain etched on her face.

We were ready. Together, we could do anything.

Printed in Great Britain
by Amazon

40109116R00320